DEDICATION

*To Joyce & Tammy for your hours of time, your gentle guidance,
your pointed reminders, and your unwavering support.*

1

It was the bridal party from hell. The gold leaf, crystal chandeliers, and acres of Italian marble of the Grand Terrace Ballroom couldn't dress up the fact that a hot mess was currently in progress. From her vantage point on the upper balcony that ringed the hotel's sunken ballroom, Frankie could see it all.

The groomsmen, in their Armani and Brioni, were overgrown frat boys destined to spend their lives reliving their prep school glory days. Their trust funds were cushy enough to buy their way out of any real trouble.

The bridesmaids were worse. All working on landing husband number two—or three in Taffany's case. They were on the prowl for men who came with a favorable prenup and a yacht in Saint Tropez.

To Frankie, it was a literal circus. But there wasn't much she wouldn't do for the bride, including standing up for her best friend in a three-ring mess of a $350,000 wedding. Pru and Chip were the golden couple of the Upper West Side. College sweethearts who had found their way back to each other. And Frankie was more than happy to be a part of their extravagantly special big day.

If this engagement party was any indicator of how fabulous the destination wedding would be, Frankie wasn't sure how a poor, sarcastic girl from Brooklyn with big hair would fare amongst the who's who in Barbados. But for Pru, she'd give it her best shot.

Besides, it gave her a chance to ogle the best man in person. She snagged a champagne glass from a passing tray, winking at the server who joined her against the balustrade. She eyed Aiden Kilbourn across the room. Impeccable, aloof, and painfully beautiful.

"I can't believe we got this gig," Jana, the server hissed. "I never in a million years thought I'd see Manhattan's Most Eligible Bachelor in person, let alone serve him champagne!"

"Don't spill anything on him, Jan," Frankie cautioned.

"You mean 'don't pull a Frankie.'" Jana smirked.

Frankie lifted a shoulder. "The guy grabbed my ass. What was I supposed to do, not drop a tray of canapés on his lap?"

"You're my hero," Jana sighed.

"Yeah, yeah. Get back down there before they start sobering up. And tell Hansen to maybe migrate away from the ladies' room. He's not getting any phone numbers tonight."

Jana tossed her a mock salute. "On it, boss."

Frankie watched Jana nimbly skip down the stairs, tray aloft. As soon as Pru and Chip had announced their engagement, she'd snapped up a second job with a catering company, knowing the cost of doing business with the privileged. She wasn't about to let Pru pay for her bridesmaid dress or her plane tickets, though the offer was there. Frankie was determined to hang with the socialites just this once without being a charity case, even if it bankrupted her.

She ran a hand over her two seasons-old Marchessa that she and Pru had found at an upscale consignment shop in the Village. It was hard to find couture that fit her curves. Pru and the rest of the bridesmaids were nymphy waifs. All blonde, all thin, all B-cups. Well, except for Cressida. Her double Ds spilled out of her size zero Marc Jacobs. Either the woman was blessed with incredible genetics, or they weren't real. But without getting a handful, Frankie couldn't tell for sure.

Speaking of good genes, she turned her attention back to the man in the white tuxedo jacket. He had a hand in his pocket in that effortlessly casual stance that the rich were born with.

At forty, Aiden was Manhattan's unicorn bachelor. Never married—just a rotating cast of arm candy, the longest of which had lasted nearly three whole months. He rarely smiled, unlike the rest of the cast of characters who pasted on their phony "great to see you" grins. It looked as though he was perhaps as uncomfortable as she was in the thick of things.

Pruitt waved to Frankie from the center of the throng. Maid of honor duty engaged. Frankie pasted on a smile of her own before taking to the stairs to join the party. She wove her way between gold cushioned chairs and ivory linen-draped cocktail tables. It's funny how good the wealthy smelled. All subtle, rich scents as if it emanated from their pores.

"You look amazing, Frankie," Pru told her, dropping the double kiss on the cheeks and squeezing her hand.

"Me? Have you looked in a mirror tonight? You look like a high-fashion model pretending to be at an engagement shoot."

"Good enough to eat," Chip, the golden groom, said swooping in to kiss his bride-to-be.

They glowed at each other, and Frankie felt like she was intruding. "Well, I should get back—"

"Uh-uh. Not until you meet Aiden," Pru said, dragging her attention away from Chip. On cue, Chip waved at the man.

"That's okay. I can meet him at the ceremony," Frankie said.

"Frankie doesn't like high-society people," Pru stage whispered to Chip.

Chip slid an affectionate arm around Frankie's shoulders. "Good thing she made an exception for us, seeing as we're classy as fuck."

Franchesca laughed. "You should have put that on your wedding invitations."

Hansen the server approached with a tray of beef crostini, and Chip snatched one off the tray. He popped it into his mouth, eyes rolling back in his head. "Ummm. Frankie, we owe you for the catering recommendation. Delicious."

Frankie gave Hansen a nod in the direction of where Pru's father was glowering in the corner. The man hadn't gotten over the fact that Chipper Randolph III had unceremoniously dumped his little girl in the months after college graduation when she'd been expecting a ring. But he was picking up the bill for this shindig, and Frankie was determined to make sure his stomach was full to prevent any hangry outbursts.

"Chip. Pru." The voice was a full octave deeper than Chip's. Smooth, cultured. Frankie considered asking him to read the grocery list she had stashed in her hand-me-down clutch just so she could listen to him pronounce edamame.

"Aiden!" The good breeding kicked in automatically, and Chip turned to his best friend to make the introductions. "Frankie, this is Aiden Kilbourn, my best man. Aiden, this is Franchesca Baranski, the maid of honor."

"Frankie," Aiden said, extending his hand. "That's an interesting name."

Frankie gripped and shook. "We've got a Taffany and a Davenport in the bridal party, and I'm the one with an interesting name?"

His already cool expression chilled a few degrees. Obviously, he wasn't used to being educated by an underling. "I was merely making an observation."

"You were pre-judging," she countered.

"Sometimes a judgment begs to be made."

She was still holding his hand. Annoyance had her tightening her grip. He returned the squeeze, and Frankie dropped his hand unceremoniously.

"So, Aiden," Pru began brightly. "I met *Franchesca* my first semester at NYU. She's brilliant—full-ride scholarship—and she graduated a semester early with a 4.0. Franchesca works part-time for a nonprofit while pursuing her MBA."

Frankie shot daggers at Pru. She didn't need her best friend trying to talk her up to a snobbish ass.

"Aiden is COO of his family's business. Mergers and acquisitions," Chip supplied. "I don't remember his GPA from Yale. But it wasn't as good as yours, Frankie."

She was about to excuse herself and track down another tray of champagne when the DJ changed it up. The first beats of "Uptown Funk" brought half of Manhattan's elite rushing to the dance floor like someone had announced the new Birkin bag was available.

Pru's hand clamped down on her arm. "It's our song!" she squealed. "Let's go!"

Frankie allowed Pru to tow her toward the dance floor. They slid seamlessly into their choreographed dance crafted two years earlier after one of Frankie's moderately disappointing breakups. They'd polished off two entire pizzas with three bottles of wine and spent the rest of the evening choreographing the perfect ass shaker.

"I couldn't tell if you two were fighting or flirting," Pru yelled over the music.

"Flirting? You're joking, right? I'm way out of his league."

2

*A*iden had a headache by the time he'd crossed the marble lobby of the Regency Hotel, one of the bride's family's holdings. And he knew an evening spent in the company of the Brat Pack of groomsmen and a few dozen people looking to marry him off, secure his investment, or beg some free advice would only make it worse.

But it was the price he paid for privilege. He handed the empty champagne flute to a passing server and wished for scotch. But drinking away his headache wouldn't do anyone any favors tonight.

"How about Margeaux?" Chip asked, jerking his chin in the direction of the model tall, waif-slim blonde. She wore a gold gown with a slit practically to her chin. She was ruthlessly styled, hair perfect, makeup impeccable. She never ate or smiled in public.

"How about not on your life? She looks like the equivalent of an ice cube in bed." Since Chip had found his lasting happiness with Pruitt, he'd made it his mission to drag his best friend Aiden along with him for the ride.

"Yeah, she's horrible," Chip agreed. "But Pru was her maid

of honor so..." he winced. "I'm going to do you a favor and skip over Taffany."

"Thanks," Aiden said dryly. The woman rebranded herself as Taffany after a second cousin named her baby Tiffany. She was the quintessential party girl. A week didn't go by when she wasn't plastered across the gossip blogs flashing her crotch in dresses short enough to be shirts and falling out of rock stars' SUVs in front of clubs.

"How about Cressida?" Chip offered, pointing his glass at yet another blonde. This one's breasts couldn't be bothered to stay within the confines of her couture corset. The rest of her was a tan skeleton. She was frowning fiercely and pacing in a short six-foot radius as she yelled into her cellphone in German.

"She seems nice," Aiden observed sarcastically.

"She seems like she'd cut your balls off and then ransom you for them," Chip said cheerfully.

"How about Frankie?" Aiden asked, warming to the game. His gaze flicked to her on the dance floor. Her hair was dark, thick, heavy with curls. Her body was lushly curved as highlighted by the simple gold slip gown she wore. Her wide mouth was curved in a generous smile as she laughed at something Pruitt said.

"Oh, she's too good for you," Chip said. "She's smart and sarcastic. She'd be too much work for you."

"I see what you're doing," Aiden said. He flagged down a server and ordered a Macallan. One wouldn't hurt. One might take the edge off a bit.

"What am I doing? I'm trying to save you from a woman who clearly isn't your type."

"What's my type?" Aiden asked, already regretting it.

"Tall, painfully thin. Doesn't smile or speak too much.

Someone looking to add you to her bedroom portfolio to make her more attractive to the next potential husband."

"That's not necessarily my type," Aiden argued. "That's just who doesn't take offense to the arrangement."

"Frankie would take offense," Chip predicted. "But I think she might also make you regret temporary. She's a hell of a girl, Aiden."

Aiden watched the woman in question as she shimmied and strutted in unison with Pruitt. She moved like a goddess, tempting mortals with her sinful body. In his experience, women tended to highlight their appeal either across the dining table or in the bedroom. And Franchesca was all bedroom.

He turned his back on the dance floor.

"When are you going to give up on dragging me into monogamous bliss?" he asked Chip.

His friend grinned. "When you find someone who makes you feel the way I do about Pru."

"I'm a Kilbourn. We're not capable of feelings. Only beneficial mergers."

"That's a sad statement to make," Chip said, slapping him on the shoulder. The server, a slip of a girl with a navy streak in her dark hair, hurried to his side. A glass of scotch clutched in her hand.

"Here you go, Mr. Kilbourn," she said in a breathless whisper.

"Thank you... Jana," he said, eyes flicking to her name tag.

Her mouth dropped open, and she backed away with stars in her eyes.

"See. Why don't you work some of that charm on Frankie?"

"I'm not interested in something that..."

"Fun? Smart? Sexy?" Chip supplied.

"Flashy," Aiden corrected. "She dances like she's got experience on the pole. And she'd probably take that as a compliment."

"No. She wouldn't," a husky voice behind him announced.

Fuck.

Chip, ever the tension diffuser, slapped an innocent grin on his face. "Frankie! Aiden didn't see you there," he said pointedly.

"Aiden doesn't seem like the type to notice much of anyone under a certain tax bracket. Why waste his time?" Franchesca announced.

She didn't hesitate to make eye contact. No, she used those blue-green eyes to bore holes into him. He'd been an ass. Usually he was much more careful about voicing his opinions in venues where they could be overheard, misconstrued. He blamed the headache, the three glasses of champagne on an empty stomach.

"Pru asked if you'd get her a drink and save her from the Danby twins. They've got her cornered by the stairs." Frankie pointed to the opposite end of the room.

"If you two will excuse me, I've got to go rescue my fiancée. No bloodshed," Chip ordered, pointing a stern finger at Frankie.

"No promises," she called after him. She turned back to him, eyes flashing with temper. "Well, if *you'll* excuse me—which I don't give a flying fuck if you do—I don't want to spend my evening looking at you."

She dismissed him, turning on her heel and whipping that curtain of hair over her shoulder.

"Hang on," he said it quietly, fingers closing around her wrist.

"Hands off, Kilbourn, or you'll be Deadbourn by the time I'm done with you."

He released her but stepped into her path. "Let me apologize."

"*Let* you?" Franchesca crossed her arms over her chest. "Look, I'm sure you're used to talking to servants and underlings, but a word of advice? Don't demand that someone listen to your shit show of an apology. Got it?"

The headache was throbbing behind his eyes. No one talked to him that way. Not even his oldest friends.

"*Please* allow me to apologize," he said, his jaw clenching. He cupped her elbow in his hand and guided her toward an alcove behind a heavy gold curtain.

The darkness made the pain in his head ease just a bit, and he pinched the bridge of his nose, willing the rest of it away.

"How about I save us both some time?" Franchesca suggested. "You don't bother apologizing because we both know you meant to be a dick, and I won't bother pretending to forgive you because I don't give a shit what you think about me. Fair enough?"

There was a cream-colored settee covered in silk, and Aiden sat. The dull throb was making his stomach roll. "Look. I'm not putting my best foot forward, and for that I apologize."

"Future reference again? 'I apologize' doesn't come across as sincerely as 'I'm sorry.' You got a headache?"

The change in subject had his head spinning. He closed his eyes. Nodded.

"Migraine?" she prodded.

He shrugged. "Maybe."

She mumbled to herself, and he opened his eyes to watch her dig through her clutch. "Here," she said, offering him two pills. "Prescription."

"You get them, too?"

"No, but Pru does when she's stressed. I didn't want her muddling through her engagement party wanting to puke."

"That's very kind and prepared of you."

"I'm the maid of honor. It's my job. Now take them like a good little boy."

He lifted his glass, but she stopped him with a hand on his wrist. "Don't be a dumbass. Alcohol makes it worse." She took the glass from him and stuck her head out of the curtain. He heard her give a little whistle, and in a moment, she was thanking someone by name and handing him a glass of ice water.

"You know the catering staff?" he asked, making conversation while he washed down the tablets.

"I am the catering staff. Second job. It's my night off." She said it as if she were daring him to find fault with that. "You want me to call you an Uber?" she offered suddenly.

"I have a car downstairs."

"Of course you do."

"Why are you being nice to me?" Aiden rubbed a hand over his temple.

"Maybe I'm doing it to rub your face in the fact that you're an ass. And maybe I gave you two birth control pills instead of headache meds just to watch you suffer."

"Maybe I'd deserve it."

The curtain twitched, and the server with the blue hair poked her head in. "Here's the soda," she whispered. Her eyes widened when she spotted him, and she backed out of the alcove.

"I make her nervous," Aiden observed when the server left.

"It's a good thing you're good-looking and rich because you definitely don't have the personality thing going for you. Here, drink this. The caffeine will help."

He drank it down and rested his head against the back of the settee. "Thanks." She was taking care of him after he suggested that she had experience as a stripper. He was an asshole and wondered when that transformation had become complete.

She took the glass from him. "Stay until it kicks in," she ordered and turned for the curtain.

"Where are you going?"

"Back to the party so I can shake my stripper ass at all those eligible bachelors."

"I'm sorry I'll miss it."

"Shut up, Kilbourn."

3

———

*T*he plane dropped like a stone onto the runway, and the violently applied brakes had everyone in coach jerking forward and back. Frankie couldn't see much of the tropical paradise outside the window from her middle seat vantage. She was crammed in between a guy who smelled like he hadn't showered in four days and a little old man who had fallen asleep at twenty thousand feet and slept on her shoulder for an hour.

She had to pee and could have killed for a roast beef sandwich, but at least the flight was over and she only had to fight her way through customs and immigration now. In an hour—two tops—she'd have her toes in the white powdery sand, a drink in her hand, and that sandwich.

Frankie waited for the elderly narcoleptic to stand and then wriggled out into the aisle behind him to help him with his carry-on.

She lugged her own carry-on with her, thankful that Pru had insisted on flying the bridesmaid dresses down on her father's plane. The rest of the wedding party had arrived on private planes they'd chartered together.

She waddled down the aisle toward the ever-smiling flight crew and the humid breeze. Frankie stepped out onto the rolling staircase and slid her sunglasses on. Eighty-three degrees with a beautiful, balmy breeze. Maybe this wouldn't be so bad after all. Even though her hair had just doubled in volume.

She followed the rest of the passengers onto the tarmac and into the long, low building of Grantley Adams International Airport. The line zig-zagged its way between the ropes. Anxious travelers ready to see paradise thumbed over the screens of their phones. But Frankie was content to people watch. The residency line for immigration was short and brutally efficient as Bajan passport holders were welcomed home. To her right was the expedited line where travelers with Louis Vuitton luggage and oversized sun hats were guided through the process by resort staff dispatched to collect them.

Frankie's line crawled along at a snail's pace as harried parents tried to juggle official questions and cranky toddlers and young backpackers zoned out on their phones, needing a prod forward every time the line moved.

One such backpacker caught her eye and gave her a smile. "Hi there," he said softly, pushing a shock of blond hair off his forehead.

Oh, sweet baby Jesus, he was Australian.

"Hi," she returned.

"Come here often?"

She laughed.

"Can I buy you a drink?" he teased.

"If you can find a bartender in here, yes, you can buy me a drink."

The line moved and the woman behind him—in a sun visor with flowers on the brim and a Hawaiian shirt—prodded him forward.

"See you around," he winked.

They caught up again when the lines froze at exactly the right place.

"We meet again. It must be fate."

"Oh, you're good. I bet that wouldn't work as well without your accent," Frankie told him.

"I like yours," he confessed.

Boca Raton Grandma gave the Aussie another push. "Sorry, honey. But I got a frozen margarita waitin' on me," she said to Frankie as they passed.

Frankie's immigration officer was an unsmiling girl in her early twenties with YouTube tutorial-level makeup. "Have a nice stay," she said, shoving Frankie's passport through the slot in the Plexiglass. Her tone implied she didn't give a damn whether Frankie's stay was nice or not. But dealing with three plane loads of grumpy tourists would do that to a person.

Frankie pushed on past baggage claim. With Pru bringing her bridesmaid dress, she'd been able to shove everything else she needed into her carry-on and saved the checked bag fee. A small victory in what had been a year of hemorrhaging money. The two bridal showers, the girls-only engagement party, engagement party, the pre-emptive bachelorette party, and now the destination wedding. She should have taken a third job. But a few more weeks with the caterer, and she'd have the credit card paid off and could stop spending money like it magically appeared replenished in her wallet every morning.

Customs was much faster. A quick scan of her bag, and she was pointed toward the exit. Her phone started ringing in the beach bag she'd dual-purposed as a purse.

"Hey, Ma."

"Oh thank, God! I thought you were dead." May Baranski was nothing if not dramatic.

"Not dead, Ma. Just in paradise." The automatic doors parted and she walked into the heat. It was a covered area rife with tourists who looked lost and cab drivers who looked like buzzards circling carrion.

"Why didn't you call me when you landed? You said you'd call me." Her mother had infused normal protective instincts with steroids until she was convinced that all of her children were in constant mortal danger or worse—destined to remain single and childless while the rest of her friends became nanas and grammas.

"I literally just walked through customs, Ma. They don't let you chit chat on your cell phones while you're in there."

Her mother scoffed. The idea that anyone could keep her from a safety report on one of her children was ridiculous to May.

"Tell me all about your flight." It wasn't a question. It was a demand. Frankie blamed herself. She liked her parents, liked talking to them, and somehow that had evolved into almost daily calls "just to check in" or "catch up." Hell, half the time she was the one doing the dialing. Her mom was a fount of information on old neighborhood and family gossip.

"It was crowded and long," Frankie said, squinting at the taxi sign. It listed island destinations and their rates, but she needed to check what parish the resort was in again.

"Your father and I went to the Florida Keys for our honeymoon forty-one years ago," May announced. "Is it as nice as the Keys?"

Frankie had never been to the Florida Keys, nor had she seen anything of Barbados beyond the tarmac and the cab line. "I'm sure the Keys are beautiful," she told her mother. "Look, Ma. I gotta go. Can I call you tomorrow?"

"Why? What's wrong?"

"Nothing's wrong. I have to grab a cab."

"Why didn't Pru send a car for you?" her mother squawked. "You're just going to get in a car with a stranger?"

"A driver Pru sent would still be a stranger." Frankie made the point in vain.

"I forbid you to get mugged or molested!"

Frankie bumped into someone and turned to apologize.

"There you are. I was worried that we were star-crossed lovers, destined never to meet again." The Australian was adjusting the backpack she'd nearly knocked off his shoulder.

"I gotta go, Ma."

"What now?"

"There's a cute guy looking at me."

The Aussie grinned.

"Hang up and flirt with him! Come back engaged!" Her mother disconnected the call to start planning the overdue wedding of her only daughter.

"Sorry," Frankie said with a soft smile. "I wasn't paying attention to what I was doing."

"You can bump into me anytime you want." He wasn't devastatingly handsome. Not like Satan-in-a-Suit Kilbourn. But he was cute and charming and very, very tan. His hair was a bleached-out blond that was in need of a cut. His clothes were wrinkled and comfortable.

"Tell me you're an Australian surfer," Frankie sighed. It had been a while since she'd had a second-party-induced orgasm. She'd been lazy in the dating field, and working two jobs hadn't left her much time for naked fun. Maybe a tropical fling with a sexy surfer would cure her sex blahs?

"As a matter of fact, I am. Tell me you're into Australian surfers and that we can share a cab so I can charm my way into a date."

Frankie laughed. Easy, charming, funny. Perfect.

She lowered her lashes. "I've never had an Australian surfer before, so I can't vouch for my preferences in the area."

His blue eyes, the same color as the sea they'd flown over, widened in appreciation. "Where are you staying?"

"Rockley Sands Resort."

"Bugger me." His face fell. "That's north of Bridgetown. I'm on the other side of the island."

"Franchesca."

A good stiff breeze could have knocked Frankie over. It had to be a mirage. She was certain of it. That was not Aiden Kilbourn leaning against a Jeep in shorts and a sexy short-sleeved button down. Boat shoes and Ray-bans. His beard looked a little scruffier than the last time she'd seen him.

"What the f—"

"I take it you're Franchesca?" the Aussie asked.

"Yeah, but... we're not together."

Aiden straightened from the fender and crossed to her. "Let's go." He reached for her bag.

Instinctively, Frankie snatched it out of his reach. "I'm taking a cab," she insisted.

"No, you're not."

"Aiden, I told Pru I'd take a cab."

"And I told her I'd pick you up."

"Franchesca, it was lovely meeting you, but I've got to go," the Aussie said, backing away.

"Oh, but..."

"Maybe I'll see you around the island." He blew her a kiss, dropped a "mate" in Aiden's direction, and sauntered off in search of a cab.

"Damnit, Aiden. I didn't even get to give him my number."

"Pity." He hefted her bag into the back of the Jeep and secured it with a tie down strap.

"So, what's this? You're doing your good deed for the day and giving a poor stripper a ride?" she shot back.

"I already apologized for that."

"And it was touchingly heartfelt," Frankie reminded him.

"Get in the damn car."

4

---

*a*iden waited until she was belted in before pulling out onto the main road. He hadn't exactly told Pruitt that he'd be picking Franchesca up. He'd overheard her talking about the maid of honor's arrival time the night before. He'd flown down with them to keep an eye on Chip. He'd screwed up Chip and Pruitt's happiness once before and wasn't going to let anything happen to them the second time around.

Besides, it gave him an excuse to spend some time alone with Franchesca. He'd thought of her—a lot—since the engagement party. She was... interesting. And damned if her headache cure hadn't worked like a charm.

He needed to do something about those headaches, about the root of them. And he'd decided to use this trip as planning time. Plotting time. It was long past time he did something about the mess.

"Did you have a good flight?" he asked.

"Great. Would have been better if I could have gotten surfer guy's number."

"That's your type?"

"Ah ah ah!" she pointed a finger at him. "You of all people don't get to comment on my type."

"Me of all people?" he asked, stepping on the gas to go around the roundabout.

Frankie grabbed on to the handle mounted on the dashboard but didn't tell him to slow down.

"If we flipped back through some of your latest conquests, we'd see one blonde skeleton after another shopping and smiling and getting her picture taken."

It was the truth. But that's what Manhattan had to offer. Hundreds of well-to-do socialites that looked alike, acted alike, and had the same goals in life.

"Conquests. Is that what Hang Ten back there would have been?"

"Shut up."

Aiden slowed abruptly to slip around a pick-up truck stopping at a roadside coconut stand. He drove rarely in Manhattan and had been delighted to find that traffic laws were more suggestions than actual laws on the island. It took him back to his racing days. The one time in his life that he'd ever really felt carefree.

"Jesus, Aide," Frankie said, gripping the handle as they entered the next roundabout.

The nickname, freely given, felt strange to him... warm, familiar. "Welcome to Barbados," he offered, slipping out the other side of the traffic circle.

She let go of the handle to harness her hair that was blowing wildly in all directions. She coiled it on top of her head and secured it with an elastic band. He let his gaze travel down her body. The pink tank top and white cotton shorts showed off the lovely olive tone of her legs. She had Mediterranean in her lineage. He'd bet money on it. No blonde skeleton was Franchesca Baranski.

"Eyes on the road, buddy," she said dryly.

"I was just wondering if it was casual day."

"This is the one and only outfit of the whole trip that didn't have to be coordinated with the bridesmonsters, and you won't ruin my enjoyment of it."

"Coordinating outfits?" He was so glad he wasn't a woman.

"Price you pay for having friends," Frankie said. "But I'm sure you wouldn't know anything about that."

And that was why Aiden kept his circle small. Miniscule really. He wasn't social, didn't enjoy attention or parties. He liked making money, rising to a challenge, finding the most creative solution to obstinate obstacles.

"Wow. Look at that water." She pointed an unpolished finger to their left and leaned closer to him to get a better view. The highway paralleled the turquoise of the Caribbean Sea. He caught the scent of her hair, something exotic, spiced. And for one glorious second, the image of Frankie naked and sprawled across his bed materialized, unbidden in his mind's eye.

"Picture perfect," Aiden agreed.

"Have you ever been here before?" Frankie asked, digging through her bag. Triumphantly, she pulled out a tube of sunscreen.

"Are you making small talk?" he asked.

"Figured we wouldn't fight as much over 'pretty ocean' and 'come here often?'" She squeezed the lotion onto the pads of her fingers and rubbed it onto her face. Aiden wondered when was the last time he'd seen a woman in anything other than full makeup and perfectly coiffed hair. The women he dated preferred to leave "natural" a closely guarded secret.

"Oh, I think we can find contention on any topic," Aiden predicted.

She hummed an answer and didn't elaborate.

"What?" he asked.

"I'm *trying* to be polite. We're here for Pru and Chip, and I'm not going to spoil their wedding by fighting with you."

"You really don't like me, do you?" Aiden asked with a grin.

"Nope. But that doesn't mean I have to be an asshole about it. Some of us were raised better than that." It was a jab at him, but rather than piss him off, it amused him.

"How were you raised?" he prodded.

"Uh-uh." She shook her head. "We're not going to play getting to know you. We don't like each other, and we don't need to. You do your thing, I'll do mine. We'll get through our formal portraits and our bridal party dance, and then we never need to see each other again."

Aiden laughed. The sound of it foreign to his own ears. "I don't *not* like you."

"I'm not biting, Kilbourn. So, you just demolition derby us to the resort in silence, and I'll sit here and pretend you're a cute Australian surfer."

"I'm not trying to start a fight—"

"Uh-uh. No words. Drive. Quietly."

He grinned, shaking his head, and let her have her way. They zoomed along the skinny highway, swerving around potholes and stopping for the occasional pedestrian. They passed sandy white beaches with swaying palms and sunburned tourists. The street narrowed as he steered them into Bridgetown. They whizzed by store fronts and sidewalk produce stands, past a handful of luxury brand stores, and on by the cruise ship port.

Frankie's attention was glued to the water view.

It was beautiful. The kind of blue that only existed on postcards. And the constant tropical breeze made the mid-eighties feel balmy, not oppressive. Not that he'd enjoy it. The long weekend was chock full of the downsides of wealth and privilege. Social obligation, familial responsibility, and—because he was closer to Chip than his own half-brother—gratuitous celebration. Was a marriage really worth this kind of fanfare? Shouldn't the bride and groom want it to be something more private, more meaningful? He accelerated up a short hill, frowning.

"What could possibly be making you make that face while you look at this?" Frankie demanded, extending an arm to the sweeping vista before them.

"I thought we weren't talking?"

"Right. I got distracted watching you look like you swallowed a lemon whole. Back to silence."

On cue, his phone rang in the cup holder. Aiden glanced at the screen, his frown deepening.

"What is it, Elliot?" he asked, keeping his tone clipped. His half-brother's calls only ever meant one thing.

"How's paradise?"

The less Aiden gave his brother, the easier the damage was to minimize.

"What do you need, Elliot?" Aiden asked, ignoring the pleasantries.

"We need to talk about the board vote." He heard the shift in his brother's voice from charm to calculation.

"We've already discussed the vote. I'm not changing my mind," Aiden said brusquely.

"I don't think you've really thought it through—"

"I'm not naming Donaldson CFO. He's under investigation for fraud from his last company. You can't expect me to put our entire holdings at his feet and turn a blind eye."

"The rumors about the fraud are completely overblown. It was just an ex-mistress with an axe to grind." Aiden heard the distinct click of metal connecting with a ball followed by polite applause.

"On the course again?" Elliot spent more time golfing and drinking and fucking his way through the city's female population than he did behind his desk in his very nice corner office one floor below Aiden's.

"Just squeezing in a quick nine with a client."

It was bullshit, but Aiden didn't have the energy to call him on it. The fact was running his family's company and extensive holdings was falling more and more on his shoulders as their father seemed to be taking a step back. Elliot could only be roused to care about business when it was something that affected him personally. He hadn't figured out Elliot's connection to the thieving, cheating Donaldson, but Aiden wasn't about to step aside and let his brother name the next CFO of Kilbourn Holdings.

"My vote stands. No on Donaldson. I have to go." He disconnected before his brother could object and then turned his phone off to avoid the inevitable barrage of calls and texts.

"Business drama?" Frankie asked without looking in his direction.

"Family drama with a side of business."

"Maybe you shouldn't do business with your family."

He shot her a glance. She had her face lifted toward the sun, a sly curve to her lips.

"It's not that easy."

She deigned to look at him now, lowering her sunglasses. "Nothing worthwhile is."

THE RESORT WAS WALLED in against the ocean behind soft yellow stone walls and a gate. He'd paid little attention to it when he'd arrived last night. But watching Frankie ooh and aah over the lush landscape and the curving drive, he tuned in and let himself forget about his family, his business. The hotel rose up three stories of stucco and stone, two wings joined by a two-story, open-aired lobby. The greenery continued inside, colorful pots clustered around a stone fountain. There was a bar on either end of the lobby and a straight through view to the water.

"Wow," Franchesca whispered behind him.

The woman behind the desk with the cheerful knotted scarf in canary yellow looked up from her computer. "I hope you're enjoying your stay, Mr. Kilbourn," she said with the subtle accent of the island adding music to her words.

"Of course," he assured her. "Ms. Baranski is checking in."

"Yes, of course. Welcome, Ms. Baranski."

"Thank you. Your resort is beautiful," Frankie said with an easy smile she'd never given him.

As if she'd heard his thoughts, Frankie turned to him. She looked him up and down and arched an eyebrow. "Thank you for the ride. You can go now."

He gave her a slow, dangerous smile. Franchesca Baranski had no idea who she was taunting. He wasn't a man who was dismissed. He stepped closer to her, crowding her against the desk, and saw the surprise, the concern in those big eyes. There was something else too. A little flare, a spark of desire.

Aiden reached for her hand and brought her knuckles to his lips.

"The pleasure was all mine." He saw the goosebumps that rose on her arm and grinned.

"I'm sure it usually is," she shot back, yanking her hand free and turning her back on him.

---

*a*iden left Frankie at the desk and followed the sound of the waves. He paused at the bar, debated, and then changed his mind and continued outside.

He'd been drinking too much. A medication of sorts for the chronic stress that plagued him. His family seemed hell-bent on making every bad decision they could with regards to the business. He'd ignored it for far too long, preferring to focus on his own responsibilities. But now he needed to be present. He'd be damned if he let anyone—family included—destroy what had been three generations in the making.

Hands in the pockets of his shorts, he strolled across the coral stone terrace, his shirt fluttering in the breeze. The infinity edge pool sparkled under the sun to his right. A handful of mid-afternoon guests enjoyed ceviche and cham-pagne at the outdoor seafood restaurant to his left.

He followed the path down the stairs and to the right where it meandered between beach and vegetation. Pruitt's father might not think much of Chip as a son-in-law, but he wasn't going to let that stand in the way of spending lavishly.

He'd been willing to rent out the cordoned off section of the resort to ensure his princess had a special and private day.

Aiden found the bride and groom sunning themselves at the edge of a freeform lagoon overlooking the beach and ocean. The bridesmaids—bridesmonsters, he corrected himself with amusement—were lounging in studied positions of perfection that best accented their appeal. He noticed the straightening of shoulders, the jutting of chests when they spotted him. They were always on the hunt.

But he was no one's quarry.

He dropped down at the end of Chip's lounger, his back to the monsters. "Your maid of honor has been delivered," he announced.

Pru peeked up at him from under the brim of a ridiculous sun hat. "Aiden! I scheduled a car to pick up Ms. I'll-Just-Take-a-Taxi."

"I canceled it," he said with a shrug. "I was already heading in that direction."

"He's just trying to get back into Frankie's good graces," Chip said loyally. His friend waved his empty glass at a passing pool server and circled his finger signaling a round. It looked like Aiden would be getting that drink after all.

"Uh-huh." Pruitt wasn't believing either of them. Not for a second.

"Did you pick up my genius best friend to pick on her? Because if you did, I'm not going to be happy with you, Aiden Kilbourn," Pruitt said, jabbing a finger into his arm.

"Pick on her? What is this? Second grade?" Aiden teased.

"What exactly did you say to her at the engagement party?" Pruitt demanded.

"She didn't tell you?" Aiden was surprised. He thought Frankie would have run tattling.

"My beautiful best friend doesn't want me to worry about a

thing. And apparently that includes whatever idiotic thing you said or did at the party."

Aiden shared a look with Chip. Neither of them were enthusiastic about repeating the insult.

Pruitt snapped her fingers. "Oh, no! Uh-uh! Don't you look at him, Chip. Spill it right now."

Chip's resolve crumbled faster than a cookie in the sticky hands of a toddler. "Aiden may have mentioned that Frankie danced like she had experience on the pole."

"You called her a *stripper*?" Pruitt's screech could probably be heard by the catamaran five-hundred yards off the coast.

Aiden winced. "In my defense—"

"There's no defense! Damn it, Aiden. She's one of my favorite people. You can't treat her like she's nothing."

"I understand, and I apologized, and I tried to make amends by picking her up today."

Pru cracked a slight smile. "Tried to, huh? She wasn't amenable?" she asked innocently.

"Not exactly," Aiden admitted. Not at all, really.

Chip slapped him on the shoulder. "Sorry, man. Our Frankie's not the most forgiving person in the world."

"So one slip up, and that's it?"

Pruitt peered at him over her sunglasses. "Why? Are you interested in her?"

"As she so astutely pointed out, I'm no more her type than she is mine," Aiden said, side-stepping the question. He wasn't interested in Frankie. He was intrigued by her, but that was different.

"Why couldn't you have been nice and polite or, God forbid, friendly?" Pruitt sighed.

"I don't want to be friendly. I don't have time for friendly."

Pruitt flopped back on her lounger pouting. "And now we have a maid of honor and best man who hate each other."

"We should have eloped," Chip said, squeezing her thigh with affection.

"We are eloping. We just took everyone with us."

Aiden bit back a quip about knowing better for next time. Thanks to him, there almost hadn't been a first time.

The server returned with a tray of pink frothy drinks with umbrellas and enough fruit to build a salad. "Mr. Randolph," he said with a flourish. Chip grinned and passed out the drinks. "Hatfield, you're the man." He slid a twenty onto the tray.

Aiden took a sip of his drink, winced, and set the glass down on the table next to the chair.

"Well, if it isn't Mr. and almost Mrs. Randolph."

Pru squealed and jumped out of her chair. "You're here!" She threw her arms around Franchesca.

She'd changed, he noted. Gone were the very small white shorts and entertainingly tight tank. In their place was a flowy cover up with a deep v that showed an eyeful of breathtaking cleavage and a hint of the black bikini beneath. Her hair was still piled atop her head. She looked exotic, curvy. And if he wasn't careful, he'd have a hard-on like a teenager in a moment.

There was nothing subtle about Franchesca.

"I made it," she said, grinning down at Pru.

"How was your flight? Do you want a drink?"

"Here." Aiden pressed his pink concoction into her hand.

She stared at the glass with suspicion.

"Oh, for God's sake. It's not poisoned. Just drink the damn thing," he ordered.

"Remember what we were talking about, Aiden?" Pru warned him. "*Friendly*?"

"You're in trouble," Frankie sang under her breath so only he could hear. She took a sip of the drink. Her full lips closed over the straw where his had been only moments ago. "Don't you worry about Aide and me. No drama. Scout's honor. Even if he did cockblock me from a sexy surfer at the airport."

Pru linked her arm through Frankie's and led her away, shooting him a dirty look over her shoulder. "Come on, Frankie. Let's go spend some time with the girls. Now, tell me about the surfer."

Aiden and Chip watched them go.

"Surfer, huh?" Chip asked.

"Shut up."

Chip laughed. "Come on. Let's play some volleyball."

6

___

"*L*adies, our maid of honor has arrived," Pruitt announced cheerily to the reclining goddesses.

"Yay," Margeaux said without looking up from her phone. Her blonde hair was rolled in a chic chignon at the base of her neck. She looked regal, even in a bikini.

Pruitt dragged Frankie toward a pair of sun loungers. She took another sip of the pink frozen tartness. It tasted vaguely of grapefruit and vodka. But it would do.

"Now, sit. And spill," Pru ordered. "The story, not the drink."

Frankie handed over the glass with a sigh. She stepped out of her sandals and pulled the cover up over her head.

She felt a heated gaze on her skin and turned to see Aiden standing in the sand looking at her. He flashed her a cocky grin and shucked his shirt. He wasn't lean like the rest of the groomsmen. He was bigger, more muscled. His chest alone made her mouth water. They stared admiringly at each other.

"Staaaalling," Pru sang, drawing her attention.

"Ugh. Fine." She turned her back on the beach, on Aiden. "What do you want to know?"

"How did your ride in from the airport go with Aiden?"

Margeaux dropped her phone and her jaw. Taffany, who had been busy swilling tequila straight from the bottle in a one-piece with less fabric than Frankie's bikini, sat up.

"You and the very good-looking best man?" Cressida wondered, her accent seeming to shift between Austrian and Russian. Frankie couldn't stop staring at the woman's breasts that seemed hell-bent on escaping the scrap of fabric masquerading as a bandeau top.

Self-consciously, Frankie reached up to adjust the ties of her own suit to make sure her girls didn't escape.

A chorus of "Ooooohs" rose from the volleyball court, and the girls craned their necks to see what had happened. Aiden, still spectacularly shirtless and ripped, was holding a hand over his eye.

"What did I tell you guys?" Pru yelled.

"No bruises!" they parroted back to her.

"No bruises, no cuts, no scrapes, no freak hair accidents. I need your faces perfect for pictures," the bride reminded them.

"Sorry," they said as one.

"Aiden was distracted," Chip added with a wink.

Aiden gave Frankie a long look, and she dropped her hands from where they were fiddling with the strings of her suit. *Had he been watching her?*

"Can't you guys just sit and read?" Pru begged.

"No more overhand serves," Davenport, the peacemaker and resident drunk, offered.

"Ugh. Fine. But keep your attention on the ball, Aiden." Pru sat back down. "It's like herding kindergartners at a candy factory. Now, sit down Frankie before Aiden loses an eye checking you out."

All attention on her, Frankie sank down on the chair and

stretched her legs out in front of her. "He picked me up at the airport," she said. She wasn't a fan of gossip in general and feeding anything to these hellhounds was a bad, bad idea.

"Why?" Margeaux asked, wrinkling her nose. "Was there a mix up?"

In Margeaux's beautiful, pristine, gold-dipped world, that was the only plausible reason why Aiden Kilbourn would offer a ride to someone so lowly. Riled now, Frankie gave a lazy one-shoulder shrug as she plucked at the ties of her top. "Nope. He was waiting for me when I got off the plane."

"He canceled the car I had scheduled to pick her up," Pru added.

Taffany picked up the tequila again but handed it to Frankie. "Way to go, Francine."

"Frankie."

"Whatever."

"I don't understand," Margeaux announced. She took her sunglasses off and arranged herself on her side, a model taking directions from an invisible photographer. "Why would Aiden go out of his way for *you*?"

"Hey, why don't we leave the cat claws at home, Margeaux?" Pru warned the woman.

"Do not listen to this angry woman," Cressida said, pointing in Margeaux's direction. "She has bet she can fuck Aiden this weekend."

"Fuck you, Cressida," Margeaux spat out.

"That was not the bet," Cressida insisted, frowning. Frankie couldn't tell if she was purposely poking at Margeaux or if the language barrier made for accidental insults.

"Ladies," Pru sighed. She rubbed absently at her forehead.

No drama, Frankie reminded herself. *She was here to make sure Pru had her perfect day.* She took a drink straight from the bottle. "Not to worry, *Margie*. Your odds are still excellent for luring him into your Venus Fly Trap vag. He was just being nice. There's no interest on either side," Frankie promised.

"Aiden isn't nice," Margeaux argued, ignoring the slam on her vagina.

"Then why do you want to bang him?" Frankie asked in frustration.

Taffany launched into a fit of giggles and hiccups. She reached for the bottle. "*Hello*. He's gorg *and* rich. What else is there? A prenup from him would set a girl up at least into her fifties."

"I have heard that he is quite excellent in bed," Cressida added. "His children would be prime specimens."

These women were from a different planet. Planet Crazy Bitch.

Frankie's parents got married because they fell in love in high school and got pregnant on prom night. They fought about toilet paper and which one of them was supposed to call the accountant. That was normal. That was love.

This? This was what happened with too much inbreeding amongst Manhattan's wealthy.

"Don't you want to meet a guy and fall in love?" Frankie asked the group in general.

The blondes shared a baffled look and broke out into a delightful cultured laughter—plus hiccups from Taffany.

"That is so *poor people*," Taffany announced. "Poor people have to look for love because they can't have money."

"So, money is better than love?" Frankie reiterated the point.

"Duh. And what's better than money?" Taffany chirped, taking the tequila back.

"More money," Margeaux and Cressida chimed in.

"To trophy wives," Taffany said, holding the bottle aloft. Margeaux and Cressida raised their glasses and Pru, looking slightly embarrassed, raised hers.

"To trophy wives," they echoed.

"Well, I've been doing this all wrong then," Frankie announced cheerfully. "Teach me your ways."

Margeaux slid her sunglasses back on. "Sweetie, no amount of education can make *this*," she circled the palm of her hand in Frankie's direction, "trophy. You're more participation medal. Anyone can have one."

Fucking asshole. Frankie hoped Margeaux would get backed over by her own limo.

Frankie smiled sweetly. "When you marry husband number two, does the prenup state that you have to have that giant stick removed from your ass, or does that get to stay?"

Taffany choked and sprayed Margeaux with a fine cloud of tequila.

"You fucking idiot!" Margeaux sprang to her feet. She grabbed the bottle out of Taffany's hand and tossed it into the pool.

"Hey!" Taffany reacted as if Margeaux had thrown her teacup Chihuahua off an overpass. She lowered her shoulder and charged, sending them both into the water.

Cressida said something that sounded like a derisive four-letter word in German and stalked off.

"How do you know these clowns again?" Frankie asked as Margeaux grabbed a handful of Taffany's hair.

"Don't fuck with my extensions!" Taffany screamed.

"Oh. Shit. Here we go again," Pru muttered. She put her fingers in her mouth and whistled. The sand volleyball game came to a screeching halt as Chip called a timeout.

"Babe?" he called from the beach.

"They're fighting in the pool again," Pru called back and pointed.

The groomsmen, ever the gentlemen, sprang into action echoing gleeful shouts of "cat fight."

Davenport, tall and skinny, took up position on a lounger and pulled out his phone. "Okay, I'm recording!" Digby, the shorter blond with eight-pack abs that he was constantly showing off dove into the water like an Olympian with Ford—Bradford on his birth certificate—hot on his heels. Ford let out a war whoop and cannonballed into the fray.

Aiden surveyed the scene from the safety of the beach.

In moments, Digby and Ford had wrestled the girls apart. "I hate all of you," Margeaux shouted, slapping the water in disgust.

"I hope your herpes flares," Taffany screeched, trying to claw her way over Ford's shoulder.

"Jesus, if my dad catches wind of this, I'll never hear the end of it," Pru lamented. Chip pulled her into his arms.

"Don't worry, babe. We'll get them drunk and make them sleep it off in their rooms."

"My hero," Pru sighed, turning to kiss her groom.

Frankie watched the groomsmen drag the girls and the bottle out of the pool. "Let's do shots," Digby decided.

"Shots!" Taffany made a mad dash toward the bar.

"Hey there, maid of honor," Ford said, flashing Frankie a wink and a grin. He was ridiculously good-looking. They all were. But Ford had a boyish charm that was hard to resist and was constantly falling in love. It never lasted longer than a week or two. But every time, he insisted that "this girl is the one." He'd tried to convince Frankie to go out with him for going on three years now and vowed that he wouldn't rest until they were married with eleven grandchildren and a house in the Hamptons.

"Don't talk to her!" Margeaux hissed, sliding her arm around his wet waist. "Pay attention to me."

Frankie wiggled her fingers in greeting and watched Ford wrangle the angry blonde away.

"God, I hope he doesn't fuck her again," Chip murmured as they watched the sloppy foursome make a spectacle at the bar.

"That would be unfortunate," Pru agreed. "Davenport, you remember you signed a non-disclosure agreement, correct?" She looked pointedly at the man reviewing video on his phone.

"Come on, Pru. This is like debutantes gone wild."

"No."

"Don't make me delete it. This is ideal blackmail material if Margeaux ends up landing a senator or something."

Pruitt's lips quirked. "Fine. Keep it, but don't post it. This is a low-key, private wedding."

Frankie shook her head. She would never understand the upper class. You could be ostracized for carrying last season's bag, but wrestle a rich bimbo into a pool over a bottle of tequila and that was fine. "I need a drink," she announced. "And not from that bar. Also, food."

"I would be honored if the lady would accompany me to dine upon whatever this humble establishment can supply, though it will surely dim in comparison to the delectable nature of one as lovely as she."

Frankie blinked at Davenport. "Oh Jesus. Are you reading Chaucer again, Dav?"

"Ladies love a man with a romantic turn of phrase. Plus, Digs bet me I couldn't pick up a chick spouting off classic literature."

"Well, it worked on me. Feed me, and tell me I'm pretty, and I'm all yours," Frankie joked.

Davenport offered her his arm. "Dost the lady care for seafood or pizza?"

"Definitely pizza. And a beer."

Pruitt moaned. "Carbs. I want."

"Come with us," Frankie told her.

"I can't. I'm vegan until the reception. Otherwise they'll have to sew me into my dress."

Pruitt had dropped twenty-one large on her custom, one-of-a-kind dresscavaganza. She'd been off carbs—except for the allotted alcohol—for sixty-four days. All of the brides-maids had done the same to ensure that their size zero designer gowns would fit perfectly. Frankie was happy with her eight and the Spanx she'd packed in her suitcase.

Life was too short to not eat pizza.

"You'll be beautiful," Frankie promised her. "Chip here will get you a salad and a yummy green juice, and you won't even miss the pizza."

Lies. Dirty, dirty lies.

"Anything you want, babe," Chip promised.

Pru sighed. "Will you eat with me?" Chip, whose metabolism had remained the same since he was twelve, looked crestfallen for just a moment before his resolve kicked in. "I'd be honored."

"Maybe you should ask your best man to join you," Frankie suggested, jutting her chin down to the sand where the shirtless Aiden was glaring at his phone. "Come on, my dear Davenport. Mama needs food."

7

*O*istins Fish Fry was the kind of human meat market that should have bothered Aiden. It was a press of bodies on all sides. Tents flapping wildly in the constant breeze. Neon lights, dancers with glow sticks, and open grills everywhere. But it wasn't the wild crowds lining up for a spot at picnic tables where they'd be served freshly grilled fish and cold beer that concerned him.

It was the fact that no one else seemed to be bothered by the fact that the bride and bridesmaids were half an hour late and no one was answering their phones.

Why Chip and Pru needed yet another bachelor and bachelorette party was beyond him. He'd attended the one in the city. A steak and scotch dinner followed by one of the more tasteful strip clubs that the groomsmen had done their best to debauch.

Today, they'd hit three rum shops and a distillery for a private tour. No strippers this time, not with the wedding less than twenty-four hours away. But the girls had been cagey about their plans, and now they were MIA. Aiden was not happy.

The band struck up another energetic song, and Aiden brushed off a few invitations to dance. Chip and the rest of them were happy to be swallowed up by the crowd, making a mockery of the dance.

"Shake your ass, Kilbourn," Digby shouted from the middle of a dozen ladies. They encircled him, moving as one, and Aiden pondered punching Digby in the face. But that would upset Pru, and Digby was drunk enough he might not notice the blow.

"Best bachelor party ever," Chip announced at the top of his lungs. The crowd around him cheered. He'd said the same thing at the steak dinner and again after a particularly creative lap dance. Chip was an effusive kind of guy. He loved everything, and it was hard not to love him back.

Aiden waded through the crowd to his side. "Where are the girls?" he demanded.

Chip closed one eye and tried to focus. Aiden, for once in recent memory, was the only sober member of the party. "Girls? They're everywhere, man." He waved a hand in a wide circle.

"Not those girls. Our girls. Your bride, Pru? Frankie? The bridesmaids?"

"Ohhh, those girls! They're awesome, aren't they?" Chip said, leaning hard on Aiden. "Well, Pru and Frankie are. The other three are kind of scary. But totally in an *al-shome* way."

"Yeah. Totally *al-shome*. Aren't they supposed to be meeting us here?"

"Oh, yeah! I forgot." He fumbled through his pocket for a phone. "Let me call my beautiful bride. I'm getting married tomorrow. Did you know?"

Aiden bit back a sigh. "I'm aware. Dial."

"Okay, okay."

Chip stabbed at the screen.

"Baaaaaaaaby!" Pru, drunk as a skunk, answered the video call. She was listing to the right on one of the blonde bridesmaids.

"Babe! I'm so drunk!" Chip shouted cheerfully.

"Oh, my God! Me too! Taffany threw up twice so far!"

The girls whooped in the background. "Puking rally," Taffany crowed.

"Jesus. Where's Frankie?" Aiden asked.

"She's right here," Pru sang. "Isn't she beautiful?" The camera switched to an extreme close up of a very sober, very annoyed Frankie.

"Yeah, I'm gorgeous. We're all aware. Pru, drink your water." Frankie took the phone from her friend.

"For the love of god, Aide. Tell me someone there is sober. I need to get food into these girls before they turn to drunken cannibalism."

"Cannonball," Taffany shouted, leaning over Frankie's shoulder and planting a wet kiss on her face.

Frankie rolled her eyes.

"Where are you?" Aiden demanded.

"How the fuck should I know? It's dark, and there's potholes so we could be anywhere on the island."

Aiden sighed. "Ask the driver where you are and how long it'll be before you're here."

From his angle, Aiden watched as Frankie climbed her way over a seat around a blonde and stuck her head between the driver and passenger seats. Her breasts were exploding out of the low neckline of her dress.

"Don't put his eye out," Aiden said mildly.

Frankie looked down, looked up, and flicked him off. "Deal with the view for two seconds, ass. Excuse me, Walter. Do you know how long it'll be before we get to Oistins?"

Aiden couldn't hear the driver's reply. He wasn't sure if it was because of the noise around him, the drunken hysteria of the women on Frankie's end, or the hypnotic view of her breasts.

"Five minutes," she repeated. "Thank God. We need food." Her eyes went wide.

"What? What's wrong?"

"Which one of you just bit me in the ass?" Frankie yelped.

"Cannonball," Taffany squealed.

Pru popped up on the screen again over Frankie's shoulder. "What are we doing? Are you two making out on my phone?" she asked.

"We're not making out," Frankie told her.

"You guys totally should. I bet it would be SO. HOT. Cause you both are SO. HOT."

Frankie stared into the camera. "Christ, can't you wealthy folk buy constitutions? Learn to hold your liquor, people!"

"I'll glue Chip to a table and meet you on the street. We can revisit the making out suggestion when you get here," Aiden offered.

"Ha." She disconnected the call, and Aiden dragged Chip and Ford out of the crowd. A flash of cash gave them an entire turquoise picnic table at Uncle George's Fish Net.

"Stay here," he ordered and waded back into the crowd. By the time he found the sidewalk, he could hear them and felt a wave of relief wash over him. *If this were his wedding, his bride would not be roaming the island. If this were his wedding, it would be him and his bride. No one else to distract or dramatize.*

"It's her bachelorette party!" one of them shouted, pointing at Pruitt who was wearing an upside down I'm The Bride sash and a tiara in case anyone had any doubt.

"Please tell me you have food for us in the next seven seconds," Frankie called, pushing through the crowd to get to him, dragging Pruitt with her. She was wearing a short black dress with a deep scoop in the front. More of her was covered than the rest of the bridesmaids combined. He could see Taffany's flesh colored underwear... or bare labia. He wasn't sure.

Aiden clamped a hand on Frankie's free wrist. "Follow me."

"Hello to you, too," she grumbled.

He surged into the crowd, nearly a head above everyone else. Uncle George's white tents were ahead. He felt Frankie stumble behind him and paused. "Why did you insist on wearing those?" he asked, surly for no reason other than he'd been worried. She wore four-inch heeled sandals that wrapped up her calves.

"Ask the bridesmonsters," Frankie grumbled. "Coordination."

"Aiiiiiiden!" An animated Margeaux threw herself into his chest hard enough that he had to catch her. "I missed you!" He saw it coming, was powerless to stop those two over-inflated raspberry lips as they came at him.

She laid a kiss on him that was sixty steps beyond friendly. She pulled back and looked up at him, squinting with one eye. "You and me are gonna have sex." She poked him in the chest with a talon-like fingernail. "S-E-X."

"Can we please get something to eat before you two decide to fuck?"

"I know what I'm hungry for," Margeaux said, saucily. She slid her hand from Aiden's chest to his crotch and squeezed. Aiden's first reflex was to swing at her. The best offense was a good defense. But before he could decide whether to hit his first woman ever or just cower in fear, Frankie swooped in.

She slipped an arm around Margeaux's swan-like neck and tightened her grip. "Get your hands off his junk or he'll sue you for sexual harassment, Marge."

Margeaux stumbled under the weight and pressure Frankie was applying. "'s not sexy harassment if I'm a lady. And I'm a fucking lady!"

"My lawyer and I would disagree," Aiden said coldly.

"Oh, hell. Get, Pru," Frankie ordered, pointing behind him. "I'll contain Slutzilla here."

Pruitt had decided to take a rest and was sitting on the sidewalk holding her shoes in her hand. Aiden was too tired to fight the shoes back on her feet, so he tossed the bride over his shoulder and hoped the scrap of white dress kept everything important covered.

She was singing "Here Comes the Bride" when he dumped her in Chip's lap. The drunken couple was ecstatic to see each other. Frankie was ecstatic to see plates of fish and rice piled on the table. She slapped the beer out of Pru's hand and waved over the server. "Is there any way we can get a ton of water?" she asked, laying a hand on his arm. The guy grinned at her as if she were asking if she could give him free blow jobs for life.

"Anything for you, miss."

"Keep the miss and call me Frankie," she insisted. "Water for everyone, and I'll be in your debt forever."

"Look! Frankie's making friends with the help again," Margeaux crowed. "It's cause she *is* the help."

"Oh for fuck's sake, why are you such a c-word?" Pruitt demanded from Chip's lap.

Margeaux apparently had built up quite an immunity to being called the c-word. She was too busy laughing at her own joke to respond and fell off the bench backwards. No one stopped to help her up.

Digby and Davenport materialized out of the crowd and pounced on the food. Davenport was sporting a hickey on his neck. Digby was wearing a hat he hadn't had ten minutes ago.

Taffany eyed the table with skepticism. She nearly tackled a server who was carting a tray of beers. "Excuse me. Where is the VIP section?"

The server laughed so loud and for so long that Taffany forgot what she'd asked and sat down next to Cressida who was enthusiastically making out with a stranger.

Aiden slid onto the bench beside Frankie, who was so busy shoveling food into her mouth, eyes rolling back in her head in pleasure, that she didn't even notice him. The moans escaping her mouth were not G-rated, and Aiden felt his blood warm.

"Nice night," he commented.

"Oh, the best," Frankie agreed with sarcasm, spearing a piece of grilled fish. "I can't think of anything I'd rather be doing."

He leaned in, crowding her. "I can."

Those big, bright eyes looked at him warily. "What? Get mauled by Marge?"

"Not at the top of my list. Not actually anywhere on my list. She's terrifying."

Frankie snorted. "Well, at least you're not completely stupid."

"Not completely," he agreed.

Aiden dropped his hand to the sliver of bench between them, his knuckles grazing her bare thigh. Testing. She jumped at the contact but didn't bite his head off. And what he read in her eyes? It was that quick spark of desire. He wanted to see it again. He wanted to watch it blaze to life.

Testing, he placed his hand on Frankie's knee under the table. Her skin was smooth, silk-like under his palm. And he wanted more.

She was still watching him. "What's your game, Kilbourn?"

"I'm not sure," he admitted. He moved his hand an inch higher, watching her watch him.

He was hard, not just half-mast but achingly, throbbingly hard, and all he'd touched was her leg. Testing again, he let the tips of his fingers trace small circles up the inside of her thigh.

She reached for her beer and drank deeply but didn't ask him to stop. Didn't call him an asshole. He didn't know what he was doing, what he hoped to gain from it. He wanted to keep touching her.

Another inch, another circle. Was it his imagination? Was she opening her legs just a little wider? Her knee pressed into his. His food was forgotten in front of him. The laughter and chatter around the table disappeared as his world refined itself down to only Franchesca. The only thing he was aware of was Frankie's silk-like skin and the hem of her dress, the way her lips were parting as if to draw a breath.

When would she stop him?

"This is stupid," she whispered, her eyelids heavy.

"So stupid," Aiden agreed.

"I don't like you."

"Yes, you do."

She dropped her hand to his thigh and squeezed. "I don't like to be left out." His cock throbbed painfully an inch from her fingers. He gritted his teeth. He felt like a horny teenager, unable to control his body in the presence of a pretty girl. But Franchesca was more than just pretty. She was a temptress.

He toyed with the hem of her dress. Another inch higher and he'd catch a glimpse of what she wore underneath. He wanted to stroke his fingers over the lace or silk or cotton whatever she'd covered herself with. Wanted to trace the edge of it until she was begging with her body. Then he'd slip his fingers underneath and trace that wet seam that protected what he wanted most—

"Franchesca, right?"

She jumped a mile, yanking her hand away from his lap. He missed the contact immediately. Aiden could practically hear his dick whimper.

"Oh, my God. Hot Aussie Surfer," Frankie breathed, shoving Aiden's hand away from her promised land.

8

Frankie was one second away from spontaneously combusting. Why had she let Aiden Kilbourn take his fingers on a walking tour of her inner thigh? And why had hot surfer guy magically appeared the second that she was going to let Aiden do dirty, evil things to her?

"It's Brendan, actually," he told her with a crooked grin. His hair was still messy, his eyes still blue, and his body was still rocking under a t-shirt and worn cargo shorts.

"Still Frankie," she said, smiling until she felt Aiden's fingers skim up the back of her thigh.

She slapped at his hand behind her while grinning maniacally up at Brendan. Aiden captured her hand and gave it a hard squeeze. Message received.

"'Scuse me!" Taffany waved and crawled across the picnic table revealing her nether region to all of Uncle George's. "I'm Taffany," she announced extending her hand, knuckles up to Brendan.

The surfer shot Frankie a "what the fuck" look before accepting Taffany's hand.

"Taffany, yeah? That's an... interesting name."

"I rebranded myself," Taffany announced proudly, shoving her hand toward his mouth. "Kiss it!"

Frankie stepped between them and broke Taffany's hold on the surfer. He shook his hand to get the circulation back.

"Anyway, I'm happy I ran into you. I was hoping I'd see you here."

"Yeah, me too," Frankie said. Her brain wasn't working fast enough. She could *feel* Aiden glaring holes into her. "You want to dance? Way over there. Away from here?"

He flashed a dimple at her. "Love to."

Frankie wrestled her hand away from Aiden. "Be back in a few minutes, Pru," she called to the bride.

"Have fun storming the castle," Pru sang.

"Feed her and water her," Frankie ordered Chip as Brendan led her into the crowd.

She'd held hands with two men tonight. One she didn't like at all and one she'd developed an insta-crush on. So why didn't insta-crush give her the pterodactyls in her stomach like Aiden had?

Brendan spun her around, and the crowd flashed by in colors and scents. He pulled her back, and she laughed.

"So, what's a pretty American like you doing in a place like this?" he asked, dimpling adorably for her.

Frankie felt... nothing. God. Damn. It. A cute, sexy, funny guy who was built to be on some kind of fundraising calendar holding a puppy was swirling her around a dance floor, and all she could think about was Aiden's finger prints on her thigh. That son of bitch was ruining her life.

"I'm babysitting several drunk women so everyone will show up for the wedding tomorrow. How about you, surf here often?"

He grinned, and again she felt less than nothing. Aiden

Kilbourn was the fucking devil, and she was going to murder his face.

Brendan launched into an explanation of his travel habits, following the surf and whatnot. She should have been charmed, excited, hell, she should have been wet. She must have had some bad rum or beer or fish. It was the only logical explanation.

"Excuse me, Franchesca." The hand on her shoulder sent a prairie fire racing through her veins. "Pruitt requires your attention," Aiden announced a bit too smugly for Frankie's liking.

Cressida, all five foot eleven of her, was peering over his shoulder. "I will dance with you," she announced, pulling Brendan into her leanly muscled arms.

"Uhhh," Brendan looked over his shoulder at Frankie as Cressida dragged him into the night.

"What the hell was that?" Frankie hissed.

Aiden gripped her around the waist. "Exactly what I was wondering. I'm not used to being thrown over, Franchesca."

"Look, we either had too much to drink, or we're coming down with food poisoning. Those are the only explanations I can come up with for why—"

He cut her off and pushed her behind a fish stand. She could hear the cooks and servers shouting at each other from the open window above her head. "I thought you said Pru needed me," she snapped.

He reached out and tucked a wayward curl behind her ear, and there were those fucking pterodactyls. *It wasn't fair.*

"Maybe it wasn't Pru. Maybe it was me."

"Aiden, this is a terrible idea. And *maybe* Brendan showing up was the best thing that could have happened. He saved us from making a huge mistake."

"Don't fuck him." He laid down the gauntlet, and despite

the lack of pterodactyls where Brendan was concerned, Aiden's proclamation made the surfer more attractive.

"I fuck who I want, when I want."

"You want me."

If Aiden put his hands on her here, there'd be no denying it. She'd be too busy climbing him like a mountain and unzipping his shorts. Distance was her friend. Distance would keep her sane.

She held up her hands. "Let's not get carried away. We're here for Pru and Chip and their wedding. That's it. Not some tropical sexathon." Though when she put it that way and Aiden was looking at her like she was a popsicle begging to be licked, Frankie had trouble reminding herself why she couldn't have both.

"Franchesca." The way he said her name sounded like a threat.

"Aiden," she shot back.

"Fuck." He took a step back, rubbing absently at his forehead. "I don't know why you're saying no."

"I'm worth more than a quick bang on the beach. I take sex seriously. I have to like the person I'm fucking."

There was a tic in his jaw.

"You were seconds away from letting me shove my fingers—"

"Stop!" She cut him off, not mentally prepared to hear what he'd been about to do with those beautiful fingers. "I made a mistake. I got carried away. But I have the right to change my mind at any time whether your dick's out or not."

"I would never force you to do anything you didn't want to do."

"Damn it, Aiden. Look. Maybe my body wants your body. But if I don't want the rest of you, then it's not happening."

"I don't do relationships. But what I can offer—"

"Christ, I'm not talking about relationships. I'm talking about liking you as a person."

"You keep saying you don't like me, but I think you're trying to convince yourself."

"My prerogative. Got it? Bottom line, you're not getting in my pretty pink thong. I don't like you enough for that. Now, I need a minute and some air. Do me a favor and check on Pru and the rest of those idiots."

She turned, ruining her exit by tripping over an empty crate outside the shack's back door. But she didn't fall on her face. Picking her way toward the sidewalk, Frankie didn't relax until she could no longer feel the burning weight of Aiden's gaze on her.

"What is with that guy?" she muttered under her breath. She didn't like him, yet she was more than happy to let him meander a trail up her thigh to her happy place. She felt like her blood had turned to electricity, zinging through her veins at impossible speeds. He was cold, judgmental, reserved. Hell, he'd assumed she was a stripper. That alone should banish him from her bed for life.

Frankie picked her way through the crowd on the sidewalk. Cab drivers catcalled fares, and drunken tourists stumbled into ZRs, the island's minivan transportation. For a buck U.S., you could get pretty much anywhere from Bridgetown to St. Lawrence Gap. A group of local girls dressed to the nines wandered by giggling as a group of boys followed a half step behind.

She spotted Chip ahead, looking around as if he was lost. He was standing on the sidewalk ahead of the cab line weaving like a man who'd ingested nothing but rum for an entire weekend.

She raised her hand to hail him. But before she could call out to him, a dirty white van roared up to the sidewalk, the rear door sliding open before it stopped. Chip leaned in, and that's when Frankie saw the hands reach out. They dragged him into the van.

"Hey! Chip!" She started running. The driver, a red cap pulled low, looked her way. "Stop! That's my friend!" Frankie yelled.

"Hey, Mami," the driver said, tossing her a wave as he floored the accelerator. Tires squealing, the door slammed shut with Chip inside, and the van sped away from the curb.

The groom had just been kidnapped.

9

*A*iden was under a full head of steam as he stormed his way through the fish festival crowd. When he found Frankie, he was going to explain that she was being an idiot. Which would probably go over well. Aiden liked having the edge, the advantage in negotiations. And Frankie's weakness was when she let her emotions off the leash. Mad, turned on, that's when she was vulnerable to suggestion.

It was callous, calculating. But he was a Kilbourn. It's what they did.

He spotted her on the sidewalk, and his calculations disappeared as if they'd never been when he saw the fear on her face. She was hailing a cab.

"Franchesca!" he pushed his way to her just as a rusty ZR van clunked to a stop in front of her. There were a half dozen people already on it.

"Aiden!" She grabbed his arm. "Get in!"

Instinctively, he followed her onto the torn-up vinyl of a bench seat.

"What's wrong? What happened?"

"Where you going?" the driver asked.

"Follow that car," Frankie announced, pointing at taillights ahead.

The ZR lurched to a start, and Aiden braced his hand on the seat in front of him. "What in the hell is going on?" he demanded.

"They took Chip." Her breath was coming in heaves as she peered over the front seat...

"What? Who took Chip?"

"I don't know. One second he was standing on the sidewalk, and the next, someone was dragging him into a minivan."

Aiden yanked his phone out. And dialed Chip's number. There was no answer.

A bell rang and the ZR jerked to a stop in front of a sports bar.

"Why are we stopping?" Frankie asked. "They're getting away!"

"Lady, this is a Zed-R. We stop for everyone."

A man dressed in all white with a hand carved cane climbed out of the back and over Frankie to the door. The van sat as he shuffled his way across the street toward the bar.

Aiden reached for his money clip. "How much for no more stops?" he questioned, handing twenties to the remaining passengers.

"I can be late," a woman with a sleeping toddler in her lap said with a smile stuffing the twenty into her bra.

"WooHoo!" A man in an orange and black Hawaiian shirt with a peeling sunburn on his nose and forehead triumphantly held up his twenty. "I love this country! I'm getting' paid to take public transportation."

"Whatever you say, mister," the driver said, accepting his bill and flooring it.

The minivan was well out of sight and Franchesca was

practically vibrating beside him. Aiden slid an arm around her shoulder, anchoring her to his side.

The ZR shuffled forward slowly building speed like a freight train. The driver cranked up the volume of a reggae song and merrily swerved around a trio of potholes. Aiden dialed Chip again. Still nothing.

He swore quietly, his brain turning over the problem. *Who would take Chip the night before his wedding, and why?*

"Franchesca, tell me everything you remember," he said, squeezing her shoulder.

"Everything I remember? Our friend was just dragged off the sidewalk into a fucking van!" Conversation in the ZR shut down as everyone leaned in to listen.

"I got that part already. Now, walk me through everything that you saw."

She went over it again and then once more as the van careened north. Her body shifting against his around turns.

"The driver—he looked at me when I called for Chip—he had a gold tooth and a dirty red cap. But he had it pulled low over his face. That's all I saw. I didn't see who grabbed Chip, but the drunk dumbass stuck his head right in the van. He made it easy for them."

They careened around a sharp turn, slipping into a traffic circle six inches in front of a city bus. The driver tooted the horn in either a friendly thank you or a fuck off. Aiden couldn't tell.

Frankie's hands were white knuckled on the seatback in front of her.

"Are you sure he didn't get in willingly?" Aiden asked squeezing her arm.

She shook her head. "I didn't hear him scream or anything, but he didn't climb into that van by himself.

Everyone he knows here is back at the fish stand. Who would do this?"

It was a question Aiden had been asking himself. Chip Randolph was squeaky clean. No gambling debts, no secret second lives. Just a trust fund kid amiably enjoying his very privileged world. Aiden scrolled through everything he and Chip had discussed in the past few weeks. Had his friend mentioned any issues? Any squabbles in the family? At work?

"You don't think Pru's dad would have done this. Do you?" Frankie asked, eyes wide.

"He hates Chip," Aiden conceded. "But I don't see R.L. Stockton plotting an abduction. He'd stick it to Chip in the prenup."

"Which he did," Frankie pointed out.

"That he did," Aiden agreed. He'd cautioned Chip against signing it, but his friend wouldn't hear of it.

"Still, maybe something Chip did pissed R.L. off?" Franchesca mused.

There was a loud bang, and the ZR slowed. Smoke rose from its engine. The driver swore over the reggae pouring from the speakers as the dashboard lit up with warning lights. He pulled off to the side of the road and jumped out, a small fire extinguisher in his hand.

"Get out," Aiden said, nudging Frankie to the door.

"How are we going to catch them?" she asked, ducking to hop out of the door and the hem of her dress rose indecently high over the curve of her ass. Aiden gripped the material and pulled down as he pushed her out of the vehicle. "We can't give up." She slapped at his hand.

"We're not giving up," Aiden insisted. "We're refocusing. Come on." They left the van and its now ride-less occupants and started walking briskly.

The night air was thick with humidity. He could hear the steady thrum of ocean waves on the beach over a thousand tree frogs chirping.

"Shouldn't we be heading north?" Frankie asked, trotting in her heels to keep up with him.

Aiden slowed his pace in the hopes that she wouldn't break both ankles.

"We're not going to be able to catch them."

"So where are we going?"

"I don't know, Franchesca. I need to think."

He hadn't brought any security with him, doubted that the Randolphs or Stocktons had either. The hotel had its own. Why would they need a personal security detail in paradise? He cursed himself for it now. His friend was missing, and he had no one but the local authorities to turn to.

Frankie stumbled and yelped.

"Your shoes are ridiculous."

"I wasn't planning on walking eighteen miles tonight."

"Clearly," he said dryly. He stepped in front of her. "Get on."

"I beg your pardon?" She sounded haughty as a queen who had just been asked to perform the Cupid Shuffle.

"Hop on and save your feet."

"You're not lugging me around Barbados on your back, Aide," Frankie argued.

"Get on my back now, or I throw you over my shoulder and show the entire island your pretty pink thong."

She hopped nimbly onto his back, her thighs settling on his hips, arms wrapping around his shoulders.

"This isn't exactly how I saw the night going," Aiden announced conversationally. He cupped his hands behind his back under her ass. "I thought I'd have you on your back."

She pinched him through the crisp cotton of his button down. "Hilarious, big guy. Fucking hilarious. Come up with a plan yet?"

"Still thinking," he said, boosting her up higher.

"I don't think it was random," Frankie said thoughtfully. "I don't think it was like 'Hey, nice watch, now get in my van.'"

"Which means he was specifically targeted," Aiden added.

"This is going to crush Pru," Franchesca said half to herself. "She loves him so damn much. Did you know that when he broke up with her after college, she couldn't get out of bed for a week? We just laid there and stared at the ceiling. She wouldn't eat, wouldn't get dressed. She didn't even really talk for days. Her dad had the family doctor visiting her every day."

Aiden felt the stirring of guilt. "I didn't realize she cared so much for him back then." He hadn't. Had thought she'd been indifferent and immature.

"He crushed her when he left, and it took her a long time to get back on her feet. Now, if I were her, I would have spent the rest of my life hating him. But not Pru. She never stopped loving him. And now here we are in paradise for their wedding all these years later, and look what happens."

"We'll get him back," Aiden promised.

"Do you think they'll hurt him?" Her arms tightened around him.

Aiden heard the fear in her tone and reacted to it. "No," he said, his voice gruff. "Odds are they took him for money. They lose their bargaining tool if they rough him up or—"

"Or worse," she finished for him.

"They're supposed to get married tomorrow. What am I going to tell her? God, why would anyone do this? Money? Ransom? Oh, Jesus. He doesn't have ties to the mob, does he?"

"Doubtful," Aiden said wryly.

They heard the groaning of brakes as a city bus eased to a stop beside them. Aiden let Frankie slip off his back to the ground. "Let's go get some answers."

10

_____

*A*s much as Frankie enjoyed seeing all six-feet four-inches of Aiden Kilbourn crammed onto a bus seat, nothing could take away the icy feeling in her stomach. Someone had taken her friend right in front of her and who knew what was happening to him right now. She hated the not knowing.

Her phone buzzed from inside her clutch.

"Oh, shit." She showed the screen to Aiden.

"Answer it. Maybe someone contacted her?"

"Hey, Pru," Frankie said.

"Where are you, Frankenstein?" It was Pru's drunken moniker for drunken Frankie.

Frankie eyed Aiden for a moment. He shrugged. "I'm with Aiden," she said.

"Ohmygod. I knew it!" Pru's shriek put a couple of pin holes in Frankie's eardrum. "I knew you two would hit it off. I'm like literally the smartest person ever."

"The smartest," Frankie agreed.

"Ask her about Chip," Aiden whispered.

Frankie held the phone out so Aiden could listen too.

"Sorry for bailing on you. Is everyone else still there?" she asked.

"Well, I think so. Margeaux passed out under the picnic table, so we had the driver carry her back to the car. And I haven't seen Chip for a little while. I think he went to the bathroom a few minutes ago."

Frankie covered the phone with her hand. "That's Pru's drunk clock. She couldn't tell time right now if there was a Birkin bag on the line," she explained to Aiden.

"We need them back at the resort with security," Aiden told her.

Frankie nodded, not wanting to consider the possibility that Chip's disappearance was just the beginning. "Is anyone there sober?" she asked.

"Oh sure. Lotsa people. There's this guy over here. He's got poodles on his shirt. I think he's sober."

"No, I mean a person you know."

"Huh?"

Oh, for the love of god. Why was talking to a drunk adult harder than prying information out of a kindergartener? "Is Cressida there?" Cressida had the tolerance of an Eastern European man, a big one.

"Sure! Watercress! Phone's for you!" Pru crooned.

"Yes? What is it you want?" Cressida answered.

"Cressida, it's Frankie. I need you to keep a close eye on Pru."

"Why? Will she attempt a crime?"

"No, nothing like that. Just... don't let anything happen to her."

"That is annoyingly vague," Cressida said.

"Yeah, I know. But I can't help it. Can you get them all back to the resort? Just tell them that's where the after party is."

"I will do this. Mainly because my feet hurt, and I would

like to swim naked in the lap pool."

"Uh, okay. Great?"

"Goodbye now."

Aiden snatched the phone out of Frankie's hand. "Just a minute, Cressida. Put Pruitt on the phone again."

They heard wild laughter and some yelling.

"Helloooooooo!" Pruitt sang into the phone.

"Pruitt, it's Aiden," he said.

"Aiden! I knew you and Frankie would fall madly in love! I totally knew it! I even told Chip so. Chip? Chip!"

Frankie covered her face with her hands. "She thinks her fiancé is going to come running."

"Pruitt, do you need Frankie or me for the rest of the night?" Aiden asked.

"Ooooh la la! No!"

Aiden glanced at Frankie. "Good, then I'll keep her to myself a little longer. Get some sleep tonight," he ordered.

"Yes, sir! I hope you two don't get any sleep if you know what I mean," Pruitt yelled.

The entire bus knew what Pru meant even without the help of speakerphone. "Great. Thanks a lot, Aide. Now she thinks we're banging on a beach somewhere." Frankie shoved the phone back in her impractical clutch.

"It's better than knowing the truth at this point."

"*At this point*?" Frankie screeched. "At what *point* do we call the cops? At what *point* do we have to sit Pru down and tell her the wedding isn't happening."

"Calm down."

"Oh yeah, because saying that to a person who's freaking out *always* helps."

"Franchesca." He gripped her chin and made her look at him. "I will fix this. I will find Chip, but I need your help. We're in a foreign country. Yes, quite possibly the friendliest foreign country in the hemisphere, but it's still different from the United States. How many drunken tourists do you think stumble off and disappear for a few hours? How many men fight with their wives and jump in a cab to go someplace else?"

"But that's not what happened," Frankie argued.

"You and I both know that. But a local cop is going to tell you to sit and wait for him to show up."

The hell she'd do that.

Half an hour and what felt like sixty-four bus stops later, they were back at Oistins. The crowds were thinner now nearing midnight and even more inebriated than when they'd left before. But the cab line was busy. Frankie suggested they split up to cover more ground, but Aiden wasn't having it. He stuck by her side like a shadow as she quizzed the first two cab drivers. Had they seen this man? She showed them a picture of Chip taken earlier that day. No, they hadn't. How about a van driver with a gold tooth? No.

It went like that for an hour. No, no, no. No one had seen anything or anyone. There was, of course, the helpful cab driver who announced that all drunk tourists look the same to him, which drew laughter from his friends. But it didn't help.

Frankie was losing hope fast. Every minute felt like Chip was getting farther and farther away from them. He could be anywhere on the island by this point.

She saw the cop whistling on the corner and remembered Aiden's warning. "Fuck it," she whispered, ducking away from Aiden as he quizzed a couple of local fish fryers near the sidewalk.

"Excuse me, officer?"

He tore his eyes away from the in-progress argument that was happening over a parking space. "Yes, ma'am."

"My friend is missing."

"Um-hm." His gaze was back on the two women and the

parking space. He clearly wasn't impressed by her story.

"I saw him get taken by someone in a van. He was kidnapped right here about an hour ago."

The cop sighed. He lifted the brim of his hat and wiped his brow. "Miss, just because someone gets into a van doesn't mean they've been kidnapped. They're called ZRs, and they're public transportation. Maybe your friend went back to the hotel early."

"No, you don't understand. He's getting married tomorrow, and he wouldn't do that. He wouldn't leave his fiancée and not tell her where he was going."

The shouting at the parking space got louder. Horns were honking in the street as the argument spilled into traffic. The yelling turned to shrieking as one woman grabbed a fistful of braids and yanked.

The cop sighed, swearing under his breath. He yanked a whistle out of his pocket and blew it furiously as he ran into the fray.

Frustrated, she turned and found Aiden standing much too close to her. He didn't say a word, but his face did the talking for him.

"Yeah, yeah. You told me so. I get it."

"They're not going to take a disappearance seriously for at least twenty-four hours."

"Fine, smarty pants. What do we do now? We lost the van. We have no idea where he could be or what they want with him or even who they are."

Aiden's phone rang and he fished it out of his pocket. "Unknown number," he read from the screen.

"Maybe it has something to do with Chip," Frankie said, eyes full of hope and dread.

"Kilbourn," he answered. Frankie snatched the phone away from him and hit the speaker button.

A garbled voice on the other end of the call chuckled. "Well, well, Aiden. It looks like we have some business to do after all."

"Who is this?" he demanded.

"That's not important. What is important is the fact that we have a mutual acquaintance."

"Where's Chip? Why did you take him?"

The voice laughed. "I'm going to fuck him up when I meet him," Frankie hissed.

"Patience. All will be revealed."

"Who does he think he is? A Bond villain?" Frankie hissed.

Aiden rolled his eyes and mouthed the words "Shut up."

"If you hurt him or so much as mess up his hair, I will hunt you down," Aiden promised.

"Then let's not let it come to that," the robotic voice on the other end said amicably. "What I want is easily within your grasp of giving. You give me what I want, I give you your friend back, and we all go home happy."

"What is it you want?" Aiden asked.

"I want you to be ready for a meeting tomorrow. I'll contact you with the time and place."

"A meeting?" Aiden repeated.

"It's just business. Nothing personal. Oh, and don't tell anyone. No cops, no security. Just you, me, and Chip."

The call disconnected and Aiden swore.

"Christ. Now what the hell do we do?" Frankie asked. "They make contact and give us nothing? Why didn't they ask for money?"

"Because they don't want money," Aiden said quietly.

Frankie stopped in her tracks. "It's you isn't it? This isn't about Chip at all. They called you because you have what they want."

Aiden wouldn't meet her gaze.

11

"*G*reat. Just fucking great. You do something stupid or illegal or whatever, and innocent people have to pay the price. My best friend's wedding is ruined, her fiancé is missing, and now we have to wait until tomorrow to find out who has him and what they want?"

Frankie ticked off the infractions on her fingers. And Aiden rubbed a hand over his forehead. He'd feel guilty if necessary later. Right now, he needed answers.

"Jesus, Franchesca. Will you shut up for two seconds so I can think?"

"Think? How about we do something? How about we find the driver with the stupid gold tooth and dirty red ball cap and beat the ever-living shit out of him until he talks?"

"By all means. Go ahead and find him. Call me when you do," Aiden snapped back.

"Do you mean Papi, miss?"

Frankie and Aiden both whirled around. And then looked down. The boy couldn't have been more than twelve or thirteen. Skinny with a big grin. He wore a white short-sleeved

Oxford and neatly pressed khaki shorts. The ball cap he wore on his head was clean but rakishly askew.

"Papi?"

"Yeah, gold tooth." The kid pointed to his own pristine front tooth. Gray hair. Greasy hat that looks like it was used to soak up motor oil? Calls all the ladies Mami?"

Frankie dug her fingers into Aiden's arm. "That's him."

"Does he drive a white van with a red square sticker by the taillight?" Aiden asked.

The kid's head bobbed. "Oh sure. He borrows it from his brother-in-law sometimes when he has a driving job."

"Where can we find Papi?" Aiden asked.

"You want a taxi? Glass bottom boat ride?" the kid asked.

"No—"

He snapped his fingers. "I know. Swim with the turtles. Snorkeling, lunch, lots of rum punch."

"No—"

"Ah, drugs then? I can get you better than Papi," the kid promised.

"Excuse me?" Frankie blinked at him.

"Ganja, coke, X—"

A natural born salesman, Aiden decided.

"Christ kid," Frankie groaned. "Look, we need to find Papi he knows where a friend of ours is."

The kid clammed up.

Frankie looked like she was going to shake him like a ragdoll until he coughed up some answers. Aiden put his hand on her arm. "Let me handle this businessman to businessman." He opened his wallet. "You look like an entrepreneur who recognizes a good opportunity."

"ARE you even old enough to drive?" Frankie asked clutching the back of the passenger seat as the little van climbed a steep hill.

The boy—Antonio, their new personal tour guide—shrugged and laid on the horn as a car swerved into their path to avoid a pothole the size of a city block in Manhattan. "What's really in an age?" he waxed philosophically. "Over there is where my grandfather grew up." He said pointing into the dark. "And Rhianna, too."

Aiden's wallet was significantly lighter thanks to Antonio's entrepreneurial nature.

"We don't need the full island tour," Aiden reminded him mildly. "We're looking for Papi."

"Papi's got five, six rum shops he hits after a good night's work."

"Does Papi kidnap people often?" Frankie wanted to know.

Aiden laid his hand over her thigh and squeezed, telegraphing a message to shut the hell up.

"Papi's like... what do you call them? A jack of all trades? He does whatever needs doing. Then he goes and celebrates."

"At a rum shop," Aiden filled in.

"Exactly. First one coming up." He pointed at the shack on their left. It sat smack against the road with six generous inches of sidewalk between its occupants and the stampede of traffic. He yanked the parking brake and opened the door.

"You can't just park in the middle of the road," Frankie protested.

"Lady, this is Barbados. We park wherever."

They piled out after him, and Aiden put a possessive arm around Frankie's shoulders. Who knew what they were walking into or how friendly the welcome would be when word got out why they were looking for Papi. Antonio pushed open the door. Its hinges creaked in protest.

"Come on."

It was surprisingly clean inside. The wood floor was neatly swept. The miniscule bar jutted out from the corner eating up most of the space in the twelve by twelve room. All five of the patrons stopped what they were doing to stare.

"Anyone seen Papi tonight?" Antonio asked.

They stared some more. The bartender spoke first. Aiden thought it was English, but the jumble of words and phrasing was beyond him. The kid answered in kind, and Frankie met Aiden's gaze over Antonio's head.

"Not here. Come on, let's go," Antonio said, grabbing Frankie's hand and pulling her toward the door.

"What was that?" Frankie asked as Antonio towed her back to the van, Aiden behind her.

"What was what?"

"That language you were speaking."

Antonio laughed and they climbed back in the van. "That's Bajan slang. Everyone speaks it. Come on, let's go. Birdspeed."

"Birdspeed?" Frankie asked.

"Yeah, quick fast." He nodded.

They barreled down the road at "birdspeed" before Aiden could ask the question. "Had anyone there seen Papi?"

Antonio shook his head, bouncing in his seat over a bump. "No. No Papi there tonight. We're trying the next rum shop."

"How many rum shops are there?" Frankie asked.

"About fifteen hundred," Antonio answered without batting an eye.

They hit four of the fifteen hundred in half an hour. It was midnight now, and Aiden was beginning to wonder if the kid was taking them on a wild goose chase. Frankie was dejected beside him. She didn't even fight it when he pulled her into his side.

At least not until the zombie-like moan erupted from

behind them. Frankie shrieked and put up her hands like she was going to karate chop the zombie while Aiden tried to push her away from the danger.

It was a man, not a zombie, that slowly rose from the rear bench seat.

"You okay back there, Uncle?" Antonio called.

The man grumbled something incoherent. He raised a small bottle of rum to his mouth, gulped some down, and then collapsed back on the seat.

"That's my Uncle Renshaw," Antonio announced.

"What the hell's wrong with Uncle Renshaw?" Frankie demanded, reluctant to lower her hands.

"He got a big fare. Six tourists. Americans. They needed a ride up north. Big money."

"Looks like he celebrated a little hard," Aiden commented.

Frankie slapped a hand on his leg. "That's it!"

"What's it?"

"He'd make more cash kidnapping someone than just driving a tourist around, right?"

"Presumably."

Frankie leaned between the front seats. "Antonio, where would Papi go if he had some real cash? Where would he celebrate?"

___

12

*B*ig Chuck's Groceries, Fish, Lotto, and Rum Shop was a ramshackle abode perched atop a steep hill with what was probably a breathtaking view of the Caribbean. However, seeing as how it was pitch dark and there were no street lights, Frankie could only assume the view was beautiful.

"I have to pee," she announced. "You two look for Papi, and I'll meet you in the bar."

Frankie found the tiny bathroom crammed in between shelves of canned goods and bags of cookies and chips. The whole place smelled like fried fish sandwiches. And when her stomach growled, she remembered how much of her dinner she'd left on her plate back at Uncle George's. A lifetime ago, when all she had to worry about was Aiden's hand on her leg. She wondered if Cressida had devoured Hot Surfer Guy.

Leaving the bathroom, she stopped and ordered four fish sandwiches and a round of Cokes to go. Holding the greasy paper bag, she went in search of Aiden and Antonio. She found them in a conference with Aiden staring at his phone in a dark corner of the nearly lightless bar. It was a ramshackle shed held together with sheet metal, wood, and prayers. The floor was dirt. The bar was greasy. And there were only a handful of wooden stools for seating.

"What's going on? Is he here?" Frankie asked.

Antonio pointed to a man holding court at the center of the bar. Dirty red hat? Check. Glinting gold tooth? Oh, hell yeah.

"What are we doing over here when he's right there?" she hissed, pointing wildly.

"He's not interested in talking," Aiden said succinctly. Clearly he was pissed. The tic in his stupid perfect jaw was working overtime.

"Yeah, he told Mr. Money Bags here to *leff he.*"

"Translation?"

"Leave him alone," Antonio supplied.

"We're going to have to do this the hard way," Aiden said, dialing the phone.

"What's the hard way?"

"I'm hiring some private security who won't ask too many questions about why we need this asshole to talk."

"Private security? Are you going all Blackwater right now?" Frankie hissed.

"Let me handle this," Aiden insisted. "We're not leaving without answers." He turned and walked out of the bar.

Fuckity fuck fuck fuck. Frankie watched Papi, the big man with his circle of friends, buying rounds, telling stories.

She shoved the bag of fish sandwiches at Antonio. "Hold these, don't eat mine, and go find Aiden. I'll meet you outside in a minute," she ordered. She sidled up to Papi and his gang. They made way for her, eagerly parting like the sea for Moses.

"Papi, Papi, Papi, you're a hard man to find." He was in his late sixties, she guessed, by the fuzzy gray hair under the hat and the softly wrinkled skin around his eyes. He had dark dots on both cheekbones, grizzly stubble on his weak jaw.

"Hey, Mami. What can ol' Papi do for you. Bradley, a drink for my lady friend."

Frankie took the vacated bar stool next to him and picked up the rum the bartender poured for her.

"Papi, you took my friend. You can tell me where he is."

Papi laughed, and after a second, the rest of his friends joined in. "I already tol' your friend. I don' want his money. I don' need his money. You get me?"

"If you don't want money, what do you want?" Frankie said, lowering her voice to a flirtatious purr.

"I've got me mates, me rum, and a good story for the day. What more do a man want?" Papi asked.

"How about another story?" Frankie offered.

"I'm listenin'."

Frankie was desperate. The man had information she needed, and if she didn't get it out of him the nice way, Aiden was going to throw tens of thousands at some mercenaries to drag the truth out of him.

She leaned in and whispered her offer to him. Papi's eyes widened to the size of the soggy coasters on the bar.

"You tell me everything you know in return?" Frankie asked, clarifying.

He nodded as if in a trance. "Oh yeah. You got a deal. But you first."

Frankie shot a glance at the door to the grocery and made sure Aiden and Antonio were nowhere to be seen.

"A deal's a deal," she said, untying the halter top to her dress.

Her unbound breasts enjoyed the temporary freedom and the weak breeze pushed down from the drooping ceiling fan above. Papi's jaw dropped, hypnotized. The rest of his cronies followed suit.

She counted to five, making sure everyone had seen what needed to be seen and then tied her dress neatly back in place. She downed the shot of rum in one swallow and slapped the glass back on the bar.

"Drinks for everyone," Papi announced coming out of his breast trance and tossing his arms in the air. The crowd cheered.

"Talk, Papi," Frankie insisted.

"Okay. Alls I know is dis guy calls me up and says he got a driving job for me. He needs me to pick up his frien' at Oistins. Oh, and his frien' might not want to get in the car so I should bring some help."

"He asked you to kidnap someone."

"No, no, no! Dis man, he gives me your friend's number. I call him and tell him I have a surprise for him. Drunk Americans are not bright, not bright!" Papi pointed a gnarled finger at Frankie.

"Preaching to the choir, Papi. Keep talking."

"So, he's like 'Cool, man. A surprise.' An I'm like, I'll see you on the sidewalk. I'm in a white van. And he went there willingly, and my frien' helped your frien' into the van, and that's that."

Poor, stupid, drunk Chip.

"Where'd you take him?"

"Rockley Ridge Resort by Sandy Lane. But good luck gettin' in dere. Some big to-do tonight. All Hollywood an' stuff. Lotsa security."

"Who took Chip off your hands when you got to the resort?"

Papi shrugged and pushed another glass of rum at her.

"Don' know. He did not feel the need to introduce himself. He pay me. I leave."

"What did he look like?"

"Big burly like guy. Like a bear. I dunno. But he was just hired muscle, I think. He said his boss would be happy."

"What did they do with Chip?" Frankie asked.

Papi tapped her glass with his and they drank.

"Ahhh, that's the good stuff," Papi hissed out. "Anyway, your friend was sleepin'. He passed out drunk on the ride. So, the big guy carried him toward the elevators like a bride."

"And you left and came here."

"To celebrate an easy night's work."

"Thanks for your time, Papi," Frankie said, sliding off the stool.

"Thanks for your boobs," he said enthusiastically.

"Yeah, yeah."

She found Aiden and the kid pacing the sliver of front porch of the shop. Aiden was dialing. Antonio was munching on a fish sandwich.

She plucked her own sandwich out of the bag and grabbed one of the Cokes she'd stashed in there. "Call off the cavalry, Aide. We got a location."

Aiden hung up the phone. "Where?"

"Rockley Ridge Resort," Frankie announced, pleased with her investigative abilities.

"Let's go!" Antonio said, waving them toward the van. "My uncle will wake up soon and want to go home."

"The fourth sandwich is his," Frankie told him.

"Thanks, Frankie. You're a hell of a girl," Antonio said, wrestling the wheel one-handed while clutching his sandwich in the other.

"Here. You might as well eat," Frankie said, handing Aiden another sandwich.

"How'd you get him to talk?" Aiden asked, peeling back the wrapper and eyeing the fish.

Frankie looked everywhere else but his face. "I asked, and he told me."

"Bullshit," Aiden said.

"I told him what information I needed, and he was happy to share," she lied.

"So, you're not going to tell me how you dragged the information out of him when he turned down a thousand bucks just a few minutes earlier?" Aiden pressed.

"I guess some things are worth more than money," Frankie said innocently.

"Kid, you know anything about the Rockley Resort?"

Antonio whistled. "FAN-cy. Good security, too," he said cagily.

Frankie whipped out her phone, praying it still had a charge. It was dead. "Shit. Gimmie your phone, Kilbourn."

He handed it over, and Frankie opened the browser. "Why were you googling me? Creeper!" She slapped Aiden's arm. His last tab was an image search of her.

"I told you. I'm interested in you, and when I'm interested in something, I do my research."

"First of all, I'm a someone, not a something, buddy. Secondly, where do these pictures come from?"

"Social media mostly," Aiden said, leaning over her shoulder to look.

"Excuse me, guys," Antonio called from the driver seat. "I think you're getting off track."

Uncle gurgled from the backseat and dragged himself into a seated position. He cleared his throat. "Ah ah HEM!"

Frankie handed him the bag with the last sandwich and Coke.

Uncle nodded his thanks and dug in.

"Right. I'll yell at Aiden later." Frankie decided. She typed in the resort's name and hit the news tab.

"Double shit. This is not good. Little Miss Trellenwy—what the hell kind of name is that? You rich people are the worst at naming kids."

"Back to the matter at hand," Aiden nudged her.

"Right. Trellenwy Bostick, Hollywood star and heiress to Napa Valley wine fortune got married there today," she said reading from a gossip site. "So far no pics because the security's too tight. How are we getting in there?"

"I can get you over the wall about a half kilometer down. You'll have to fight your way through some vegetation, but you can come out on the beach," Antonio put in.

"Antonio, I hope you only use your powers for good," Aiden said to the boy.

"Mostly good," Antonio promised.

"We can't sneak into a wedding like this," Frankie said looking down at her mini dress.

"What else do you have with you?" Aiden asked.

"Nothing good enough to crash high society except for my bridesmaid dress."

He stroked a hand over the hair on his chin. "That'll do."

13

___

rankie didn't know who Aiden called or how they managed it, but as Antonio buzzed up to the front door of their hotel, the concierge was waiting outside with two garment bags.

Aiden swung the side door on the minivan open just wide enough to grab the bags and throw cash at the man, and then they were off again.

Uncle was snoring peacefully in the backseat having washed down his fish and Coke with the rest of the rum.

"If this dress gets wrecked, Pru is going to kill me, and then she's going to kill you because I'm going to tell her this is all your fault," Frankie announced. She slid onto the bench seat behind Aiden and unzipped the bag to reveal the reason behind her second part-time job. The two-thousand-dollar bridesmaid dress. The one Pru had offered to buy for her. The one Frankie insisted on buying herself even though her fingers physically cramped while signing the credit card slip. The gold sequined V-neck gown cost more than the entire rest of her wardrobe combined.

He turned around. "What makes you think this is my fault?" Aiden demanded.

"Eyes up front, mister. Both of you," she said, when Antonio adjusted the rearview mirror. "I'm saying it was your idea to use the wedding clothes to sneak into another wedding. I'm sure Pru's no bruises, no cuts, no hickeys also extends to no destroying your couture."

Aiden slid over in his seat to block the kid's view. Frankie did her best to shimmy into the dress while keeping everything important covered with her mini dress. Finally in the gown, but without the proper undergarments, she twisted in the seat.

"Zip me, Aide?" she asked, offering her back to him.

She peered over her shoulder as he abandoned the buttons on his Oxford shirt, leaving it delectably open. Regrettably, she'd missed him getting into his pants.

She felt his hand at her hip, holding her in place while he guided the zipper up to the middle of her back. Her flesh burned where his hand still lingered, and she scooted away from him.

She'd already come to her senses once tonight. Once was more than enough where kajillionaire ladies' man Aiden was concerned. Besides, they had a groom to find.

"Rockley straight ahead," Antonio announced, pointing in the direction of the van's headlights.

"Drive past it and then turn around," Aiden ordered peering through the window into the night.

The resort was walled off quite literally by a tall stucco wall painted a soft, sandy yellow. It seemed to go on for a mile. Not only was the gate closed, but there were half a dozen security people standing at attention in front of it.

"Who did you say was getting married?" Aiden asked Frankie.

Frankie consulted his phone. "Trellenwy Bostick. Technically she and her groom got married last weekend in Napa at her family's vineyard. This is the party. Ultra-exclusive, all the non-wedding guests at the resort had to sign non-disclosure agreements," she read. "Private security to ensure Trellenwy's privacy. Blah blah blah. Basically, we're screwed."

Antonio drove past the resort and pulled into a gravel parking lot that flanked the beach. "I can get you in," he announced confidently.

"What are you going to do? Forge us an invitation?" Frankie asked.

"Me and my brother used to walk to the resort on the beach. Sold a few bracelets before security chased us out."

"The beach will be crawling with security," Aiden pointed out.

"Yeah, but between the road and the beach is like a jungle. Trees, bushes, no lights," Antonio grinned.

"And if the gate is guarded and the beach is guarded, no one will be looking in the jungle," Frankie said triumphantly.

"Exactly. Hang on, guys." Antonio floored the old van past the hotel gate as if he were a man on a mission.

"Slow down, desperado," Frankie yelled.

"If we go by all slow and pokey, they're gonna get suspicious."

Aiden laughed softly.

"I'm going to let you out down here, further away from the hotel in case you make a lot of noise climbing the wall."

"Let's do this." Frankie wedged her feet into her incredibly impractical wedding heels. She hoped the jungle was more of a neatly trimmed landscape that she wouldn't break both ankles exploring.

Aiden eyed her in the dark interior of the van. "Maybe you should stay put. Let me go find Chip."

"Please. Like I'm going to let you go in there alone. Besides, a couple dressed for a wedding will be a hell of a lot less suspicious than James Friggin' Bond wandering up the beach in a tux. You're not leaving me."

He looked like he wanted to argue further but wisely shut his mouth when Antonio swerved across the road and pulled up to the curb. "Good luck, guys."

Aiden pulled out another bill from his billfold. "You've been immeasurably helpful tonight, Antonio."

The kid pocketed the money cheerfully. "If you get caught, don't mention my name."

Frankie threw him a salute as she stepped out the door. "Thanks, kid."

"Here's my card." Antonio shoved a business card out the window at her. "Call me anytime you need anything."

Frankie took it and tucked it into her clutch. "That kid is either going to end up running a drug cartel or a small country someday," she predicted as she watched the taillights recede in the dark.

"Uh-huh," Aiden said, noncommittally. "How good are you at climbing walls?"

It turned out not very. She ended up needing a boost from Aiden, whose hand lingered a lot longer than necessary on her ass. But in the end, she made it up and over, landing hard enough to knock the wind out of her. The sound of snagging chiffon on the way down made her wince. She was still gasping for breath when Aiden nimbly landed beside her, her shoes in his hand.

"You okay?" he asked, pulling her to her feet.

"Fine. Totally fine," she wheezed. She stepped away from the flowering shrub she'd flattened with her comical landing and brushed the dirt off of the skirt of her dress. She'd felt the fabric tear as she flopped over the wall graceful as a humpback whale and hoped she hadn't done any real damage. Pru would kill her... if there was a wedding to be killed over. "Crap! I tore the skirt. It's okay. I can fix it."

"Come on," Aiden whispered. He grabbed her hand and led the way into the dark.

Frankie couldn't see shit. But Aiden seemed to have night vision, pulling her through the vegetation and around trees in the scant moonlight. The peepers chirped in a loud, never-ending serenade to the night. The air was thick with exotic fragrances. Aiden's feet were sure beneath him while she tripped over roots and branches and god knew what that weird squishy thing was. All that she could see was the broad shadow of Aiden's shoulders in front of her as he towed her through the forest.

They were getting closer to the ocean. She could hear the waves, taste the tang of salt on the air. Aiden stopped in front of her and she walked into his broad back.

She heard the far-off beat of club music.

Up ahead, through leafy palm fronds and a smattering of moonlight, Frankie could see lights. Purple and silver flashes seemed to pulse to the thrumming beat of music. Someone had brought L.A.'s hottest club to paradise or at least a very expensive DJ to an heiress's second wedding.

"I think we've found the party," Aiden said quietly.

"Okay, so what are we supposed to do?" Frankie asked. "Roll up out of the shrubs and order a round of shots?"

"Tequila or whiskey?" he asked.

"Tequila is always the answer."

"Let's try to get a little closer," Aiden said. "Then we'll discuss our bar order."

"Wait, what's our backstory? Who are you? Who am I? How do we know Trell?"

"Trell?" Aiden asked, his lips quirking on one side.

"Obviously if we're her friends we don't call her Trellenwy." *Duh.*

"Fine. I'm an old friend of Trellenwy, and you're my date."

"Why aren't I an old friend of Trellenwy?" Frankie demanded. Her foot caught on a thick root and she went sprawling to the ground. "Oh, man! How am I going to get poison berry juice out of this?" she rubbed at the stain from the plant she'd landed on. It looked like the period fairy had pointed her wand all over Frankie's hip. "Crap. Okay. I can fix this. I'll soak it in... something."

Aiden sighed. "Franchesca, what's more believable? A socialite has an acquaintance with a wealthy New York business owner with a reputation for dating women just like her or the daughter of Brooklyn deli owners?"

"Excuse me. Are you saying I can't pass for upper class?" Frankie challenged.

"Shut up."

He clamped a hand over her wrist and dragged her forward, skirting the lights and music.

It was nearly one a.m. in paradise, and she had a sexy, crazy rich bachelor who could have made a lucrative career out of being beautiful dragging her around in the dark. Frankie should have been squealing with joy on the inside. Instead? She was pissed. Annoyed at the whole thing. That someone would take Chip. That she couldn't "pass" for being some dumb socialite with more money than street smarts. That some security guard would potentially believe Aiden would have a better chance of knowing Trellenwy. That they didn't exist in the same worlds. And she didn't know why that mattered.

Sure, she could let Mr. Big Deal Kilbourn put his hands on her. But in the eyes of the entire world, she was the lesser partner here. He had the power, the control. He'd tire of her and move on, as he had with every other woman in his life.

The sound of the waves was louder now. The lights and thump of the music was behind them. She could see moonlight dancing on the ocean through the trees that separated them from the beach. There was no more talking now. They were just a billionaire and his nameless date out for a late-night stroll.

A twig snapped under her foot, and Aiden swore quietly. He turned and pulled Frankie against him. She wanted to tell him to get his damn hands off of her. To go to hell.

He took her down to the sand in a move so smooth she barely felt the shift in her gravity.

"What are you doing?" she hissed as he covered her body with his. She shoved at his shoulders and froze when she felt his cock twitch against her as it hardened.

He didn't bother answering her before his mouth crushed down on hers. She wasn't prepared. Couldn't have prepared. Not for the rush of heat that washed through her, the electricity that coursed through her. His lips were strong and firm, demanding. But Frankie wasn't one to give up the upper hand. She gripped his lapels and fought for control of the kiss. When he opened his mouth, it was her tongue that surged forward. Aiden growled low in his throat and stroked into her mouth, tasting and toying.

She felt dizzy with power, with madness.

His erection was thick and hard against her center, and Frankie opened her legs so he could settle between them. When he grinded against her, Frankie's world went black. She could come like this, dry-humping a billionaire on a beach.

She should have been embarrassed, should have had better judgment. But before those thoughts could take hold,

Aiden trailed one large, capable hand down over her breast and surged against her again.

She murmured meaningless words against his mouth. *This. Now. Here.* She didn't care.

"Fuck," he whispered, before diving back into the kiss. Her blood had gone molten. Lava flowed through her veins now. More was the only word left in her vocabulary.

Aiden abandoned her breast, and when Frankie moaned her disappointment, he made up for it. That hand was now shoving the skirt of her dress higher. Her body sang to the heavens. If he didn't shove a part of him inside of her in the next thirty seconds, Frankie knew she'd die a slow and agonizing death.

He was grinding against her thigh now, prodding her with what felt like a painful erection.

"More, Aide," Frankie whispered. Begging. She never begged. But in this second she was happy to plead her way to orgasm.

"Hang on, baby," he murmured against her lips. "I want you so fucking bad."

This was not the ice-cold man she'd met in the ballroom. Or the game-playing chauffeur from the airport. No, the man whose hand danced over the satin of her thong was a sinful lover, all heat and dark promises.

"Fuck," he whispered again when he pressed the tips of his fingers to her center.

She cried out, softly, brokenly as he started one of those tiny circles he'd worked his way up her thigh with under the table. He knew how to touch her. Whether it was instinct or obscene experience, she didn't give a good damn.

"You're so damn wet, Franchesca. So wet for me."

Frankie bucked against his hand. "Touch me," she commanded. When he looped two fingers under the seam of her underwear, when his knuckles brushed her soft folds, she reached for him.

He grunted his approval when she gripped his hard cock through his pants. "I want your hands on me, your mouth," he growled.

"Right back at you, Kilbourn," Frankie murmured.

His knuckles brushed her again, and she melted under him.

"*I'm* going to fuck you, Franchesca. Not that surfer, not Davenport. Me."

Her body thrilled at the words while her mind reeled at the possession in his tone.

"Shut up and kiss me."

His fingers were poised at her entrance, her tongue buried in his mouth when Frankie found herself squinting into a blinding light.

---

14

*A*iden contemplated killing the security guard with his own two hands. If the man continued to shine his flashlight in the direction of Franchesca's nipples that were trying to cut their way out of her gown, Aiden was going to break his fucking neck.

Franchesca stood full of fury, hands on hips. He'd forgotten himself, forgotten where they were and why they were here. He'd heard the guard's approach and had gone with the lovers out for a romantic stroll-slash-fuck story. Touching her? Tasting her? It had wiped out all instincts besides the need to take her.

He could tell by the way she refused to look at him that she thought he'd taken advantage of her. And he had, or at least he'd taken advantage of the situation.

Now, he was going to kill a security guard, and then Franchesca was going to kill him.

"Look, sir," Franchesca said, her cheeks still flaming. "We just slipped away from the party and got carried away.

Aiden stepped in front of her. He couldn't tell exactly

where the guard's gaze was falling, but he imagined it had to be somewhere around Frankie's heaving chest.

"It's my fault. I got carried away," he said, offering the man a chagrined smiled. "I'm sure it's not the worst you've seen tonight."

The guard stared blankly for another moment. Aiden felt Frankie grab the back of his jacket with both hands.

"I just caught two girls skinny-dipping in the lobby fountain ten minutes ago," the guard announced. "Go on back to the party, and keep your clothes on."

"Will do," Aiden promised. Frankie's eyes were as wide as big screen TVs as they hurried past the guard onto a path that led to the crowded terrace that served as a dancefloor. "Well that was easy," he said. He reached up and picked a leaf out of Frankie's hair. He was starting to wonder if he was obsessed with her hair. The thick, dark curtain that fell in curling waves. He wanted to bury his face in it.

"Easy?" she hissed, slapping his hand away.

"Well, you didn't have to flash anyone this time," Aiden pointed out.

Her gasp was worth the anticipation.

"You saw me?"

"I saw quite a bit of you." Aiden decided not to mention that he'd been a split second slow in covering Antonio's eyes.

Frankie slapped him in the shoulder.

"What? You're the one who decided to flash half the island."

"Yeah, but that didn't mean you had to look, too!"

"I wasn't about to miss out on that view, Franchesca." He reached for her, and she held up her hands.

"Keep your hands off of me, or I'll break off that hard-on you've been sporting all night and slap you in the face with it."

How could he not want more of her? How could she

believe that he'd leave her alone?

"Are you trying to draw attention to us?" he asked, pulling her into him. Those blue-green eyes narrowed at him. "We're on the dance floor. So dance."

She glanced around them and seemed to notice for the first time that they were surrounded by the upper echelon of California royalty. Aiden recognized a few faces here and there. A half dozen politicians, a handful of celebrities, but mostly it was a collection of heirs and heiresses to various fortunes who had clearly had more than enough to drink.

"What's wrong with these people?" Frankie asked, allowing Aiden to draw her further onto the dance floor. Even the band was trashed, judging by the limping tempo to their song. "Oh, my god. Is that Meltdown?"

"The band with that song that you hear on the radio every six seconds? It would appear so. And what's wrong with everyone is they're wasted."

It was like witnessing last call at an all-you-can drink gun raffle. The over-fifty crowd was straight up drunk. One man was projectile vomiting over the stone balustrade. A woman in her mid-sixties was sloppily pouring a homemade champagne fountain, pausing now and again to swig out of the open bottle.

There was a couple on the dance floor drunkenly leaning in time to the offbeat music and taking their clothes off.

It appeared that the younger set had graduated from alcohol to something harder. There were four women in couture gowns sitting in the shallow end of the pool laughing like hyenas. Further into the deep end a "who can break their neck first" diving competition was in full swing.

The bride was standing on the bar mainlining cosmos and shouting "I'm married, bitches!"

The third cosmo spilled like a waterfall down her bejeweled dress.

"Classy as fuck," Frankie whispered to Aiden as they danced and dodged their way toward the hotel. "That's a twenty-six-thousand-dollar dress."

"Wonder where the groom is? Running for the hills?"

Frankie pointed toward a large potted palm. "I think he's the one with his tongue down that groomsman's throat."

"Ah." Aiden said.

Frankie shook her head. "This is like the Great Gatsby with a drug and alcohol problem."

"And you thought Pruitt's bridesmonsters were horrible," Aiden teased.

A finger poked him hard in the shoulder. "Hey! Who arrrre yoooou?"

Aiden twirled Frankie around so they could face the poker together.

"I'm Aiden. Who are you?" he asked the woman. She looked to be in her forties and trying desperately to hang on to her twenties. Her lips had been done, badly. The tight skin around her eyes and forehead screamed BOTOX or facelift. One strap of her ivory colored dress was broken. She held a bottle of champagne in one hand. Her hair extensions were coming out of some intricate knot at the back of her head and hung over her eye.

"I'm Priscilla." She swayed as she said her own name. "Are you fren of bride or the broom?"

"We're friends of the broom," Frankie said, stepping in smoothly. "I'm Druscilla, and this is my paid escort, Aiden. I met the groom on Season Eight of Trust Funds and Trophy Wives."

"'Zat a reality show?" Priscilla asked.

Frankie nodded. "Oh, yeah. And the exposure was great. It really launched my career as a foot model. I can give you the producer's number if you're interested. It was the best eighteen months of my life if you like living on a yacht near the UAE."

"Druscilla, we really should be going," Aiden said, pinching Frankie in the waist.

"Call me," Frankie sang as Aiden propelled her past the frowning Priscilla.

"We're trying *not* to get noticed," he reminded her.

"Aide, the only thing these people are going to remember tomorrow is a big, fat nothing."

He hustled her into the hotel's open-air lobby. With the ocean and debauchery at their back, the lobby was rather quiet. He made a move toward the front desk but was thwarted by the foot-dragging Frankie.

"Franchesca, come on. We've got work to do."

"Sorry. Geez. Does being wealthy require you to ignore awesomeness?" she asked, admiring the thatched ceiling two stories above them. Gold and white statues and heavy potted palms filled in the expanse of stone floor. Her eyes widened as they approached the front desk. "Is that gold leaf?" She pointed to a grand staircase that winged off into two different directions one level up.

"We can ask after we find Chip."

"Right. Okay. I'm focused," she promised. "What's the plan here?" Frankie asked, nodding at the woman behind the desk.

"Charm first."

"Good evening, sir. How may I be of service?" Hilde, according to her name tag, was tall and reed slim. She looked as though nothing in the world could ruffle her.

"Hello, Hilde. I'm looking for my friend's room, and I'm embarrassed to say I can't remember the number." Frankie, pretending to be bored, wandered away from the desk over to the koi pond and out of Hilde's line of sight.

"I see. What is your friend's name, please?"

Aiden did his best to look chagrined. "My friend's name is Chip. But the room is registered to someone else. Chip is about this tall. Blonde hair. This is his first night here."

Hilde gave him a wan smile. "I'm sorry, sir. But I'm not permitted to divulge guest information. What is your room number, please?"

Aiden patted his jacket as if he were looking for a room key. "Let me look... Babe, do you have our room key?"

At that moment, two women, sufficiently intoxicated, stumbled past Frankie. "An' then I poked a hole in the condom, told him I was on birth control, and vi-ol-a! I'm a millionaire, and he paid to fix my tits."

"You're like the worst human being ever," the other crowed.

"I know, right?"

Frankie's move was so fast Aiden almost missed it. One moment Millionaire Tits was stumbling across the marble floor, and the next, she was falling face-first into the koi pond.

The woman's screeches combined with Frankie's calls for help had Hilde grabbing a walkie-talkie from behind the desk and scurrying off toward the hub-bub.

"Hurry up," Frankie hissed, appearing at his side. "Stand guard." She shimmied behind the desk and sat in the vacated chair. "Shit. Password protected."

The screaming had yet to quiet down, so Aiden poked his head over the desk. "Option one, we crack the password ourselves. Option two, we make Hilde give us the password." He was weighing the pros and cons when Frankie's fingers flew over the keys.

"Ha. Got it."

"You cracked the password?" Aiden asked. Did the woman have no limits?

She snorted. "Don't have to crack it when they tape it to the monitor for me. Okay, I'm in. Who are we looking for? No one's registered as Kidnapper or Wedding Ruiner."

Aiden skirted behind the desk, hopeful that the koi pond distraction would hold. "Scroll through the reservations," he ordered, scanning the monitor.

"You think you're going to magically recognize the name of the kidnapper?" Frankie asked.

"Shut up. There," he pointed at the screen. "Room 314. Three nights. Who's it registered to?"

"No name. Just a business. El-Kil Corporation," Frankie read out loud.

Fuck. Aiden felt the sucker punch to his gut. He should have known.

"Oh, look! It's gotta be them. Two hours ago they ordered a tuna salad sandwich with crushed up chips on it. Chip's favorite! At least we know they're feeding him. That's good, right?"

"Good. Yeah." Aiden murmured.

"Oh, shit." Frankie exited out of the program and grabbed him. He heard the click of heels on the marble. They only made it as far as the marble column next to the desk. When Hilde and the fish pond woman appeared with a small entourage.

"Let me call housekeeping and get you some fresh towels and a robe," Hilde offered a soaked and shrieking celebutante.

"A fish swam *down my dress.* Do you think a robe is going to make me feel better after I was attacked by sushi?" the woman howled.

Hilde's eyes narrowed when she spotted Frankie and Aiden standing next to the desk. Aiden thought about kissing Frankie again since it had worked so well the first time, but Frankie was faster.

She slapped him across the face so hard his head snapped backwards on his neck.

"You know it bothers me when you slip your sister the tongue. I don't care how many years you spent in boarding school in Europe. That still doesn't make it right!" Frankie's voice echoed off the marble drawing every eye in the lobby.

"A. She's my half-sister," Aiden said, jumping on the crazy train that Frankie was engineering "And B. I can't help it if I come from an *affectionate* family!"

"Oh, puh-lease!" Frankie's scoff nearly knocked her off her feet. "Affectionate? Your grandmother grabbed my ass at Thanksgiving."

"She wanted to see how the butt lift I paid for turned out." He nodded toward the exit.

"Excuse me. I earned this butt lift!"

They kept up the argument for posterity's sake, storming away from the front desk. As they passed, Aiden heard one of the audience whispering.

"What can you expect from a reality TV star and a male prostitute?"

News traveled fast.

He hauled Frankie outside. She started laughing the second their feet hit the resort's grand circular drive. "You're insane," he told her.

"Oh, please. I saw that look on your face. You were thinking about kissing the hell out of me back there. And it wouldn't have worked the second time around."

"Why not?" he asked, rubbing a hand over the cheek she'd so efficiently slapped.

"I don't make the same mistake twice, Kilbourn. And you're a big, fat mistake. Now, come on. I think room 314 is that way." Aiden watched in fascination as Frankie pulled a map of the resort out of her cleavage.

"Where did you get that?" Aiden snatched the map from her.

"At the desk."

"We're not going after Chip."

"Excuse me? We know where he is, and all of the sudden, you want to call it a night?"

"What do you want to do? Knock on the door and demand that they give him back?"

"It's a start! I'm not leaving my friend here."

Aiden gripped her upper arm and started pulling her toward the cab desk. "We have the upper hand here. What we need is a plan. I have to go figure out who has him, and if I can do that, I'll know why they took him." The lie was easy. He already knew the who and the why, but he wasn't about to add Frankie into the mix. He wasn't sure who she'd murder first.

"I'm not leaving Chip here with some kidnapping asshole! Let's call security or the cops!"

"We're not calling anyone," he said, tightening his grip on her arm.

"Why in the hell not? We know where he is!"

"We don't know who took him or why. We know that he's here and they're feeding him. And that means he's safe. For now."

"For now?" She tried to wrestle her arm free. "Did you just track down his abductor because you were curious where they took him? And now, curiosity appeased, you want to go back to the resort for some margaritas and see how this plays out?"

Aiden rounded on her. "Look. Believe me when I say your loyalty is admirable. But we need to regroup. I need a plan. If we go in there half-cocked, it could be disastrous."

When her gaze slid to his crotch, Aiden rolled his eyes. "Stop looking at my cock. We're leaving."

15

*H*e walked her to her room as if she were a prisoner. They'd spent the entire ride in silence as Frankie stewed and Aiden plotted. She understood that there was a time and a place for planning and manipulation, but when a friend was in danger? That seemed like the ideal time to kick in a door and start making noise.

With barely controlled rage, Frankie swiped her keycard. She intended to storm into the room and slam the door in Aiden's face, but he was faster. He caught her by the arm and forced her to look at him. "I appreciate all your help tonight. But I've got this handled now."

"Excuse me, Lone Ranger?"

"Franchesca, I need you to trust me to fix this. I promise you, I'll get Chip back before the wedding."

She opened her mouth ready to verbally punch him in the face, but as usual, he was quicker. He brought his mouth down on hers for a fast, hard kiss. Just when she was deciding between dragging him into her room or kicking him in the balls, Aiden pulled back. "You were amazing tonight."

He ran a finger down the tip of her nose and walked off.

"What in the fuck was that?" Frankie asked the empty room as she shut the door and added the chain in case Mr. Kilbourn decided to try his luck again.

She looked down at her dress and groaned. There was a tear in the waist and one in the skirt. Those damn berries had smeared their bloody red massacre over the right breast and hip. She looked like a murdered starlet in Monique Lhuillier.

Pru was going to kill her.

Frantically, she dialed the front desk and begged for a super emergency cleaning. The figure they named made her wince. It meant at least another month of catering gigs. But at this point, she had no choice. It was either pay the exorbitant fee and hope for the best, or walk down the aisle and get stabbed by the bride.

If there was a wedding. If Aiden didn't come through, there would be no groom for Pru to marry, she thought bitterly as she changed into sleep shorts and a tank.

Frankie handed over the dress to the bell hop that knocked and then texted Pru.

Frankie: You up?

Pru's response was practically instantaneous.

Pru: OMG, get over here!

Frankie padded down the hall to Pru and Chip's room. Before she could raise her knuckles to knock, Pru opened the door and dragged her inside. Frankie blinked. Her best friend was wearing a silk pajama set... and her veil.

Clearly the rum and beer hadn't worn off yet.

"I know. I know. I look like a crazy person," Pru announced leading the way back into a marble on marble on marble bathroom the size of a football stadium. "But I started thinking. We're in paradise. It's hot. Do I really want to wear my hair down tomorrow? Have a seat," she said, pointing toward the ledge of the soaker tub.

"And do you?" Frankie asked, feeling like the worst human being in the world. Her best friend's fiancé had been kidnapped in front of her face and not only did she know where to find him, she had walked away without trying to rescue him. She was scum. The chewing gum on the bottom of someone's shoe. The kind of person who faked diseases to set up phony crowd-funding campaigns. She, Franchesca Marie Baranski, was a bad, bad person.

She sat on the lip of the tub.

Pru was discussing the merits of a sexy chignon when she abruptly cut herself off. Her blue eyes going wide in the mirror. "Here I am yammering on and on about my hair and you've just come back from a tryst with Aiden! What kind of a friend am I?"

"The best. You're the best kind of a friend, Pru," Frankie lamented. "You're a wonderful person, and you deserve all the happiness in the world." She had to tell her. If she were in Pru's shoes, she'd want to know.

"What's wrong?" Pru demanded, whirling away from the mirror. "You look like you're gonna cry."

Frankie let herself slide backwards into the tub. "Before we talk about Aiden, we should talk about Chip." *How in the hell was she going to explain to her best friend that she didn't call the cops, didn't kick the door in and drag Chip home? That she was the worst friend in the world.*

Pru got a soft, faraway look in her eyes. "I can't believe I finally get to marry him, Frankie. I just... I love him so much. He's funny and sweet and kind and smart, and he looks like a Ken doll. But when I look at him, I can see us fifty years from now. Chasing grandkids, hosting parties, summering in the Hamptons with our huge family."

Pru clasped her hands together and sighed. "He's everything I've been dreaming about since I was five. I have my dream dress, my best friend, and I get to marry the man of my dreams in paradise." Her eyes glistened with tears.

"Don't cry, Pru," Frankie pleaded. At least not before she'd told her the shitty part about having an MIA fiancé.

"I can't help it." Pru dabbed at her eyes with a tissue. "I'm so happy. And that's what I want for you, Frankie. I want you to find someone who makes you feel like you're flying. Someone who makes you look forward to the next fifty years."

"I can't focus on the next fifty minutes let alone years," Frankie teased.

Pru crossed the bathroom. It took about ten minutes given the expanse of marble between them. She perched on the edge of the tub and toyed with her veil. "I think Aiden will be that for you," Pru confessed.

Frankie smacked her head off the back of the tub. "Ow! What?"

"I know you two got off to a rough start—"

"The man called me a stripper!"

"After the engagement party, he asked Chip a thousand questions about you."

"Maybe he wanted to find out where I dance and if I give BJs for an extra fifty," Frankie shot back.

"He picked you up from the airport. I saw the way he was looking at you during dinner. Like he wanted to eat you instead of what was on his plate. And then he whisks you away? Don't think for one second that just because I'm getting married tomorrow that I don't want every single detail of what you two have been doing for the last five hours."

Frankie rubbed the bump on the back of her head. "Let's

get back to this getting married thing tomorrow for a second. How upset would you be if something happened and you couldn't?"

"Couldn't what? Get married tomorrow?"

"Yeah. What if something... came up?"

"Franchesca Baranski, a mother-fucking hurricane could blow over this island leveling every building on it tomorrow, and I would still be marrying Chip."

Ah, hell.

"Yeah, but—"

"Listen. You'll understand this once you and Aiden really start getting to know each other," Pru said, patting her arm. "Chip and I lost each other after college, and I was devastated because I knew he was the one. I never stopped believing that. Not once in all those years. And we found our way back to each other. We've paid our dues. That separation was heartbreaking for me, for him too. So we are going to have a magical day tomorrow because we deserve it. I deserve it," her voice cracked.

Frankie grabbed her friend's hand. "Of course, you deserve it. I know that Chip is all you've ever wanted, and you'll have him. You'll have your perfect guy on your perfect day. I promise."

Pru nodded, her veil rippling. "I should text him! Text him and tell him how much I love him and can't wait for tomorrow! Oooh! Or I could call him!"

"Uhhh—"

But Pru was already scampering back to the vanity for her phone.

16

Frankie: Pru thinks we made out for five hours tonight. Also, she's texting and calling Chip to tell him how excited she is about tomorrow. In about thirty seconds, she's going to start to panic.

Aiden: I've got it covered.

rankie wanted to reach through her phone and strangle him. Or at the very least punch him in his smug "I've got it covered" face. She was debating whether or not to bite the bullet and tell Pru everything when Pru's phone signaled a text.

"Is it Chip?" Frankie asked, aghast. Was Aiden really that good?

"No. It's Aiden," Pru said, beaming at her phone. "He said that Chip is sound asleep in his suite, and he didn't want me to worry that Chip wasn't returning my texts."

Pru hugged her phone to her chest, her eyes glistening with unshed tears of happiness. "I'm getting married tomorrow."

Hell yes, she was. Frankie vowed that she would do whatever it took to get Pru down the aisle to the man of her dreams.

"Enough about me. Tell me about Aiden! Is he really an orgasm master?"

~

PRU'S WEDDING day dawned bright, beautiful, and hot. With no groom in sight.

The evening ceremony called for hours spent at the spa with the rest of the bridesmonsters. Frankie had tossed and turned the rest of the night away in Pru's room seeing Chip's abduction over and over again in her head.

Aiden hadn't bothered checking in, and with this seaweed wrap sucking the fat out of her, she couldn't just get up and go find him. All she knew was he had better be mounting a rescue with tanks, ninjas, and mercenaries. Whatever it took to get Chip Randolph back to the resort and in a tux before six.

Cressida sauntered by in a short, silk robe and mud mask. "Here. Have zis," she said, wielding a bottle of Cristal. "You look tense."

Frankie looked at her arms pinned to her side with green slime. "Got a straw?"

Cressida shrugged. "Open your mouth. I will pour."

Frankie laid back and did as she was told. Cressida poured with precision, and Frankie swallowed the bubbles like a first-string sorority pledge.

"Did you take care of what you needed to take care of last night?" Cressida asked without moving her lips, careful not to crack her mask.

"It's being managed," Frankie said evasively. She wasn't about to trust any of the bridesmaids with a brown bag lunch with her name on it let alone sensitive information that would ruin Pru's wedding day.

"Ze bride is getting anxious. She has not heard from ze groom since last night," Cressida announced, nodding her blonde head in Pru's direction.

She had her feet in a spa tub and was staring at her phone in her lap as if willing it to ring.

Frankie prayed that Aiden was handling it. "What's Chip doing today?" Frankie asked Pru, already dreading the answer.

"Apparently he's fishing with Aiden this morning." Pru bit her lip.

"That sounds like fun," Frankie prodded.

"Yeah, I'm just getting a little... nervous."

"Butterflies," Margeaux announced knowledgeably. "I was that way the first time. The second time around you won't feel a thing."

"Nice, Marge," Frankie snorted.

Margeaux scoffed. "Please. Like anyone believes this marriage will last. Hey, watch the cuticles," she screeched at the woman doing her manicure.

"Don't listen to her," Frankie pleaded with Pru, inch-worming her way into a seated position. The seaweed ripped down her back, and she could breathe again.

"I haven't heard from him since the fish fry last night. What if..." Pru didn't finish the sentence, and Frankie was the only one in the room who knew the truth was even worse than all the scenarios that Pru was running through.

"If they're fishing offshore they probably left early, and there's no cell reception," Frankie said, shrugging back into her robe.

Pru chewed on her lip. "True. But if I haven't heard from him by lunch, I'm going to send my dad to check on him."

Wouldn't that go over well? R.L. Stockton storming around

the resort looking for the future son-in-law that he hated. One whiff of trouble with Chip and R.L. would have Pru on a private plane flying back home while his team of attorneys worked out the best way to sue the shit out of Chip and his parents.

"Trust Aiden," Frankie insisted. "He won't let you down." And if he did, Frankie would be first in line to kick him in the balls.

"There's my baby girl!" Addison Stockton stormed into the treatment room in her matching robe and slippers. "She's going to be the most beautiful bride," she announced to the room, fluttering her hands like hummingbird wings.

"Someone enjoyed their laser hair removal appointment," Taffany said, cracking her gum.

At noon, the spa served up a vegan spread for the party. Chip's mother, Myrtle, took one look at the hummus topped cucumber rolls and ordered a burger, rare, with extra fries. *Can't take the Texas appetites out of a cattle ranch baron's daughter.*

Frankie would have done the same if she could stomach the thought of food. Every time Pru picked up her phone, Frankie cringed inwardly.

She volunteered to go first for hair and submitted to the violent hair stylist who seemed intent on embedding pins into her skull.

"I don't see why we all have to change our styles because Pruitt did," Margeaux whined, slapping away the stylist as the man tried to sweep her thick curtain of honey blonde hair off her neck. "And wax my eyebrows while you're at it."

"Christ, Marge! Can you shut your mouth for one day and do something for someone else? It's not your fucking day. You'll probably have eight or nine wedding days by the time a husband holds a pillow over your face and puts the rest of us out of our misery. So put your damn hair up and shut your damn mouth!"

It was exactly the wrong approach to take with a sociopathic asshole.

"Do you even know who I am, you piece of shit from Brooklyn?"

Margeaux spat out the word Brooklyn as if it were sulfur flavored.

"Do you even know what a black hole of a human you are?" Frankie shot back.

Her stylist, unfazed by the exchange, spun her around to show her the results of eight thousand hairpins and six cans of hair spray. She'd tamed the dark curls into submission, wrangling them into a rock-hard bun at the nape of her neck.

"Looks amazing," Frankie said, jumping out of the chair and throwing cash at her before she could reach for more hair pins.

"You're just jealous because you're nothing. You're literally the help. Pathetic with your hand out for tips so you can pay your dry-cleaning bill."

"You better watch how you talk around people, Marge. A lot of us are help, and without us, you'd have a dirty toilet, bikini burn, and no food at your stupid parties."

"Someone like Aiden Kilbourn would never give you a second glance. Unless it was out of pity or to wonder how you managed to shove your Kardashian-sized ass into your dress. You're going to look like a whale in the pictures next to the rest of us." She laughed an unhinged, diabolical Dr. Evil kind of laugh.

The stylist working on Margeaux reached for the hot wax and slathered it over the entire brow. He gave Frankie a commiserating look and slapped the waxing strip on top of the wax.

"I might not be the only one people are staring at tonight," Frankie predicted. She turned and marched out of the room to the music of Margeaux screaming.

"What did you do to my eyebrow you fucking idiot?"

In the hallway, she pulled her phone out of her robe pocket and fired off a text to Aiden.

Frankie: Status update. Where are you with Operation Free the Groom? The bride is getting nervous.

His response was terse.

Aiden: I have it handled.

She'd like to handle him... out of a ten-story window and into a dumpster full of broken glass.

She dialed him as she walked. If he didn't tell her he was breaching the door to Room 314 right now she was going to get Chip herself.

"What?" he answered brusquely.

"Where are you?" she hissed. She marched down the sun dappled hallway that connected the spa to the main building.

He sighed. "Franchesca, I'm in the middle of something, and every time I have to check in with you, I have to stop working."

"Will Chip be back here before the wedding?" she asked.

"I'm working on it," Aiden answered tersely.

"Have you even heard from the kidnapper today?"

"Yes. We have a meeting scheduled."

"A meeting?" Frankie stormed past the doors to the resort's library bar and stopped in her tracks. She backed up two steps and glared through the glass doors. It was a spacious room with tall bookcases and ladders straight out of *Beauty and the*

Beast except for the large L-shaped bar with the spectacular ocean view. The bar that played host to one Aiden "Dead Man Walking" Kilbourn.

Disgusted, Frankie ended the call and flicked off the unseeing Aiden through the glass. Under a full head of steam, she approached the front desk. "Excuse me," she said to the concierge. "My dress is in for an emergency cleaning."

"Yes, Ms. Baranski. We're working on the damage right now."

"I'll need it ready in time for the ceremony. Because nothing is going to ruin this wedding. Not a missing groom, or an asshole best man, or a stained dress." She was pointing her finger in the air like a movie heroine making a proclamation.

"Of course, Ms. Baranski." The concierge gave Frankie the "you're a crazy person and I have to be nice to you" smile.

"Um. Thank you," Frankie said. "I'm going to go away now."

The concierge smiled pleasantly again, and Frankie backed away from the desk. She jogged to the bank of elevators. Once in her room, she shucked the robe and dragged on a sundress. Antonio's business card fell out of her clutch when she dug out her money.

Maybe she didn't have to do this entirely on her own.

17

"Where's your uncle's van?" Frankie asked, eyeing the doorless dune buggy-like vehicle.

"He's driving it," Antonio announced sliding out from behind the wheel. "Your chariot awaits, madam." He was wearing a prep school uniform of navy blue shorts and a white short-sleeve button down. His tie was a clip-on.

"Did you steal this? And I feel like I have to repeat my question from last night. Are you even old enough to drive?"

"You wanna stand here and ask questions, or do you want to go to Rockley?" Antonio asked.

"Oh, my God. Just drive." Frankie climbed in next to him and fastened the safety harness.

"Yee haw!" Antonio gunned the engine, jumped the curb, and tore down the winding drive to the road.

"Do *not* kill us!" Frankie shouted over the rumble of the engine.

Antonio approached the highway like a villain in a car chase. Frankie covered her eyes with her hands and said her prayers. She heard horns and braced for death. But the impact and death never came. She peeked through her fingers to see they were tooling down the highway weaving in and out of traffic.

"Okay. We're not dead. This is a good start."

"So, what's the plan, lady? You find your friend last night?"

"The plan is you're driving me to Rockley, I'm rescuing my friend, and you are driving us back to the resort in time for the wedding."

"Good plan," Antonio nodded. "Where's Money Bags?"

"Aiden?" Frankie glared out the windshield. "He had business to take care of."

"So, you're going to rescue your friend by yourself?"

"If you want something done right..."

Antonio nodded sagely.

"Speaking of Money Bags," Frankie began. "My pockets aren't as deep as his."

"That's okay. You can pay me by flashing your boobs again."

Frankie cuffed him on the back of the head. "Hey!"

He grinned.

Frankie's phone rang. "Oh, hell." It was Pruitt.

"Hey, bride!" Frankie answered. She sounded like a complete phony.

"Where are you? We're ready for bridesmaid pictures."

Frankie slapped herself on the forehead. Shit.

"I'm not there actually. I'm, uh, heading to the... dock?"

"The dock?"

Frankie could hear the note of panic in Pru's voice.

"Yeah, I wanted to get down here and check in on Chip for you. Just so, you know... you'd know," she finished lamely.

"You're the best friend a girl could have," Pru sniffed. "I didn't want to say anything, but I'm tied up in knots. I need to hear his voice and know that everything is still good."

"Everything is going to be better than good," Frankie

promised. "I'm going to have him call you as soon as I see him. He probably just dropped his phone overboard or something. You know how he is with those things."

"Yeah," Pru sniffled. "I do. I just... come back soon, okay? I can't wait for you to see Margeaux's eyebrow. They had to draw it back on."

Frankie rubbed her temples. "I'll be back before you know it," she promised.

She hung up and buried her face in her hands. "Oh, my god. If I can't pull this off I've ruined not only her wedding day but our friendship."

"It'll work out," Antonio said cheerfully.

"Is that a school uniform?" Frankie asked, eyeing the loafers working the gas pedal.

"Yep. You got me out of a geography test."

"You're skipping school to drive me around?"

"Sure! I do it sometimes. It beats sitting behind a desk and listening to teachers blah blah blah all day."

Frankie tried not to think about all the laws they were probably breaking at this exact moment. Her phone rang again, and she picked it up without thinking.

"Franchesca! You're alive! I've been so worried."

"Mom?"

"Oh, thank god you remember me," May said, laying on the sarcasm. "I thought you went paragliding and hit your head and got amnesia."

"Ma. Now's not a good time."

"What could possibly be more important than reassuring your mother that you're alive and well?" May insisted.

"Ma, it's Pru's wedding day, and I'm running an errand for her. I really have to focus, okay?"

"Pruitt's parents must be over-the-moon excited." Reality didn't exist in May Baranski's world. She'd met R.L. and

Addison Stockton on dozens of occasions. The Stocktons weren't an overly excitable bunch. "You know, I'd love if *my* daughter had a wedding day someday," May sighed.

"Yeah, yeah. Poor you. No grandbabies except for the one on the way from Marco and Rachel. I'll get knocked up next time I go out with a guy on Tinder. I promise."

"Franchesca Marie, you wouldn't dare—"

"I gotta go, Ma. I'll call you."

"When? You've been gone for so long already!"

"Soon." Probably. "I gotta go. Bye!"

She hung up before her mother could deliver yet another guilt trip with the precision of a surgeon.

Antonio snickered. "Your mom sounds like fun."

"Shut up, underage felon, and drive."

She had Antonio get as close to the gate as possible. She couldn't waste time crawling through jungle this time. After three embarrassing attempts, she finally made it over the wall scraping the shins of both legs on the sharp stone of the wall.

She grunted and groaned her way out of the flowering bush with the sound effects of an elderly person. *At least her hair helmet hadn't moved.*

Now, to stealthily—shit!

Three maids were catching a smoke break at the back of the building closest to her. They were all watching her warily.

Frankie brushed the dirt and leaves off her of dress and strolled toward them casual as can be.

"Good afternoon," she greeted them smiling like a normal person. "So, here's the thing..."

18

Frankie tied the apron around her waist. "Thank you again for this, Flor," she said to the woman she'd swapped clothes with. The bust was a little tight and the shoes were a little big, but other than that, Frankie was confident she could pass for a resort maid. At least temporarily.

"Is no problem," Flor said, straightening Frankie's collar. "That man is an ass. I'm happy to help."

"Do you know if there's anyone else staying in the room with him?" Frankie asked as her new friends hustled her down a back hallway.

"He's got an assistant who hovers around. Big man," Bianca told her. "But he stays in a different room."

Okay, so hopefully only one potential hired gun to get around. Frankie pressed a hand to her stomach as Wilma punched the call button for the elevator. She was either going to die today or pull off the greatest wedding day miracle of all time. And she was really hoping she wasn't about to die. Not without slapping the shit out of Aiden Kilbourn first.

They got off the elevator in the basement. Flor played

lookout while the other two stocked a room service cart with liquor.

"Just tell Mr. Hasselhoff you're there to restock the bar," Bianca instructed.

Hasselhoff. At least the kidnapper had a sense of humor.

"And don't make eye contact with him. He hates that," Wilma suggested.

They returned to the elevator with a white sheeted cart and half a dozen bottles of liquor.

"Keep your head down to avoid the cameras," Flor said, ushering them back into the elevator car. "And if you need help hiding the body, call 101 from the room phone and say you'd like to order room service."

"Cameras. Body. Room service. Got it," Frankie said. Her heart was thudding in her ears like the bass in her high school boyfriend's Chevy Cavalier.

Was she doing the right thing? Should she have trusted Aiden to handle it? Would she at least see Chip before she was gunned down in the prime of her life?

It was the longest elevator ride of her life, and that was counting the one with the guy who was breaking up with his girlfriend on speakerphone. The longest elevator ride was followed by the longest, creepiest walk down a hotel hallway. 302, 304, 306. As the room numbers counted up, Frankie's heart started pulsing in her head. She should have written up a will before this trip.

What if her brothers fought over her NHL memorabilia collection? She could see Gio and Marco coming to blows over her signed Kreider jockstrap. She hoped whoever took her apartment would be a good neighbor to the Chus across the hall. Mr. Chu was constantly losing his glasses, and Mrs. Chu thanked Frankie for finding them with gift cards to their

Korean restaurant around the block. She'd never again get to taste their bulgogi.

Tears swam in her eyes as 314 loomed in front of her. She took a deep breath. She was doing this for Pru. Her best friend deserved her happily ever after. And she'd totally get over the death of her best friend.

She was lousy at pep talks. Frankie raised her knuckles to knock and hesitated for a second. "You can do this," she whispered to herself. "You can go in there and show him that nobody kidnaps your friends and gets away with it."

Her pep talk was interrupted by the questioning glances of a hungover couple dressed to the elevens. The nines were so last year.

"She looks a little like that reality star that threw Kennedy in the koi pond last night," the woman said in a stage whisper.

Frankie put her head down and, eyes clenched shut, knocked.

The door wrenched open. "Can you read the 'Do Not Disturb'? Or are you all illiterate and stupid?"

All rich assholes tended to look the same. And this guy was no exception. He was medium build, medium height, spray tanned complexion with medium brown, carefully coiffed hair.

"I am here to restock dee barrr." God, her fake accent sounded more pirate than Bajan. Only an idiot would fall for it.

"It's about damn time. I called hours ago," the idiot said.

He ushered her inside, making annoying flapping motions like a chicken trying to take flight. "Come on. I don't have all day."

The suite was dark, heavy curtains closing out the tropical sunshine outside. It looked as though he was trying to make the room resemble a bad guy's lair. But there was too much mess—room service trays, empty liquor bottles—marring the luxury. It looked like a crew of trust fund babies had gotten together on daddy's dime to trash a hotel suite, not execute an abduction.

Kidnapping Asshole didn't look much better than the room itself. His hair was messed up like he'd been shoving nervous hands through it. His tie was loosened. *Who the hell wore a tie to lounge around a hotel room in Barbados, anyway?*

She headed into the main living space of the suite and did her best to guess where the bar was hidden. She guessed wrong, finding the TV sequestered in a cabinet. Wealthy people didn't like to stare at blank screens.

Kidnapping Asshole snapped his fingers. "The bar is over there. What, are you new here?"

She was saved from having to bite back a response by the man's phone ringing.

"Christ. What's taking so long? Get back here. He's going to be here any minute, and I'm not doing this without backup." He stormed out of the living room and into one of the bedrooms, slamming the door behind him.

"Oh my god. Oh my god. Oh my god," Frankie chanted. She surveyed the room and ran for the next closed door. It was a bathroom. The next one was a freaking walk-in closet. Finally, she spotted another closed door on the far side of the room. When she jiggled the handle she found it locked.

She yanked out the keyring Flor had loaned her and fumbled with the lock. She got it on the fifth try and ducked into the room. It was dark in here too, and it smelled like old eggs.

Frankie quietly closed the door behind her. "Chip?" she whispered. "Are you here?"

She tripped over him before she saw him. He was laying on his back on the floor beside the bed.

"Oh, my god, Chip," she hissed. *Was he dead? Had that sono-fabitch killed Chip?*

She reached a tentative hand toward him knowing that if she touched cold skin, she was going to throw up and then go commit a murder so heinous she'd go down in Barbados history. "Please don't be dead," she whispered.

19

*F*rankie prodded Chip hard with two fingers. It wasn't the cold flesh of a corpse that greeted her but a still-warm armpit and a snore.

"Chip!" She shook him again.

"Huh? What?" he struggled to wake up.

She breathed a sigh of relief so big it almost brought her breakfast back up. Her phone vibrated in her pocket. A text from Pru.

Pru: Where are you? Where's Chip?

Shit.

"Chip, it's me, Frankie. Are you okay?"

"Frankie?" he asked, groggily. "Does Elliot still have me? Does he know you're here?"

Frankie looked back toward the door. "No time to talk. We have to get you out of here. Can you walk?"

"Of course, I can walk. I fell asleep doing sit-ups. They gave me something to knock me out. Plus, super hungover. How's Pru? Is she mad? Is her dad—"

"Pru's fine. She's anxiously awaiting you in a poufy white dress."

"She didn't cancel?" Chip lit up like the Rockefeller Center Christmas tree.

"She doesn't know you're missing yet."

Frankie's phone vibrated again and then again. A rapid succession of texts she imagined.

"Why were you doing sit-ups?" Frankie asked, grasping his hand and pulling him into a seated position.

"Didn't want my six-pack to suffer just because I got abducted. I'm good. I swear." To prove it, he bounded to his feet and promptly fell on the bed. "Sorry. My foot's asleep."

Frankie pulled him back up. She could hear a voice in the other room and footsteps.

"Hide," Chip whispered.

Frankie ran around in a circle panicking and was eyeing the bedspread as a potential hiding spot when Chip opened the closet door and shoved her inside. He had just shut her in the dark when she heard the room door open.

Was Asshole Kidnapper coming to kill her? Reflexively, she hunkered further into the closet and hit her head on something large and metal.

"Mother f—"

Frankie clapped a hand over her own mouth when she heard the bedroom door open.

"Stay in here until I tell you to come out," Asshole Kidnapper insisted.

"Look, Elliot. Let's work this out. I'll get you whatever it is you want if you let me leave."

"Nice try, Randolph. But there's only one person who can give me what I want."

"Aiden is not going to let you get away with this."

Frankie froze. This guy had to be someone Aiden knew.

Was that the reason he hadn't let her kick in the door last night? She rubbed the knot on her head.

She was reaching for the door, ready to burst through it and demand answers when she heard a faint knock.

"Stay here and this will all be over soon," Asshole snapped, slamming the bedroom door.

The closet door flew open, and Frankie jumped back, hitting her head again in the same spot.

"Are you okay?" Chip asked when she doubled over.

"Ouch!" Frankie's hair snagged on a clothes hanger. She felt a half dozen bobby pins explode out of her head. "Oh, my God!"

"What?"

"My hair! My head! We have to get out of here!"

They both stopped, listened. There was more than one voice in the living room now, and it was only a matter of time before someone came back in.

Frankie rushed to the wall and pulled back the heavy curtains. "Oh, thank God," she whispered when she spotted the balcony. As quietly as possible, she muscled the sliding glass door open. The noise of ocean and resort life immediately filled the room, and she winced. If they stopped talking outside the bedroom, they'd hear.

Ugh. Three floors up, she confirmed, looking over the balcony edge. There was no way down, but perhaps there was a way out. The railing banister was wider than the railing itself. Some enterprising architect had probably realized people would want to put their crystal martini glasses down to take sunset selfies. And it connected every balcony on the floor.

"Chip, get out here," Frankie hissed.

He hobbled into the daylight like a hungover vampire.

"Why's the sun gotta shine all the time here?" he groaned.

"Oh, my God. Climb up here."

"You're bleeding!" he said, gaping at her.

She touched her fingers to her hair. "I hit my head on the safe. It's fine.

"It looks like..." Chip doubled over and breathed deeply.

"Pull it together, Chip." He'd been pre-med at NYU until he realized that blood made him vomit and faint. "Don't make me slap you."

"Okay. Maybe if I just don't look at you."

"For the love of god, Chip. I need you to climb up on this railing and shimmy your ass to another room with an open balcony door. We need to go. Now!"

Chip peered down to the terrace below. "Jesus, Frankie, that's like instant death!"

Frankie grabbed his face in her hand and squeezed his cheeks until he made fish lips. He closed his eyes so he didn't have to stare at her head wound. "Chip, do you want to marry Pru today or not?"

"Yesh."

"Then get your ass up there and shimmy over to the next balcony."

"Okah."

She released his face and pushed him toward the railing.

"You're coming too, right?"

"I'll be right behind you. Out of curiosity, what did Aiden have to do with all this?"

Chip paused on all fours balancing. "It's not his fault."

They heard raised voices coming from inside the suite. "Go. We'll talk later." Frankie shooed him further down the ledge and ran back into the room.

She'd barricade the door to buy them a little time. At least that was her plan when she tried to pick up the nightstand. The bedroom door burst open.

Asshole Kidnapper stared at her for two full seconds before losing his shit.

"Who are you, and where's—"

"Your kidnapping victim? My friend Chip? You want to know where he is?" Frankie's voice was rising. Her fingers closed around the alarm clock and iPhone charger on the nightstand.

"Yes!" he shrieked, tearing at his hair. "And why is there blood everywhere? Did you kill him?"

"What's going on—" The man in the doorway didn't get a chance to finish his sentence because Frankie hit Asshole in the face as hard as she could with the alarm clock.

He doubled over, screaming. More blood rained down on the white carpet. Frankie gave him another whack for good measure that knocked him to his knees.

"I tried to keep this civilized," Asshole shrieked.

Frankie turned on the second man and hefted the alarm clock.

"You want a turn, Kilbourn?"

Aiden held up both hands. "Hang on there, slugger. Why are you bleeding?"

"Why am I bleeding? Why am I bleeding?" she laughed. "I'm bleeding for the same reason your best friend is missing his wedding. Because of *you*."

"Franchesca, I can explain."

"I don't want an explanation! You're too late. Chip's already long gone—"

"Uh, Frankie?"

"Chip! What the fuck?"

Chip peeked through the patio door looking sheepish.

"So, I found a room that was open, but it was occupied, and I think they're calling security."

"Back up, Kilbourn. Just back the fuck up," Frankie ordered, wielding the alarm clock.

"Hey, Aiden."

"Good to see you, Chip."

"Don't talk to him. And don't you come near us!" Frankie inched past Aiden, dragging Chip with one arm while holding the alarm clock pointed in Aiden's direction.

Asshole Kidnapper moaned on the floor. "She broke my nose."

"Good," the three of them answered.

"Now, Chip and I are going to walk out of here, and you both are going to let us, or I'm going to start screaming bloody murder, and all of resort security will be breaking down that door in thirty seconds."

Frankie backed them toward the door to the suite.

When Aiden made a move to follow, she shook her head. "Uh-uh, buddy. You're persona non-grata. You stay here with your pal. We've got a wedding to get to."

"You should probably do what she says," Chip suggested to Aiden. "She's terrifying when she's mad."

"I can see that," Aiden said, looking more amused than terrified.

"Don't you dare laugh," Frankie growled. "I'll make sure you regret this. Let's go, Chip."

"Hey, do you want a ride, Aiden?" Chip offered.

Frankie slapped him on the arm. "No, he doesn't want a ride. Kidnappers don't get rides from their victims."

"Awh, Frankie, he didn't really kidnap me."

"Then he conspired to kidnap you."

"No, I didn't!"

"No, he didn't!"

"We'll talk about this later," Frankie said, finally understanding just exactly how mad a parent had to be to use those words.

She pushed Chip out into the hallway. "Stay," she said, pointing at Aiden who was helping his brother to his feet. "If either of you try to follow us, I'll kill you."

"I think the crazy maid means it," Elliot stage whispered, still clutching his nose and looking terrified. "Lo siento, lady. Lo siento."

"Seriously? We're in Barbados, you idiot!"

She pulled the door shut and then pushed Chip toward the stairs. "Go! Go! Go!"

They sprinted to the basement and burst through the double doors. Footsteps sounded a floor or two above them. Flor in Frankie's sundress was stocking a cart with mini shampoos.

"Can you lock that door?" Frankie asked, as she worked her zipper down her back.

Bianca raced to the stairwell door and locked it. "Someone's running," she reported, stepping away from the window.

"Thank you so much for everything," Frankie said, shoving her way out of the dress. "Sorry about the blood. Those closet safes are sharp."

Something, a good-sized body from the sounds of it, hit the doors at a run.

Frankie winced. She'd have nightmares forever of being chased down the stairs.

Flor stripped down quickly and handed the dress back to Frankie. "I hope you showed that asshole in 314 who's boss."

"I'll apologize for the blood up there too," Frankie said grimly.

Flor gave her a curt nod and clapped her on the shoulder. "Good luck, my friend."

"May the force be with you," Frankie offered. She was no good at pep talks or thank yous. "Let's go Chip."

They tiptoed out a side door and then half ran, half crawled, into the vegetation. The open scratches on her shins sang as she packed more dirt into the wounds. Her head throbbed and her hair was being picked apart by branches. But she had the groom.

"Ouch!"

Frankie looked back. Chip was holding a hand over his eye. "Are you okay?" she hissed.

"I got a branch in my eye."

"Just look with your good eye. We're almost to the wall."

Finally, the great stucco monument rose before them. "Okay, we're going to climb over, get in the car, and go get you married, right?"

"Right," Chip said, still clutching his eye.

"Let me see your eye."

He dropped his hand. There was a red welt that continued on either side of his eye. The eye itself was as red as a blood-hound's.

"Oh, God." She clutched a hand to her mouth. Frankie's stomach could handle a lot of things. Wounded eyes were not one of those things.

"Why are you *still* bleeding?" Chip gagged. "It's smeared all over your face." He bent at the waist and dry-heaved.

"Let's just stop looking at each other and climb the wall."

Frankie shoved Chip up and over, and when he leaned down to offer her a hand, he wisely squeezed his eyes shut tight.

They landed unceremoniously alongside the highway two hundred feet from Antonio and his stupid little car. The engine roared to life as they approached. Frankie stuffed Chip in the backseat.

"Buckle up," she warned, before jumping in next to Antonio.

The kid sped away from the resort with the vigor of a NASCAR driver in a brand-new sports car. Frankie pulled out her phone.

"Oh, my god." She had nineteen missed calls. All but two from Pru. The others were from Aiden. She played her friend's most recent voicemail and winced. Pruitt was sobbing uncontrollably.

Frankie hit redial with one hand and clung to the dash with the other. "Pru? Can you hear me?"

"Where are you?" Pru wailed. "Chip is gone. Aiden's missing. And you *abandoned* me! My dad is looking for a weapon, and Chip's mom already broke into the cocktail hour appetizers. I'm supposed to be getting married in twenty minutes, and I don't have a groom or a best friend."

"You have both, Pru. I have Chip with me, and we are on our way back."

"You have Chip?" At least, that's what Frankie thought she said. It was too high-pitched and blubbery to be sure.

"He's right here. And there's no rules about talking before the ceremony, right?"

"No, I don't think so," Pru sobbed.

"Here," Frankie said, shoving her phone into Chip's hand. "Talk to your bride?"

"Pru, baby?" Chip crooned into the phone.

"Is there always this much drama at weddings?" Antonio asked, veering around a pothole big enough to swallow their buggy.

"Really this is par for the course for most American weddings," Frankie said.

"Really?"

"No! Jesus, Antonio. This is a complete shit show. Kidnappings and rescues—"

"And car chases," Antonio added looking in the rearview mirror.

Frankie twisted in her seat to look. A big, black SUV was glued to their tail. She didn't recognize the driver, but she sure as hell knew the passenger.

20

Frankie released her safety harness and leaned out her open doorway to give Aiden a better view of her middle finger.

"It's just Aiden," Chip said, trying to juggle the phone and eye injury while shooing her back into the vehicle.

"*Just* Aiden? His brother kidnapped you!"

"That's kinda the way they do things."

"Your friends are horrible people," Frankie yelled.

"Pru, baby?" Chip said into the phone. "Yeah, kidnapped. I know, right? Look, I gotta go. Aiden's calling, and Frankie's hanging out of the car, and we'll be there so soon. I'll explain everything after you're my wife. I can't wait to see you in your dress. I love you," Chip shouted over the wind.

"Don't you dare answer that call—" Frankie's warning did no good.

"Oh, hey, Aiden. Oh, good. You're right behind us... No, I don't think it's a good idea for me to tell her that right now. She's pretty mad at you... I don't know. We haven't really had time to talk."

Frankie reached behind her and snatched the phone back.

"What the hell are you going to do, Kilbourn? Run us off the road? Shoot us in the back of the head?"

"Sit your ass down, buckle your seatbelt, and try to stay alive," he growled into the phone.

"Excuse me? I don't take orders from kidnappers."

"He didn't kidnap me!" Chip said.

"I didn't kidnap him!"

"Whatever. Don't even think about trying to keep us from the wedding. It won't go well for you."

"I'm not trying to keep you from the wedding, you irresponsible, exasperating idiot. I'm on your side."

"Bullshit. You knew your brother had Chip."

"I did," he admitted. That temporarily shut her up. "I realized it when you read the business name on the room register last night. It's a subsidiary of the family company."

"Well, good news for you."

"I promise you, I'll deal with Elliot later. For now, let's try to get the groom to his wedding in one piece."

"You are the worst human being in the world, and I know a lot of people," Frankie shouted into the phone.

"Sweetheart, you have no idea." He disconnected before she could have the satisfaction of hanging up on him.

"Agh!"

"So Money Bags kidnapped you?" Antonio asked as he skirted through an alley.

"Yes," Frankie said.

"No," Chip said. "Hey, are you old enough to drive?"

They made it to the resort in one adrenalized piece. The big black SUV maintained its course and pulled up to the hotel behind them. Frankie tossed every bill she had in her wallet at Antonio, blew him a kiss, and dragged Chip out of the car.

Aiden burst out of the passenger door of the SUV, and the three took off at a dead run through the lobby.

The concierge and front desk manager gaped after them.

"We have to get you dressed," Frankie said, pushing Chip toward the elevator. The doors miraculously opened, but Aiden slid in behind them. The close quarters were what pushed her over the edge. She launched herself at Aiden. Her hands were so angry they didn't know whether to slap or punch and instead flopped uselessly against his chest.

"She's going Solange on you," Chip observed.

"Thank you. I can see that," Aiden said dryly, wrestling Frankie into the corner of the elevator. "Stop. Hitting."

He held her there with the weight of his body. Frankie's rage kicked up another notch when her body reacted as if it was happy to have six-plus feet of lying asshole pressed against it. Stupid, traitorous body.

"Hold still, Franchesca. I'm just trying to look at the cut on your head." He gripped her chin from behind as she flailed against him. "Stop." He gave the order softly.

She winced when his fingers prodded the cut.

"It's not too deep. But you should have it looked at."

"Oh, sure. I'll make an appointment with a doctor in the next, oh, two minutes before the ceremony starts."

"What happened to your eye?" Aiden asked Chip.

"Tree branch during the escape. This is going to be some story for the grandkids someday."

"Yeah, just remember who rode to your rescue and who was the bad guy," Frankie muttered.

The elevator doors opened, and they spilled out into the hallway. Chip jogged toward his room, one hand clamped firmly over his eye. Aiden stood rooted to the spot. "We need to talk," he said to Frankie.

"Yeah, well, that's not happening either. I have nothing to say to you."

"Let's go Kilbourn. Gotta get me married," Chip called from the end of the hall.

"Don't get abducted again," Frankie called after him. She whirled on Aiden and stabbed him in the chest with her finger. "He trusts you. But I don't. And if you do anything to fuck this up for him and Pru, I'll be taking your balls home with me in my carry-on," Frankie warned him.

"I'm rather attached to them."

"Don't be cute with me."

"You're beautiful when you're covered in blood and pissed off."

"Then I must look like a fucking super model right now."

She flipped him off one more time for good measure and stormed down the hall to her room. She'd forgotten until she got inside about the dress. The mangled, stained dress. The garment bag was hanging in the closet. She was too nervous to look to see if the hotel laundry had been able to work a miracle. She shucked off her now ruined sundress and shoved herself into the strapless bra and friggin' forty-seven dollar satin briefs that *had* to go with the dress.

With shaking fingers, she unzipped the bag. Oh god. There were still visible berry stains. The tears at least looked... better-ish. It still looked like the dress had been run through a garbage disposal.

Her phone rang again and she stabbed the speakerphone button as she shimmied into the dress.

"Yeah?"

"Frankie, you've got to get down here. My dad and Chip's dad are fighting in the aisle."

"Fistfight or wrestling?"

"Ha. Basically, screaming at each other about how the other's kid is a selfish asshole."

Frankie could hear shouting in the background. "What are the groomsmen doing?"

"Putting action on it. Most of them think my dad can take Mr. Randolph because of the years of pent up rage."

"Ugh. I'll be down in two minutes. In the meantime, have your wedding coordinator do literally anything."

"Hurry!"

Frankie hung up and stared in horror in the mirror. The left side of her face was covered in blood. Only some of it was dried. Her carefully coiffed hair was exploding out of the last of the torture pins that were still hanging on. She had an entire vine stuck in there somehow. And the dress?

The dress was cleaner now but still destroyed. Did bridesmaid dresses come in distressed fabric? Pru was definitely going to kill her.

There was a knock at the door, and Frankie tripped over the hem in her haste to get to it.

"What the hell do you want?"

Aiden was standing there in an annoyingly pristine, perfectly tailored tux. No blood or bruises on his face. Just a ghost of a smile and a garment bag slung over his shoulder.

"I thought you might need this," he said, handing over the bag.

"Like there's anything you could give me that I'd accept right now," Frankie snapped. Her head hurt and so did her heart.

Seeing that she wasn't going to, Aiden reached over and unzipped the bag himself.

It was her bridesmaid dress. Or at least an exact replica. "How in the hell—"

"Do you really want to know how, or do you want to put it on?" he asked.

"On." Anger and shyness be damned. She had a best friend to please. Frankie slid out of her dress, shoving it into a pile on the floor.

Aiden lost that smug smile and simply stared.

"Like you haven't seen a thousand tits before," she muttered, stepping into the new dress.

He steadied her when she wobbled and zipped her up in the back.

"Perfect," he said.

"How did you know my size?"

"Did you forget I've had my hands on you?"

"That was eighteen hours ago. How did you get a gown in my size here that fast?"

"Why don't we take care of the blood and the hair instead of focusing on the hows?" he suggested.

"How did you get dressed so fast? Is Chip ready? Oh, God. You didn't leave him alone did you?"

Aiden pushed her into the bathroom and wet a washcloth.

"Why are hotel towels always white?" Frankie winced, as he began to clean her face. "Those stains aren't coming out."

"Do you always babble when you're nervous?"

"Nervous? I'm not nervous. I'm a freaking rock over here. I didn't almost die or give myself a concussion or ruin my best friend's perfect day."

"Shhh." Aiden worked the cloth gently around her temple.

"Look. You don't have to be all gentle about it. We gotta get down stairs and keep Win and R.L. from killing each other. They were four seconds away from wrestling when Pru called."

"Got it covered."

"You have everything covered, don't you?"

"I would if you'd let me."

"You could have told me. That you knew who had him. That you were working on a plan."

"I didn't want to involve you in Kilbourn business. It's messy and ugly, and I'm trying to impress you. So, how appealing would I have been if I told you my half-brother orchestrated this entire thing to ensure my vote for a new chief financial officer?"

"I find honesty a lot more attractive than someone who never gets dirty, Aiden."

She turned to look in the mirror. He'd done the best he could with the cleanup, and she no longer resembled a car accident victim. "Oh, my hair."

"Leave it down." He pulled a pin out before she could object. "Don't try to tame it."

Their eyes met and held in the mirror. She was still mad. But marginally less mad. It must be his pheromones that he was giving off. Sexy, wealthy pheromones.

"We better get down there," she said, grabbing a stick of deodorant and her lip gloss and shoving them in her clutch. "I can finish in the elevator."

She made a dash for the door only to turn around. "Shoes!"

Aiden held up his hand, her sandals dangling from his fingers.

21

The wedding was, despite the events leading up to it, picture perfect.

Well, after Pruitt's father, R.L. tried to take a swing at Chip when he handed off his daughter to her groom. But besides that, it had been rather nice, Aiden decided.

Pruitt glowed in her gown and didn't even seem to mind that Chip was wearing an eye patch. A scratched cornea, according to Dr. Erbman, an optometrist who was attending the wedding. The couple said their vows and sealed them with the requisite kiss. It appeared as though all transgressions had been forgiven and everyone was ready to enjoy the party. Everyone except Franchesca.

There was no forgiveness in those blue-green eyes. He'd watched her throughout the ceremony. He tried to put his finger on exactly what it was about Franchesca Baranski that held his attention like a hand closing around his throat. She wasn't his usual cookie-cutter beauty. She wasn't refined. And she certainly wasn't used to high society.

He made sure the women he dated were all of those things. It made it easy, uncomplicated.

There was nothing uncomplicated about Frankie. And she was dismissive about his wealth, something else Aiden wasn't used to.

But he longed to touch her again. It had been a test of both his and her reactions at Oistins. He'd pushed his luck on the beach at Rockley. But now that he had his answer, there was no way he was giving up the chase. He wanted her under him, naked and begging. Wanted to fist a hand in that curtain of curls and bring her to her knees. There was something dangerous about those desires. He wanted to own her, consume her.

He wanted her to complicate the hell out of things.

He watched her throughout the ceremony. While the other bridesmaids looked bored or practiced the perfect pose for the photographer, Frankie cried tears of sincere joy for her friends and the commitment they were making. She was a romantic, and he knew he'd spoil that in her if he touched her. If he got her to say yes. He wasn't capable of love or romance. He excelled at winning.

And even with the blood, the bruises, the lack of makeup, Franchesca was a prize worth winning. She outshone the rest of them, all posing like clothes hangers. The same hair, the same makeup, the same drive.

He'd have her, Aiden decided, for purely selfish reasons. She didn't make sense. She didn't fit in his life. But he wanted her all the same. He'd have her even if it meant ruining her.

He'd caught her eye during the vows, and the soft happiness in her eyes had shifted to steel. No, she hadn't forgiven him. Nor should she. However, if that grudge was going to keep her out of his bed, Aiden was willing to grovel to destroy the obstacle.

They spent the rest of the ceremony locked in a staring contest. His focus zeroed in until there was nothing but

Frankie, her hair blowing in the breeze, her dress hugging her curves like she were a pin-up.

"Knock. It. Off," she mouthed to him. He grinned wickedly. Yes, this conquest would be more than satisfying.

When the bride and groom linked arms in celebration and marched down the aisle to the cheers of their audience. Aiden felt the anticipation ratchet up.

And then he was touching her. Frankie stiffly slid her arm through his.

He reached into his jacket pocket and produced a handkerchief. He handed it to her. She frowned down at it. "You soak this in chloroform?" she hissed.

His laugh surprised them both and drew the eyes of the ceremony guests.

"You are one-of-a-kind, Franchesca."

"Ugh. Let's get this over with, you steaming pile of shit," she muttered.

"Smile pretty for the cameras, sweetheart," he said as they started down the aisle.

"How about I break your nose like I did for your brother?" she offered sweetly, beaming up at him as if he were the most fascinating man in the world.

"Half-brother. And if it gets you to forgive me, my nose is yours."

"Don't tempt me."

They smiled and nodded their way down the white carpet, and Aiden captured her hand with his free one. A photographer darted in front of them, and Aiden squeezed her hand until Frankie pasted on a "fuck you" smile. They grinned at each other. His hand crushing hers, her nails digging into his wrist.

He'd never wanted a woman this badly before in his entire forty years. Not even the voluptuous and unattainable Natalia when he'd been a fifteen-year-old virgin in private school. Two years older than Aiden, Natalia hadn't remained unattainable, and Aiden hadn't remained a virgin.

However, Frankie was just stubborn enough to deny them both what they most wanted on principle. He couldn't have that. He was a Kilbourn, and Kilbourns did whatever it took to get what they wanted by any means necessary as embarrassingly evidenced by his half-brother's dim-witted move.

Reluctantly, Aiden released her when Pruitt threw her arms around Frankie.

The women hugged rocking side to side, and the tears returned.

Aiden slapped Chip on the shoulder. "You did it."

"Thanks to you and Frankie," Chip said, prodding his eyepatch. "So, you going to kill Elliot?"

"I've got some plans for him," Aiden said darkly. He was used to his family's manipulations to some extent. But Elliot had crossed a line, and there was no going back.

"What did he want out of you?" Chip asked.

"A vote."

"Family, right?" Chip shrugged good-naturedly.

"I'm sorry he dragged you into this. Rest assured he'll pay."

"I had no doubt, Kilbourn. Now, let's party."

Chip swept Pruitt out of Frankie's arms and spun her in a circle. "Mrs. Randolph!"

"Mr. Randolph," she cooed back at him. "Now, tell me everything that happened."

Davenport appeared with Margeaux attached to him. She slinked over to Aiden and smiled slyly. "How do you feel about bagging a bridesmaid before cocktail hour?"

He frowned and leaned in a little closer. "What happened to your eyebrow?"

Margeaux growled. "That low-class, fat bitch Franklin bonded with the help, and they waxed it off."

"Oh, hey, Marge," Frankie strolled by, plate of hors de oeuvres in hand. "You've got a little something right here." She pointed to where the fake eyebrow that wasn't fooling anyone had been sketched onto her forehead.

"Why don't you fuck off and go scrub someone's toilet?" Margeaux snapped.

"Actually, I'm in catering, so you should ask me to get a plate of food. But I can see how you'd get those confused, being a spoiled, selfish dumbass and all."

"Ladies," Davenport said jovially. He threw an arm around both bridesmaids. "Can't we all just get along?"

"Sure, as soon as someone sends her back over the wall to Mexico where she belongs," Margeaux sneered.

"I'm Lebanese and Italian, you fuckwit."

"Whatever. Your people fold my laundry and cook for me."

"Margeaux, why don't you do us all a favor and go off and fuck some poor schmuck who doesn't yet know what a soulless harpy you are?" Aiden said succinctly.

Frankie and Margeaux stared at him, open mouthed.

"Don't insult Franchesca again, or you won't be happy with the consequences."

"Come on, doll. Let's get you a drink and some appetizers that you can throw up later," Davenport said, steering Margeaux away from Frankie.

"I don't need you defending me," Frankie reminded him.

"And I don't need you being treated like shit."

"I can handle myself."

"I can see that. Nice job on her eyebrow by the way. She's going to look perennially surprised in every photo."

Frankie's full lips curved ever so slightly. "It wasn't my idea. I wish it had been."

Cressida and Taffany joined them. Cressida snapped her fingers at a waiter bearing a tray of drinks. "You may leave these here," she said, taking the tray from him.

Taffany was a shocking shade of fuchsia. She reached for a glass and winced as her dress rubbed her raw skin.

"What happened to you?" Frankie asked.

"I fell asleep in the sun this afternoon after the spa," Taffany said trying to lift the drink to her lips without stretching any skin.

"Passed out actually," Ford said, leaning over Taffany's shoulder and grabbing a drink. He'd already loosened his tie and slapped on a pair of Ray-Bans. "Let's get this party started!"

"I agree," Cressida said fiercely.

"Woooo," the burnt Taffany said without moving.

Digby strolled by on his phone muttering about "not missing this IPO" and "restricted shares."

"Let's talk," Aiden told Frankie. He was pleasantly surprised when she let him guide her away from the festivity, his hand at the small of her back.

Night was falling. The sunset cast a spectacular show of pinks and reds over the sky and ocean to the west. Behind them, the band warmed up with an old favorite.

"You wanted to talk, so talk," Frankie said, crossing her arms in front of her. The move made her breasts swell dangerously against the fabric of her dress.

"I'd like to explain what happened."

"To me or to my boobs," Frankie asked.

Rather reluctantly, Aiden raised his gaze to her face. She was smirking at him, her hair spilling over a shoulder, the curls lifting in the wind.

"To all of you, if you'll let me."

She made a sarcastic and sweeping gesture with her hand. "The beach is yours. Talk."

"My family isn't normal," he began. She rolled her eyes but didn't interject. "We don't ask for things. We take them. We manipulate and maneuver until whatever it is that we want is ours or until we lose our interest."

"I thought you were trying to get into my pants?" Frankie quipped.

"I'm trying to be honest. And I have a feeling honesty will get me farther than painting pretty pictures."

"So, you're all selfish, manipulative assholes. I got it. Why did your selfish, manipulative asshole brother take Chip?"

"Elliot is my half-brother. He's spent years trying to prove to our father that he's the better son." Despite their ten-year age difference, Elliot had been born trying to keep up with Aiden. "I'm favored for whatever reasons my father has. But Elliot is constantly trying to outdo me, undermine me, prove his worth."

"Uh-huh. And abducting your best friend would help him how?"

"We're all on the board of Kilbourn Holdings. We're looking for a new CFO. A powerful and lucrative position. Elliot wants me to vote for the candidate he's backing. His candidate is... lacking. And I told him so, repeatedly." It was the polite way of saying Boris Donaldson was a sexual harassing, egotistical, asshole who left his last position under the shadow of an insider trading scheme. Aiden wasn't letting the man near his family business.

"So, he took Chip to strong-arm you into it?"

Aiden nodded. "It sounds stupid, but the business of it is complicated."

"It is stupid, but it's not that complicated. Obviously, Elliot has a reason he wants this guy in place whether it's personal or professional. CFO for Kilbourn Holdings. That's a lot of money, not to mention prestige, and a voice as to what happens within the company. He either really likes this guy, or it's a 'I'll do this for you, if you do this for me' deal."

Aiden nodded, pleased that she grasped the situation. "I knew Elliot was behind it when you named the company listed on the room. He thinks it's a secret shell corporation, but I know everything that happens under the company umbrella. I've kept an eye on him and his business."

"This is the part that really starts to piss me off. You knew where Chip was and who had him, and you could probably guess the reason. Yet you decide we have to leave him there and 'regroup.'"

"I told you I didn't want to involve you."

"I could have held your coat while you kicked in the door, punched your brother in the face, and dragged Chip out."

His lips curved. That was probably the way Frankie would prefer to conduct business.

"That's not how Kilbourns react to threats."

"Let me guess," Frankie said, tapping a finger to her chin. "You came back to the hotel, did a little digging, and found out why this Boris guy is so important to your brother so you could use it against him."

He nodded again. "Essentially. You're not running away screaming yet," Aiden pointed out.

She shrugged. "It's no kicking in a door and punching him in the face, but at least you were willing to do something vindictive. However, you were *also* willing to leave my friend at the hands of an idiot kidnapper for more hours than necessary. What if Elliot had hurt him?"

Aiden shook his head. "That's not Elliot's MO. He doesn't get his hands dirty. You saw the setup. Chip was locked in a room and fed."

"But you couldn't know that for sure," Frankie reminded him. "People go crazy all the time."

"Chip dabbled in mixed martial arts after college. I think he could take a sniveling idiot like Elliot without breaking a sweat."

She stepped closer. Her chin came up defiantly. "Your brother could and did hire other people to do his dirty work. You shouldn't have assumed that they would have qualms about harming a rich, drunk American. You were so cocky in your assessment, you left my friend in a potentially dangerous situation and me in the dark. That's not how you treat people, Aiden."

He frowned, her words striking a direct hit. "There's no point in reviewing 'what-ifs.' I was confident that Elliot wouldn't harm Chip, and he didn't."

"You were willing to risk it."

"I got where I am today by listening to my instincts."

"Please. You got to where you are today because your daddy gave you a position and a big, fat trust fund. Maybe you've worked hard since then. Maybe you're good at what you do. But you fucked up here. Chip could have been hurt while you and your brother were playing human chess. This wedding might not have happened, and a whole lot of other people would have gotten hurt."

"But it didn't happen that way," Aiden pointed out, his frustration rising. He wasn't used to being lectured by anyone other than his father.

"You were careless with other people, Kilbourn. That's a pretty damning character flaw. I don't go to bed with people who treat me or anyone else like shit."

"Franchesca," he began. Defending himself was getting him nowhere. Time to change tactics. "I'm sorry. You're right. I was careless and cocky, and my decision could have hurt people."

"Hmm."

"What does that mean?"

"Aide, you tell me you're a champion manipulator, and then you go and give me the perfect apology? Please. I didn't just fall off a turnip truck. I know how far a man will go to get in my bed."

He didn't particularly care for being called out for his tactics or having to think about any other man lucky enough to land in Frankie's bed.

"You wanted answers, you wanted an apology. And none of that's good enough. What more do you want from me, Franchesca?" he demanded, crossing his arms.

"I want you to be real. Don't play games. Don't paint me a picture. Be honest. Don't try to strategize your way between my legs." She turned and started back toward the party and then paused. "Oh, and you owe Chip and Pru a pretty massive apology. Make it a good one."

22

_F_rankie marched back to the reception ready for a good, stiff drink. She was exhausted. Chip was safe, Pru was married, and she'd knocked the great and powerful Aiden Kilbourn down a peg or two. Her work here was done.

She was flying back in the morning. Back to normal life. Work, school, her insane mother. And as far as she was concerned, she'd be just fine if she never saw Aiden again.

"There you are!" One of the photographer's lackeys grabbed Frankie's wrist just as she was reaching for a glass of something cold and alcoholic. "Time for portraits," the woman said cheerily, dragging her away.

"But, but tequila!"

"I'll have a hot cocktail waiter spoon feed you tequila if it means you'll run, not walk," the woman said through gritted teeth.

"You don't have to be afraid of the bride. There's no zilla there," Frankie said, warming up to a jog.

"It's not her. It's Wannabe Annie Leibovitz," the lackey said, nodding in the photographer's direction. The woman was wearing diamonds and silk as if she were one of the higher end guests. "She's terrifying."

"Send me that waiter," Frankie hissed as the woman shoved her toward the photographer.

"You!" The photographer pointed an accusing finger in her direction. "Makeup!"

As if by magic, a hotel employee with a palette of gels and goops and glosses appeared in front of Frankie and started applying things to her face.

"And you!" The photographer pointed at Aiden who had trailed in, a glass of something manly in his hand. "Your hair is a little long on top for my vision. We need to cut it."

"Or you'll take me as I am," he suggested calmly, his gaze finding Frankie.

"Bah!" the photographer spat out a laugh. "Fine. Stand there and look broody. Perfect," she said when he didn't move a muscle. She pointed at Frankie again. "You. Go there."

"Where's my tequila?" Frankie whispered to the assistant.

"I'll share," Aiden offered, holding up his glass.

She wasn't getting through this without alcohol. She sipped, her eyes widening at the slow, smooth burn at the back of her throat.

"Scotch?" she asked, taking another sip. A team of assistants appeared and shoved her at Aiden, arranging them for the photographer.

Aiden nodded. His hand skimmed the small of her back, fingers curling around the curve of her hip.

One of the assistants snatched the glass from her hand and Frankie glared, mutinously at the man. "I must have only had the bad kind before."

"I'll give you a case," Aiden promised.

Frankie looked up at him sharply. "Don't start with me, Aide." One of the stagers grabbed her hand and laid it flat on his chest. "Hey!" Frankie didn't care to be arranged like a Barbie doll. Especially not when her Ken was Aiden.

"Perfect! Don't move!" The photographer flew around them snapping away. Flashes blinding them both. "Stop looking at me. Look at each other."

Frankie didn't obey the command swiftly enough and Aiden nudged her chin up to meet his gaze.

"Oh, hell yes. Inferno over here," the photographer shouted. "Give me more."

"I want you," Aiden announced quietly.

Frankie tried to withdraw, but he wouldn't let her. He held her in place with those two big, capable hands.

"You wanted honesty. You don't want games. I'm giving you that. I want you in my bed, Franchesca. I want to see you when we go home."

"God! The smolder on you two," the photographer crowed.

"I want you, and we both know that's not one sided," he pressed.

She shivered, thinking about those probing fingers under the table at dinner the night before.

"Giving in to every craving your body has is a stupid idea," she shot back.

"Craving. What a perfect word for it." He brought his hand up and smoothed her hair away from her face.

"Oh, yeah. I'm having orgasms over here," the photographer shouted. "Way better than Sunburned Fake Tits and Mr. Roboto."

"I just told you I don't sleep with guys who treat people like shit."

"Then I've changed my ways."

She gave him her best "shut the fuck up" look.

"I'll be whatever it is you want me to be."

"Aiden! How is that not playing games?"

"I'm trying to be honest with you."

"Then try this on for size," she suggested. "'Frankie, I like you. A lot. And I want to fuck you, and I promise to make it worth your while.'"

"I want to do more than fuck you," he admitted.

Frankie shook her head. "I know what you do. You play with women like toys until something newer and shinier comes along."

"I don't do long-term relationships," Aiden agreed. "But I won't play with you. I'll be good to you."

"While it lasts," she shot back. "I'm not interested in being someone's toy. And what makes you think I'd want a relationship with you anyway?"

"Then spend tonight with me."

"Just tonight?"

"Let me have you tonight. All night. Then decide."

"Jesus, Kilbourn. You want me to fuck you and then decide if I want to be your plaything?"

He looked pained. "I'll give you anything you want."

"Newsflash. You don't buy me, asshole. You earn me."

The camera shutter clicked incessantly. "Why don't you grab her leg and hook it over your hip," the photographer suggested to Aiden.

"I think we're done here," Frankie said, pushing out of Aiden's arms. She needed tequila to cool the slow burn in her blood. Every damn time he put his hands on her, she couldn't think of anything else but how good it felt.

She couldn't trust him. Wouldn't trust him. She had standards. She wasn't some walking horn dog like Margeaux. And she wasn't an idiot like Taffany. She knew exactly what she'd be getting into, and it wasn't just Aiden's bed.

~

THE PARTY MOVED to the expansive stone terrace for dinner and more drinks. Frankie noted that Pru looked a little shell-shocked over Chip's description of recent events. But she was a Stockton-Randolph now. Appearances had to be kept.

Still, Frankie watched her closely for signs of migraines or minor freak-outs. And while she watched Pru, Aiden watched her.

She avoided him. But it wasn't easy. There was the group photography. The bridal party dance. And she couldn't completely ignore him now that he was giving a toast.

He rose from the chair on Chip's right, the microphone in his hand. The long bridal party table was swagged in ivory cloth and tens of thousands of dollars of cream-colored flowers. Strands of silver and gold crystals dripped from the table top down to the floor. Frankie half expected Gatsby himself to stroll out with a goblet of champagne.

And Aiden Kilbourn in a bespoke tux looked as if he belonged here.

He didn't need to quiet the crowd. When Aiden spoke, everyone listened.

Frankie tried not to look at him, but it was like telling an elementary school student not to look directly into the sun during an eclipse. It made her want to look more.

"Chip and I met on the polo field several years ago when my rather aggressive pony tried to take a bite out of his shoulder," Aiden began warmly. "He was quite nice about it as Chip is about everything. I, on the other hand, am more like my pony."

The crowd chuckled, and Frankie rolled her eyes.

"Despite that, we became friends. I thought my influence would harden him. Make him more aggressive to better suit me. However, it didn't work out quite that way. Despite my best efforts, Chip remained kind-hearted, friendly. And I found myself softening a bit. Chip reminded me that there is more to life than conquering the world. There's living and loving to be done. And he and Pruitt are a shining example of exactly that."

Chip grinned up at Aiden.

Stupid eloquent bastard. He wasn't even reading from notes.

"Now, I'm not saying you and Pruitt have changed my mind about marriage. But you do make love look appealing. I've never had someone in my corner the way Pruitt is in yours. Well, except for you, Chip, and you're already taken."

The crowd laughed eagerly.

"I'm honored to be in both your corners today. And for the first time in my life, I worry that I might be missing out."

Every woman on the terrace swooned. It was an audible sigh, like a flock of birds taking flight at once.

"To Chip and Pruitt. I wish you all the happiness that comes with living and loving," Aiden said, raising his glass of champagne.

"To Chip and Pruitt," the guests echoed.

That sexy rat bastard. No one would have guessed that just a few hours ago the man had allowed his so-called best friend to be used as bait. Aiden came to her, the microphone in hand. He leaned down and in, his lips brushing her ear.

"Quit glaring at me, sweetheart. You'll spoil the pictures."

He handed over the mic, winked, and returned to his seat.

Frankie cursed him. Her pulse rate was running at jack hammer speeds. One brush of his lips against her ear lobe, and she was ready to take his pants off under the table and grip his cock with both hands.

How was she supposed to give a speech when her nether-region was throbbing like a volcano about to erupt? The man was leaking pheromones, nature's roofies.

Grateful for the cover of the table and the long gown,

Frankie rose and stood with her legs crossed tight. She cleared her throat and focused on Pru's pretty face.

"I have two loud, obnoxious brothers at home. My whole childhood was spent wishing for a sister. Someone to even the odds. Someone who didn't leave the toilet seat up."

The crowd chuckled. *See? She could be funny, too.*

"I didn't get my wish until I moved into my dorm freshman year. I walk into my new room, carting all of the freshman necessities like cheese curls and a straightening iron with my brothers bickering about who was carrying more stuff. And there she was," Frankie smiled down at Pru who was already crying.

"My sister. She told my brothers to quit whining and to go order us a pizza. A good one, not one crapped up with onions and anchovies, if I recall. We were there for each other through mid-terms and finals, and boys and late nights, and hangovers, and more boys. Pru taught me to ski. I taught her to flip the bird to cabs in the crosswalk."

Pru laughed and wiped her eyes.

"But for me, the absolute best thing about our relationship," she paused to shoot a look at Aiden, "is being here today and seeing you two so happy. When you love someone, when you really care about them, nothing is more important to you than seeing them happy. And seeing you and Chip here today, I couldn't be happier or more proud. You found your way back to each other, earned it. And together you'll face the future as a team. I love you two. Salute."

"Salute," the crowd echoed and the air rang with the clinking of the finest crystal Barbados had to offer.

23

$\mathcal{H}$e caught her on the dance floor. Frankie was sharing a dance and laughing with Chip when Aiden appeared with Pru in his arms.

"Care to trade partners?" Aiden offered.

"Get your hands off my wife, Kilbourn," Chip teased, reaching for Pru and reeling her in.

"There ye be, my pirate husband!"

Frankie started to step away, but Aiden held out his hand to her, daring her to take it. *Fine. She could deal with a dance. One dance. It didn't mean she'd end up naked with him doing magical things to her body.*

"Sorry about ruining our pictures," Chip told Pru.

She shook her head at him. "Everything was absolutely perfect. Think of the story we'll have to tell our grandkids someday," Pru told him. "I'm just glad you're safe."

"I have Frankie and Aiden to thank for that."

"Ahem!" Frankie cleared her throat, staring pointedly at Aiden.

"Almost entirely Franchesca," he admitted. "In fact, I'm

afraid I'm due the blame, not the thanks. It's my fault Elliot took Chip."

Pru stopped mid-dance and prodded Aiden in his impeccable lapel. "Make him pay."

"You can count on it," Aiden promised.

Pru nodded and melted back into Chip's arms.

"Wait, wait, wait. That's it?" Frankie demanded, squirming against Aiden's hold. "He gets your groom kidnapped, lets him almost miss the wedding, and you're totally fine with it?"

Pru stared up into Chip's one good eye. "Aiden will take care of whatever needs taking care of."

"Where is the girl who made me grovel for three days after I ate the last cannoli junior year?"

"Those cannoli were freaking amazing! Heaven in my mouth," Pru argued.

"I know! *My* father made them!"

"Yeah, well, you said I could have as many as I wanted, and I was on my period. And I wanted that last one."

"Three days. Over cannoli. You get her husband kidnapped and 'oh, it's fine.' Life is not fair," Frankie announced to Aiden.

"Shut up and dance with the handsome man while I make out with my pirate husband," Pru said, shooing them away.

"You should listen to your best friend," Aiden said, his voice was a rumble low in his chest.

She tilted her head back to look at him and regretted her decision. Why? WHY did he have to be so beautiful? His cheekbones were sculpted like a team of angels had weighed in on the exact right proportions. His beard was neatly trimmed moving him from clean cut to rakish. And all that dark curling hair? She wanted to shove her hands into it and grip while she shoved his face between...

Fuuuuuck.

She was no better than stupid Margeaux. Why did she want him? God, was she so desperate she'd fuck a guy just because he was hot?

As if reading her mind, Aiden drew her to the side of the dance floor and pulled her a little tighter against him.

"I'm not a bad guy, Franchesca. I've made mistakes, but I'm not some heartless villain."

"Would you have felt the least bit bad if your brother had ruined their wedding?"

"Of course I would have. And he *will* pay for what he did with more than just a broken nose."

"Is it really broken?" Frankie asked hopefully. She'd thrown more than her fair share of punches, growing up with two brothers that lived to torment her. And when she sprouted boobs, those same brothers wanted to make sure she could fight off any guy not good enough for her.

"Definitely," he said. His hand cruised over her back until it met bare skin.

She ignited. She never wanted something that she wasn't sure she'd survive before. She didn't like it.

"I need some air," she breathed, pushing out of his grip. What she needed was more tequila. A bottle of it. And a flight home. She couldn't afford to play with the rich and famous anymore. She wouldn't get out unscathed.

He let her go, but she felt the weight of that hot stare on her until she jogged down the steps and disappeared onto the sand. The moon glimmered over the water, another perfect slice of paradise.

"What the fuck is wrong with me?" she murmured, stalking toward the ocean. *Was there a friggin' cupid mosquito down here that she wasn't aware of?* She'd had sex before. Plenty of it. She liked it. But one look from Aiden and her underwear melted off of her body. "Stay mad," she coached herself, pacing down the beach. It was safer. Maybe Pru was feeling forgiving, but that didn't mean she had to.

Someone had to keep their wits about them.

She felt him before she saw him emerging from the shadows. Frankie's breath caught in her throat as Aiden walked toward her.

"I've never chased anyone, Franchesca." The moonlight played over his perfect face, shadowing the hollows beneath his cheekbones. He had his hands in his pockets, deceptively relaxed. But there was no doubt that he was a hunter and she was the prey. Another challenge.

"Why do you want me, Aiden? And don't give me some bullshit about me being beautiful and special. I already know I am, just like I know that I'm not your type. So ask yourself why it's me you're chasing and not some high society princess who'd beg to be ass up in your bed."

"That is exactly why it's you and not Margeaux or Cressida or whatever the fuck the other one's name is. I want that smart, wicked mouth of yours wrapped around my cock as you take me to the back of your throat. I want to hear my name from that mouth when I make you come with mine. I want the challenge, the chase. I live for it. You'll make me work for it, earn it. And I'll worship you for it."

Frankie blew out a breath and bent at the waist. "Well, that was at least honest."

"I'm not offering forever. It's not on the table. But what I can give you is time that we'll both remember."

"Fondly or 'I spit on your grave' memories?" Frankie quipped.

Somehow, he was in front of her, moving like a ghost. He threaded his fingers through her hair, and she shivered at the contact. "I'm not going to stop until you give me what I want. You need to understand that. I'll push your buttons, manipulate you. Whatever it takes. I won't fall for you. But I'll be good to you."

"Oh, I've seen how the Kilbourns do business," Frankie snapped back.

He was a breath away. She could smell him, feel the heat pumping off of him. His presence drowned out the steady roll of the surf behind her.

Aiden didn't know, couldn't know, that he was waving a red flag in front of an enraged bull. He wasn't the only one who loved a challenge. She bet that if they tangled, she could get in a few shots of her own. Maybe even make him fall just a little.

"So, I agree to be your shiny new plaything, and you give me—"

"Anything and everything you want."

"And what do you get out of it?"

"You."

She wanted to laugh, to make a joke. This didn't happen to Franchesca Baranski. She met nice guys in coffee shops and offices, and they went to plays and bars and had fun, energetic sex. *This* happened only in the dog-eared novels on her bookshelf. Billionaire sweeps regular girl off her feet.

God, she at least hoped the orgasm count of fiction would come true.

"I'm going to kiss you," he said, his voice low and rough.

Frankie slapped a hand to his chest. "Uh-uh. You're going to kiss me when I say you can kiss me. I'm not a 'submit to the alpha' kind of girl. I'm a 'kick him in the balls and take what I want' woman."

"What do you want?"

"To break you."

She caught him by surprise. That much was clear when her mouth met and took his. He stilled beneath her lips, her hands, for the span of a heartbeat. And then the beast was out of its cage. His hands on her felt so right. He pulled her into him, and she felt the heat, the hard of his body.

There was nothing soft or gentle about him. And she didn't want him to be.

She wanted to jump off that jagged edge of pleasure they'd been dancing on. She wanted to throw herself to the wolves. *The wolf.* Aiden's teeth raked her lower lip, and she whimpered. He used it to gain access to her mouth, his tongue sweeping inside, claiming new territory.

She shoved at his jacket, needing far fewer layers between them. Then it was her hands splayed over the thin material of his shirt. She felt the steady thrum of his heart under her hand. It gave her a little thrill to know that he was nearly as revved as she.

With one hand, he dove into her hair, closing his fist around her curls and pulling. The pain at her scalp should have been a warning to slow down, to back off. But it only heightened her craving. He growled into her mouth, and the sound went straight to her belly.

Frankie's nipples were begging to be released, to be stroked and tasted and sucked. And her panties were so wet there was no way they could catch fire now.

"Don't play with me, Franchesca," Aiden said, leaving a millimeter between their mouths. "Don't torture me."

"Shut up and kiss me, Aiden."

"Tell me I can have you. Tell me you're mine."

24

*A*iden kicked open the door to his room so hard it bounced off the wall. But he pushed them through the doorway before it flew back to hit them. He shoved it closed behind them and felt blindly for the lock without breaking from Frankie's mouth. Her mouth, God, that mouth.

Everything she did with those lush lips and wicked tongue drove him insane. They should have talked. The expectations should have been made clear before this.

Frankie slipped her hands between the buttons of his shirt, her fingers flexing on the fabric.

"You're rich, right? You can afford a new shirt?"

"Oh, yeah," he breathed.

It was all the incentive she needed. She yanked, sending buttons flying in all directions. One stroke of his chest, and she sent her busy fingers to his belt.

"Franchesca if you don't get out of that dress now, I'm going to destroy it."

"You bought it for me," she reminded him.

"Right. I'll get you another dress and me another shirt."

He didn't destroy the entire thing. Just ripped one of the

straps and ruined the zipper trying to get his hands on her faster.

She worked just as quickly, just as impatiently. She had his belt off and his pants unhooked before he got the dress to her waist.

He'd thought of little else since he'd seen her in that strapless bra and gossamer thin panties before the ceremony. And now she was his for the touching, the taking.

One more shove and her dress pooled at her ankles. She was curvy like a goddess. So different from the waiflike size zeros he usually took to bed.

Her body made him salivate. She was made for sin, and he was happy to oblige.

He wanted to stop, to enjoy the view. Aiden wanted to stroke and kiss his way over every inch of her beautiful body. But his pants were sliding down his thighs, and she was wrestling his throbbing dick out of his briefs.

"Let's see what we're working with here," she said, dropping to her knees.

The picture of Franchesca on her knees in front of him, staring at his cock, nearly leveled him. It was so much more than any fantasy. And if he thought about it for one second longer, he was going to come before her red lips even parted over his cock.

"Fuck." He needed to reel it in, to take control. He didn't let anyone dominate him. Ever.

It was a rule.

She was looking up at him, a submissive vixen with fingers curled loosely around his erection. "Nice equipment, Aide," she said, her eyes twinkling.

He nodded, incapable of words. Every ounce of his focus was on not coming on her face, in her hair.

Jesus.

"You okay up there?" she asked. "You having a stroke or something?"

"You and your fucking mouth," he groaned. And then she was using that fucking mouth on him.

She knew, had to know, how close to the edge he already was. When she took him to the back of her throat, it was slow and teasing, giving him precious seconds to get used to the drag of her tongue, the glorious wet of her mouth.

Those eyes. More green than blue now, stared up at him triumphantly as she licked and sucked him. She was a witch, and he was her victim. He fisted his hand in her hair and regulated her strokes. Keeping them slow and controlled. But there was nothing he could do about that tongue. Those incredible noises at the back of her throat. He wanted to do this and nothing but this for the next year, watch her like this, feel her like this.

She *could* break him, he realized. With nothing more than that smart mouth, she could break him and make him grovel.

It was that thought and that thought only that had him hauling her to her feet by her hair. She licked her lips and made his cock twitch against her stomach.

"I was just getting started."

"So am I," he promised. He stepped out of his pants, kicked off his shoes. "Bed. Now."

She didn't move fast enough for his liking. So he picked her up, draping her long legs over his hips. Her breasts taunted his mouth. "Take off your bra," he said, crossing the living room.

By the time he hit the bedroom, he had one of those caramel nipples in his mouth, and she was begging him loudly to fuck her.

"Aiden!" She swore at him when he dropped her on the mattress. But he followed her, not wanting to be away from the body that tempted him like he was under a spell. He slapped at the lamp on the bedside table and reached into the drawer. Thank fucking God he never traveled without condoms. He wouldn't have survived the hunt for one. And it would have taken zero convincing for him to drive himself into her bare. Something he'd never done in his entire life.

Kilbourns didn't father bastards.

But Frankie could have batted those long-lashed eyes at him, and he would have happily shot his load inside her, thanking his lucky stars.

She was fucking beautiful, sprawled across his mattress, her hair spreading out beneath her, her nipples swollen and straining. She still had her sandals and underwear on, and Aiden planned to remedy that.

"You gonna look all day, or are you gonna make me come, Aide?"

"Just taking in the view, sweetheart. If I don't get myself under control, you won't be able to walk tomorrow."

"Challenge accepted." She rose up and grabbed him by the back of the neck, yanking him down to her. She kissed him like he was the only man in the world, and it was a heady thing. His cock was weeping with the need to bury itself in her. Precum leaked from the tip.

"Fuck," he rescued himself from the kiss and slid down her body pausing to worship both breasts with their perky, needy nipples. She hissed in pleasure as he closed his mouth over each one, sucking until she writhed under him.

This wasn't a woman faking her way to a picture-perfect sexual experience. This was a goddess chasing an orgasm that would eclipse the sun. And he would give her what she wanted.

"Finally," he said, settling between her legs. He let his lips graze her inner thigh and watched her tremble. Aiden dragged those air-thin panties down to her thighs. He left them there. The final barrier prevented him from ramming himself into her wet pussy. He wanted to torture her the way she had him.

"Aiden if you don't do something right this second, I'm going to take matters into my own hands," Frankie threatened. He grinned. He didn't know what love was, but he sure liked Franchesca Baranski more than any woman he'd ever taken to bed.

He took two fingers and traced them through the soft wet folds.

"Oh God. Oh fuck. Aiden!"

He held out for his name and then thrust his fingers inside her.

She cried out, and he nearly came on the sheets that touched his cock. He fucked her with his fingers, and when she started to grind her hips up, he leaned in and slid his tongue through her slit.

Rather than the scream he'd hoped for, she went deathly silent. He peeked and saw her, eyes squeezed shut, mouth open in a silent O. "You okay up there? Are you having a stroke?" he quipped.

"Aiden, talking is *not* what I want you doing with your mouth right now!"

He licked his way to her center. His tongue and fingers working her clenching pussy and her sweet, little clit. She rode his hand, his mouth, determined to steer him toward her orgasm. But he could get there without the road map.

He added a third finger and traced his tongue down to her tight asshole and back to her clit again and again. She was sobbing his name. Everything else was incomprehensible.

He felt her walls tremble against his fingers and then the first pulse squeezed against him. He licked and fucked her through every contraction of that beautiful release. She clenched his fingers with those slick muscles, pulling him in as deep as he could go, and he wanted more. He wanted her coming on his cock, wanted those hungry squeezes to milk his own orgasm out of him.

"Aiden!"

He ground his hips into the mattress, desperate for the friction.

Her orgasm went on forever, and by the time she went limp beneath him, he was afraid he might black out if his brain lost any more blood. There was a pulse hammering in his head.

He raised up onto his knees and fisted his hard-on to roll on the condom.

"Franchesca," he snapped. "Look at me. Open your eyes."

She did, hazily at first. But when she saw him, fisting his dick between her legs, her gaze sharpened.

"What are you waiting for?" Her voice was hoarse.

"Tell me you want me. Tell me I can have you."

"Take me, Aiden."

"Are you mine?" He didn't know why he was asking. He wasn't possessive about women. But he wanted her to say it, say the words. And then he'd know he won.

"You get me for tonight. Don't fuck it up."

It was enough for him. For now. He spread her thighs and gripped her hips and had the satisfaction of hearing her voice break on his name when he pushed into her. She was so fucking tight, even after the warm up he'd given her. He buried himself to the hilt, pinning her to the bed with his hips.

Something snapped. Something he didn't understand triggered, as if he were one man a second ago and now a brand-new one.

Her eyes, so bright and glassy, stared into him, into his

soul. And she could see into his. Into the emptiness there that he was never free of.

But he wasn't so empty now. They were connected. They were one. He could feel the aftershocks of her orgasm tremoring around his cock. He could read her thoughts if he tried hard enough.

He wouldn't last long. Not with her eyes glazing over like that and those round tits tempting him. "Franchesca," he whispered her name as he finally began to move in her.

She brought her hands up and stroked over his shoulders, down his arms. A gentle, soothing touch. It felt like something had broken inside of him and now there was light getting in through the cracks.

She had bewitched him. Or he had contracted some kind of tropical fever.

She cried out, and he saw tears in her eyes. Her fingers dug into his shoulders, nails carving into his skin. He'd treasure the marks, hoped they'd stay.

He was done thinking. Done doing anything but feeling because she was getting tighter around him and he was swelling impossibly thicker in anticipation of a release that could wreck him.

Franchesca's breath was coming in short bursts, and he felt sweat dot his skin. It was heaven, moving in her, being surrounded in her heat. He leaned down and closed his mouth over one pert nipple.

She arched against him, and all sweetness, all tenderness, was gone. They were animals in heat, clawing at each other, blindly scrabbling for a pleasure too intense for words. He released her breast and grabbed her hair, burying his face in her neck. She hiked her thighs up around his waist drawing him in deeper, and when he bottomed out in her, when she screamed his name brokenly, he felt it.

The detonation.

His own orgasm was on a hair-trigger, and when she closed around him, he exploded inside her. Pump after pump, he couldn't stop coming, and neither could she. Every thrust, every hot rush of come, she met him, squeezed him, pleaded for just one more.

He emptied himself into her welcoming center, but he felt anything but empty now. There wasn't cold, calculation at his center. No. There was something warm and bright and dangerously real.

He felt wetness against his shoulder, heard Franchesca sniffle.

His gut tightened. "Franchesca? Frankie? Are you okay?" *He was still inside her, and she was fucking crying. It gutted him.*

"Oh, my God. I'm so embarrassed."

He wiped a fat tear from her cheek with his thumb. "What is it? Did I hurt you?" *What had he done?*

"No. I think it's because the wedding, and I was stressed, and those were the two most powerful orgasms of my entire life. And now I'm blabbering and embarrassed and holy fuck, Aiden. What was that?"

He dropped his forehead to hers, relief coursing through him.

"Are you sure you're okay? I didn't cross a line or something?"

"You didn't shove your dick up my ass without asking first, so I think we're fine. Can we pretend this part never happened?"

"What part?"

She laughed and another tear escaped. "Oh my God. Maybe you don't suck so bad after all, Kilbourn."

"Are you hungry?" he asked.

"I could eat an entire buffet in under ten minutes."

He wanted to kiss her on that tear-stained cheek. Kiss her and stay buried inside her where he felt something *good*. But he didn't do that sort of thing. And she wouldn't trust it if he did.

"Let's see how many dishes we can order from room service," he said, reluctantly sliding out of her and reaching for the phone.

25

*T*here was nothing like a walk of shame to make Frankie feel like she was twenty years old again. Except this time, she was thirty-four, and she was sneaking out of a man's room wearing his Yale t-shirt because he'd ripped her dress in his desperate haste to fuck her to five mind-altering orgasms.

She clutched her shoes to her chest and balled up the remains of her gown and slipped out the door.

They'd dined on champagne and tender steaks in bed and ended up naked and panting again. She had every intention of leaving, of going back to her room to pack and regain whatever shred of sanity she had left, but had instead fallen asleep next to Aiden, a tangle of limbs and sheets.

She woke with a start, sunlight beaming obnoxiously in her face between the slice of curtain they hadn't bothered closing. She'd been horrified to find her face snuggled into Aiden's neck. Her hand resting on the smattering of chest hair above the slow and steady beat of his heart.

Her leg was thrown over his crotch, and his erection was digging into her thigh. The magnitude of last night, of not just giving in to his chase, but demanding he take her, hit her like a heavyweight champ. And the things she'd let him do to her? The things she'd done to him? *Hell.*

Apparently, she was as forgiving as Pru. Or as hormone driven as ol' one-eyebrowed Margeaux.

She must have forgotten to pack her dignity.

"Well, well, well."

Frankie jumped a mile in the hallway as she pulled Aiden's door closed.

"Jesus, Pru. You scared the ever-living hell out of me."

Her best friend was still in her wedding gown, her hair a disaster, her makeup smeared. She smelled like a distillery and was grinning like a kindergartner turned loose in the Hershey Chocolate Factory.

"You and Aiden?" Pru squealed at dog whistle frequency.

"Shhh! Jeez. Keep your voice down."

Pru listed hard to the side as if she were walking the deck of a boat. "I'm super drunk but not drunk enough to not be really, really excited."

"Have you even been to bed yet?" Frankie asked.

Pru shook her head violently from side and side and walked into a wall. "Nope. 's my party. Hey! Wanna hold my hair while I throw up? You can tell me why you're sneaking out of You Know Who's room with sex hair and teeth marks on your neck."

PRU COULD BE A PROFESSIONAL VOMITER, Frankie observed. She tucked her knees under her neatly in front of the toilet and gracefully sighed up the contents of her stomach.

"You know, when I barf, I sound like I'm trying to bring up a foot of intestine," Frankie pointed out.

"Blaaaaaah," Pru crooned to the toilet. She sat back on her heels looking proud of herself and flushed. "Barf drunking is so much easier than barf sicking. I prolly won't even remember this tomorrow... or today."

"Yeah, but you were like this with the stomach bug of 2005 too."

"The trick is not to fight it," Pru said sagely. "When you fight it, it makes it so much harder."

Vomit lessons from a cheerful zombie bride. At least this was keeping her mind off of the satisfied ache in every well-used muscle. Off of the naked man down the hallway who had shown her things in the dark that she couldn't comprehend in the daylight.

"Where's your husband?" Frankie asked, handing Pru a glass of water.

"My husband is sleeping under the head table on the terrace," Pru said proudly. "Now, tell me exactly how you got beard burn on your neck.

Her neck wasn't the only place she'd gotten it. But she wasn't about to mention her inner thighs right now.

"Aiden and I had sex," Frankie admitted.

Pru started cackling.

"Geez, what? You laugh any harder, and you're gonna spew again."

"I was jus' thinking that I can't wait to tell this story at your wedding!"

"Why would you tell this story at my wedding?" Frankie asked, horrified.

"'Cause you're gonna marry Aiden, and I'm gonna be your matron of honor!"

"I'm not marrying Aiden! We had a one-time momentary lapse in judgment."

"Uhhhh, judging by the orgasmic look on your pretty,

pretty face, you had a life-altering one-time momentary lapse."

Frankie slumped against Pru's vanity. "Okay, it was good. Really good." So fucking good every sexual experience from now on was going to pale in comparison. That was a cheery thought.

"And?" Pru prodded, fluffing the skirt of her dress around her.

"And the key phrase is 'one-time.' We are not each other's types no matter how good in bed we are together."

"Okay, okay. On a scale of Jimmy Talbot and Tanner Freehorn, where does Aiden fall?"

This was the problem with having a best friend who knew everything about you. She created sex scales based on your worst and best experiences. Jimmy had been her first and sweetly awkward. Tanner was a random hookup at a New Year's Eve party ten months ago who had given Frankie her first multiple orgasm.

"Ugh. Don't make me do this!" Frankie begged.

"You have to," Pru ordered. "It's in the friendship rules. Jimmy to Tanner. Go!"

"Tanner plus three," Frankie mumbled under her breath. She traced the grout line with her finger, refusing to meet Pru's eyes.

"Tanner plus wha?" Pru asked. Her post-puke voice echoed off the marble.

"Three."

She watched drunk Pru do the math very slowly on her fingers. "Oh hell. Five. I had five orgasms, okay?"

"Is that even physically possible?" Pru shrieked. "Wait, hang on." She leaned over the toilet bowl and blahed again. She bobbed back up, perky as a morning TV show host who hadn't just thrown up a carafe of champagne. "Five orgasms in one night?"

"Yeah. I think it's like a super power or something."

Or something all ridiculously rich dudes could do. Could money buy sexual prowess? No wonder women were always chasing them.

"I. Am. So. Happy. For. You." Pru stabbed the air with her finger to emphasize every word.

"Again, one-time thing," Frankie pointed out. "But let's talk about how happy I am for you, Mrs. Stockton-Randolph."

"Did you see my ring?" Pru asked.

Frankie had seen it approximately nineteen times since the ceremony.

"I would love to see your ring."

"What kind of ring do you think Aiden will get you?" Pru asked, closing one eye. She slid down to lay on the marble floor, her dress puffing up around her.

"No ring. No more sex either."

"But he's good enough for you, Frankie."

"Okay, you're clearly all heart-eyes and alcohol-ed because you're telling me to marry the guy whose brother kidnapped your fiancé on the eve of your wedding."

"I forgot about that. But still, Aiden is amazing."

"He's also a perennial bachelor who likes to swap out his women every month. And again, brother kidnapped Chip."

Pru waved a dismissive hand. "Details, details."

FRANKIE FOUND herself in the middle seat of the plane wedged between a tiny Asian lady with very nice headphones and a guy whose chest hair was woven around the thick gold chain visible because he had the first four buttons of his shirt open.

The lady smelled like vanilla. The man like half a bottle of Drakkar Noir. It was going to be a very long flight. But at least she'd escaped Barbados without facing Aiden. She wondered if he'd been pissed or relieved when he woke up to find her gone.

She plugged her earbuds into the seatback entertainment and randomly selected a music station. So maybe she was running away. And maybe she was a coward, but had she spent one extra second next to Aiden's perfect, naked body, she would have literally died. Could one die from perfection? She'd come close. Or maybe it had been too many orgasms.

Frankie knew that had Aiden woken up and brought up the subject of a temporary relationship, she would have sat up and begged like her parent's cocker spaniel. Out of sight, out of her sore yet satisfied pussy. *Mind. She meant mind.*

A hasty exit was for the best. Aiden would forget about her and their few hours of mind-boggling, flesh-searing, soul-shattering pleasure.

Chest Hair gave her the side-eye, and Frankie realized she'd moaned out loud. If this is what five orgasms skillfully doled out by Aiden Kilbourn did to her, she couldn't imagine what a temporary dalliance would do.

Her phone was off, and she had to work tomorrow. It was back to normal... with a few erotic memories that she could relive for the rest of her life.

26

*A*iden took the stairs two at a time, his heart pounding. He'd been revved since waking up that morning. And all those hours in between, he'd been ready to snap.

She'd left him. He'd woken up to an empty bed with no trace of her in his room. And by the time he'd pulled on a pair of shorts and stormed down the hall to bang on her door and drag her back to bed, the maids were already cleaning it. *Checked out. Sorry sir.*

Franchesca had a thing or two to learn about just how he did business.

This place smelled like mothballs and dust. The stairs creaked ominously under his feet. There was no security on the door, and half the streetlights on the block were dark. And it had taken no more than a "please" to get Mrs. Gurgevich in 2A to buzz him in.

Everything pissed him off.

And that translated loud and clear when his closed fist met the door that stood between him and the source of his annoyance.

"Jesus, break down the door, why don't you, Gio?"

Frankie's eyes widened in surprise and, very possibly, fear. She probably would have slammed the door in his face had Aiden not shoved his way inside.

The apartment was small, on the shabby side, but clean. There was a kitchen, a living/dining room, and what Aiden assumed was a bedroom. Her TV, a pathetic thirty-inch, was on, and there was an open beer on the coffee table. The couch was deep and cushioned.

He turned to face her, and he felt it, that magnetic connection. It hadn't been the tropical setting or the adrenaline. It was the way she reacted to him. He was used to attraction. He used it as a snare when necessary. But what echoed between them? It was elemental. It was the primitive lust of one body desperately needing the other. She didn't want his money or his family name. She wanted *him* and how he made her feel. And that was more potent to him than any aphrodisiac.

"What the fuck are you doing in my apartment?" She stood, hands on hips, wearing leggings and a thick sweater that draped over one shoulder. She had her hair pulled up in a thick tail.

He fisted his hands at his sides so he didn't reach for her and strip the tie out of her hair. "Why did you run?"

"I didn't run. I had a flight." She was cocky, self-righteous, and lying.

"Why didn't you wake me or say goodbye?"

He saw the shadow of guilt in those big eyes. "It was a one-time thing, Aiden. That's all."

"Bullshit." His voice rang out sharply. He was tired, angry. And despite that, he wanted to touch her. Punish her. Please her.

"Oh, come on, Kilbourn. We had a good time. Now it's back to the real world."

"We are *not* done, Franchesca."

"I think once was more than enough," she snapped back, eyes flashing.

"Twice," he corrected. "And do you really?"

"Go the hell home, Aiden."

He closed the distance between them and forced himself to take a gentle hold on her shoulders. She was melting into him even as she swore. Aiden felt relief, swift and sharp, knowing that she still felt that need. Even if it was only pure biology, body-recognizing body. It was enough, and somehow more.

"Last night?" he began. "That doesn't just happen. And running away from it is cowardly."

"Are you suggesting that I'm afraid of you?" Frankie's voice was low.

"I'm suggesting that what we shared was a first for me. That... connection. I don't want to walk away. And I don't think you do either." If she wanted honest and real, then that is what he'd give her. Aiden only hoped the price wouldn't be too high.

"I don't want to be some guy's plaything. I deserve more than that," Frankie shot back.

"You do," he agreed. "You're the one who labeled it as such. Just because I'm not interested in marriage doesn't mean I'd be disrespectful or callous toward you."

She chewed on her lower lip, staring intently at the top button of his shirt. "So how exactly would this kind of arrangement work?"

He scented victory, knew it was within his grasp. "We spend time together. I give you anything you want."

"Temporarily," she added.

"It's not like there's an expiration date, Franchesca."

"But you always lose interest."

"I might point out that you happen to be single, too. Is that because you've always lost interest?" He let his fingers roam up to the back of her neck, toying with the curls there.

She sighed and finally, finally raised her gaze to his.

"Look, I'm not looking for forever either. I don't know where I want to be in five years. I'd rather figure that out before I have to take someone else's wants and needs into consideration. And God help the woman who wants it with you."

He ran his hands around her tight shoulders. He turned her slowly in his arms, kneading her tense muscles. She sagged back against him.

"Then why aren't you saying yes?" he whispered darkly in her ear. "Are you making me work for it?" He didn't know why that made him hard. A Kilbourn never willingly relinquished control.

"Whoa! Am I interrupting?"

The man lounging in Frankie's doorway looked more interested than angry to find her wrapped up in another man's arms. He was broad shouldered and muscled. He wore a tight Henley that showed off that fact and ignored the thirty-degree weather outside. He was holding a bag of food that smelled better than any five-star meal in Manhattan.

"Gio," Frankie greeted the man as she tried to shrug out of Aiden's grasp. He didn't care for that. "Are you early?" she asked, shooting a panicked look in Aiden's direction. He *really* didn't like that.

"Huh?" Gio asked, fishing a phone out of the pocket of his track pants.

He held up the phone and snapped a picture.

"Don't you fucking dare!" Frankie wasn't nervous anymore. She was a snarling lioness.

"Oops. Too late," he shrugged. "You wanna introduce me to your friend?"

Aiden went from trying to keep Frankie in his grasp to holding her back as she took a swipe at the smugly grinning man.

"You are such an asshole!"

Gio's phone dinged, and he grinned, glancing at the screen. "Ma's looking forward to meeting your friend Sunday."

Aiden had to grab Frankie around the waist when she lunged for him. He picked her up and spun her around while Gio laughed.

"I'm Gio," the man said, extending a hand well out of Frankie's reach. "This hellion's brother."

Aiden shook with his free hand.

"Aiden," he said.

"So, you two dating?" Gio asked.

"Yes," Aiden said.

"No," Frankie countered.

"Well, either way, you just got me out of awkward fix up attempt number sixteen. Mary Lou Dumbrowski."

"Mary Lou's single again?" Frankie said, ceasing her attempts to kill her brother.

Gio crossed to the tiny table and dumped the bag of food on it. "Yeah. Husband number three keeled over last month at the dry cleaners. Bam. Dead before he hit the floor."

"Ma must be getting desperate if she's moving on to fresh widows for you," Frankie pointed out.

Aiden squeezed her hand and then released her. She didn't seem murderous anymore.

"Ma don't like having a 36-year-old bachelor son," Gio explained. "She also doesn't like being the only one of her sisters without grandbabies."

"Marco knocked up Rachel," Frankie reminded him. "Marco's our other brother and Rachel's his wife," she explained for Aiden's benefit.

"Well, don't worry because you just gave her even more grandmotherly hope," Gio teased, unpacking the bags.

Frankie shook her head. "I hate you. What did you bring?"

Gio unpacked four deli sandwiches, pickles wrapped in wax paper, and a large bag of barbeque chips. "The usual. You hangin' out, Aide?"

No one in his entire life had called him Aide before Franchesca. It appeared that the Baranski family enjoyed assigning nicknames.

"We taped the UFC fight from last night," Gio said, wiggling a sandwich at him.

"Mixed martial arts?" Aiden asked, eyeing the glorious stacked sandwiches.

"Ugh," Frankie rolled her eyes. "Fine. You can stay. But I call dibs on the roast beef."

"You got beer?" Gio asked.

"Yeah, yeah. Keep your pants on." Frankie headed into the kitchen, and Aiden followed her.

"We still need to talk," he told her, reaching out to grip her slim wrist.

"Yeah, we do," she sighed. "But not around the big mouth singing bass out there."

"Have dinner with me tomorrow."

She eyed him for a moment, and he thought she might be trying to come up with an excuse. "Fine," she said. "But I'm picking the place."

"Done." He leaned in and brushed his lips against her cheek. "See how easy this is? You tell me what you want, and I give it to you."

He had the pleasure of seeing goose bumps raise on her neck and arms. Aiden grabbed the beers she pulled from the fridge and wandered back to the living room.

They settled on her couch with Gio in the ratty armchair

and ate sandwiches built by a master while watching men and women pummel each other into bloody submission. Frankie and Gio had action on nearly every match and enjoyed ribbing each other throughout. Aiden tried to imagine doing the same with his half-brother. It was unfathomable. They'd never had an easy relationship like this.

"So, how'd you two meet?" Gio asked, biting into a pastrami on rye.

Franchesca took a quick swallow of beer. "Well, Aide here called me a stripper five seconds after we were introduced. I told him he was an asshole. And then his brother kidnapped Chip the night before his wedding, and we had to track him down."

Gio's sandwich fell out of his hands into the wrapper in his lap.

"You serious?"

"Unfortunately, yes," Aiden admitted. "But I didn't really mean the stripper thing."

"Good," Gio said good-naturedly. "I'd hate to have to beat you down on a full stomach."

"I'd hate to be beaten down," Aiden agreed.

Frankie picked up her beer and watched until Gio took another bite of his sandwich.

"Oh, and we had awesome sex last night. Crazy awesome."

Gio choked on his sandwich, coughing until Frankie got up to slap him on the back.

"Goddammit. I hate when you do that shit."

27

The restaurant Frankie chose was a hole-in-the-wall Portuguese place sandwiched between an empty storefront and a hot yoga studio on a quiet street in Brooklyn. The tables had no cloths, and the menus looked as though they'd been printed from a back-office printer. But the smells coming from the kitchen were nothing short of heavenly.

Aiden silenced his phone and slipped it inside his jacket pocket. He didn't want anything trying to steal his attention from the woman across the table. Frankie had worn her hair down and, in keeping with the casual atmosphere of the restaurant, she was wearing tight jeans, a sweater with a neckline that kept drawing his eye to her delectable cleavage, and soft suede boots.

She seemed... comfortable, perusing her menu, resting her chin in her hand. He tried to remember the last woman he saw who didn't maintain perfect posture and actually asked for and remembered the names of the waitstaff.

"What?" Frankie asked, frowning at him over her menu.

"I was just..."

"If you say admiring the view, I'm going to throw up on the table."

Aiden shook his head. *The words that came out of her mouth...* "Well, we can't have that now."

"Then why were you staring at me?"

"Because I like looking at you. You're interesting to watch."

"I'm going to assume that's a compliment so we don't have to start our first date with a fight," Frankie decided.

"It was very much meant as a compliment. You're different than—"

"What you're used to." She closed the menu. "Which brings me to my first point in what I hope will be a civil discussion."

"You're not going to threaten to rip my face off and feed it to me like you did your brother last night, are you?" Aiden asked.

"Har har, smart guy. Let's put this on the table. We have literally nothing but pretty spectacular orgasms in common."

The word "orgasms" had his cock stirring. "I find it hard to believe there's nothing else. How do you feel about puppies and apple pie?"

Her lips quirked. "Okay, let's try this. What's your goal this week? What do you plan to accomplish by Friday?"

The waiter returned with their glasses. It was a BYOB place so Aiden had raided his collection and settled on a decent bottle of cabernet. They placed their orders and handed over the menus.

"By Friday?" Aiden asked, filling her glass and then moving on to his own. "The board vote is this week. I plan to make sure it goes my way. Elliot needs to be reminded of his place in the family and the business. And I have a new acquisition that is experiencing some, shall we say, growing pains that need my attention."

"Uh-huh," Frankie said smugly. "You know what I'm doing this week?"

"I'd love to know."

"I'm trying to ace my Corporate Social Responsibility exam on Thursday."

"Exam?"

"I'm getting my MBA. Should have it by May if I can focus hard enough. The catering thing was a side gig so I wouldn't go broke on Pru's wedding. I work part-time for a small business development center."

"You're interested in business?" he ventured. Common ground that didn't involve orgasms.

"Very. It's what happens when your parents run a business. I'm sure you get that."

He nodded. "Of course. At times, it can seem as if it's in the blood."

"Yeah, well maybe the business part for me but not the lunchmeat."

At his questioning glance, Frankie laughed. "My parents own a deli in Brooklyn just down the street from their house. My brother Marco runs it now. I grew up in that shop. I can slice a pound of corned beef better than Marco or Gio."

"But you didn't want to take over a deli?"

Frankie shook her head. "I like the numbers side of it. The accounting, the planning, the tracking."

"What will you do with your MBA?"

She shrugged. "I really like what I do at the small business development center. Some people think that big business, huge corporations, are where America works. But it's not. It's the second-generation plumbing company or the ice cream shop that's been open for forty years or the machine shop start-up or the florist. I help those businesses do business."

Fascinated, Aiden leaned forward and rested his elbow on the table.

"And you think we have nothing in common," he pointed out.

"How much does this bottle cost?" she asked, lifting her glass to study the wine.

He shrugged. "I have no idea."

"Well, I do because I Googled it when you were in the restroom. My rent is cheaper than this bottle."

"Why do I get the feeling that money is going to be an area of contention with you? I don't care what you have or how much you make or owe. Why should you care about my financials?"

"Aiden," she laughed. "Your financials put you in an entirely different world than mine. I don't think those worlds are going to mix well."

"We won't know until we try."

The waiter returned delivering the chicken skewer appetizer with a flourish.

"What do you want me to do, go to galas as your arm candy? Because I'll be honest. What you saw last night? Sweat pants and UFC and greasy sandwiches? I'd much rather be doing that on a weekend than strutting around like one of Pru's friends, dressed to the nines and 'being seen.'"

"In this arrangement, Franchesca, you don't have to do anything you don't want to do. I'm not interested in you as another Society Barbie. I like you the way you are."

"Hmm."

"What?" he asked.

"I'm thinking."

"You're trying to come up with another excuse. Try it, Franchesca. Date me. Fuck me."

"You know how to sweep a girl off her feet," she joked, taking another sip of wine.

"I'm just being honest."

She picked up a piece of bread from the plate and studied it. "Fine. I don't want to be paraded around like one of your other 'dates.' And my life is here. I don't want to be trekking all over Manhattan at your beck and call."

"Deal. I don't do messy. I don't do drama. If you can adhere to those two things, we'll get along just fine."

"Monogamy?" Frankie asked, arching an eyebrow.

"A requirement for us both."

She nodded. "Good. I guess we have a deal."

He reached across the table and picked up her hand. But instead of shaking it, he brushed a kiss over the knuckles. "I have a feeling it's going to be a pleasure doing business with you," he predicted.

They ate and talked over spoonfuls of fish stew and bites of salt cod fritters and lingered over their coffee. It was strong, not bitter but not quite sweet, on his tongue, and Aiden couldn't help but think of the flavor of Franchesca. He'd only begun to sample it, and he wanted more.

She picked up the check before he could stop her. "Uh-uh," she said, snatching the paper away. "Money isn't an area of contention, is it?"

"I pay, Franchesca."

"You can get next time. This one's on me. And stop frowning like that. If it means that much to you, you can get dessert."

Dessert. The word brought dozens of images of Frankie's naked body to mind.

"Gelato, Kilbourn. I see what you're thinking."

The server returned with Frankie's change. "I'm leaving

the tip," Aiden announced, laying down a bill roughly the value of the entire tab for dinner.

"Show off."

They rose, and he helped her into her coat. It was a wool trench that had seen better days. "You're missing a button," he said sweeping into his own cashmere coat and eyeing the gap in her coat's closure.

"Ugh, I know. I lost it last winter when my brothers dared me to sneak out of my old bedroom window at my parents' house and shimmy down the tree like I used to. In my defense, we were three bottles of wine into Thanksgiving dinner. Still can't find the button."

"So, where's this gelato place?" Aiden asked. He was pleased when she took his hand as they exited the restaurant. He wanted to ask her what she had in mind after dessert. He had an overnight bag in the car and a respectable stash of condoms. He was just being prepared... and maybe a little hopeful.

Frankie led the way around the block. "Did you work today?" she asked.

He nodded. He hadn't been planning to. Hell, he wasn't supposed to have flown home from Barbados until this morning, but Franchesca had changed that plan when she left his bed. "I did. Had to make sure nothing catastrophic had happened while I was gone."

"Did you decide what you're going to do about Elliot?" Frankie asked.

He tensed, wondering if this was a trap. Another excuse for her to go back to hating him. "I hit him where it hurts the most."

"His broken nose?" Frankie asked.

Aiden laughed. "No, but he has two black eyes and can't

breathe, so that was entertaining to see as he groveled to our father."

"You went to your dad?" Frankie asked.

"Elliot was always a problem child. He makes rash decisions, often with large amounts of money. He was given a position in the company because it was only fair in my father's eyes. But Elliot's money is tied up in a revocable trust. My father didn't want him gambling it away or loaning it to a prostitute to start her own brothel."

"Or a girl who dances like a stripper," Frankie said, batting her lashes at him.

Aiden nudged her shoulder. "I'm sorry for that. I'd had a long day, and the last thing I wanted to do was spend my evening at a party with friends trying to hook me up."

"And you had a migraine."

"That too."

"Do you get them often?"

"Only on special occasions. Usually when dealing with Elliot."

"So, what did your father consider a punishment for committing a felony?" Frankie asked.

"He froze Elliot's accounts for a month."

Frankie stumbled. "Your brother kidnaps someone in some whack job power move, and your daddy takes *his allowance* away?"

Aiden wasn't about to tell her he'd had a similar reaction when his father had meted out the punishment. It was private family business.

"My father felt that was what the situation called for."

"And what do you feel like 'the situation' called for? Keep in mind your answer will determine if you get past the gelato portion of our evening."

"In that case, I'd like to bring back tarring and feathering."

"You're learning, Aide. You're learning," she said, eyes twinkling. It was a victory sweeter than any in recent history. And without thinking, without maneuvering her into it, Aiden pulled Frankie against him.

"Do I get to kiss you anytime I want now that we're dating?"

She looked up at him, hooking her fingers into his lapels. "Within reason, I suppose."

He saw the heat in the narrowing of her eyes, the parting of her lips. And when he brought his mouth to hers, he tasted that victory again. Franchesca Baranski had submitted, temporarily. She was his to kiss, to fuck, to tease. And he wasn't going to waste a second of their time together.

She was backing up, and he followed her until her shoulders met the cold brick of the building. Holding her there, Aiden cupped her chin in his hands and seduced her mouth. Her lips were full and oh so soft. He remembered them sliding over his dick, remembered them going round in the shock of her release. And now they were feeding hungrily on him.

Her hands moved from his chest inside his coat to his hips. She pulled him against her and groaned when she felt his erection.

"How married are you to gelato?" she asked, breaking free of his mouth.

"I hate gelato."

"My apartment is three blocks from here."

"I have condoms in the car."

"I have some at my place."

His father's warning to his teenage son echoed in his head. Rich kid rule number seventeen. Never use a woman's condoms. She may be trying to trap you by getting pregnant.

"Let's go."

28

hree blocks felt like miles when her clit was swollen with need and there was a sexy man holding her hand who could do something very efficiently about it. They barely spoke, the tension between them skyrocketing by the second.

Every brush of his body against hers put Frankie further on painful, needy edge.

Would it be as good as it had been in Barbados? Would it be better? Would she survive?

There was only one way to find out.

She fumbled with her keys at the door, nerves visible in the way her fingers shook. Aiden took her keys from her and unlocked the door. It was the last civilized thing he did for the rest of the night.

Frankie dragged him inside and shut the door behind them before Mrs. Chu could stick her head out into the hallway and offer them snacks or sex advice. Aiden was already shedding his coat and suit jacket by the time she slid the chain on the door.

She joined him, shucking layers and shoes until they had

the barest of essentials between them.

"Come here," he said, his voice a gravelly order.

She could have sauntered to him, making him wait, keeping the upper hand for a bit longer until he stole it from her with those sinful lips and magic cock that was straining to escape the confines of his sexy, tight red underwear. But she didn't. Frankie launched herself at him. Aiden, to his credit, didn't buckle under her weight.

He picked her up, lifting her by her ass cheeks, and settled her against his hard-on.

She was beyond grateful that she'd dressed with the potential for sex on the mind. For once, her underwear matched her bra. Black and lacy were about as sexy as she got effort-wise. And they seemed to be doing the job.

Aiden fed on her mouth as he carried her into the bedroom. This time, he lowered her slowly to the mattress, covering her body with his. Her bed was small, nothing like the acreage of mattress they'd indulged themselves on in Barbados. But Aiden didn't seem to mind.

"Condoms?" he asked, his voice rough.

She pointed to a box on her nightstand.

"I hope you put those there thinking of me," he said dryly. She was amazed that he could tease her with as hard as his cock was against her.

"No, I always keep a jumbo box of extra-large for-her-pleasure rubbers on my nightstand."

He pinched her ass, and she squealed. His mouth muffled any further comment.

"I want you in every way possible," he confessed.

"Gotta start somewhere," she breathed, half laughing, half ready to plead. "How do you want me, Aiden?"

As she'd expected, the question had carnal need lighting his beautiful blue eyes. He clenched his jaw.

"Show me," she insisted. She was giving him permission. The last time it had been a war for the upper hand. This time, she wanted to see exactly what dark fantasies went on behind that angel's face.

He growled low in his throat and flipped her over onto her stomach. He held her head down by grabbing a handful of hair and slid an arm around her waist, lifting her hips so that she rose onto her knees.

"Is this okay?" he whispered.

"I'm greenlighting you. Whatever you want is okay tonight." Sure, she was testing him. But if he didn't slam his cock into her in the next ten seconds, she was probably going to die.

"Whatever I want?" he repeated.

"Well, I'm not into threesomes or dudes pissing on me."

"What about…" he trailed a finger down her spine to the cleft between her ass cheeks. When he stroked the tip of the finger over her asshole, Frankie tensed.

"Let's see how the evening goes," she said.

"I think we should get married," Aiden joked.

Frankie laughed into the pillow. "Aide, seriously if you don't stick a body part inside me right now, I'm throwing you out and going for gelato by myself."

"We can't have that, now can we?" He took those magic fingers and brought them between her legs.

"God, yes." Frankie's groan was muffled when he dragged her underwear down her thighs. And then she was soundless with shock and pleasure when he finally drove two fingers into her tight, wet core. Finally, she wasn't empty anymore.

She pushed her hips back against him, begging for more. Aiden's hand left her hair and slid down her shoulder and around to cup her breast where it hung.

Kneading her with one hand and fucking her with the

other, he slowly escalated the torment. And Frankie chanted her words into the pillow.

"You are such a beautiful girl, Franchesca," Aiden whispered, raining kisses down her back.

God, she loved the feel of him curling over her. Of him pumping his fingers into her and tugging on her nipples. She needed *more*.

And he was willing to give it to her.

Frankie felt his thumb probing between her ass cheeks and tensed at the touch.

"Trust me?"

The question was strained.

She didn't trust Aiden to not bend the rules until he got what he wanted or even possibly abduct someone like his brother had. But she did trust him to give her body pleasure like she'd never known before.

"Yep. Okay. Yeah," she said, her voice husky.

He didn't need reassurance. In moments, she was back to begging as he fingered her in ways she'd never experienced. That thumb. Those magic fingers. The feel of his thick shaft probing her through the material of the briefs he'd yet to remove. His heavy breath that she could not only hear but also feel against her bare skin.

There was only so much build up a girl could take before she exploded.

Frankie cried out into the pillow on a particularly masterful crook of his fingers. She was going to explode and take the entire apartment building down.

Aiden groaned, low and guttural. "I feel you getting ready to come." He leaned down and bit her on the shoulder.

That quick slice of pain was all it took to snap her like a guitar string. She let go and hurtled into the orgasm. This? This was otherworldly, and Aiden was her new universe.

Chanting praise, he continued to pump his fingers and thumb into her and she shuddered and trembled through her release.

Aiden played her body like a maestro.

She felt his weight shift behind her, sobbed out a plea when he pulled out of her. And then she heard the foil wrapper.

He stroked himself against her, priming his cock, and Frankie spread her knees just a little wider, inviting him in. It took nothing more.

Aiden notched the crown of his dick against her, gripped her hips, and drove into her.

Decadently full, Frankie welcomed the invasion. The noise he made at the back of his throat drove her wild. Frankie reared up, arching her back.

He closed his fist around her hair and used it to hold her still while he began torturously slow, measured strokes. She was so glad she hadn't insisted on gelato.

His other hand was never still, stroking and squeezing her flesh as if he wanted to explore every inch of her body. Aiden's grip on her hair disappeared, and when he gripped her by the hips, she tossed her hair over her shoulder and looked back at him.

He looked like a god lost in the throes of passion. His jaw was clenched. The cords of his neck stood out against the strain. His eyes were hooded.

"I love when you look at me like that," he gritted out the words.

"Like what?"

"Like I'm the center of your universe."

That connection, gaze to gaze, held them prisoner. His pace quickened imperceptibly at first before speeding up, faster and faster. His thrusts were so powerful they were forcing her forward until finally she was flat on her stomach accepting his full weight on her back.

"Aiden!" she called out his name. The climax building again inside her was terrifying.

He grunted softly into her ear, lost to the wild rhythm. *Take*, his body told hers. And Frankie was only too happy to obey. He was crushing her to the mattress, giving her no room to move. All she could do was take the pleasure he was delivering.

Aiden slid his hand between her legs, cupping her exactly where she needed his touch. "I'm coming, and I need you with me," he told her.

He slammed into her—once then twice—and, on the third thrust, held as he shouted victoriously. She met him there, her walls closing around him as her body fell into spectacular freefall. "Fuck, Franchesca. Baby," he groaned against her ear.

It only made her come harder. His cock pulsing inside her, his labored breathing against her neck, the weight of him on top of her. Her fingers were white knuckled on the sheets even as the waves began to mellow.

He fucked her until she was done and vibrating beneath him, and then he collapsed on top of her.

"I know I'm crushing you," he said, "but moving is not an option right now."

"It's fine. I've accomplished all I've set out to do sexually. Dying like this is totally acceptable," Frankie said into the pillow. "My mom will be so proud."

"Speaking of your mother—"

"Aiden, you're still inside me. I don't like where this is going."

He laughed softly against her neck. "Am I still invited to Sunday lunch?"

29

*F*rankie hadn't exactly meant to let him spend the night. But lounging in her bed with naked Aiden Adonis wrapped around her was too decadent to put a stop to. Plus, the heat that his ridiculously perfect body pumped off was more than enough to keep her warm in her Arctic breeze apartment. The windows were drafty, and the building's furnace had been on its last legs for years. But the rent was affordable, and it was close to her parents.

So she dressed in layers and piled blankets on her bed. The bed that Aiden had dominated last night with his large frame. The bed that he'd been too polite to complain about with its lumpy mattress and sagging box springs. It was on her list of things to replace when she was finally done paying for grad school. Sure. She'd have some student loans, but for the most part, she'd shouldered the burden up front, paying as much of her tuition as she could out of pocket.

Frankie poked her head out of the bathroom and eyed the damage a vigorous night of lovemaking caused while she brushed her teeth. Her blankets were in a pile on the floor, and at one point, someone's foot or arm had swept the nightstand clean. It looked as though she was going to need a new lamp.

Worth it.

Aiden had pressed a kiss to her forehead on his way out at the ungodly hour of five.

He had early meetings and needed to get home to shower and change.

She, on the other hand, had lounged about in her bed on sheets that smelled like him until her alarm sounded two hours later.

She'd showered, leisurely, and then decided to treat herself to a coffee—the expensive kind—at the hipster café on her way to work.

"Good morning," Frankie said as she breezed through the glass door of the office. Brenda, the receptionist and part-owner of the Brooklyn Heights Small Business Development Center, shivered at the draft of winter air that followed Frankie inside and huddled closer to the space heater under her desk.

It was a cheery if not chic space. Just last year Frankie had come in on a Sunday to help Brenda and her husband Raul paint the industrial gray walls a nice, clean white. They'd decorated with art by local Brooklynites. Paintings of store-fronts, sketches of the skyline and streets. Brenda had added a veritable garden of plants for pops of green and "air filtering."

"Girl, you are going to freeze to death walking to work," Brenda tut-tutted.

Frankie laughed and unwound the wool scarf from her neck, looping it over the coat rack. After last night, she felt she had heat to spare for the six-block walk having taken so much of Aiden's.

"I *like* walking to work. Because the walk allows me to do

this." She handed over the small green tea she'd picked up for Brenda.

The woman wiggled her fingers and reached for the cup. "Gimmie! Forget what I said. Walk all you want. Who cares about frostbite when you bring me green tea?"

"How did Daisy Scouts go last night?" Frankie asked, shrugging out of her coat and carrying her bag over to her desk.

Brenda had been called to babysit her granddaughter's Daisy troop when the scout leader—Brenda's daughter—came down with a case of front row seats to see Bon Jovi.

"I drank half a bottle of wine after they left. Thirteen seven-year-olds." Brenda shook her head and then patted her hair to make sure it was still in place. She wore her dark hair in dozens of tiny braids coiled in a bun at the base of her neck. "My dining table looks like a glitter bomb went off."

"I warned you not to do sparkly or sticky crafts!"

"Lesson learned," Brenda sighed. "What about you? How was your mysterious dinner date?"

Frankie had been cagey about her evening plans, which had raised Brenda's red flag immediately.

"It was uh... good."

"Mmm-hmm," Brenda said.

Frankie felt the color on her cheeks rising. She'd donned a turtleneck today to cover the bruise between her neck and shoulder where Aiden had gotten a little overzealous with his mouth. *She'd have to lay down the law before next time: No visible hickeys.*

The thought that there would be a next time? Now her cheeks were flaming.

"Girl, the shades of pink you're turning are making me *very* curious."

"I had dinner with... the guy I'm... my boyfriend?" That's

technically what he was. Wasn't it? It was too much of a mouthful to say *the guy I'm seeing temporarily and enjoying naked.*

"Boyfriend?" Brenda perked up. She popped the lid off her green tea and blew on the steam. "Details, please."

"Don't we have to get ready for the social media workshop?" Frankie asked hopefully. She pulled her laptop out of her bag and booted it up.

"The one you have given every month for the past year? I think we've got it down to a science. Spill."

What could she possibly say that wouldn't sound like she'd lost her damn mind? *My boyfriend and I are having sex until he gets bored and moves on. But it's cool because he's promised me a ton of orgasms and anything I want.* Nope. That wouldn't do.

"His name is Aiden, and we met at the wedding."

"He must be one of the hoity-toity crowd if he was at Pruitt's wedding," Brenda guessed.

"I don't really know what he does," Frankie said evasively. It wasn't exactly a lie. Just because Aiden had more money in his couch cushions than she did in her savings account didn't mean that she exactly grasped what he did to earn those piles of cash.

"That's not like you. Usually you have a dossier of every dateable candidate before you even say yes to the first date," Brenda pointed out.

"I'll have to get on that dossier," Frankie promised.

"What's his last name?" Brenda asked.

"Kilbourn. Aiden Kilbourn." Shit was about to go down.

Brenda shoved a finger in her ear above the neat rows of tiny gold hoops that she wore in her lobe. "I'm sorry. It sounded to these old ears like you said Aiden Kilbourn."

"You've heard of him?" Frankie asked innocently. Of

course, she'd heard of him. Everyone in the five boroughs knew of the Kilbourns and their Manhattan domination.

Brenda bustled back to her desk, her nails clicking on the keyboard. She was shaking her head and muttering. Frankie slunk into the tiny kitchenette and stored her lunch in the fridge. "Morning, Raul," she called through his open door.

Raul was a man of small stature and big heart. He also dressed to the nines in vibrant colored pullover sweaters and nerdy glasses. His hair was going silver. He always made time for anyone who graced his doorway and considered himself an aficionado on bottles of wine below twenty dollars.

"Morning, Frankie. You ready for the workshop today?"

"All set. We've got ten signed up, which probably means eight will show." One of Frankie's specialties was teaching social media marketing to local business owners or employees that were hired to take care of Facebook pages and Instagram accounts. She ran the Facebook account for her parents' deli after her father had blatantly refused to learn how to turn on a computer. Her mother was quick on an iPad but had no desire to "blab about every damn thing" she did in her day.

But it gave Frankie a special insight into the mind of a small business owner. It was just one of the areas she focused on at her job. But it was usually more fun than grant writing and accounting software tutorials. The people the business development center served couldn't afford a pricey accountant, and if they could, they wouldn't trust one. Small business was as different from the corporate level as, well, Frankie was to Aiden.

She slipped back to her desk and found a stack of freshly printed papers.

Brenda had started the dossier for her.

She intended to ignore them, but a headline caught her eye. And then a picture of Aiden and another man at a charity auction. She skimmed the caption and promptly fell down the rabbit hole. Aiden was COO for Kilbourn Holdings, a mega corporation that specialized in mergers and acquisitions as well as corporate finance. Aiden on his own also dabbled in real estate. The man owned buildings. In Manhattan.

And he still played polo but only for charity. *Of course.*

She flipped to another picture, a group shot on the carpet of some gala. He looked like his mother, one of the women under Aiden's father's arm. The same thick, dark hair, the same patrician nose. Spectacular cheekbones. His father had the Irish auburn hair that was going silver. Cozy family, she thought. Aiden's parents had divorced years ago. Yet they still socialized in the same circles.

Aiden's stepmother and Elliot the Fink were also in the picture. The women were dressed in stunning gowns, the men in tuxes they'd been born to wear.

Frankie was suddenly beyond relieved that she'd laid down the law on dabbling in his life. No arm candy appearances. She'd done enough catering gigs to see how the whole trophy date thing worked. Stand there and look beautiful but keep your trap shut. Drink but not too much. Don't eat anything that crunches or crumbles or ruins your lipstick. Smile but not too much.

Barf.

She was not about to sign up for a life that treated Tuesday nights like it was prom.

She checked her watch. She still had an hour before she needed to head upstairs to set up. They had a conference room on the second floor where they hosted educational seminars. Frankie was working on building a set of online classes for business owners who were too busy to take time out of their day to attend. But it was slow going with the grad work and the catering. Just a few more jobs that she'd already committed to and her credit card balance would be gone. Then a few more months and she'd have that shiny MBA in hand.

And then?

Then she wasn't sure. She'd love to stay here, working for Brenda and Raul. They were the heart of the business community in Brooklyn Heights. But their budget was already stretched near to breaking. If they lost even one grant, cuts would have to be made, and unfortunately for Frankie, she'd be first in line. It was another reason she wanted to make sure they had the online classes to offer.

She'd find something that excited her, that challenged her. And she'd finally be able to claw her way up from the paycheck-to-paycheck existence she'd known her entire life.

She was startled out of her reverie by the door. A courier popped in hefting a large black box. "Looking for a Ms. Baranski," he said, popping an ear bud out of his ear.

Brenda pointed an index finger in Frankie's direction. "You found her."

"Cool," he strode over and dropped the box on her desk. "Just need your signature here." He whipped out a tablet and Frankie signed the screen with her finger.

"Who's it from?" she asked.

"Big guy at Kilbourn Holdings downtown. Later," he said, flashing a quick salute before heading back out the door.

Frankie stared at the box, half scared to open it. What could he possibly have had the time to send her in the scant hours since they'd been wrapped up naked in each other's arms? Even Prime wasn't that fast. *Oh, god. What if it was a box of sex toys?*

Brenda leaned over Frankie's desk. "Hurry up. I'm dying over here!"

She'd be dying if it was a value pack of dildos. But there'd be no getting rid of Brenda until the package was open. Carefully, Frankie lifted the lid and peered underneath.

"Well?"

Frankie dumped the lid to the side and parted the delicate layers of tissue paper. Seriously, who had a gift wrapper on hand first thing in the morning?

"Oooh," Brenda crooned as Frankie pulled the coat out of the box. It was black like her current one, but the similarities ended at the color.

Wool—and was that cashmere?—with a plaid silky lining.

"It's so soft," she murmured.

"Put it on," Brenda ordered.

"Holy crap. It's Burberry."

Brenda shoved her into the coat. It *felt* luxurious. She stroked her hands over the fabric. The coat nipped in at the waist and fell to mid-thigh.

Brenda nodded approvingly. "You look fabulous."

"Don't you dare look up how much it costs," Frankie warned her. This was no hundred-dollar coat from a department store.

Brenda shoved her hands in the pockets.

"What are you doing?"

"I'm looking to see if he stuffed the pockets with loose diamonds."

Frankie laughed. She felt lightheaded. Was she just supposed to accept this as a gift? How could she possibly reciprocate in kind?

"Aha!" Brenda pulled her hands out of the pockets in triumph. "No diamonds, but I did find these." She held up a sleek pair of gloves.

Of *course* they were cashmere lined leather.

"Oh, look! There's a note in the box!"

Nestled in the tissue paper, Frankie snatched up the envelope before Brenda could get to it.

To keep you warm when I'm not around.
   A

Holy. Shit.

"What's it say? What's it say?" Brenda was practically dancing from foot to foot.

Frankie cleared her throat. "It just says, 'To keep you warm,'" she fibbed.

Brenda squealed. "This is so exciting! Our Frankie lands a jillionaire!"

Raul poked his head out of his office door. "How's the workshop setup going?" he asked, eyeing them with suspicion.

"Great," Brenda said sweetly. "And thank you for asking!"

"I'd better go set up," Frankie said, reluctantly sliding out of the coat.

"You go ahead. I'm going to pet your coat for a few minutes."

Frankie put the coffee on in the kitchenette and then headed up the narrow staircase to the second floor. In the conference room, she turned up the thermostat and set out the notebooks and pens. And then flopped down in one of the chairs. She pulled out her phone.

Frankie: Where did you find a Burberry coat before 9 a.m. on a Tuesday?

He answered immediately and she guessed he must have been waiting for her to text.

Aiden: You're welcome. I told you. Anything you want.

But she hadn't asked for it. Gifts like this? A coat that cost at least a grand and probably more? There was no way in hell she could keep up with him on this side of their relationship.

Aiden: Do you like it?

She hadn't thanked him, and that made her rude in addition to being poor. They had to talk about this side of things. That she wasn't comfortable being the beneficiary of his deep pockets. But for now a little gratitude was due.

Frankie: It's stunning. I want to say I can't accept it. But I think my boss threw my old one in the trash can with the coffee grounds. Thank you for thinking of me.

Aiden: I have a feeling I'll be doing a lot of that.

30

"*Y*ou're bringing your young man to lunch on Sunday, aren't you?"

Frankie's mother had caught her between work and class on exam night, guaranteeing the highest amount of stress.

"Ma! He's forty. We're having sex, not going to junior prom!"

"Even better. He'll be wanting to settle down and give his mother-in-law a half-dozen grand babies."

"Do you torture Marco and Rachel like this? They're actually pregnant," she pointed out.

"If I have to listen to my smug sister tell me one more time how smart Baby Nicky is or how she couldn't wait to spend the day taking little Sebastian to the park, I'm going to set her on fire."

May Baranski was never just a tiny bit dramatic.

"I don't know if he can come, Ma," Frankie sighed, running up the front steps of the building. It was the only class she had to physically be on campus for. The rest were online, thank

God. So once a week she schlepped her ass downtown for Corporate Social Responsibility.

She started for the stairs.

"Well, you won't know until you ask him," May sniffed.

"Fine. I'll ask him."

"Good. We'll see you both on Sunday." Her mother hung up, and Frankie cursed family and its complications.

She was five minutes early. And rather than reviewing her notes one more time like she should have, she opened her texts.

Aiden: Good luck tonight.

How had he remembered that she had an exam? With as packed as she presumed his calendar to be, the fact that he was storing little personal details about her both delighted and unsettled her.

Frankie: Thanks. You're going to need some luck now. You've been summoned to Baranski Sunday Lunch. You can say no. It's loud, cramped quarters. People yell a lot. I can tell her you're busy buying a country or something.

When he didn't respond immediately, Frankie silenced her phone and stowed it in her bag. It was for the best if he didn't go. It would be a mistake to take him to her parents'. Her mother would start building castles in the sky and "finally" planning her "only daughter's wedding." And when it ended, when she and Aiden went their separate ways, May would be more devastated than either of them. Plus, she didn't want to complicate things. And that's exactly what family usually did.

They were doing a good job of keeping it uncomplicated.

They'd had dinner and (phenomenal) sex on Tuesday and had been texting off and on since then. See? Minus the expensive coat and gloves she loved so much that she wore them watching TV in her icebox of an apartment, they were basically a Tinder hookup.

That, she could handle.

Professor Neblanski shuffled into class clutching a latte and dumped his briefcase on his desk. "All right, let's get this over with."

FRANKIE HATED TO ADMIT IT, but she was disappointed that she didn't get to see Aiden Friday or Saturday. Friday night, she already had plans to go out with friends, hitting a new wine bar in Clinton Hill. Saturday Aiden spent half the day in the office and the other half juggling rich guy responsibilities. Something about a fundraiser appearance and a dinner with clients. Now, she was curled up on her couch with Netflix reruns on in the background and her thesis draft in her lap, ignoring both in favor of thinking about Aiden.

What they lacked in physical attention, they made up for in texting. Frankie was delighted to find that Aiden was funny over text.

Aiden: Dinner companion mentioned having his hands full of wood. Exactly how am I supposed to respond? (Full disclosure: client owns several lumber mills).

Aiden: I was going to stop by your place tonight and surprise you, but Brooklyn.

Aiden: I've been disappointed by every single sandwich since the one your brother made.

And then there was tonight's message.

Aiden: Preparing for lunch tomorrow. What's the best way to take your mother's attention off of Gio and the fresh widow? Should we tell her we're adopting a child or that our sex tape was leaked?

Frankie laughed out loud at that one. She fired off a response.

Frankie: When is the last time you met a girl's parents?

Aiden: I meet most of them.

Frankie didn't care for that particular tidbit. It certainly didn't make a girl feel special.

Aiden: However, I'm feeling a lot more pressure having heard about your mother. What's the best way to win her over? Asking for a friend.

Frankie laughed again. She started to text back and then threw caution to the wind and dialed his number.

"Franchesca." He answered the phone sounding both smoldery and delighted.

She felt like a damn teenager talking to her crush on the phone.

"Hello," she said, wondering why she called him. Now they had to make conversation. "Are you really worried about meeting my mother? Because you should be. She's terrifying."

"You underestimate my charm," Aiden insisted.

Frankie laughed. "You underestimate my mother's lack of sanity. She's going to ask you about weddings and babies."

"And what should I tell her?"

Frankie flopped back on the couch cushion. "Well, she already knows that we're having sex, which she thinks makes me a diabolical genius for hooking you on sex and then tempting you to put a ring on it."

Aiden laughed softly.

"You don't have to go, Aide," she reminded him. She was more nervous about him meeting her parents than any legitimate boyfriend she'd had since high school.

"I'd like to go."

"I can't imagine why. They're messy and loud and nosy, and you're guaranteed to leave with a headache and probably a buzz and indigestion. My mom will keep refilling your plate while my dad keeps the booze flowing."

"Are you trying to talk me out of it? Because never-ending food and alcohol are doing the exact opposite."

"It's not going to be what you're used to."

"Franchesca, just because I haven't experienced something yet doesn't mean I'm not going to like it. But if you don't want me to go, say the word. Anything you want."

She paused, chewed on her lip. "Come. Meet my crazy family."

"I'll be there. Besides, someone has to save Gio from the widow."

"You're awfully loyal to my brother."

"The man made me a sandwich that I'm still fantasizing about."

"Just wait 'til I make you a sandwich. You'll forget all about Gio and his wilted lettuce and soggy bread."

"A sandwich artist, too? Is there nothing you don't do?" Aiden teased.

Was he taking a dig at her blue-collar roots? Sandwich maker and catering help?

"Well, if you wouldn't be so busy making all that money,

you could learn to make yourself an acceptable sandwich," she said lightly.

"How was your week?" he asked, changing the subject suddenly.

"It was... good."

"What did you do?" he asked.

"Why?" Frankie laughed.

"I'm interested in you," he said dryly. "Tell me about your week. How did your exam go?"

So she told him, and he listened. She couldn't get a read on him. It was as if he were treating this as a real relationship. Something she couldn't afford to do. Get used to late night calls with the gravel-voiced Aiden Kilbourn? Then what exactly would she do when those calls stopped?

It played on an endless loop in the back of her mind. Even as she enjoyed the conversation, the banter, the interest.

31

*F*rankie glanced out the front window of her parents' house for the ninth time in two minutes.

"Someone's waiting for her *boy*-friend," her brother Marco sang in an annoying falsetto.

"Shut up, Marco," his wife and Frankie's new best friend, Rachel, snapped.

"Babe, don't yell. The doc says it's not good for the baby," Marco said, rubbing his hand over her rounded stomach.

"Oh, hang on there, buddy. Why don't you stop doing things that require getting yelled at for?" Rachel was her brother's match in everything... including volume.

"Both of you stop yelling so I can hear Drew." Frankie's father was a short and stocky man whose favorite place to be was ass-first in his recliner with the volume cranked on the TV. He DVR-ed *The Price is Right* all week long and binge watched it every Sunday. "For shit's sake, two dollars? Whatsa matter, lady, you never do your own shopping?" he grumbled in disgust.

"Ma! When are we eating?" Gio called from the back of the house where he was probably sneaking scraps in the kitchen.

"When Frankie's boyfriend gets here! Get your hands off of that roast!" May Baranski had the gift of sight when it came to the goings on in her children's bedrooms and her kitchen. The first time Frankie had snuck a boy into her room, May had suddenly needed to "borrow" a sweater from her teenage daughter and had scared the shit out of the guy in her closet.

"Is that him?" May threw herself at the couch in front of the window and peered outside.

Frankie's family didn't go to church, but her mother still believed in Sunday best and was wearing her very best elastic waist slacks and turtleneck purchased from JC Penney in 1989.

The car that pulled to a stop was worth more than the house they were in. It had to be him. Her phone dinged, and Frankie dove for it.

Aiden: I'm here. Is it safe to come in?

"Is it him?" May was clamoring over the couch to get a better view. The woman did aquacise classes three times a week at the YMCA and was in better physical shape than most of the rest of them combined.

Frankie: I'll be right out to escort you in. Did you bring any security with you? My ma is humping the couch trying to get a better look at you. I'm not sure if I can hold her back.

Frankie dropped her phone on the coffee table and dashed out the front door and down the two steps from the cement stoop. Aiden got out of the car looking good enough to eat in charcoal gray slacks and a burgundy sweater. Her mother would think he dressed up to meet them and give him bonus points. Frankie didn't want to admit it, but she'd changed twice, matched her bra to her underwear again, and applied work day makeup.

She met him on the skinny concrete walk that led up to the house and stopped short. Every single family member, minus her father, would be plastered to the front window. She wanted to kiss him, but she didn't want to give them a show.

Sensing her hesitation, Aiden gave her a smile. "If you shake my hand it's just going to make them talk more."

"I'm going to go ahead and apologize now. Because this was a huge mistake, and I'm so sorry I got you into it."

"Relax, Franchesca. We're going to lunch, not war."

She snorted. "Shows what you know. In this neighborhood, they're usually the same thing."

"I'm going to kiss you," he warned her. "And then we're going to go inside and have lunch. And then I'm going to take you home and fuck you."

The thrill rushed over her as he reached for her.

"Fine, but no tongue. You know my pants fall off when you do that."

He was grinning at her with something like joy. He laid a very chaste kiss on her mouth before pulling back.

"How was that?"

"My pants still want to fall off. Let's get in your car and drive away and jump straight to the sex," she suggested.

"After," he promised. "We've got business to attend to first." He held up the flowers and wine.

"Jesus, Aide. You didn't bring a thousand-dollar bottle of wine, did you?" Frankie was appalled. The flowers were no grocery store impulse buy either. White lilies and glossy green holly leaves. *Ugh. Her mother would love them.*

"Relax. I went to a store and paid a respectable price."

"It better be under a hundred dollars."

"If I tell you it was, will you please let me in the house?"

She sighed and straightened her shoulders. "Just remember, I gave you the opportunity to run away."

She led the way inside through the rusting storm door that hit Aiden in the ass when she stopped suddenly because every member of her family was crowding around the twelve slate tiles that acted as the home's foyer. Geez, why hadn't she noticed the dust bunnies on the floor trim? And when had the coat closet door started peeling?

"Oh, great. You're all lurking like turkey vultures. Everybody, this is Aiden. Aiden, this is everybody."

"Aiden, it's so nice to meet you," Frankie's mom crooned as if she were meeting Frankie Fucking Valli.

Her father grunted and looked over his shoulder at Drew Carey's face, his version of a "pleasure to meet you."

"Hey, nice to meet you, man," Marco said, offering a hand. "This is my girl, Rach."

"Wife actually and future mother to his child," Rachel said pointing at her belly.

Aiden shook all the appropriate hands and greeted them more warmly than Frankie thought they deserved.

"Hey, good to see you again, Aide," Gio said, pulling Aiden in for one of those one-armed buddy hugs.

"Again?" True to form, May latched onto that statement with a talon. "You've already met."

"Yeah," Gio shrugged. "He was at Frankie's apartment last week."

"And you didn't think to mention it?" May's voice was accelerating into dog whistle range. She cuffed Gio upside the head.

"Ouch! Ma! I sent you the picture of them!"

"I forgot! I'm sorry!" She smacked him again.

Aiden looked on in what Frankie hoped was amusement. Her mother was a few cards shy of a full deck.

"Can we please, for the love of God, act like regular people for one afternoon?" Frankie screeched. She turned to Aiden. "I wish I could say they don't usually act like this. But this is the family that got permanently banned from an Applebee's on Atlantic Avenue."

Aiden squeezed her shoulder and stepped in. "Mrs. Baranski, thank you for inviting me to join you today." He wielded the flowers and wine like they were a shield that would keep the little Italian woman at bay.

"Oh, my! What a gentleman," May sighed in approval. "So very nice. Why don't you boys ever bring your mother flowers?" she asked, admiring the lilies and managing to lay a guilt trip at the same time.

Gio and Marco spouted excuses that earned them both a cuff to the back of the head.

"Mr. Baranski," Aiden began, "Gio brought some sandwiches to Franchesca's this week. He said they came from your deli. Best sandwich I've ever had."

Hugo puffed out his chest in pride. "It's all in the meat. You've got good taste in sandwiches. You're okay by me." He immediately returned his attention to the TV.

Frankie rolled her eyes. "Welcome to the sixth circle of hell," she whispered.

Aiden winked. "Wait until you meet my family."

32

"*I*t's so good that you met Frankie when you did," May was saying as she helped herself to another glass of wine. "Her eggs are only a few years from drying up."

"Ma!" Frankie looked more annoyed than aghast. "Would you shut up about my eggs? We literally just started dating. Aiden could be an axe-murdering clown."

"He's not an axe-murdering clown!"

"How do you know?"

"He brought flowers and wine. Clowns don't have manners like that." It appeared that no one could argue with May Baranski's logic, Aiden decided.

"I appreciate your faith in my character, Mrs. Baranski."

"Call me, Ma."

"Ma!" Franchesca covered her face in her hands, and Aiden hid his laugh behind his beer. "Why don't you write him into your will already?"

"As soon as there's a ring on your finger, I will," May challenged with a stubbornness that had clearly been passed down to her daughter.

"So, Aiden. What do you do?" Hugo's attention span had expanded since *The Price is Right* had ended.

Frankie gripped his thigh under the table. She was sending him a silent message, but unfortunately for her, it was intercepted by his cock.

He cleared his throat and took a sip of beer. "I'm in business, too."

When she snorted next to him, Aiden brought his hand to the base of Frankie's neck and squeezed.

To him, a business was a business no matter how many employees or office buildings it laid claim to. Frankie's father wanted to be his own boss and provide a service for the community. Aiden could appreciate and respect that.

"Dad, Aiden is COO of Kilbourn Holdings" Frankie explained. She didn't sound like she was bragging. She sounded like she was apologizing.

Marco whistled. "Damn. You own entire city blocks downtown."

May's eyes widened and she reached for her wine glass. "Franchesca, may I see you in the kitchen?"

Aiden and Frankie shared a glance.

"All the food's already on the table, Ma," Frankie pointed out.

"Now." May's tone left no room for arguing.

Aiden felt the dull throb of the headache that Frankie had promised him begin in the base of his skull. Here it comes, he thought. There wasn't a mother in the world whose eyes wouldn't light up at the thought of her daughter landing a Kilbourn.

Frankie squeezed his thigh and followed her mother into the kitchen.

"What in the hell have you gotten yourself into?" May Baranski yelled from the confines of the kitchen.

"Uh, Ma likes to think the kitchen is soundproof," Gio said.

"You're probably going to want another beer," Marco predicted.

"You might as well get us a round," Hugo sighed. "Sorry, Aiden."

"Should I go in there?" Rachel wondered.

Marco's arm landed on her shoulders. "It would be a danger to the baby, believe me."

"Gotten myself into? What the hell, Ma?" Frankie yelled back.

"He's a *millionaire*," May said. "You can't handle a husband like that."

"I hate to break it to you, Ma, but you probably have to change that 'm' to a 'b,' and I'm not looking for a husband. He's a nice guy. We're having a good time."

No one in his entire life had described him as a "nice guy."

"You're thirty-four years old, Franchesca. Just how long are you going to wait to settle down?"

"Until I find the right guy, Ma! Not all of us get lucky and find our soulmate in junior high." Apparently, Frankie thought the kitchen was soundproofed too.

"He's from another world! You can't expect to be an equal partner in that relationship!" May shouted.

"Ma! Do you think there's any man on the planet I'd let treat me like less than?" Frankie demanded.

"I don't like this, Franchesca. Not one bit. It's one thing to be friends with Pru, but dating a man who owns half of Manhattan?"

"Now you're exaggerating."

"Exaggerating? Me? I never exaggerate!"

"She always exaggerates," Rachel said, smiling sympathetically at him.

"Hey, Aide," Gio said suddenly. "How you feel about the Knicks?"

"The Knicks? I think they have a shot at the semis if not the finals this year." Aiden was grateful for the rope.

"Me and Marco have an extra ticket for the game Tuesday. You wanna go?"

Aiden tried to remember the last time someone invited him somewhere that wasn't related to business. He couldn't come up with anything.

The shouting from the kitchen reached a crescendo. "He's a nice guy that I'm not marrying, Ma. Chill the hell out."

"Don't you swear at me, Franchesca Marie!"

"You're the one acting like a crazy person in front of a really nice guy that I like a lot."

"I'm not acting crazy! I'm making sure my daughter isn't getting in over her head with a crowd that runs too fast! What if he wants you to go to Monaco or St. Barths? What if he gets you hooked on drugs? All the celebrities need rehab, you know."

"Jesus, I'm not thirteen, Ma! And Aiden isn't hooking me on drugs."

"I don't want you losing your focus on your degree for a handsome face with deep pockets."

"*Mother!* All you've talked about since I was twenty-two was me getting married."

"I meant to a nice guy from Brooklyn who could offer you a family and a nice home within a three-block radius of our house. Not some kajillionaire who would treat you like some trophy."

"Oh, I'm not a trophy?" Frankie challenged at full volume.

"I thought you said you weren't marrying him?" May demanded.

"You know how I operate! You say no, and that's what I want to do!"

"Tuesday would be great," Aiden said.

"Awesome," Marco shrugged.

"Meet at the Garden?" Gio suggested.

"Works for me," Marco nodded.

"Me, too."

"Who's gonna sneak in there and get another round of beers?" Hugo wondered.

"Oh, my God. I'll do it," Rachel said, pushing back from the table.

"Be careful in there, babe," Marco warned her, no longer as concerned with the welfare of their unborn baby since beer was on the line.

Rachel headed down the hallway supporting her belly.

"Everyone can hear every word you both are saying," she announced.

"No, they can't," both Baranski women said.

"Yes, we can," the Baranski men called back from the dining room.

"See what you did, Ma?"

"Me? You're the one who brings a trillionaire to lunch!"

"We can still hear you," Gio yelled.

"No, you can't," May insisted.

But the yelling ceased, and after a few stage whispers from down the hall, Frankie, Rachel, and May reappeared. Frankie and May had topped off their wineglasses.

Rachel was juggling four beers that she doled out at the table.

Aiden guzzled the last of his beer and reached for the fresh one. "This roast is delicious," he announced.

Marco snorted and choked.

"We're so happy to have you here to enjoy it," May said, smiling sweetly.

Frankie flipped her brother the bird.

Marco flipped it back but not before his mother caught him. May got out of her chair and walked casually behind her son, and just when his shoulders seemed to relax, she cuffed him on the back of the head.

"Manners!"

"Frankie started it," Marco argued.

Frankie flipped him another bird.

"See, Ma? Look!"

Frankie picked up her fork and ate innocently. "Marco, you're hallucinating."

May slapped Gio on the back of the head on her way back to her chair.

"What was that for?" he whined.

"I saw your finger twitch," she pointed out. "It was a preemptive strike."

May sat down primly. Frankie and her brothers watched carefully, and the second the woman's attention was on her plate, three middle fingers shot up around the table.

"Oh, for Pete's sake. When did you all turn into assholes?" Hugo sighed over his plate.

"What? What did they do?" May demanded.

"Nothing," the three Baranski siblings announced.

"You sure you want to deal with this?" Rachel asked Aiden from across the table. "There's still time to get out."

Aiden turned his laugh into a discreet cough.

"Don't try to scare off the trillionaire. He's Frankie's last shot at non-test tube babies," Marco joked.

Aiden shot Marco the finger, and the table erupted in laughter. Except for May. She very calmly got out of her seat and smacked him upside the head.

"Ma!" Franchesca was horrified.

"I don't care if Aiden is a trillionaire. No one flips the bird at my dinner table!"

As soon as she glanced down at her plate, six middle fingers shot up.

33

When all was said and done, Frankie had to drive Aiden to her place in his car because he'd had one or three too many with her dad and idiot brothers. He was a sweet drunk, complimenting her on her braking and turn signals the whole eight blocks back to her place.

Frankie slid the key in the lock and gave him a push into her apartment. She dropped her keys on the kitchen counter and kicked off her shoes. "Well, *that* was eventful," she announced.

"I couldn't tell. Did I pass?" he asked, sliding out of his coat and hanging it neatly on the dubious coat rack that leaned like the tower of Pisa.

"Pass what?" Frankie asked, fishing two glasses out of the cabinet in her kitchen.

"Your parents' inspection."

She laughed. "My mother hit you upside the head. That's a gold star seal of approval if there ever was one."

"That's not what it sounded like from the kitchen."

Frankie handed him a glass of water and some ibuprofen.

"You heard that, huh?" She curled up on the couch, tucking her feet beneath her.

Aiden flopped down next to her and stared at the pills in his hand.

"Go on. They always give me a headache," Frankie joked.

"You're very thoughtful," Aiden said, smiling sweetly at her.

She indulged herself and ran the fingers of one hand through his thick hair.

He leaned back against the couch cushion and closed his eyes. "Feels good," he murmured.

There was something irresistible about tipsy, vulnerable Aiden.

"Do you really care if they like you?" she asked, wondering if he could be playing her.

"Of course I do," he said, lolling his head to one side to study her. "If they're important to you, they're important to me."

"Did you and my dad sneak into the bourbon?" Frankie asked.

"Only one or two times," Aiden said, listing toward her. "Hey, you know what I heard some people do on Sunday afternoons?"

"Buy small countries?" Frankie offered. His head hit her in the chest and she continued the slow stroke of her fingers through his hair.

"Ha. You're funny. I heard some people nap."

She closed her fist in his hair and gave a tug until he was looking at her. "Have you never had a Sunday afternoon nap?"

"Sure. When I was like three," he smirked.

"Sunday afternoon naps are the best. And if rich people can't take them, I don't ever want to be rich."

Aiden nestled into her, his face pressed against her breast. "Will you take a nap with me?"

"Take your shoes off, Aide," she told him.

"'K." He shoved his Ferragamo loafers off, and they hit the floor one at a time.

"Are you always this adorable when you drink?" she teased, tugging the blanket off the back of the couch to cover him.

"I drink too much," he murmured. His eyes were closed.

"You do?"

"Self-medication."

"I've never seen you drunk before," Frankie pointed out as she adjusted the pillow behind her.

"I don't like to get sloppy," he yawned.

"You're not a sloppy person," she agreed.

"Hey, will you come to a dinner with me this week?"

"Where?" she hedged.

"At some museum. It's a reception for a nonprofit. My mom is on the board."

"Your family will be there?"

"Mmm-hmm. Everybody. Even that asshole Elliot."

Frankie laughed softly. "I'm gonna have to pass."

"Why?" he sounded disgruntled.

"I don't think that's a good idea, Aiden. It's better if we keep our relationship... private."

He lifted his head and looked at her frowning. "But I just met your family," he pointed out.

"I know. But that's different. I don't think I should dabble in your world. Okay?"

It was all temporary, and she didn't want either one of them to forget that. Meeting her family was one thing. It drove her mother batty. Mission accomplished. If she met Aiden's family, it would be making a statement. And she wasn't really a statement kind of woman.

"I wish you would. I liked meeting your family, and mine doesn't hit as much."

Frankie laughed again. "That just means Ma really liked you."

"Even though I'm a trillionaire?"

"She wouldn't have smacked you if she didn't like you."

"Promise?"

"I promise." Despite her better judgment, Frankie dropped a kiss to the top of his head. His hair was soft, silky to the touch.

"What do you use on your hair?" she asked.

"Mmm, stuff. Can we sleep now?"

"Yeah, we can sleep now."

His arms came around her waist, and he was out like a light in seconds.

Frankie tried not to think about how good this felt. A Sunday nap on the couch with her sexy boyfriend. It wasn't real, but that didn't mean that it didn't feel damn good.

She woke slowly in stages to a gentle stroking. She knew without waking that it was Aiden's hands in her hair.

"Mmm," she sighed.

"I can't remember the last time I took a nap," Aiden murmured.

Somehow, they'd shifted during the nap and Aiden was now spooning her and stroking his hand through her thick, wild hair.

"You are missing out," she said, giving herself over to the luxury of a whole body stretch.

"I had no idea just how much," he said, his lips moving against her ear. She wiggled back against him and felt the reward of his exceptional hard-on.

"Do you always wake up with wood?" she asked.

His hand slid down to capture her breast through her sweater.

"When I wake up next to you I do."

He sounded sleepy but sober. And there was something irresistible about his lips moving over her hair, her neck.

"Are you sure you won't reconsider coming to dinner this week?" he asked, his hand squeezing the tender flesh of her breast.

"Mmm. Meeting the family? Facing photographers? Sitting around while you wow the room? No thanks."

He sighed behind her. Was that disappointment? Relief?

"But maybe there's something I can do to make it up to you," she said rolling to face him and reaching her hand between them to cup his erection.

34

———

*A*iden shoved his gloved hands in his pockets and watched the crowd fighting their way into Madison Square Garden. There was no sign of the Baranski brothers yet, and he had a brief, unsettling flash of concern, wondering if they weren't actually serious about the invitation.

That sort of thing didn't happen to him. Not with the last name Kilbourn. Growing up, there hadn't been a birthday party, a bar mitzvah, or a wedding he hadn't been invited to. However, those invitations usually came with strings. It was the reason he'd been looking forward to the game. Gio and Marco didn't seem like string-holding guys. And what would it be like to spend an evening being just one of the guys?

Frankie had been entertainingly shocked when he told her he couldn't meet her for her booty call tonight because he was hanging out with her brothers. It was good to keep a woman on her toes. And lately, he'd been feeling like Franchesca was holding all the power in their relationship. Turning her down tonight made him feel like he'd taken a step to restore the balance of power.

"Hey, Kilbourn!"

He turned with relief at his name and spotted Gio and Marco making their way through the crowd to him.

"Good to see you, man," Gio said, slapping him on the shoulder.

They all exchanged greetings. The brothers were decked out in Knicks apparel. Aiden, not sure of girlfriend's brother's hangout etiquette, had kept it simple with jeans and a sweater.

"We ready to get out of this ball-freezing cold?" Marco asked, digging into his coat pocket for the tickets.

"Where we sitting?" Gio demanded, blowing into his hands and rubbing his palms together. Aiden wondered if anyone in the Baranski family ever remembered gloves.

"Well, we're not nosebleed, but we ain't front row," Marco said, waving the tickets.

Aiden debated for a second before digging into his own pocket. "Actually, we are," he said, producing the tickets. He didn't want it to seem like an over-the-top gesture. But when they'd invited him, he'd actually been excited and not in a conquer-the-business-world way. Besides Chip, Aiden's friends were few and far between, and there was something entertainingly normal about Frankie's brothers.

"Are you fucking kidding me?" Gio snatched the tickets out of Aiden's hand.

He couldn't tell if the man was going to hit him or hug him.

"Front fucking row?" Marco whooped.

"I hope you don't mind—"

"Mind?" Aiden found himself enveloped in a male embrace and actually lifted off his feet.

"This is like a real fucking dream come true," Gio said, still staring at the tickets. Aiden wasn't sure, but it looked as though his eyes had gone a little misty.

Marco released him back to the ground and slapped his

brother on the shoulder. "Can Frankie pick 'em, or can she pick 'em?"

"I wish you'd tell her that," Aiden said before he thought better of it.

"She giving you a hard time?" Gio asked sympathetically.

Aiden hesitated. Family loyalty dictated that Frankie's brothers would be one-hundred percent on her side.

"She's great," Aiden said evasively.

"She's a slippery one to nail down," Marco said. "If you want to be in it for the long haul, she'll make you work."

"Overtime," Gio added.

"Tough nut to crack," Marco said.

"I can't tell if she wants to be in this relationship, or if she's just waiting for it to end."

The brothers shared a look and a laugh. "How about we get inside and talk over a beer and some steak sandwiches?"

"Real quick, hang on," Gio said, snatching the old tickets out of Marco's hand. "Hey, kid." He stopped a gangly teenager in a jersey. "You got tickets?"

The kid shook his head. "No, man."

"Now you do." Gio handed them over with a flourish.

"Are you serious?" The kid gaped down at his hand as if Santa himself had just bestowed a magical gift.

"Pay it forward," Marco announced cheerfully. "Let's go." He led the way inside.

"I feel like Oprah," Gio mused, bringing up the rear.

THE GAME WAS action-packed for a basketball game. The courtside seats were worth the astronomical price when Gio and Marco couldn't stop hitting each other in excitement.

"This is the greatest night of my life," Gio announced when one of the Knicks City Dancers blew him a kiss.

"Top ten, definitely," Marco said through a bite of steak.

Together, they razzed the players and shouted along with the rest of the crowd. And Aiden felt like he was part of the unit. He couldn't imagine spending an evening like this with his half-brother. He and Elliott had never had much, if anything, in common. They were loyal because it was required. But they weren't tight-knit like the Baranski siblings.

"Are you excited about being a father?" Aiden asked Marco.

"Shit yeah," Marco shrugged. "Never thought I would be. But Rachel? She makes my life a thousand times better than before. And I had a damn good life before."

"You know what you're having?" Aiden asked.

"Little girl," Marco puffed up and then shoved a finger in Aiden's face. "But Rachel wants to be surprised, so she didn't open the envelope. And *neither did I*. Got it?"

Aiden smirked. "Your secret is safe. Does Frankie know?"

"Not yet." The way Marco said it made Aiden think there weren't many secrets the Baranski siblings kept from one another.

It was an appealing dynamic, he thought. He'd spent his life with family that ruled decisions, friends that he could rarely trust, and hundreds of acquaintances who would sell him out at the drop of the hat. It was nothing like the bond Gio and Marco shared.

Between plays, the brothers helpfully schooled him on all things Frankie.

"You gotta understand, Frankie's looking for what our parents have," Marco said, washing down the rest of his sandwich with overpriced beer.

"A partnership," Gio added. "She's not settling for less."

Less is exactly what they'd agreed upon.

"So, how would someone prove they'd be a good partner?" Aiden asked.

"First of all, don't be a pushover. Don't give her everything she demands. Like when she calls you tonight and suggests you come over, tell her you can't, and don't give her an excuse."

"That will drive her friggin' nuts," Marco grinned in approval.

"You're not giving me bad advice to sink me, are you?" Aiden asked wryly.

Marco leaned in, the epitome of seriousness. "With the seats you could get us for the Jets? Nah, man. We wouldn't lead you astray. Hell, we're hoping you get married and have eight babies."

"Frankie grew up with us. She's basically a guy without the equipment," Gio pointed out, leading them back to the topic at hand. "Talk to her like you would a VP in your company. Don't be all like 'Not now, baby, men are talking.' She'll have your balls in a peanut butter jar for that."

Marco nodded. "Yeah, she's a smart girl. Talk to her like she's one."

The crowd exploded as a breakaway was foiled.

Gio put his hand on Aiden's shoulder. "Listen, man. Don't be dicking around if forever isn't what you're after. You want to keep it light? Fine, do that. But don't be getting into her head if you're looking to jump ship next week, got it?"

"Fair enough," Aiden agreed. He didn't know if forever was what he wanted, but he sure as hell wanted more than just next week.

"Good. Because I'd hate to have to beat the shit out of you after courtside seats," Marco chimed in. "I mean, I'd still do it. But I'd probably be pulling my punches a bit."

"Hey, so what's it like being able to buy whatever you want?" Gio asked.

~

"HELLO, BEAUTIFUL," Aiden answered Frankie's call, plugging his other ear with a finger so he could hear her over the din.

"I saw you and the two stooges on TV," she told him.

"I hope you recorded it."

"I did. I even took some still shots of them climbing you like a tree on that last second three-pointer. You do remember which member of the family you're dating, don't you?"

He grinned.

"Is that, Frankie?" Gio hissed.

Aiden nodded. Marco grabbed a pen off of a waitress and scrawled a note on a beer napkin.

Don't say yes to the booty call.

"So, where are you guys?" Frankie asked.

"Celebrating with apparently half of Madison Square Garden in a bar," Aiden told her.

"You drinking?" she asked.

He had a vague recollection of his confession before falling asleep on her Sunday afternoon. He didn't know whether to be annoyed or pleased that she was looking out for him.

"One beer at the game. One beer here," he reported.

"Good boy."

He wanted to hate the way the praise she gave him made him hard. Made him want to see her, touch her, taste her.

Marco shoved another napkin in his face.

Stay strong!

"I live to serve," he said lightly.

Dismayed, Marco and Gio shook their heads.

"Are you coming back to Brooklyn with them?" she asked innocently. "I might have a cute, lacey nighty on."

He knew her better than that. She was in a tank top and leggings curled up under a mound of blankets.

"I don't think so, but you're more than welcome to come into the city," he offered. Thinking of her in his bedroom, her dark hair spread out on white sheets, the city lights shining through the windows. Aiden wanted her to say yes. Wanted it more than anything.

"I've got an early morning," she said. "Don't stay out too late."

"I'll talk to you tomorrow," Aiden said, wishing she'd change her mind.

"Goodnight, Aide."

"Goodnight, Franchesca."

35

*a*iden opened the front door of his apartment and, ignoring the fresh flowers on the foyer table, headed down the hallway to his bedroom. He deposited his wallet and cufflinks in their special compartments in his closet. He slid out of his suit jacket and shoes, returning both to their appropriate places before changing into jeans and his favorite Yale sweatshirt.

Comfort clothes.

It had been another tough day at work. The board had finally settled on a CFO candidate that they could all stomach. All except for Elliot. He'd stormed out of the meeting like a child having a tantrum. Their father ignored the show of temper and moved on to the next agenda item.

They'd all been far too lenient with Elliot, ignoring his absolute uselessness. Uselessness Aiden could deal with. He didn't like it but could accept it. However, the willful harm his half-brother was committing against the family and their business? That was a different story. Kilbourns were a lot of things. Manipulative bastards, cold-hearted sons of bitches, competitive enemies. But they never turned their back on family.

Aiden had broached the subject with his father after the meeting. Ferris had shut him down with a "Not now, son," and ushered him out the door.

As much money as he made Kilbourn Holdings, as much value as he added, his father still thought of him as a child to be guided.

But the unease that had settled into his gut had less to do with work and more to do with Franchesca. She was holding back with him everywhere but bed. It irritated him to extend invitations only to be consistently shut down. She acted as if she couldn't care less about his life. Yet when they were together he *knew* she felt it. That magnetic pull that had them orbiting around each other. There was a connection and while she seemed only interested in exploring that connection when he was shoving his cock into her, it wasn't enough for Aiden.

And that unsettled him.

He padded into the living room, his gaze settling on the decanter on the side table. It had become his habit to have a glass as soon as he walked in the door. And another one while he worked for another hour or two in his home office cleaning up what he hadn't gotten to during the day. And a third while reading or catching the game.

He didn't drink to get drunk. He drank to numb himself. It wasn't pain that he felt. It was something more nebulous. Dissatisfaction? Emptiness? Loneliness?

Looking around the rest of the room, was it any wonder? He'd hired a designer. People of his stature didn't choose their own furnishings. The company had done a reasonable job filling the place with things that he mostly liked or at least didn't have to think about. The leather couch was a little too modern, a little too hard. But it looked right in the space.

His father always commented that the wealthy didn't have

time to sit around on their furniture. They were too busy making money.

Aiden's mother had always rolled her eyes at the sentiment and insisted that Ferris sit and talk. They'd usually get five, maybe ten, minutes out of him before he heaved himself out of the silk upholstered wingback chair and headed back to work. Everything to his father was work. Success was defined by the number of hours a man put in and the number of zeroes in his portfolio. It was a cold way to look at the world. And Aiden had fallen into the same trap.

He traced a finger over the marble surround of the fireplace he never sat in front of. The leather club chairs flanking the fire had never held guests. The fully stocked bar built into the bookcase served only one.

He'd considered this place to be his sanctuary, but today it felt like a two-dimensional replica of a home, a life.

Aiden's gaze flicked back to the scotch. There was no siren's song coming from the crystal. Only a habit. He hated weakness, and the fact that he'd managed to develop a crutch without noticing it was embarrassing. He'd confessed to Frankie that he thought he drank too much. *Why had he told her that? Why had he given her that weapon?*

He scraped a hand over his face and wandered over to the piano he didn't know how to play. He didn't feel safe sharing things with her. Not when she'd clearly marked it as a one-way street. But he couldn't stop from offering up pieces of himself to her. Sacrifices to a cruel goddess, he mused.

Only she wasn't cruel. She wasn't disinterested. She was... careful. And maybe she had the right idea to remain distrustful.

The buzzer to his door sounded, and Aiden frowned. Very few people were cleared to this floor. His mother would have called first.

He crossed to the door and found his father on the other side of it.

Ferris Kilbourn strolled inside, hands in his pockets in a deceptively casual stance. Ferris and his wife, Elliot's mother, lived two blocks over in a stunning two-story penthouse. But despite the proximity, they rarely made social calls.

"This is a surprise," Aiden said, closing the door behind him.

"I thought it would be good to talk away from the office," Ferris told him, perusing the space as if he were a bored guest in a museum.

"Would you like a drink?" Aiden offered.

"Macallan?"

"Of course."

Aiden led the way into the living room and poured a glass. He hesitated and then poured a second. He handed one to his father and deliberately took a seat in one of the club chairs.

Ferris unbuttoned his jacket and sat down on the couch, stretching his arm across the back of it. Aiden had gotten his looks from his mother, all dark hair and blue eyes. His father had the gingery hair of his Irish heritage, most of it gone now. What remained was trimmed short. He was clean shaven and always, always in a suit. His father was the type of man who wore a tie on Christmas morning. And not a silly Santa tie, either. He preferred Hermès.

Aiden waited while his father gathered his thoughts. Neither appreciated the banality of small talk, and there was power in silence.

"I'm thinking of retiring," Ferris announced without preamble.

"Thinking about?" For his father to verbalize such a bombshell, he'd gone past the considering stage and into planning and implementing. But retirement shouldn't be in Ferris's vocabulary.

Ferris eyed his glass. "I've given my life to this company. We've achieved something your great-grandfather and grandfather couldn't have envisioned."

"And you're comfortable just walking away from it?" Aiden asked. He sat his untouched drink on the walnut side table and rested his elbows on his knees. His hands dangled between his knees.

"Jacqueline and I are getting a divorce," Ferris said, dropping the next boom as though he were casually commenting on the weather.

"I beg your pardon?"

"I've met someone else. My relationship with your stepmother has run its course. We've already spoken to our attorneys and are letting them hash out a settlement."

"Dad, what the hell is going on?"

Ferris sipped his scotch and sighed. "It might be a mid-life crisis, but son, this is the most fun I've had in my life. I think it's time I had some."

"I'm happy for you," Aiden said. He probably was. He wasn't entirely sure. He'd never developed more than a superficial relationship with his stepmother. And she'd rightfully favored her own son over Aiden. He couldn't say that he'd be sorry that he would no longer suffer through her incessant to-do lists that she nattered on about.

"I have to go to the salon and then the dermatologist. Then it's lunch with so and so's club. Soul Cycle afterwards. Then there's the board meeting for such and such. I don't see how I'm going to find the time to have dinner. People ask me how I do it. They just don't realize that I'm hanging by a thread!" Always a martyr.

"Her name is Alice, and she's a clothing designer. Not high fashion but outdoorsy, athletic lines. Smart, vivacious. We're going to take the boat down the coast and cruise the Bahamas this spring and summer."

Aiden made a mental note to contact the family law firm immediately and have an iron clad prenup drafted before Alice became a Kilbourn.

Aiden stared at the man who looked like his father but sounded like a complete stranger. However, as Ferris had taught him, it didn't pay to show surprise or confusion in any situation. Even if his father was losing his damn mind.

"Congratulations," Aiden said.

Ferris raised his glass in a toast. "I've built an empire. I think it's time I started enjoying the perks."

Mid-life crisis? Or perhaps an undetected brain tumor? Maybe a visit with the concierge doctor his father favored was in order.

"You certainly deserve to use your time as you see fit," Aiden responded.

"I wouldn't be doing any of this if I wasn't one-hundred percent confident in your ability to step into my shoes as CEO. You've been groomed your entire life for this, Aiden. I know you won't let me down."

"What about Elliot?" Aiden asked.

"I know you're not pleased with how I handled him over the Barbados situation—"

"He abducted someone, Dad."

Ferris at least had the good grace to look embarrassed. "It was a family matter that got out of hand."

"It was a felony no matter where it happened."

"He's always wanted to be you, son. And, unfortunately for him, he'll never be. You can't blame him for being rash with his decisions living in your shadow. He acts out because he's not you, and I can't see punishing him for that fact."

"Elliot does not put this family first. He doesn't put the business first. He puts himself first."

"And that's why I'm counting on you to lead him. Groom him into a Kilbourn man. I'll be the first to admit that he's an embarrassment."

An embarrassment? Aiden suddenly wanted that drink, but he forced himself to ignore it.

"He's not just an embarrassment. He's a danger. He wanted to put Boris Donaldson in our company for a reason." A reason Aiden had yet to discover.

"Elliot is harmless and misguided. I need you to take him under your wing. I need you to do this for me, Aiden. I know it's not easy. But when my father stepped down, I had to make tough choices, too. It's part of passing the torch. Someday you'll ask something of your son."

Aiden bit back a reply. He was forty fucking years old. His girlfriend wouldn't even consent to meet his parents, not that he could blame her now. Building a new generation to carry the weight of a family legacy was not on his to-do list.

"I'm about as far away from having a family as I can be," he told his father.

"Aren't you seeing someone?"

Aiden lifted an eyebrow. His father always had his fingers on the pulse whether it was business or family. "Where did you hear that?" he asked.

"I know you've been spending time in Brooklyn."

"And?"

"Defensive about her," Ferris mused. "Just make sure you're making the responsible choice for the family."

Aiden bristled. "Dad, you walked in here and told me you're leaving your socialite wife for a woman who makes cargo pants."

"I've served my time. I've made every decision for the last

fifty years with family and responsibility in mind," Ferris said coldly. "It's your turn now. And we both know this Baranski woman isn't the kind of wife a Kilbourn needs by his side."

Aiden shook his head in disbelief. No, Frankie wasn't a woman to stand quietly in the wings. She belonged on center stage.

"I'm asking you to give me this, Aiden." Ferris wasn't a man who wasted time on please or thank you. "I'm asking you to choose family first."

36

*A*iden stared at the glass on the side table. His father had gone home to get ready for some event or another with Jacqueline. They'd decided to continue their appearances together through the end of the month before quietly parting ways. Jacqueline would go to the no-longer family home in Provence for a few weeks. Ferris would announce his retirement and then whisk Alice away to the home in St. Barths. Everything would blow over while they were gone.

And Aiden would be left to pick up the pieces.

He picked up the glass and took it into the kitchen. It was all dark wood and white marble. A room he rarely if ever used. Every once in a while, if he couldn't sleep, he'd whip up a grilled ham and Brie. He had a feeling tonight would be one of those nights.

His father had lost his sense of familial duty. The man had confessed that running the company had killed his soul and then turned the keys over to Aiden without a thought as to the effects on his son's. There was no "there's more to life than business, son." No "you've done so much for us, you deserve to take a step back and focus on something you care about." But that was his father: selfish with zero self-examination. Why would Ferris think about others when he paid them to think about him?

He had assistants getting him his afternoon almond toffee snack. He had a personal chef that made his favorite meals in a specifically choreographed rotation. He had a wife who organized his social calendar to include only the most advantageous events. And he had a son who would run the family business while he abandoned all responsibility for a new girlfriend who made fucking windbreakers and cargo pants.

He glared at the glass, channeling all of his anger into the crystal and McCallan. He didn't feel much better after he shattered the glass in the sink. But at least he hadn't felt some overwhelming desire to drown his sorrows.

He thought of Frankie. Of the departure from this life that she offered. She was a respite from Kilbourn business. From the constant battle for success. Maybe there was something more productive he could do with his time.

He left the mess for later, grabbed a water from the refrigerator, and headed down the hallway into his private office.

The file was where he'd left it, front and center on his desk. He opened it and propped his bare feet up on the corner of the desk. One of their holdings was a small security firm that did an excellent job quietly digging into people's lives.

Frankie had twenty-one thousand dollars in student loan debt. Not bad considering the fact that she'd returned to NYU for her MBA. He could make that disappear within hours. He planned to. If he could get the slightest inkling of interest out of her. It was a point of pride that he could take care of those closest to him. But when one of those select few did everything she could to shut him out, he would tread lightly.

Perhaps there was another gift that would be more beneficial to them both? He picked up his desk phone and dialed.

"It's Aiden Kilbourn. How soon can you make a delivery for me?"

~

AIDEN PUSHED ASIDE the contract his team of very well-paid lawyers had spent weeks dissecting and moved on to the newest candidates for chief information officer at another holding. For a software firm, their management was woefully antiquated. He fired off an email to the current CEO saying he found it hard to believe the only candidates for the position were white men over the age of fifty. He suggested they restart the search with a more "interesting and energetic" crop of candidates.

The Knicks game was on in the background, drawing his attention more often than usual as he'd found himself added to the text message conversation between Frankie's brothers about the game.

It was after ten, not nearly late enough to consider turning in. He slept on average five, possibly six, hours a night. But the day, the evening, had taken its toll.

His phone vibrated from under a stack of papers. Reflexively, he checked the TV to see what was happening with the game, but it was a time out.

Frankie: Why are there three men with a mattress at my front door at 10:30 at night?

Aiden: Your bed is a disgrace to beds everywhere.

Frankie: It's my bed!

Aiden: Well, you're not the only one sleeping in it now.

Frankie: Don't you think you should have run this by me?

Aiden: And this is how that conversation would have gone. You: No. Me: Yes. You: Fuck you, Aiden. Me: Fine, but it's going to be on this nice new king-size. You: *has several orgasms on new bed* Okay, we can keep the bed.

Frankie: You're insane.

Aiden: You're welcome.

A few seconds later she sent another text. It was a selfie on the new mattress.

Frankie: I'm willing to give this bed and the aforementioned orgasms a shot.

He laughed despite himself. He knew what she needed. He was eager to give it to her. But everything with Frankie was a battle.

He started to type a reply and changed his mind. He'd take a shower and read until he got out of his own head, he decided.

He made it as far as the bedroom before his phone rang. Frankie.

"Hi," he answered.

"Hello, secret bed buyer. Where do you even get a king-sized bed and mattress at 10 o'clock at night?" Frankie asked.

"I have a guy," Aiden joked.

"Are you okay? You sound... off."

Aiden sat down on the edge of the bed and stretched out. "Nothing I can't deal with," he said, flippantly.

There was a pause on her end. "Wanna talk about it?" she offered.

Did he?

"I wouldn't even know where to start," he admitted.

"You're not just patting me on the head and shooing me away so the menfolk can talk business, are you?"

It was exactly the kind of behavior Ferris treated his wives to.

"Gorgeous, you know more about business than I do."

She laughed huskily, and it went straight to his chest. "Let's hope my Corporate Social Responsibility professor thinks like you do. So, what happened?"

"My dad came over tonight."

"Hmm, not enough information for me to make snap judgements and offer unwarranted advice. Keep going."

Aiden covered his eyes with his free hand and soaked in the sound of her voice.

"He announced that he's retiring at the end of the month."

"Holy shit. Stepping down as chairman of the board?"

"Walking away from everything. Oh, and he and my step-mother are getting a divorce."

"Mid-life crisis?"

"If you can have one at sixty-five. There's a girlfriend."

"Of course there is. Let me guess, a dancer? No, wait, not classy enough. Oh! A museum docent?"

"An athletic apparel designer."

"Nice! You finally have an in for all the sports bras you've been wanting."

Aiden's lips curved. "I wish you were here." The words were out in the world before he could stop them.

She sighed into the phone. "Maybe sometime. But for now, I wish you were here in this big bed with me."

Just imagining her stretched out, her wild hair fanning out in all directions, stirred him.

"So, what does this mean for you? You're COO—I Googled you—what happens next?"

"I make the move to CEO, take on more responsibility, including the care and maintenance of one Elliot Kilbourn."

"You're shitting me. That man-child is an epic asshole. Why would your father let him within five-hundred yards of the company?"

"He's blinded by Alice the sports bra designer."

"Funny. So your dad is dumping all his responsibilities on you so he can what? Retire on a topless beach in Boca?"

"Sail down the Intercoastal Waterway and spend the summer in the Bahamas."

"Is he going to change his mind?" Frankie asked hopefully.

"I don't think so. He wants me to carry on in the business and family."

"Oh," she said flatly. "You mean find a nice billionaire debutante and create perfect male heirs."

It was amazing exactly how much Frankie understood about the inner workings, the expectations of his life.

"Something like that."

"Did you buy me a bed to break up with me?"

Aiden laughed, and the sound echoed around the quiet room. "I bought you a bed to fuck you on without dumping us on the floor."

"I'm not mistress material, Aide."

"No, you're not. My father also wants me to groom Elliot for a VP position. Something respectable."

"Eeesh. Sounds like your dad's asking for a unicorn for Christmas. Never gonna happen."

It was simple for her. When presented with a decision, if it wasn't satisfactory, turn it down, move on. But his life was so much more complicated than that. Where was the gratitude for everything the previous generations had built that he now enjoyed? Shouldn't he be happy to sacrifice for that legacy as his father had?

"So, you're not out shopping for a wife right now?" Frankie asked.

"They don't exactly have stores for that," he said dryly.

"Oh, I don't know. Everything can be bought for a price."

"What's your price, Franchesca?"

"Hmm. I guess it depends on the currency."

37

J anuary gave way to the icy fingers of February. New Yorkers spent the month shivering their way from building to building on gray, slushy sidewalks. But Frankie stayed warm enough with Aiden in her apartment at least three nights a week.

They were getting along better than she would have imagined. He was smart and funny and horrifyingly generous. The new bed had been broken in, and now when Frankie went to bed alone, it was in the middle, hugging the pillow he'd used last.

She tried not to think of the countdown clock. His relationships usually lasted between two and three months. They'd been going strong for six weeks. It was longer than she thought they'd survive. In fact, neither one of them was showing any signs of slowing down.

Frankie finished up the email she was working on and fired it off. It was her half-day today, and with her evening class canceled for the evening, she had a luxury she wasn't used to. Several unfilled hours. She thought about texting

Aiden to see if he would come out tonight, but as he'd been there last night, it wasn't likely.

She turned to eye the flowers he'd sent this morning. Raul liked to joke that if Brenda had turned the office into a greenhouse with her pretty plants everywhere, Frankie's boyfriend had turned it into a tropical rainforest.

These were exotic and colorful with green spikes.

Wild and beautiful. Just like you.
    —A.

Frankie's phone rang from the desk drawer, and she retrieved it.

"Well, if it isn't my old married friend Mrs. Stockton-Randolph," she answered.

"Frankie! Tell me you don't have plans for lunch," Pru squealed into the phone. "I haven't seen you in a thousand years, and I need you to tell me if I look like an old married lady."

"Send me a selfie so I can see first. I don't want to be seen in the city with some old lady," Frankie teased.

Ever the obedient friend, Pru sent her a selfie with crossed eyes and a scrunched nose.

"Yeah, I'm definitely not being seen with that."

"Har har. It's your half-day, isn't it?"

"It is. I get off in twenty."

"Well get off and get your ass downtown. I want all the dish on you and a certain most eligible bachelor who's been seen smiling from time to time since he got back from my wedding."

"Smiling you say?" Frankie asked. So maybe she wasn't the only one walking around with a stupid grin on her face.

"Meet me at The Courtyard in an hour," Pru ordered.

"Yes, ma'am."

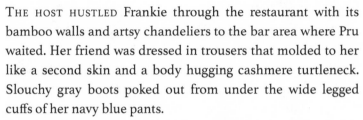

THE HOST HUSTLED Frankie through the restaurant with its bamboo walls and artsy chandeliers to the bar area where Pru waited. Her friend was dressed in trousers that molded to her like a second skin and a body hugging cashmere turtleneck. Slouchy gray boots poked out from under the wide legged cuffs of her navy blue pants.

They hugged as if it had been years rather than a few weeks.

"Well, marriage certainly agrees with you," Frankie quipped, sliding into the leather backed booth.

"I'd say that dating Aiden agrees with you," Pru said, eyeing her coat.

"Yeah, keep it down, okay?" Frankie glanced around the restaurant. It was one of the places where important private conversations were often overheard for the gossip columns.

"Tell me everything," Pru demanded.

"There's not much to tell," Frankie fibbed. She wasn't exactly prepared to put into words the feelings she had surrounding Aiden. They weren't identifiable at this point, and she was in no hurry to hash them out.

"You've been dating the most eligible bachelor on the eastern seaboard for six weeks, and there's yet to be a picture of the two of you together. You never bring him up. You only don't talk about men when you're really serious."

"We're not serious," Frankie said. "We're just having fun, enjoying the ride."

Pru snorted into her still water at "the ride." "Oh, I bet you are."

"He's great. Okay? He's smart and funny, so much more

than the gorgeous son of a bitch I thought he was. Happy?" Frankie asked.

The waitress appeared and rattled off the daily specials. Pru ordered the kale salad with steamed chicken. Frankie ordered a beer and a turkey panini with fries.

"Why do you do this to me? All my snotty rich friends order green juice and plates of air," Pru lamented.

Frankie took a bite out of one of the breadsticks the waitress delivered. "I'm your snotty poor friend, and I love carbs. I thought your stupid diet was over the minute the dress came off?"

"I'm on a new diet called fat blast the honeymoon weight."

Frankie shoved the breadstick in Pru's face and waved it from side to side. "Eat me. Eat meeeee..."

"God, I miss you," Pru sighed, snatching the breadstick out of her hand and taking a tiny nibble out of it.

"You rebel, you," Frankie teased. "I miss you, too."

"So, tell me about Valentine's Day. What did Aiden the perpetual bachelor do for you?"

"Well, he tried to surprise me with a long weekend in San Francisco. He had to go for business, but I couldn't get away. So he ended up bringing over take out when he got back, and he got me a bracelet."

A very *nice* bracelet. One that was too nice to actually wear. But she did open the swanky case and stare at the diamonds every night.

"Jewelry already? Margeaux would be impressed and dying of jealousy. What did you do for him?"

"I got him a Knicks hat."

Pru sat waiting expectantly. "And?"

Frankie shrugged. "And that's it. Well, I did flash him from the fire escape when he got to my place."

Pru looked like she smelled something funny. It was her

concentrating face that Frankie recognized from a few years of finals weeks.

"What?"

Pru shook her head, her honey blonde hair never moving from its sleek knot at the base of her neck. "Nothing. Hey, let's do dinner tonight! The four of us! We can go to The Oak Leaf."

Frankie wrinkled her nose. "Eh. Doesn't Page Six camp out there?"

Pru rolled her eyes. "Who cares? Their crab puffs are to die for, and I miss you, and I want to see you and Aiden together so I can give you my official seal of approval. I'm texting Chip right now."

"I don't know what Aiden's doing tonight," Frankie began to argue.

"So text him. Find out," Pru said without looking up. "It's Friday night. You're already here. You can stay at Aiden's."

"I've actually never been there," Frankie said, taking a bigger bite of breadstick. It lodged in her throat.

Pru dropped her phone on the table with a clatter. "I'm sorry, what? You've been dating him for almost six weeks, and you haven't seen his place yet? Is he taking you to hotels like some skank?"

A few of the closer diners shot glances their way.

"I'm not a skank," Frankie promised them. "She's just running lines for a play." Everyone went back to their meals. "Can you try to keep it down, please?"

"I can't believe he hasn't invited you to his place. I really thought this was different. Chip said he's never seen Aiden so—"

"Relax, Cujo. He's invited me plenty of times."

"And?" Pru looked at her like she was talking to an idiot.

"And I live in Brooklyn. By the time I get over here and we do our thing, I'd have to spend the night or go straight to work.

Take the train..." She trailed off, feeling a sliver of something uncomfortable.

"I see. So, when do you see each other?" Pru asked.

Frankie shifted uncomfortably. "When he comes to Brooklyn."

"And how often is that?"

"Three or four nights a week," she said. Five times last week.

"I see," Pru said primly. "And what kind of events have you gone to with him? Any fundraisers? Galas? The theater?"

Frankie shook her head to each one.

"Have you met his family?" Pru asked.

"Uh, no. He wanted me too, but the timing wasn't right. He did meet mine."

Pru brightened considerably. "Really? How did it go?"

"Well, I mainly did it to piss my mom off. Like 'Hey, Ma, here's this gorgeous guy I'm seeing. But guess what, we're just fooling around. No future here. Burn.'" Frankie laughed nervously but quit when Pru didn't join her.

Pru pinched the bridge of her nose. "Frankie, I'm going to say this with love because I do love you, and I want you to be happy. But you have got to quit the Frosty the Bitch Queen routine before you ruin something amazing."

"Excuse me?"

The waitress reappeared with their meals. "I'll leave you two to it then," she said when the silence at the table grew awkward.

"Frosty the Bitch Queen?" Frankie repeated.

"Don't even pretend you don't know what I'm talking about. You are freezing Aiden out. Why in God's name, I have no freaking clue. But you're trying to sabotage this thing. Do you want to be right that badly?"

Frankie's jaw was on the table.

"And while I'm talking and you're listening, Aiden inviting you to his home, to meet his parents, to go to San Fran? He's trying to share his life with you, jackass. And you're basically kicking sand in his face."

"That's not what I'm—"

"Bullshit." Pru stabbed her salad with such violence Frankie thought she saw the kale shrivel. "I get that you're protecting yourself, but you don't need to hurt him to stay safe."

Frankie swallowed hard.

"It's just a fling." She said it to remind Pru and herself.

"That's no excuse to treat him like Margeaux treats her housekeeper."

Frankie brought her hands to her face. She was trying to protect herself. But that was no excuse for purposely rejecting him. Had she hurt Aiden? It wasn't her intention. Though if the tables were turned... "I'm such an asshole."

"Frosty bitch queen," Pru corrected with less vehemence.

"He's done everything for me, and all I've done is reject him."

"Good," Pru said, pointing her fork at Frankie. "That's the guilt I want to see. This is not like you to treat someone as less than."

"How do I fix it?" Frankie asked.

"We start with dinner tonight."

"You still want to go with me even though I'm Asshole the Frosty Bitch Queen."

Pru looked down her nose piously, "My dear, some of us can afford to forgive."

"Oh. Nice. Now who's the asshole?" Frankie asked.

"I didn't want you to feel all alone up there on your high horse."

"I'll ask him about dinner tonight. But I'll do it in person," Frankie decided.

"Good girl. You can meet me at the salon afterward, and we'll go shopping so you have something amazing to wear to start your apology tour."

Frankie eyed her sandwich. "You, uh, wouldn't happen to know where he works, would you?"

"You are the worst."

38

---

*A*iden left the conference room feeling vaguely annoyed. He didn't care for the old adage, 'If you want something done right, you'd better do it yourself.' However, with the fresh crop of new hires in human resources and marketing, he felt like it would be faster to do their jobs for them.

He made it a point to meet with new hires periodically throughout their first year with the company. He found that flattening the layers of the corporation led to more natural communication and a better absorption into the corporate culture.

But the early meetings were always a pain in the ass. No, Kilbourn Holdings didn't need its own podcast. And no, they were not replacing all of the desk chairs with bean bags and exercise balls and opening a juice bar downstairs.

He nodded at his admin, Oscar, a thin, fashionable dictator with a French accent who ruled Aiden's calendar with an iron, manicured hand.

"Well, that ran long," Oscar announced, glaring at his

Rolex watch, a gift from Aiden for the man's tenth anniversary of dealing with Kilbourn drama.

"I don't suppose you have lunch waiting for me like a good admin," Aiden shot back. Their relationship was closer to that of Frankie's brothers than boss and employee.

"Ah, I have something better than that waiting for you," he said, pointing at Aiden's closed office door. "I approve, by the way."

Aiden frowned and let himself into his office. The sight of Frankie sitting behind his desk swiveling in his chair jarred him hard enough that he froze to the spot for a moment. Oscar closed the door behind him with a stage whisper. "Have fun."

"Hi," Frankie said, ceasing her swiveling.

"Hi," he responded, still shocked to find her in his office. She was dressed for work in a neat little suit that made him want to unbutton the jacket and slide his hands inside. She looked nervous. Something he wasn't used to seeing on her face. Not his confident, energetic Franchesca.

"I hope you don't mind me dropping by," she began, rising from the chair.

"No! Not at all! I mean..." He couldn't seem to regain his composure. He was so damn happy to see her. "I'm really happy to see you," he admitted.

"Yeah?" she asked beaming at him. "I was in town for lunch with Pru, and I well, we... Do you have dinner plans?"

He did. Business ones. But having Frankie here in his office asking him for anything trumped that.

"I'm yours," he said. He meant it.

She flushed and crossed tentatively to him, a paper bag in her hand. "I was hoping you'd be free for dinner with Pru and Chip tonight."

"What's in the bag?"

"I know you don't get a lot of time for lunch, so just in case you didn't get it yet today I brought you a sandwich."

"Is it a Baranski sandwich?" he asked snatching the bag from her.

She laughed. "Gio really made an impression on you, didn't he? Remind me to make you a club sometime. You'll worship me."

He already did.

His gaze must have told her as much because she looked down at her shoes and then the bag in his hand. "It's not one of ours, but it's a deli a few blocks away that's almost as good as us. Don't tell Dad."

"Your secret is safe," he promised.

"Why did Oscar let me in?"

"I told security and reception that you had free rein to come and go as you pleased."

"When did you tell them that?" Frankie asked.

"The day after I got home from Barbados."

She bit her lip and dipped her head.

"Is something wrong?" Aiden asked, nudging her chin up to look at him.

"There was, but now there isn't," she said firmly.

"Can I ask what?"

She shook her head. "Uh-uh. It's better that you just go with it."

"Then that's what I'll do." He grabbed her wrist and towed her back to his desk where he spread the sandwich out on the bag. Hot roast beef, and was that a whiff of horseradish?

"I had them leave the onions off in case you had meetings today," Frankie said. She was back to chewing on her lower lip.

"Do I have to share this with you, or am I good to inhale the entire thing?" he asked, keeping the tone light.

"Inhale away. I had a turkey panini and watched Pru choke down six pounds of kale."

"How are the newlyweds?" he asked.

"Glowing like all the lights in Paris," Frankie sighed and perched on the edge of his desk. "She looks great and says Chip's eye is all healed. Is The Oak Leaf at eight good for you?"

He would rearrange whatever it took to clear his schedule. Oscar would whine about the last-minute changes, but Aiden finally had a social occasion that trumped any business.

"That's fine," he promised.

"There's one more thing," she said. Frankie was watching him closely. "Is it okay if I stay the night at your place? Since I'm already here and all—"

"I'd love that," he said, taking her hand and kissing her knuckles. His blood was already roaring through his veins with the thought of Franchesca naked on his bed. Franchesca eating breakfast at his table. Franchesca lounging on his couch or arguing with him over something in his office.

He didn't know what had caused this abrupt about-face, but he was grateful.

She glanced at her watch. "I should probably head out soon. I'm meeting Pru and we're going shopping."

Aiden reached for his wallet and stopped when Frankie pressed her stilettoed foot to his chest. It gave him a direct line of sight up her skirt. "I can buy my own dinner dress, Kilbourn."

He didn't know whether to be incredibly turned on with the heel pressing into his pec or annoyed that, once again, she was rejecting him. He decided it was okay to be both.

"Fuck it. Franchesca, this is the one thing I have to offer you, and when you refuse it, it cuts at me."

"Aiden!" she gasped his name in shock and some anger if he wasn't mistaken.

Damn it. Why did he have to open his mouth? It never paid to show someone your vulnerability.

Frankie moved her shoe and surprised him by sliding onto his lap. "You think your wallet and your cock are the only reasons I'd be with you?"

He felt his cock thicken at her words. He knew she had to feel him lengthening under her, her skirt pushed up around her hips.

"Do you think that?" she asked again. Those eyes were more blue than green here under the office lights. And they tore at pieces of his soul.

He shrugged. "I don't know. Maybe." Yes.

"Then I haven't done a very good job at being your girl-friend," she sighed. She gripped him by the tie, and he went fully hard under her.

"New deal, Aide. I'm not doing all the taking anymore. Starting now."

She slid off his lap, and he was still reaching for her when she shoved his chair away from the desk.

When her fingers met his belt buckle, the breath left his body, and he seized up like rigor mortis. "What... we can't... what if..."

All thoughts and corresponding words left his brain with the last ounce of blood that plummeted to his aching cock. How could one woman make him feel this free, this terrified?

In seconds, she had his cock freed from his pants. "Are you sure your man out there will keep people out?" Frankie asked. But she wasn't looking at him. She was looking at his erection that she held firmly in her hand.

Aiden couldn't even find the words to answer her, and Frankie didn't seem to need them because she was opening her mouth and slicking her tongue over his dick from root to sensitive crown.

He crashed back against his chair and watched in fascination as she did glorious things to his dick with her mouth.

"I want to touch you," he gritted out when she took him to the back of her throat.

"Mmm, tonight. For now, this is just for you." Frankie focused her mouth on things much more important than words.

She was slick and hot, and the feel of bottoming out against the back of her throat nearly did him in.

In ecstasy, Aiden's head fell back against the leather cushion of his chair. She was pumping him with her fist and using her mouth, a heady combination. He'd walked into this room frustrated and tired, and in seconds, she'd turned his entire day around.

Her tongue did something particularly insane to the tip of his dick, and he felt his balls tightening.

"Franchesca," he hissed.

"I've got you, baby," she promised, kissing his cock before resuming her attention with her mouth. She was no longer languid with her strokes. No. Frankie was hollowing her cheeks and sucking hard enough that he saw stars.

He couldn't close his eyes though. He wanted this vision of her on her knees in front of him sucking him off. Wanted it forever.

Aiden dug his heels into the rug for traction, fearing that he'd become weightless and float away. He felt it build at the base of his spine and marveled at the witchcraft that brought him to orgasm so quickly.

Giving up all pretense, he gripped her head with both hands and let loose a guttural groan when she let him take over. Fucking her mouth with short, shallow thrusts, he lost himself in the moment. He meant to pull out. But then he was coming, jerking convulsively and pouring his release down her throat.

He went silent as the orgasm ripped through him, hollowing him out even as it filled her mouth.

Nothing. *Nothing* in this world could have prepared him for the sight of Franchesca at the receiving end of his cock, taking everything he gave without asking for anything in return. He shuddered and collapsed back into the chair, blood rushing in his ears.

She rose from her knees, a goddess no matter her position. She crossed the room and peered inside, finding his private bathroom. Aiden would have directed her to it, but he was a shell of a man right now. Leveled by beauty and desire.

She returned with a warm, damp washcloth and cleaned him thoroughly.

"I haven't been a very good girlfriend. I'm hoping to improve my score," she confessed, gently tucking him back into his underwear. "You're a good man, Aiden. You're smart, you're funny, you're unbelievably patient. If I asked you for Cleveland, Ohio, you'd find a way to deliver it to me. You're insanely generous and surprisingly sweet, and I'm sorry I haven't been appreciative of it."

"Gah." It was the best he could provide verbally after having been completely decimated.

"So I'm going to do a better job, and I'm going to expect you to hold me to a higher standard." She perched back up on his desk, and he swore he could smell her arousal. He would have fucked her. He would have given her anything she wanted just for visiting him. But she wanted to change the way things were.

Aiden managed a shaky breath and then another one,

slowly feeling the life return to his body. "I have an addendum to our deal as well," he told her.

She watched him warily.

"I'm not suggesting forever," he began. "But I would like to table the 'temporary' aspect of our relationship."

She stopped breathing, freezing in place like a rabbit in front of a predator.

Aiden reached out, shifting his chair so he was in front of her. "You're special to me, Franchesca. And I don't foresee a point when you won't be."

"Jesus," she blew out her breath. "That must have been some BJ," she said.

"See? That's what I'm talking about."

"The blow job?" she asked cheekily.

He pinched her.

"Ouch! I'm kidding," she said.

"Forget the fact that you're beautiful beyond belief. You're sharp and mean when you need to be. You have no filter. I've never known anyone who didn't carefully weigh every word. You're a breath of fucking fresh air in my life."

"Aide, you've got me shaking in my boots here," she admitted.

"All in, Franchesca. You and me."

She blew out a slow breath and stared at the ceiling. "What if we fuck it up?"

He squeezed her hips. "I won't let you."

She laughed. "Ass," she said.

He saw the shimmer of tears behind her long lashes. "I'm asking you to take me or leave me," he told her.

"You ever have this conversation with anyone else you dated?" she asked.

He shook his head. "Not even close. You and me, Frankie."

"I feel like I'm gonna throw up," she admitted, clutching her hand to her belly.

He saw it then, the fear, the nerves. And he made the conscious choice to push the button. "I never would have thought I'd see the day when Franchesca Marie Baranski was too scared to go after what she wanted."

It was a manipulation, but damn it, he needed this. He needed her.

She nodded, her lips pressed tight. "Okay. All in."

He rose, lifting her off the desk in a tight embrace.

"You won't regret it, Franchesca."

39

"Judging from the fingerprints on your neck, things went well with Aiden," Pru said, eyeing Frankie as she flopped down in the salon chair next to her.

Frankie was too emotionally drained to argue. "You were right, and I was a horrible person," she admitted, pouting in the mirror.

"When you know better, you do better," Pru chirped from under her foils.

"We're officially in a 'real' relationship, and I threw up my panini on my way out of the building."

"You have a cast iron stomach," Pru pointed out.

"Yeah, okay, so that part didn't actually happen. But thanks to you, Aiden and I are," she swallowed compulsively, "a couple."

"I have the perfect way for you to thank me."

"I just made it up to Aiden under his desk. What the hell do you want from me?"

Pru pointed at Frankie. "Oh, Christian! My friend here needs something done with her mop."

A man dressed in head to toe black with a shaved head—irony of ironies—magically appeared behind her.

"Babe," he said plucking a curl and holding it between his fingers. "We can do so much better."

Places like this charged four-hundred dollars just for planting your ass in the chair, Frankie thought. She tried to stand, but Christian had some muscles under that tight black t-shirt.

"It's my treat," Pru sang out.

"You know I don't like when you do this," Frankie reminded her.

Christian whirled a cape around her and tightened it at her neck. "Now, what are we thinking?" he asked, holding her hair at varying lengths and glaring in the mirror as if looking for creative inspiration.

"We're thinking a nice little trim," Frankie said, snatching her hair out of his hand.

He grabbed another fistful. "A trim?" he scoffed examining the ends. "You have what? Eight months of damage."

"Don't you think she'd be gorgeous with some highlights?" Pru suggested.

"That tin foil is messing with your brain waves," Frankie shot back.

"Don't mind her, Christian. She's not usually this surly. Also, she's from Brooklyn," Pru said.

Christian spun her chair around and caught it by the arms. They were inches apart. "I need you to trust me. I do not do bad hair days. I do not deliver subpar cuts. If I give you highlights, you will wish you would have been born with them. I will make your hair into a miracle, but I need you to trust me."

"Do it!" Pru hissed in a stage whisper.

Frankie pointed an index finger at him. "If you fuck up my hair, months from now when you've forgotten all about me, when you're complacent, I'll wait for you in the alley, throw you into a dumpster full of human hair and perm chemicals."

"And if I make you look like the kind of woman who doles out whiplash from second glances, you'll come back and let me touch up your highlights," he bargained.

She offered her hand. "Deal."

"Her boyfriend likes it long and wavy," Pru added helpfully.

"Oh, so I have a boyfriend now, and I need to wear my hair to please him?" Frankie shot back.

Pru and Christian rolled their eyes heavenward in the mirror.

"I've got this," Pru sighed. "Look Frankie. When you're in a relationship, you don't live your life to please your partner. But you sure as hell don't figure out what they like and then run in the opposite direction to maintain some semblance of independence."

Christian shoved his fingers into her hair like he was hand washing laundry in a river, turning her head this way and that. "One of the greatest gifts to give in a relationship is something very small that costs you nothing."

Well, it was costing Pru four-hundred dollars.

Awesome. She was getting her hair cut by a Manhattan fashionista version of the poet Pablo Neruda.

She closed her eyes and let him do his worst. Flinching at the snips of the scissors and the tugs of the comb. She couldn't stop thinking about Aiden's face when he found her behind his desk. He'd lit up like Times Square. As if her mere presence was a gift.

She'd been holding on to the thought, the hope that Pru had been wrong. That she and Aiden were just having fun as they'd agreed. That he wasn't looking for more. That she wasn't secretly hoping he'd disappear so she could be right.

Would right have soothed her bruised heart if she'd succeeded in pushing him away?

She wasn't a cruel, callous person. She wasn't someone who crushed a person because she could. Yet, she'd been so determined to keep Aiden at a distance she'd rejected him every step of the way. And he'd stuck.

Seeing him *see* her? Unguarded joy. And if he was willing to be that vulnerable, the least she could do was meet him there.

After what felt like hours of fussing, she felt her chair spin around.

"Okay, open your eyes and take in my genius."

She opened one skeptical eye, prepared to see a purple Mohawk or something equally garish. But it was her own hair. A few inches shorter, curls more defined and certainly shinier, but it was her.

"Are those caramel highlights?" she asked, turning her head.

Christian scoffed. "Caramel highlights are for amateurs. "Those are macchiato lowlights."

She looked sleek, put together yet still herself. No longer did the static electricity of winter rule her head.

"Damn it, Christian. I really wanted to throw you in a dumpster."

"AIDEN IS GOING to drag you somewhere dark and semi-private within five minutes of seeing you in that," Pru guessed, poking her head into Frankie's dressing room. For an upscale boutique, there was a surprising lack of security in the dressing room area.

Frankie turned to the side to look at her ass in the scarlet red dress. It hugged her curves, dipping low at the breasts and skimming over her waist and hips.

"It's February. I can't wear sleeveless," she argued. Besides, this freaking swatch of fabric cost just under a grand. Aiden had slipped a credit card into her hand on the way out and ordered her to use it. But it felt... weird. A blow job and a credit card? They'd happened too close together. She needed to make it clear to herself that she wasn't Vivian from *Pretty Woman*.

"You'll have a coat, and I requested a table by the fireplace. You'll probably be sweating by the end of dinner," Pru predicted, sashaying around in a sleek black sheath.

"Why aren't your boobs on display for the world to see?" Frankie asked, glancing down at her own overflowing cleavage.

"I'm a married woman and a B cup, babe. There isn't much to display. And you're insane if you don't buy that dress."

Frankie studied herself in the mirror, barely recognizing herself. The hair, the dress, the diamond and—God, was that platinum?—bracelet that she'd just happened to have in her bag.

"You know what we need now?" Pru asked.

"I'm hoping you're going to say froyo, but I have a feeling it's shoes," Frankie sighed.

"Shoes!"

When Pru ducked back into her own fitting room, Frankie checked the price tag on the dress again. It made her feel ill.

She pulled out her phone.

Frankie: When you gave me this credit card, what kind of budget were you thinking?

Aiden: I doubt very much that there's anything you'd buy that would cause me to so much as blink.

Frankie looked down at the dress again. *Wanna bet?*

Frankie: I'd feel better if you could give me a number to stay under. I found a dress, but there are more digits than I'm used to. And Pru is chanting "shoes, shoes, shoes," one dressing room over.

She could picture him chuckling to himself at his back-woods girlfriend panicking over pennies.

Aiden: I love seeing you treat yourself. And I love it more that I can be part of it. How about keeping it under fifty grand for today?

He *had* to be fucking with her. Frankie couldn't begin to imagine a world in which fifty grand was blow money. Of course, knowing Aiden, he'd named a sum lower than usual to appease her.

Frankie: Oh, so I can't get this seventy-five thousand dollar dress? Too bad.

She added a disappointed meme.

Aiden: Maybe if you'd send me a picture of the dress, I could make a judgment call.

His playfulness eased her tension the tiniest bit. And maybe she could give him some tension of his own.

She snapped a selfie of mainly her boobs and sent it.

Aiden: I've never gotten an erection in an analyst meeting before. This is interesting.

Frankie laughed. She didn't know if he was kidding, or if he really was texting her during a meeting. Either way, she felt lighter. And if he thought fifty-grand was an acceptable level of spending, then her pretty dress and a pair of shoes wouldn't kill either of them.

"Okay, Pru. Where are we going for shoes?"

40

*F*rankie spent more time prepping for this double date than she had her senior prom and the two weddings she'd been in combined. She had been plucked, glossed, lotioned, and smoothed and was starving to death by the time their car pulled up in front of the restaurant.

Chip and Pru extracted themselves from the permanent embrace marriage seemed to have sewn them into.

"Aiden's here," Pru said, pointing at the limo in front of them. All limos looked the same to her, so she took their word for it.

Frankie felt her blood sing. She wanted to see him here on his own turf. See what she'd been missing out on. She wanted to watch his pupils dilate when he got his first good look at her in this damn dress. She wanted him to be proud to have her on his arm.

And she wanted to eat some goddamn dinner.

"Just two photographers," Chip said, glancing out the window. "They must not have seen Aiden yet."

Frankie gulped. "Why? Does he get a lot of attention?"

Pru and Chip exchanged a look. "You'll be fine. Be you," Chip said, patting her on the knee. He exited the car first and held a hand out for Pru.

Frankie saw the flash of a camera and rolled her eyes. Who in the hell in their right mind would camp out in front of a restaurant in February to snap a few pictures of people?

She stepped out next and immediately forgot about the photographers. There on the sidewalk in front of her was Aiden Freaking Kilbourn, and he was closing in on her like a lion on a slow, fat gazelle. The look in his eyes told her he was hungry, too. Just not for dinner.

Frankie felt a cold rush of air and realized she'd forgotten to button her coat. Aiden noticed too as the wind opened the cashmere, parting it.

She swore he licked his lips, and then his hands were on her and then his mouth. His touch ignited every nerve ending in her body as if they'd been waiting for this exact moment. It was chemistry, biology. Something hardwired into them both, and Frankie couldn't get enough of it.

He kissed her hard, licking into her mouth to stroke his tongue against hers, leaving no doubt to any witnesses exactly who she belonged to. Laying claim to her.

She didn't like being on display. Didn't like the attention. And she would have told him so if she hadn't been so busy clinging to him like a vine.

"So, we'll go get some drinks then," Chip said, pointing toward the restaurant and dragging the grinning Pru after him.

"Meet you crazy kids inside," Pru called after them.

"We'll be back," Aiden answered without looking away from her. There were flashes of light, and Frankie was dimly aware of questions being hurled at them both. And then

Aiden was tucking her under his arm and guiding her back to his limo. He opened the door and ushered her inside.

"Drive until I say so," he ordered tersely and then raised the privacy glass.

"What about dinner?" Frankie asked, sliding across the bench seat to accommodate him.

"We're having dessert first," he breathed, freeing her of her coat. His hands cruised her dress, stopping reverently just beneath her abundant cleavage.

"Do you know what happened after you sent that picture today?"

"What?" she breathed, needing him to touch her. Afraid that when he did, she'd cease to exist. She ran her palms over his thighs.

"I had to excuse myself from the meeting to jerk off in my bathroom.

Her breath was a shiver. "Did you think of me?"

"Gorgeous, I'm always thinking of you." He reached down and palmed his hard-on through his pants.

Frankie was instantly wet. "In a limo?" she hissed. She hated to admit it, but limo sex was on her bucket list.

"It has to be now, or I won't make it through dinner. Not with you in that dress."

His blunt honesty was as attractive to her as the predatory look in his eyes.

Game, Frankie slid a leg over his lap, leaving enough room that he could free himself from the confines of his pants. His thick length fell heavily into her hand. He was already leaking, and Frankie felt a thrill of power. Steadying her on his lap, Aiden reached around her into a compartment and produced a condom.

He'd probably had sex in this car a hundred times, Frankie

thought. But she'd be damned if this wasn't the only time burned into his brain forever.

While he rolled the condom on and stroked himself gratuitously, she inched the skirt of her dress up until it bunched around her hips. She shoved at the wide V-neck until it slid off her shoulders down her arms. The material hanging precariously from her breasts.

The low rumble in his chest was her reward.

He leaned over and pressed his face to her breasts, his beard rough against her skin. Frankie moved closer so the powerful strokes of his hand brought his cock in contact with where she needed him most desperately.

"It's going to be hard and fast, Franchesca," he warned her. "Once I'm inside you, I'm not going to stop until you're coming on me."

"Fuck me, Aiden," she breathed. It was an order, a plea.

He gripped her hips, positioning her with his tip probing her center, just outside her weeping entrance. With one hand, he yanked her thin-as-air underwear to the side.

His chest was heaving, his jaw clenched, and he hadn't even started fucking her yet. Aiden Kilbourn over the edge was a heady sight.

It was her last coherent thought as he thrust his hips up, driving into her with brutal force. He didn't give her a moment to get used to him, to relax around him. He jackhammered into her and used one hand to free her breasts from the dress. It had a built-in bra, so there was nothing left separating him from her heavy, needy tits.

"Aiden," she hissed when he closed his mouth over one nipple and sucked it hard. His thrusts never ceased. He growled into her breast, his hands gripping her hip so hard it made her cry out again.

It only made him fuck her harder.

He was out of control, suckling and thrusting, driving her completely mad. Frankie dug her hands into his shoulders and held on for dear life.

She couldn't breathe, couldn't think. She could only take what he was giving her. Life. Fire. Desire.

"So fucking perfect," he murmured against her flesh.

This dress had been the best extravagant purchase of her life.

She felt him thicken inside her, heard his breathing go ragged, and knew he was close. Aching to orgasm. Hanging by a thread.

He held her against him, shortening his thrusts to grind against her. It was beautiful, primal.

He released her nipple with a pop and moved to her other breast, his eyes bright and hard on hers. She watched him take the tip in his mouth, felt his tongue stroke over her. She had molten gold flowing through her veins. Her world went white hot and brilliant as her orgasm exploded without warning.

"Aiden!" She sobbed out his name as he thrust in to the hilt. His moan was low and guttural as he emptied himself into her. Even through the condom, she could feel him pulsing inside her, releasing his seed in a never-ending climax.

She came again, or still, as he rode out his orgasm. And when he finally went still beneath her, Frankie collapsed against him.

He wrapped his arms around her waist and held her close, pressing her breasts against his crisp shirt. He stroked her bare back with soothing sweeps of his hand. The praise he whispered in her ear made her blush. Her boyfriend was one dirty talker. And that was coming from a woman whose second word as a child was "fuck."

She felt like he'd taken her apart and put her back

together again. There was nothing like feeling Aiden inside her. Even now, after an orgasm that had hollowed him to the core, he was still semi-erect.

"Thank you for the dress," she whispered, her throat too raw for any volume.

He laughed softly against her hair. "Thank you for you."

41

$\mathcal{A}$iden clearly had clout at The Oak Leaf. The host didn't even blink when the limo pulled up in the alley. He merely led them through the kitchen, past the bar, to their table where Chip and Pru were arguing over tapas.

Frankie tried to ignore the curious glances in their direction. He was the most recognizable Kilbourn in the family and a permanent bachelor. There was bound to be interest.

Frankie slid into the booth first, and Aiden followed her, his hand clamping on her thigh under the table. She picked up the menu and pretended to peruse it, ignoring the expectant weight of Pru's stare.

"How are the clams here?" she asked innocently.

"Uh, *hi*. How was your limo sex?"

Frankie looked up at Pru who was resting her chin in her hands and grinning smugly.

"It was nice. Right, Aiden?" Frankie said haughtily, looking at him. His hair was mussed, but it could pass for purposeful styling. His tie was crooked. And the rest of him was, of course, flawless. She, on the other hand, looked as though someone had run a vacuum cleaner over her and then bit her in a few key places.

"Very nice. Highly recommended," he said, reaching for his water goblet and downing half of it.

He squeezed her thigh and moved his hand a millimeter higher on her thigh.

Teasing him, she hooked her shoe over his shin, opening her knees.

No one else would know just by looking at him, but he was already displaying his turn on tells. There was the flush at the neck, the flaring of his nostrils. She wished she could get a look at his crotch, betting money he was sporting wood again. The man was a freaking marvel. His orgasms probably had orgasms.

"So..." Pru began pointedly. "How's life?"

They dined on fabulous food, drank astronomically expensive wine and, in general, had a lovely time. Frankie eventually forgot about the curious stares and enjoyed watching Aiden relax. His reserved façade slipped around Chip. And he laughed more, smiled more, those sexy-as-hell crinkles showing at the corners of his eyes. Even while deep in conversation with his friend, Aiden still maintained a physical connection with her. Toying with her hair, stroking her shoulder with his thumb, or coaxing his fingers higher on her thigh.

Pru filled them in on their honeymoon. When residents of the Upper West Side marry in Barbados, they can't very well vacation there, too. Pru and Chip had spent another ten days in the Maldives. Frankie wasn't exactly sure geography-wise where the Maldives existed, but the pictures on Pru's phone were stunning.

It felt... normal. Blissfully so.

Well, as normal as a $73 pasta entrée could feel. A Friday

night with friends. For the first time, Frankie felt like they were a real couple. She wasn't the poor girl from Brooklyn. He wasn't the CEO and newly appointed family head.

He was very simply hers. Aiden, the man who drew every woman's gaze and snagged the check from Chip claiming the meal was a welcome home gift, belonged to her.

Frankie felt a rush of teenage girl giddiness sweep through her. Like she'd just spotted Pre-Jessica Simpson John Mayer across the restaurant.

"Girl bathroom break," Pru announced pushing Chip out of the booth so she could escape. "Let's go, Frankie. Give the boys a chance to miss us."

Pru all but hauled Frankie into the bathroom and then mauled her in a fierce hug.

"Okay. What the hell is this?" Frankie asked, awkwardly patting her friend on the back.

"You love him!" Pru squealed. "I've been waiting for the day when you look at a man the way you sat there and looked at Aiden."

"I don't love him," Frankie argued.

"You have this glow," Pru said, twirling around and checking her makeup in the mirror.

"It's a post-orgasm glow. He dragged me into his limo for sex, Pru. We're not decorating summer homes and naming babies."

"And the way he looks at you? I swear to God it singed my eyebrows off. He wants to eat you alive."

"Stop. You're all clouded with newlywed bliss, and you want everyone else to be in love right along with you."

"We should have babies together," Pru decided, reapplying her lipstick. "We could share a nanny."

"I love you, Pruitt, but you're fucking insane."

Pru grinned at her in the mirror. "I like seeing you happy. That's all. I promise. I'm mostly just teasing."

"You're such an ass," Frankie laughed.

"I may be an ass, but you sure photograph well," Pru said, handing over her phone.

"Are you kidding me?" Frankie scrolled through the post. It was a gossip blog with a series of pictures of Frankie and Aiden pawing each other on the sidewalk. "Oh my God, my mother is going to see these!"

"Your mother and anyone who's anyone in the city," Pru said, unsympathetically gleeful.

"This *just* happened! How is this even a story with..." she scrolled up again, "*three* updates since it was posted?"

Pru rolled her eyes. "Uh, don't you teach social media workshops?"

"To business people about businesses!" Frankie waved her arms at her friend. "Not some vapid readership that has an opinion on... my food order? What the hell is wrong with these people?"

"You're an exotic unknown on the arm of everyone's favorite bachelor. What did you expect?" Pru asked.

Pru's phone vibrated in Frankie's hand, and a text message popped up.

"How is that ethno-mutt dating Aiden Kilbourn?" Frankie read out loud.

"What?" Pru shrieked. "Is that in the comments?"

Frankie held up the phone. "Uh, no. That's your best pal Margeaux texting you."

"She's the worst human being in the history of human beings. The world is lucky she has no ambition besides getting another husband because, if she had any kind of drive, she'd be the new Hitler."

"How are you two friends?"

"We're definitely, definitely not. My father and her father are business partners. I was in her first wedding to a cocaine-snorting, prostitute-buying gambling addict. They made a lovely couple."

Frankie slumped against the wall. "Someone is telling the paparazzi what I'm eating for dinner. And hundreds of people are freaking out about it, including Hitler Junior. I'm not ready for this."

Pru marched up to her and stabbed a finger in her shoulder. "You listen to me Franchesca Marie, you can and will handle this. You are the one person in this world who has the ability to be completely immune to this kind of attention. And if you can survive it, your prize is Aiden. So suck it up. You're dating a guy who gives you an excuse to hang out with me and Chip in Manhattan on a Friday night. I'm not letting you make a mess of it."

"Don't tell me you were tired of schlepping to Brooklyn for cheap pizza and movies?" Frankie joked, but she felt the familiar unease return. It was another reminder that she didn't belong in this world. At the end of the day, she was just a girl playing dress-up for the night.

Could she really survive keeping a foot in both worlds?

42

"It's still early," Pru said, checking Chip's watch.

There was nothing early about a dinner that wrapped at 11 p.m., Frankie thought, stifling a yawn. "Do you guys want coffee, or do you want to hit a club?" Chip offered.

Frankie slid her gaze to Aiden's. "No thanks," they said together.

"They're going for Round Two," Pru explained with a wink at Chip.

"That's not a bad idea," he said, winking down at his wife.

"You know, I kind of miss the eyepatch," Frankie mused to Chip.

Aiden texted his driver from the table to bring the car around and helped Frankie into her coat. The restaurant was much less crowded, but the crowd outside seemed bigger than before. The maître-d whispered something in Aiden's ear, and he frowned, nodded. Two gentlemen in suits appeared.

"What's going on?" Frankie asked.

"There's more paparazzi outside," Aiden said, glaring through the glass. "Security is going to clear the way for us."

"Clear the way? How the fuck many people are out there?" Frankie asked.

"Not that many," he said dryly. "I'm not in a boy band."

There were enough people milling about to Frankie's way of thinking. Sure, Bieber would have caused a fan frenzy, but there were still two dozen curious passers-by and seven guys with cameras when they left the safety of the restaurant. Security barreled their way through the crowd forcing the cameras back as Aiden tucked her under his arm and guided her to the waiting limo.

She was blinded by the flashes but otherwise unscathed. And the second Aiden slid in behind her, the door closed, sealing them off from prying eyes.

"Why do you eat here if you get that kind of response?" she asked, flopping back against the head rest.

The back of the limo still smelled faintly of sweat and sex.

"They're more interested in you and who you are to me," Aiden told her.

"Well, they better prepare for disappointment," Frankie shot back.

Aiden tugged her into his lap and reached inside her coat to hold her around the waist.

"It goes with the territory. Just like your mom slapping everyone. It's one of those things we all have to tolerate."

Frankie laughed and rested her head against his chest. She'd half expected him to jump her again the second they got in the car. But this was nice too. Very nice.

"You're breathtaking, Franchesca."

"Aide," she said softly.

He shook his head. "I'm not trying to give you a compliment. I'm warning you. They're going to find out who you are. They're going to want to know everything about you and put it up for public consumption."

"Why?" she asked.

"Because you're mine."

It was arrogant the way he stated it as fact. But damn it if she didn't like hearing that claim a little bit.

She opened her mouth.

"Don't argue with me," he warned her.

"It's what I do best," she teased, toying with the buttons of his shirt.

"Don't argue about not belonging to me. I belong to you. I'm yours. All in, remember? It goes both ways."

"All in," Frankie murmured.

AIDEN'S BUILDING was in the middle of everything important. Only three blocks from his office, he could walk should he choose to brave the masses. Though after witnessing the attention he attracted, Frankie didn't blame him for hiring a car. Not much fun feeling like a goldfish in a bowl on the commute to work. Where everyone else in the city was an anonymous stranger, Aiden's face and name was known far and wide.

And now Frankie was stepping into that orbit. Willingly.

The lobby was guarded by a uniformed doorman and a smartly suited woman in black behind a sleek U-shaped workstation. "Good evening, Mr. Kilbourn," she greeted him with a professional smile.

"Good evening, Alberta. This is Ms. Baranski," he said, nodding at Frankie as he pulled her along, never slowing his pace.

"A pleasure, Ms. Baranski," Alberta said.

"Nice to meet you," Frankie answered over her shoulder as she jogged to keep up with him.

Aiden was towing her toward the bank of elevators like a pack of hyenas were on their heels.

They stepped inside, and Aiden pulled a key from his coat pocket.

"Don't even," Frankie said, shaking her head.

"Don't even what?" he asked, sliding the key into the elevator control panel and pushing the P.

"Oh, come on! The penthouse? Really? Can't you at least pretend to be a normal guy?"

He stared at her with amusement in those blue eyes. "You are the first person who has ever complained about the penthouse," he observed.

"I'm not a fan of reminiscing about the horde of ladies you brought back here for naked times, Aide."

"Exactly how many women do you think I've been with?" he asked with a laugh.

"Enough."

One second he was standing in front of the button panel, and the next he had her pinned to the wall of the elevator.

"You know what I've never done?"

He planted his hands on either side of her head. He was a whisper away, as close to touching her from head to toe without actually making contact.

"What?" she whispered.

"I've never kissed anyone in this elevator." He trailed his lips over her jaw line to her neck and back again.

"Aren't they watching?" she asked, nodding toward the security camera.

"Does it matter?"

The soft of his lips, the rough of his beard—a contrast of sensations.

Frankie held on to the rail behind her. And when his lips closed over hers, she was glad to have the support. It wasn't a wild, passionate kiss. It was something different, something that ran deeper and sang in her bones.

The kiss bloomed like a rose under the heat of the sun. Opening and reaching for more.

His tongue slid lazily against hers, stroking, exciting, and soothing all at once.

"I'm so glad you're here." He said it like a confession. A dark one.

"I'm glad to be here. I get to find a flaw in you tonight. Maybe you're a hoarder. Maybe you have horrible taste in velvet paintings. Maybe you've got sixteen cats." She brought her arms around his neck. "I'm going to find what makes you human, Kilbourn."

The elevator doors slid open, and Aiden led her by the hand into a spacious foyer. White on white on white.

"Hmm, so far no cats," she observed.

He unlocked the door and pushed it open. "Maybe they're all hiding inside with my yard sale collection of eighties cassette tapes."

She slapped him on the shoulder. "See? There's my normal guy."

"Your version of normal is woefully odd."

She stuck her tongue out and sauntered past him inside. His foyer was the size of her entire apartment with about an acre of glossy white marble with gray veining. There was a pedestal table in the middle of the space with a vase of flowers. She touched a petal. Fresh flowers.

There was no mail piled up, no magazines scattered about, no jumble of keys and coupons. The living room stretched out in front of her. One open space with a wall of windows. Of *course* he had a killer view.

They were part of the city skyline from here.

The furniture was dark, leather, and arranged just so. He

had a bar stocked with every top shelf liquor known to man. A marble fireplace. Bookcases housed books and framed photos. Everything was neat, tidy, and maybe a little cold. There were no pillows or blankets on the couch. The white rug under the sitting area was thick as a cloud. The walls were dark—a contrast, she imagined to the white of the floor and the sunshine that would pour through that wall of windows.

He followed her as she wandered into the kitchen. It was a long galley style. Sleek, modern, and most likely never used. The island that divided the kitchen from the dining area stretched on forever. She could have climbed up on the granite and stretched her arms over her head and still not been able to touch both ends.

The dining table was just as long. Glass with metal legs. High-backed chairs ringed the table, ready and waiting for a party of twelve. There were more shelves in here. More photos. Some art, carefully colorful.

She glanced down the hallway but decided to stick to the main living space. In this dress, they wouldn't make it out of his bedroom until morning.

It was cool, beautiful, just like him. It also felt a little empty, a little lonely. And she wondered if that too reflected the owner.

Aiden was watching her, leaning against the island and working his tie free. He slid the silk out of his collar and coiled the tie on the counter.

"What do you think?" he asked.

"It's very beautiful." And it was. A showplace. She did not want to know what it was worth. Real estate in this part of the city was beyond astronomical. It would have been cheaper to build a summer home on the moon. But there was a lifelessness here, and it made her sad. The idea of Aiden coming home alone to the cool museum-quality beauty... She wondered if he felt at home here, if he ever relaxed here.

"Thank you," he said.

She picked up a gilt frame. It was a photo of Aiden's father behind his desk in an office, the city skyline outside the windows behind him.

"Tell me about your family," she said.

"Why?"

"So, I know what I'm getting myself into with this gala thing this week."

.

43

*a*iden wasn't one to count on luck. Luck, as far as he was concerned, was a fickle bitch. Timing, preparation, and aggression usually worked more in his favor. But for some reason, that fickle bitch was smiling on him today. Frankie was in his home, making plans to step into his world.

All in.

"This is your first time in my place, and you want to talk about my family?" Aiden teased, stripping out of his jacket. He saw the hungry look in her eyes and reveled in it. Wanting, being wanted, with that intensity was new. And humbling.

"Would you like a drink?" he offered.

"Do you want one?" she countered.

"How about water for us both?"

She followed him into the kitchen and snooped through his refrigerator and pantry.

"Well, there's some actual food in here," she said, sounding surprised.

"What did you expect? Bags of blood?"

"Ha, vampire diet. No, I mean, I wasn't sure if you actually *lived* here."

He eyed her as he filled two tumblers with ice.

"Of course, I live here."

"Oh, I don't doubt you sleep here. But do you put your feet up on the coffee table? Do you make eggs at midnight on this fifty-burner stove? Do you pay bills and swear at the TV when the Giants are playing?"

Her definition of living fascinated him.

"I sleep here. I work here. Occasionally I eat here. I can't recall ever putting my feet on the coffee table, but that might be because the designer referred to it as 'priceless and one-of-a-kind,' so that kind of billing most likely kept my feet on the floor."

"Do you lounge around in suits all the time, sitting up straight and counting gold coins?"

He laughed and handed her a glass of water. "Your mind is a fascination."

She wandered back into the living room and flopped down on the sofa. She wriggled onto the cushion and then pulled her feet under her.

"This isn't the most comfortable piece," she complained.

"Your couch tries to swallow its victims whole," he pointed out.

She studied him over the rim of her glass and sighed. "You're just so perfect I want to mess you up and see what happens."

"What's wrong with me as I am?" Aiden asked, amused.

"Nothing. Absolutely nothing."

He sat next to her and tugged her feet into his lap.

"I'm trying to wrap my brain around how we can fit together. Because if you think I'm going to prance around in sexy dresses and four-inch heels with my hair and nails done when we're home alone, you're going to be seriously disappointed."

He shook his head. When he envisioned her here, it wasn't in designer apparel and flawless makeup. He pictured her in sweats and bare feet, eating takeout off the coffee table. Or laying her head in his lap while they read or watched TV. Or naked and sighing in his bed.

"Are you trying to ask what my expectations of you are?"

She nodded, looking apprehensive.

"Franchesca," he reached out to tuck her hair behind her ear. "I want you to be you. I enjoy spending time with you. Not some carbon copy of every other celebutante in the borough."

"I can't believe you know that word," she joked. But she was rubbing her cheek against his palm, and he saw the nerves in her beautiful face.

"Tonight was fun. And not just the limo. I enjoyed taking you out, showing you off, and spending time with people who are important to us both."

She nodded, looking wary.

"But I also love being with you in Brooklyn. Exploring those hole-in-the-wall restaurants, sleeping in your drafty fire trap. Hanging out with your brothers. I like all that, too."

"You'll still do those things even though I've crossed the river?"

"Sweetheart, did you think I'd stop giving just because you started?"

He didn't know who was more surprised when her eyes clouded with tears. "Hey, what is it?" he asked, pulling her into his lap.

She shook her head, curls shivering from the movement.

"I feel awful. I want to say that I was only trying to protect myself, but I think part of me wanted to make you eat your words about all this being temporary. I wanted to prove to you that I'd be important to you."

"Well, mission accomplished. Franchesca, you're very important to me. Don't doubt that."

"I feel like I Aidened you."

He laughed softly. "I don't know what that means."

"It means I know that you get off on the chase, and I made you work hard. I think I manipulated you whether I consciously meant to or not."

"And you think now that the chase is over I won't be interested," he guessed.

"I don't know. I just, it's not like me to hurt someone on purpose. And I'm sorry, Aiden. I truly am. The more I get to know you, the more clear it is that you're... great."

"Great?"

She nodded, blinking back the tears. "Really great."

"This doesn't have to be complicated, Franchesca."

She stiffened in his arms.

"Hang on. Before you get all fired up. I mean, *all in* doesn't have to be complicated. You don't want to give up your life just to be with me, and I want you to know I wouldn't ask you to."

"I don't know if I'm going to fit in on your side of the tracks."

"If I tell you a secret, do you promise it goes no further than this apartment?"

"Don't you dare call this sublime chunk of Manhattan real estate an apartment. And yes, I promise."

"I don't exactly fit in either."

"I call bullshit. Your family basically built this side of the tracks."

"Very true. My great-grandfather blackmailed and swindled his way into a bank presidency, and the Kilbourn story began there. His son, my grandfather, added to the family fortune by leaving his wife and two children for a very wealthy heiress whose father needed someone to step in and run his business. My father continued the great Kilbourn legacy by cheating his way to a business degree at Yale and then bribing admissions with a very hefty donation to accept his son with less than stellar grades and a few scrapes with his private school disciplinary committee."

"You? A bad boy? We're going to need to circle back to this."

He smiled at her, shifting her in his lap. "I wouldn't call the Kilbourns sociopaths. But I would say we prioritize business over all else. But in our case, family is inextricably tied to business. For my father, it was the amassing of trophies and successes. For me, it's the hunt, the chase, the kill. Then there's everyone else. I have friends, Chip included, who don't actually work. Their money is managed for them, and they just live. They marry beautiful women and have beautiful families and extend the family line."

"But you all have money," she reminded him.

"Yes, but my point is, I feel like I don't fit in. I don't want to make small talk with someone over their new race horse or the Van Gogh they got at auction. I don't want to compare portfolios or fuck a stable full of women. I don't want to party like I'm a 20-year-old with my father's black American Express card. I want to win."

"Why?" she asked.

"Because I don't know how to do anything else."

Kilbourn Holdings announces heir to the throne is dating Brooklyn student

Five things you need to know about Aiden Kilbourn's Brooklyn girlfriend

Meet the Parents: Aiden Kilbourn introduces family to new girlfriend

.

44

"*T*his is way too *Pretty Woman*," Frankie complained inside Aiden's closet.

"Are you calling yourself a prostitute?" he asked from the bedroom.

Frankie pulled the dress on and studied herself in the full-length mirror. She hadn't had time to go shopping for a gala-worthy dress... or to even find out what gala-worthy dress code was. So, it had fallen on Aiden to find her the right dress.

It was midnight blue with elbow length lace sleeves and yards of skirt. And, of course, her size. "Am I going to freeze my ass off there tonight?" she asked.

Aiden poked his head in the doorway and stared appreciatively at her in the mirror. "Freeze your ass off?" he repeated.

"Yeah, like you know how some restaurants are drafty, so you dress warmer if you're going there? Or certain offices have the heat blasting, so you make sure you can strip down and not sweat to death?"

He laughed. "Your practicality is refreshing. I once escorted a woman who chose a dress she couldn't actually sit in. The ride to the event was quite memorable." He leaned back against the shelving, keeping his body ramrod straight imitating the woman's position.

"She did not!"

"I swear she did. Then she smiled for the cameras for twenty minutes and complained the entire rest of the evening and refused to eat."

"Ugh. What's the point of wearing something if you can't sit down or, worse, eat in it?"

"I promise to always pick clothes for you that allow for both."

"My hero. So, what do you think?" Frankie asked turning from side to side.

Aiden came up behind her and zipped her up in the back.

"Oh, that's better."

Her waist was slimmer, her breasts were supported and the full skirt floated around her. "Damn good job, Kilbourn."

"Can I pick 'em, or can I pick 'em?"

"Mmm, the way you're looking at me I'm wondering if you're not just talking about the dress."

He leaned in and dropped a kiss to her shoulder.

"Isn't this the part where you shower me with a quarter-million dollars'-worth of jewelry?" she joked.

"As a matter of fact," he reached into his pocket and pulled out a small jewelry case.

"Get the fuck out. Don't come near me with whatever that is. I'll lose it or get robbed or break out in a rash. This skin isn't used to platinum."

She backed into the corner of the closet warding him off with her hands.

"You're being ridiculous."

"You have expensive jewelry in that case, and it's my right to refuse it. I'll be a nervous wreck with something sparkly you rented for the evening."

He opened the case.

"Oh," she breathed, reaching out. "If you shut the case on my fingers, I'm going to punch you in your very sexy nose."

"I wouldn't dream of it. Do you like them?"

It was a pair of chandelier earrings. They weren't dripping in diamonds but rather a rainbow of glittering gemstones."

"Aide, they're beautiful."

He handed them over one at a time, and she slipped them into her ear lobes.

"They're not rented. I saw them and thought of you. Colorful. Interesting. Warm."

"Oh, sweet baby Jesus, Aide! Exactly how much of your money am I wearing right now?" she asked, admiring the glitter in the mirror.

"Are we going to do this every time I buy you something?"

"Yes. Unless it's a candy bar or a slice of pizza or any other item under ten dollars."

"Then I guess we'd both better get used to this conversation. Also, those were some specific food references. Do I need to feed you before we leave?"

"Definitely."

"I'll have something sent up." He paused in the doorway. "Or I can make you a grilled cheese."

She perked up. "A grilled cheese?"

He nodded.

"That would be perfect."

He turned to leave again, but she called him back.

"Hey, Aide? Thank you."

He gave her that warm smile that crinkled his eyes, the one that she was starting to think he reserved just for her.

She turned back to her reflection and took a deep breath, barely recognizing herself. Money really did buy style.

"Who does this on a Thursday night?" she murmured to her reflection in the mirror.

EVER SINCE KILBOURN HOLDINGS had released a PR statement announcing that Aiden was dating business student and small business professional Franchesca Baranski, the attention had noticeably ramped up.

Brenda had to screen Frankie's calls at work, and her email and social media accounts had blown up with interview and friend requests. She'd actually spotted a photographer outside her building twice, but her neighborhood wasn't exactly friendly to lurkers. One of her neighbors had called the cops, and the problem disappeared.

But none of it had prepared Frankie for the frenzy outside The Lighthouse at Chelsea Piers.

There was a literal red carpet under her feet. And Aiden's arm was wrapped around her waist, anchoring her to the spectacle of camera flashes and shouted questions.

"Aiden, what's your connection to Big Apple Literacy?"

"My mother has been a long-time supporter of the cause. And our family is proud to support its educational initiatives," Aiden answered smoothly.

"Franchesca, who are you wearing?"

She looked down at her dress. "I don't know. Whoever Aiden picked out for me."

The crowd of photographers chuckled like she was a stand-up comedian in the middle of a routine.

"Carolina Herrera," Aiden filled in. "Now, if you'll excuse us." He towed Frankie away from the call line.

"There. That wasn't so bad, was it?"

"Am I supposed to answer them when they ask questions?" Frankie frowned.

"You're supposed to do whatever you want to. I'm not going to treat you like a puppet and feed you sound-bites."

"But you'll tell me if there's something I shouldn't say?"

"It's always safe to avoid the word 'fuck' on the red carpet."

She rolled her eyes. "You're so helpful."

She accepted his arm with a death grip. If she didn't fall off of these sexy as hell icepicks and take a header into an ice sculpture or billionaire, it would be a damn miracle.

Miraculously, they made it inside unscathed. Aiden helped her straighten her skirt for her. "Ready?"

She looked beyond him to the crowd. At least she wasn't underdressed.

"Yeah, let's do this," she said.

"You're going to be great. You might even have the smallest bit of fun."

She didn't believe a second of his pep talk, but Frankie appreciated it all the same.

"Yeah, you too."

"And when this is all over, I'll take you through any drive-thru you want, and we'll eat in pajamas at home."

"Deal."

She recognized Ferris Kilbourn from his photo at Aiden's. He skimmed in just under six feet tall, and his Irish roots showed in the red hair going silver that ringed his head. He wore a tux and seemed as comfortable in it as if he were wearing sweats. He had his arm around a skeletal platinum blonde who had brushed a little too closely to having too much work done. She was dressed in gold and decorated in diamonds.

"My father and step-mother," Aiden whispered in her ear as they approached.

"Aren't they getting a divorce?"

"Appearances."

"Of course."

"Dad, Jacqueline," Aiden greeted them. He offered a hug for his father and a stately kiss on the cheek to his stepmother. "This is Franchesca or Frankie if you prefer."

"Frankie?" Jacqueline eyed her like a wad of chewing gum someone spit on the sidewalk. "Isn't that... cute?" Her tone made it clear she found it anything but cute.

Frankie ignored the dig. It was hard to take offense to a woman who had been traded in on a younger, hipper model.

Frankie offered her hand to Ferris. "It's nice to meet you."

"I've heard my son has been smiling for weeks now," Ferris said amicably. "I assume we have you to thank for that." Instead of shaking her hand, he lifted her knuckles to his lips.

Oh. Okay, so this is the 1800s.

"I'm sure there are other factors at play," Frankie guessed.

Aiden slid his arm around her waist. "Not at all. Ah, and this lovely woman is my mother," he said, offering Frankie up to a lovely brunette in hunter green.

"Cecily, Franchesca. Franchesca, Cecily."

Cecily was a stunning woman in her early sixties. Her face had yet to show signs of an intervention by scalpel. She was tall, regal, and lovely.

"Franchesca. I've heard so much about you. May I call you Frankie?"

If Jacqueline was the frosty Arctic air, Cecily was a Bahama breeze.

Frankie accepted the woman's hand and shook it.

"And I believe you already know my half-brother," Aiden said.

Frankie could hear the tension in Aiden's voice and slid her hand up under his jacket. She wouldn't be breaking any noses this evening and embarrassing him. At least not without provocation.

Elliot sauntered into the group, hands in his pockets and an insolent expression on his face.

"Franchesca," he said, running a finger down the bridge of his ever so slightly crooked nose. "So nice to see you again."

"Hey, Elliot. How's the nose?"

She felt Aiden stiffen next to her, but then he covered his laugh with a cough.

"He broke it playing polo," Jacqueline announced firmly. Either she was an idiot or an idiot in denial.

Frankie wasn't sure who started it, but soon the Kilbourns were all laughing. Not the genuine belly laugh that was contagious around her parents' dinner table but the stifled, embarrassed "I know something you don't know" chuckle she imagined was probably common on this side of the East River.

The Kilbourns were a remarkably civilized lot for people who had done so much damage to each other. It seemed as though everyone knew their particular role and was secure in it.

"And you thought my family was weird," she whispered in Aiden's ear.

"Why don't we find our way to the silent auction?" Ferris said jovially, offering an arm to both his ex-wife and his soon-to-be ex-wife.

45

Franchesca let Mr. Fast Feet drag her on another lap of the dance floor. The man was in his early thirties and very energetic. He also had an ulterior motive. If he said, "I think Aiden would really be interested in hearing about this investment opportunity," one more time, she was going to stomp on his fast feet and go find some tequila.

"You know, I can't help but think Aiden would—"

Frankie brought the dance to a halt. "Yeah, you're not being even remotely subtle. You want to talk to Aiden about something to invest his gazillions in, go to him. Don't go through me."

Fast Feet looked chagrined. "It's a really exciting opportunity—"

"Dude, seriously." Frankie scanned the crowd for Aiden, and when his gaze met hers, she waved him over. "Tell him what's in it for him and why you think he'd like... whatever it is you're doing," she instructed. "If he says no, I'll buy you a drink. Just, for the love of God, stop talking to me about it."

Aiden arrived at her side.

"Aiden, Mr. Uh..."

"Finch. Robert Finch," Fast Feet supplied.

"Right, Finch has something he wants to talk to you about." She winked at Aiden as she sailed in the direction of the bar. She didn't know if tequila was classy to order at a swanky event like this.

"What can I get for you, miss?" the bartender asked, all professional politeness.

"Listen, I'm new here. Is there a way that I can order a shot of tequila and not have half of this crowd gossiping about me?"

His smile warmed a few degrees. "How about I put it in a rocks glass, and you pretend it's top shelf scotch?"

"Sold," she said, slapping the bar. She slid a five-dollar bill into his tip glass.

He made a show of tossing the bottle over his shoulder and catching it behind his back. Bartender flirtations.

Frankie watched appreciatively and hid her smile when she saw he was catching the eye of a few other ladies in the crowd. There was always someone drunk enough to screw the staff in a closet or a restroom before the end of the night at events like these.

Frankie had been propositioned often enough at the events she worked to accept it as par for the course. Unless those propositions got a little too aggressive.

She accepted the glass that he handed her with a flourish. Clearly a double pour. And gave him a smile and a nod as she left him to his new admirers.

The event felt like someone's wedding. White and crystal and sterling silver everywhere. A winter wonderland, she believed the theme was. It had to be $500 a head, which made her wonder exactly how many people here would have been happier to cough up $250 just for the privilege of staying home.

But she supposed being seen supporting a worthy cause was part and parcel of the responsibility of wealth. Aiden and Fast Feet were still chatting near the ice sculpture on the canapés buffet.

A suit sidled up next to her. "So, Franchesca, when are you going to apologize for breaking my nose?"

Elliot might have been trying to be charming, but he came across like a slug oozing slime. He was blond like his mother with finer features than Aiden. He was pretty, not handsome. His presence wasn't commanding like Aiden's either. It was more of an afterthought.

"Maybe when you apologize for committing a felony and nearly ruining my best friend's wedding."

He gave an elegant shrug of his slim shoulders. "No harm, no foul."

She swung around to face him. "Lots of harm, lots of foul," she countered.

"I came over to clear the air. Now that you're part of the family, we can't have any bad blood between us. Now, can we?"

"I'm completely fine with lots of bad blood."

He laughed, but it sounded forced to her ears.

"I think you should dance with me," Elliot announced.

"Did you get a concussion when I hit you?"

"It's all about putting on a show." He held his arm out toward the dance floor. "Don't you want to prove that you can play the game?"

Frankie downed the rest of her tequila and pointed the empty glass at the bartender. He gave her a nod and started pouring.

"One dance, and you will not grab my ass or piss me off or abduct anyone, got it?"

"My word," he said, crossing his heart.

He led her onto the floor and settled his hand at her waist.

She didn't particularly care for it. There was only one Kilbourn whose hands she wanted anywhere near her.

She followed his lead, grateful for the three weeks of remedial ballroom dance her high school gym class had forced on students every year.

"So, what do you want, Elliot?"

"Maybe I just want to spend time with my brother's girlfriend."

"Or maybe you want something. I like people who cut to the chase and don't waste my time with flattery or threats."

"I need something from my brother."

"So ask him," Frankie said.

"It's not that simple," Elliot argued.

"Yes. It is."

"I need a favor that's he's not going to want to give to me."

"So why are you dancing with me? You going to twirl me into a van and chloroform me until he agrees to whatever you want?"

"Where did my brother find you?"

"Dancing like a stripper at an engagement party."

Elliot laughed. "You're refreshing."

"And you're stifling me. Don't use me to get to Aiden. Be a big boy and talk to your brother."

The song ended, and Frankie abandoned Elliot in the middle of the floor and headed for the bar. She made it within six feet before she was intercepted.

"Franchesca, my dear. There you are," Ferris Kilbourn said. "Allow me. A glass of wine for the lady," he said chivalrously.

Frankie stared mournfully at her two fingers of tequila sitting behind the bar.

"Walk with me, will you?" Ferris suggested, handing her a glass of white wine.

"Certainly."

She followed him to the edge of the room where a wall of windows and doors overlooked a stone courtyard. He held out a chair for her at an empty table.

Grateful to get off her feet, Frankie flopped down and kicked off her shoes under the table.

"I wanted to make sure you didn't take offense to the concerns I voiced to Aiden," Ferris began.

Frankie caught on to his game quickly.

"Concerns?" she said innocently.

"I'm sure you're a lovely girl," Ferris began.

"I'm an even better woman." Frankie didn't like it when older men tried to put her in the same category as her thirteen-year-old cousin who was obsessed with Harry Styles and Snapchat.

"Of course, of course. What I mean to say is I don't want you to take it personally that I believe you don't quite fit into our world. In fact, I'd be very surprised if you didn't agree with me." There was no malice behind his words. Manipulation, yes. But no real desire to harm.

She'd spent forty fucking minutes on her makeup for this. She could have troweled on blue eye shadow and bronzer in five minutes instead since they saw her for who she was. A *girl* from Brooklyn with student loans and no portfolio.

"Then I guess you'd be surprised. I'm not on my way out like some other family members," Frankie said, staring pointedly across the room at Jacqueline.

Ferris looked flustered for a moment.

There, didn't expect that, did you smarty pants?

He'd dropped the Aiden bomb knowing full well his son wouldn't have discussed that particular conversation with her. But she'd gotten a piece back.

"I really don't think I'm the right person to be having this conversation with. If you're so concerned with your family, maybe you should plan to stick around."

Ferris sighed and lifted his glass. "I've given enough. It's my time to enjoy. My father never got the chance. Heart attack in his office at age 71. I don't want that to be me."

Frankie turned in her chair to face him. "Ferris, I don't think anyone would begrudge you your chance to do what you want. But don't try to dictate Aiden's life. He's your son, not just a business partner. Trust his judgment and not only when it comes to broads from Brooklyn."

He sighed. "I don't expect you to understand the complications of our family," Ferris said. "Our business, our family, are inextricably intertwined. There is no one without the other. My son has a responsibility to make choices that will benefit both our company and our family." Again, his words lacked spite. He was simply a man sharing his truth.

"And which one of those don't I fit?" Frankie asked.

"Do you even want to fit?" Ferris asked, turning it back on her.

"I want to see Aiden happy."

"Sometimes, happiness is a luxury that no one can afford."

Frankie smirked. "I'm pretty certain the Kilbourns could find a way to pay for it." If Aiden's deep pockets were any indication of the family coffers, they could all quit working to live in a multi-million-dollar commune in Dubai without ever feeling the pinch.

"I'm only trying to save you some time and heartache," he added. "I don't see how a woman who could give a damn about appearances would willingly fit into this world. There are expectations that we must live up to."

"Would your world really come crumbling down if the girlfriend of your CEO didn't spend five hundred dollars on her hair and nails every two weeks? Would anyone really care if I show up to a family meal in $25 Target jeans?"

"Frankly, yes," he laughed. "There are certain expectations that we uphold. To the Kilbourns, work comes first. I missed out on most birthdays, baseball games, even some Christmases. It was the price I had to pay. But I built something that they can have long after I'm gone. Aiden will do the same. And he'll need a woman by his side who understands that, accepts that, embraces that."

"Did you ever think that maybe Aiden would rather have a piece of you instead of a legacy?" Frankie suggested. "Maybe he'd rather have dinner with you than you pulling his strings from a goddamn yacht because now he has to suffer for the next twenty years of his life while you finally live."

"You think I'm very selfish, don't you?" Ferris asked.

Frankie put her glass down. "I don't know you well enough to judge you yet."

"Touché."

"Thank you. For the record, I don't care who you're divorcing or where you're sailing. But if you care for your son more than you do a bunch of zeroes and buildings and whatever the hell else, don't lock him in the same prison you just busted out of."

Ferris eyed her. "I may have underestimated you."

"Usually the case. But that makes it easier to win."

Ferris raised his glass to her. "Maybe you would fit in."

Frankie tapped her glass to his. "For future reference, I prefer tequila to wine."

"Franchesca." Just the sound of Aiden's voice was like a caress on her skin.

She rose, forgetting that she'd kicked off her shoes under the table. "Oops. Sorry. Too many dances," she said, fishing the heels out from under the table.

He tugged her into his side. "Are we having a private meeting?" his voice was guarded.

"Your dad and I were just discussing our beverage preferences."

Ferris rose. "Franchesca, it was... refreshing talking to you."

"Illuminating," Frankie agreed. They watched him walk away, joining a group of men clustered around a painting of what looked like a roman orgy.

"Was my father bothering you?"

"Not really. He's quite polite with the 'you're not good enough for my son' spiel."

Aiden's eyes narrowed. "I'll speak to him."

She shook her head. "You don't need to. I told him he better get used to me because I've been poking holes in our condoms for weeks, and it's only a matter of time before he has a grandchild to deal with."

His booming laugh drew the attention of guests nearby. "Are you ready to go?" Aiden asked, lifting his fingers to toy with one of her earrings.

"God, yes. My feet hurt, and if one more idiot tries to get to you through me, I'm going to break a bottle of Cristal over their smug face."

"Give me a head's up so I can have my attorney on call."

"Why can't people just talk to you and ask you for shit?" Frankie muttered.

"Because I'm very powerful and intimidating. And because they see that you have influence over me."

"Can I influence you to pick up some Thai food on the way home?"

46

"*W*as it a blood bath?" Oscar asked, handing Aiden a bottle of headache meds as he passed his desk.

"Worse," Aiden said, fighting the pain that bloomed behind his eyes. Worthington Financial, an accounting consulting firm, hadn't taken his CIO candidate search criteria seriously and had presented him with the same old, white guys. It had pissed him off enough that Aiden pulled a team off of the sale they were neck-deep in so they could dissect the corporate structure.

With a little digging and some precisely applied pressure, Aiden discovered a rotting culture of harassment and misogynistic behavior. He'd fired seven of the company's top managers within half an hour. With the newly departeds' threats of lawsuits still echoing in his ears, Aiden had called a company-wide meeting and announced an immediate restructuring. Two administrative assistants had burst into tears while thanking him. And a junior vice president—exactly the kind of person he wanted for chief information officer—rescinded the resignation that she'd tendered two days ago.

He ordered an independent HR consultant into the wreckage to deal with the internal fallout and warned Kilbourn Holdings lawyers that there was a situation.

"Sacked them all?" Oscar asked. The man loved two things in life. His partner Lewis and juicy corporate gossip.

"Most of them." Aiden noted the time on his watch. His two afternoon meetings had been juggled into a hasty conference in the car and a late dinner, during which his headache prevented him from eating anything. "It's late. You should go before Lewis comes looking for you."

"I'm meeting him for drinks to celebrate another week of his mother not moving in with us." Oscar pulled his coat from the rack and slid into it. "Don't work too late," he reminded Aiden. "I'm sure there's a Brooklyn girl waiting for you somewhere."

Just the thought of Frankie lifted Aiden's spirits. She had a catering gig tonight. One of her last, so they wouldn't see each other. But that didn't mean he couldn't call her.

"Go home, Oscar," he said again. "And first thing in the morning, you can help start the search for all new senior management. Maybe we can cherry-pick from our own backyard first."

"Of course. I'll also be happy to make sure the ones you sacked are unemployable anywhere else."

"You're a mean Frenchman, aren't you?" Aiden said, with a weak smile.

"The meanest."

Aiden watched Oscar saunter toward the elevators. The rest of the offices were dark. It was nearly nine, and Aiden still had a few hours of work to catch up on. If he could get ahead of the headache... and stop thinking about the events of the day.

Two of the men had cried when he'd pulled the trigger.

None were innocent, but there was something unsatisfying about punishing someone who felt like a victim.

"I have two kids in college," one had pleaded.

"Then you shouldn't have ordered HR to ignore the complaints against you and your colleagues," Aiden had said briskly. He was efficient and cold. Merciless. It was more intimidating that way when he treated people like gnats who mattered too little to bother getting angry over.

On the inside, he was anything but cold. These men had created a work environment so hostile that it was a wonder they had any employees left.

It was the right decision. Perhaps a bit abrupt, but it would set the tone for the coming year. They were a new acquisition, and this was the fastest way to send the message that Kilbourn Holdings would not tolerate anything less than equality, anything other than fairness.

Having to defend his decision to his father on the phone hadn't helped.

Ferris agreed that "something" should have been done, just not now and certainly not by making such a statement. "We're already dealing with enough transition," he'd argued. "I don't see why you would have taken on a project of this magnitude that will only take your attention away from more important things."

In other words, Ferris felt like the women should have toughed it out a little longer, at least until he was on his boat smoking a cigar without a care in sight.

Aiden not-so-respectfully disagreed and said as much.

He wanted to go home. Scratch that. He wanted to go to Franchesca's and lay next to her in bed until everything felt right again.

"Well, if it isn't my all-work-and-no-play brother," Elliot said snidely from Aiden's doorway.

And just like that, Aiden's night got worse.

"Look who stopped avoiding my calls." Since their father had made his decision to step down, Aiden had been trying to schedule a meeting with Elliot. And, until tonight, his half-brother had been avoiding him.

He was dressed for going out. A blazer with velvet lapels and a jaunty plaid bow tie. He looked like an overindulged idiot.

Elliot brushed a speck of lint from his shoulder. "Sorry, *boss*. I've been busy."

"Doing what, exactly?" Ferris had allowed Elliot to hold a title and kept an office available to him should his brother show any signs of interest in the business.

Elliot slunk into the chair in front of Aiden's desk and propped his shiny loafers on the surface. "A little of this. A little of that."

"Let's cut to the chase. From now on, you're required to be a contributing member of this family, of this business."

Elliot sneered at him. "You want more work out of me? I want a bigger office and an assistant. I want to have a say in operations."

Aiden remained impassive. "You *earn* those things by proving yourself. Not by having the right last name."

"Fine. Then buy me out." Elliot crossed his arms smugly. He named a figure that was far too precise to have come from thin air. "That's the price to get me out of your hair."

"That is not an option." As much as Aiden would love to write the bastard a check right here and now, he'd promised his father a year. An entire year to give Elliot the chance to prove himself and fail.

"Then I'll sell them to someone else."

Aiden stared his brother down. "You'd better think long and hard before you do anything irreversible. Kilbourns hold

317

the majority. If you sell off your percentage, that would no longer be the case. It would put the company at risk."

Elliot shrugged, but Aiden saw the beads of sweat on his forehead. Elliot was many things, most of them terrible and offensive, but his desire to be recognized as a valuable Kilbourn came first at all times. If something had him scared enough to sell off his only piece of the pie, it must be quite the threat indeed. It made Aiden almost curious enough to start digging.

"If you want to continue to see a paycheck, you're going to have to do something to earn it. I don't care if that means you're making coffee in the breakroom or you're emptying trashcans in the conference room. You will contribute, or you won't have a place here."

"You've been dying to get rid of me since I was born," Elliot whined. "Now's your chance."

"One year. You know where this company is going. What the future looks like. You'd be an idiot to sell now."

"Some of us don't have a choice," Elliot hissed, he dropped his feet to the floor and leaned forward in his chair. "Some of us were never the favorite. Some of us had to settle for scraps. And some of us do what we have to in order to survive."

"You've been handed everything you ever wanted," Aiden pointed out.

"Not everything. And the rest was never enough. So you're going to buy me out, or I'm going to that pretty little girlfriend of yours and tell her exactly why your friend Chip broke her best friend's heart all those years ago."

Aiden stilled in his seat. "What makes you think I had anything to do with that?"

Elliot sneered. "You've been ignoring my existence my entire life. I overheard a lot of things in that house."

Aiden's hand tightened on the pen, but he kept his face impassive, disinterested.

"Do you really think that information would have any effect on my relationship with Franchesca now? If you'll recall, Chip and Pruitt are happily married now. No thanks to you."

"Ah, but imagine how Franchesca would feel knowing that you were the reason her best friend in the whole world was nearly hospitalized? There were plenty of rumors back then about how hard she took the breakup. Chip didn't know what you were doing, but I did. I recognize manipulation when I see it. How do you think he would feel knowing you orchestrated his breakup?"

"You have nothing. I'm offering you the chance to finally be a real part of this company." Aiden kept his words clipped.

"You have a week to decide. Buy me out, or I'm spilling your dirty little secrets to Franchesca." With that, Elliot stormed from Aiden's office in a fit of temper.

And now Aiden's headache was full blown. He glanced at the blinking voicemail indicator, at the dozens of new messages in his inbox, at the neat stack of contracts awaiting his signature and rose.

By the time he got there, Frankie would likely be getting home. He wanted her. Needed her. He called his car service. "We're going to Brooklyn."

AIDEN CLOSED his eyes in the car and let the dark and the quiet relax him. By the time he got to Frankie's front steps, it was ten, and he just wanted to lay down on that big bed, wrap his arms around her and sleep.

He pressed the buzzer for Frankie's apartment and wasn't

surprised at the lack of response. He pressed the buzzer for Mrs. Gurgevich in 2A.

"Sorry to bother you so late, Mrs. Gurgevich," Aiden said when she answered. The world was spinning in halos and nauseating visual disturbances around him.

"That girl hasn't given you a key yet?" she grumbled.

"Not yet, ma'am."

"Have you tried flowers?" she suggested through the crackle of the speaker.

"I'll try that," he agreed.

"I'll keep my fingers crossed for you." She buzzed him inside, and Aiden trudged up the three flights of stairs praying that his head didn't fall from his shoulders. He'd sit in the hallway and wait for her. He should have texted her, but part of him wanted to test her. Would she be happy to see him? Annoyed? He needed to know before he went any farther. He could feel himself getting pulled into her. And he needed to know exactly how far she was comfortable going before he could give any more pieces of himself.

The door across the hallway cracked open. "Oh, it's you. I thought it was Mr. McMitchem down the hall stealing my paper," Mrs. Chu said, glancing down to make sure her decoy newspaper was still there.

Aiden caught a glimpse of pink house coat and plush puppy slipper through the crack in the door.

"Sorry for startling you, Mrs. Chu. I'm just waiting for Franchesca—ah, Frankie—to get home."

"If you're lurking out here, Mr. McMitchem will get scared off. Here." She disappeared for a moment and then returned, shoving a key at him. "We have a spare."

He needed to get Franchesca into a building with better security. Her neighbors would happily welcome an AK-47 wielding bank robbery suspect inside.

But it would be more comfortable than sitting in the hall. He unlocked the door, returned the key, and went inside.

He was always struck by the contrast between his home and Frankie's. Hers screamed lived in, if somewhat messily. There were dishes in the sink, mail on the table, and a lump of clean laundry on the floor just outside the kitchen as if she'd dug through the basket in search of a particular piece in a hurry.

With a ridiculous amount of gratitude, he noted she'd washed a pair of his sweats and a t-shirt. He changed out of his suit, thought about raiding her cabinets, and decided his headache would be better off with rest over food. He lay down on the couch and tried to put his brain to work on the problem at hand. He knew how it would go if Frankie knew what he'd done. How he'd pushed Chip into breaking up with Pruitt. And from comments Frankie had made, the breakup had been devastating to Pruitt.

How was he going to fix it all? It was his last thought as the dark and the quiet enveloped him.

47

---

*H*e was sprawled on her couch, a pillow over his face, his t-shirt showing a sexy peek of abs above the low waistband of his sweatpants.

Frankie would have screamed when she walked through her front door, but there was no mistaking that gorgeous, god-like body for some stranger who broke in to rob and rape her. Aiden Kilbourn was her mysterious guest, and judging by his bleary eyes, he wasn't here for sex.

"Hey," she said softly.

He winced at the light and closed his eyes again. "Hi," he said, his voice raspy. "What time is it?"

"Not quite 11."

"Sorry for breaking in."

"Seeing as how my door's still intact, I imagine Mrs. Chu let you in," Frankie said, brushing her fingers through his thick dark hair.

"You need better security." He nuzzled his cheek against her hand, and Frankie melted on the inside.

"Headache?" she asked.

"Yeah."

"Hang in there, tough guy." She pressed a gentle kiss to his forehead and headed into the kitchen. She returned with a glass of water and two caplets. "I don't have any of Pru's good prescription stuff, but this is over-the-counter."

He worked his way into a seated position, and she could see that it pained him.

"How was your night?" he asked her, downing the pills and water.

His hair was disheveled from sleep, the ends curled softly at his neck. How was it that arrogant and demanding Aiden could make her blood sing, but vulnerable, sweet Aiden turned her cold steely heart to mush?

"It was fine," she lied. It hadn't been fine. It had been a pain in the ass. And a bit of a culture shock to go from attending a huge charity function one week to working one the next. She felt as if she didn't belong in either place now.

Perhaps she was two people too. Franchesca the entrepreneur's girlfriend and Frankie the grad student from Brooklyn who sprinkled the f-bomb like fairy dust.

"How was your day?"

He pressed his fingers to his eyes, but she could still see the grimace.

"You don't have to talk about it if you don't want to." She took his empty glass back to the kitchen and opened a can of Coke.

"I do. That's why I came here." Now he sounded just the slightest bit surly, and she found it endearing.

She handed the can over. "Here. Let's double up on the caffeine."

"Thanks," he murmured.

"Come on," she said, gently tugging on his hand. "Let's go."

"Where are we going?"

"To bed."

"I don't know how well I'll perform—"

"To sleep, Aide. Just to sleep. I promise not to jump your bones until you feel better."

"Oh."

She led him into the bedroom and tucked him in on his side of the big king bed. His side. He had a side in her bed, a drawer in her bathroom, and it was probably time he had a key too instead of depending on the kindness/nosiness of her neighbors.

Frankie brushed a kiss to his forehead. When she tried to move away, he grabbed her hand. "Where are you going?" he asked.

"Honey, I'm going to change and then I'm coming to bed."

"You're probably not tired yet."

She wasn't. After running around like a fool for four hours feeding rude people and cleaning up their messes she was usually a little revved.

"I'm going to read in bed, right next to you."

"Okay." He pressed his face into his pillow.

God damn it. Vulnerable, needy Aiden was still sexy as fuck and all she wanted to do was bundle him up in a quilt and baby him until he felt better. It was making her feel weird in her chest area. Warm and... happy. She didn't like it.

She took her time brushing her teeth and washing her face. When she came back into the bedroom in search of pajamas, he was asleep, a pillow pulled over his head.

Poor indestructible Aiden had found his limit. It must have been a very rough day indeed. She'd caught peeks at his work calendar before. He was scheduled down to the minute on most days. Aiden Kilbourn got more done before ten than most people did all day—hell, all week. But she recognized a pattern.

Work was his life, and he pushed until he burned out, and then he got back up and pushed some more.

She could admire that kind of dedication, Frankie thought as she pulled back the covers and slipped between the sheets. She settled back against the pillows with her eReader.

It was something they had in common. Sure, his work life involved him running a multi-billion-dollar conglomerate. Her work life was two part-time jobs and grad school. But still, they both had their eyes on the prize, and neither would stop at anything. Him: world domination or the corporate equivalent. Her: a master's degree and a financially secure future.

It was funny how similar two people from opposite sides of the tracks could be.

He shifted on the mattress. Without opening his eyes, he rolled to her side, curling around her and pressing his face against her arm.

The most eligible bachelor in the city was in her bed, holding on for dear life, and her heart was doing something funny and fluttery.

"Son of a bitch," she murmured. She was falling for him. And this was not going to be a soft landing.

She picked up her eReader and opened the novel she'd started. At least on the page she was guaranteed a happily ever after.

Aiden Kilbourn's new girlfriend a cocktail waitress?

Just the tip: Waitress bags billionaire

48

Frankie swung through the crowd, a tray of pancetta crisps in her hand. It was her next to last catering gig. With the cash from tonight, she'd have almost enough to pay off her credit card that was still sobbing from Pru's wedding.

The rich were raising money for manatees or sea turtles or some kind of endangered marine life in an Upper West Side art gallery. They were scribbling checks with one hand while downing signature cocktails and stuffed mushroom caps with the other.

"These are *divine*," a woman in black sequins sighed, plucking another appetizer from Frankie's tray. "The only reason I come to these things is for the food," she confessed.

Frankie gave her a smile. "In that case, don't miss the brie toast points."

She made a lap around the far side of the room, smiling politely and pointing out the restrooms when asked. And was completely surprised when Cressida's considerable rack came into her line of vision.

Shit. She'd been hoping to remain as under-the-radar as

possible. Her catering boss already had reservations about letting Aiden Kilbourn's girlfriend hand out apps to her new peers. The last thing she needed was a run-in with Pru's bridal party.

Frankie ducked behind a tall, stooped gentleman and peered around his elbow. Cressida wasn't alone. She was on the arm of groomsmen and day-trading boy genius Digby. Frankie was so surprised that she didn't notice when her cover wandered off toward the bar.

"Frankie?" Digby asked, cocking his head to one side.

Crappity crap crap.

Frankie plastered a bright smile on her face. "Hey, Digby. Cressida. It's nice to see you," she said for once wishing she was in a nice dress holding a fundraiser program and not a tray of pancetta snacks.

Cressida eyed Frankie's uniform. "You are working?" she asked.

Frankie straightened her shoulders, daring them to say anything. "Yep. So, what brings you two here?" she asked.

Digby snatched a piece of toast off her tray. "Cressida owns the building," he said, chewing happily.

"And I like the manatees," she added pointing at one of the informative banners hanging from the ceiling.

The big-boobed blonde was a real estate mogul, and Frankie was pushing appetizers for a living. Sometimes life wasn't quite fair.

Digby reached into his pocket.

"You use your phone, and I will have you killed," Cressida purred.

Digby sheepishly ended his search and reached for another appetizer.

"I am training him to not be an asshole," Cressida announced. "Good luck with your training of Aiden."

"Uh, thanks?" Frankie said.

Digby grinned. "I heard Margeaux didn't take the news of you two dating well."

"Why Margeaux thinks it's any of her business is beyond me."

"That one does not like to lose," Cressida announced. "We must go make love now."

Digby's face lit up, and for once, it wasn't from the backlight of his phone. It looked as though he was trading in his day-trader ways.

"Great seeing you, Frankie. Tell Aiden we said hi," he said in a rush, grabbing Cressida's wrist and dragging her toward the door.

"Huh," Frankie said, watching them leave. Maybe there had been something in the water in Barbados. She shivered, pitying whatever man ended up with Margeaux.

She moved on, circulating like a ghost through the crowd until her tray was empty. Back in the cramped kitchen, she restocked. Jana slid through the door with a tray of dirty glasses.

"Another hour, and we start packing up," she sang. Her blonde hair was streaked with turquoise today.

Frankie couldn't wait for that hour to end, and with it this portion of her life so she could step into her newly favorite role. Aiden's bed warmer. Since she was already in town, it only made sense for her to stay at his place tonight. Especially since tomorrow was Saturday. The plan was to sleep in and have a lazy Saturday brunch. Then dinner with Aiden's father, his new lady friend, and Aiden's mother. As always, the Kilbourns kept it quite civilized. Though not civilized enough to invite the step-mother/soon-to-be-ex. News of the divorce had leaked early. And the gossip was rampant even here.

Rumor had it that Jacqueline had been on the guest list for

tonight but was too humiliated to show her face. Frankie guessed the woman was probably reviewing her prenup with a magnifying glass rather than suffering any actual humiliation. It was funny serving food to some of the same people she'd danced alongside of last week. But as was typical, no one looked a server in the eyes unless they were after something more than food or drink.

The anonymity was more comforting than anything. Aiden hadn't mentioned anything about her catering gigs, but she imagined it must be odd for him to have a girlfriend who cleaned up after his peers.

"Franchesca?" Cecily Kilbourn cocked her head to one side. "It is you!" She was dressed in a simple yet stunning yellow dress that only a woman with her coloring and bearing could begin to pull off.

"Mrs. Kilbourn," Frankie said, nearly bobbling her tray.

Her ghost status had just been revoked.

"Please, call me Cecily," she said with a genuine smile. "Is Aiden here?"

"No. He was working late tonight."

"Ah. My son is *always* working," Cecily sighed. "He takes after his father in that area."

"He's very dedicated," Frankie agreed.

"That's a very polite way of saying he needs to be careful before he starts following in the rest of his father's footsteps. I'm very glad he's found you. He seems quite taken with you."

"Same. I mean, I feel the same way."

"I may be biased," Cecily said, "but he is quite the prize."

"We're enjoying our time together," Frankie said, not knowing how to make small talk with her boyfriend's mother when she was supposed to be handing out miniature shrimp cocktails served in ceramic spoons.

"What did you find now, Cecily? You're going to end up

ten pounds heavier when you leave here if you don't stay away from the food." Jacqueline, neither humiliated nor glued to her prenup, sidled up to them and plucked a sample from Frankie's tray. She sampled it and wrinkled her pretty nose. "Ugh. Disgusting. I hate shrimp." She dropped the half-eaten shrimp back on the tray in a masticated lump.

Asshole.

"Where's the girl with the brie?" she demanded.

"Jacqueline, you remember Aiden's girlfriend Franchesca, don't you?" Cecily said pointedly.

It took Jacqueline a moment to realize that Cecily was talking about the tray-wielding Frankie and not someone else. "You're a *waitress*?" Jacqueline asked with a laugh. Her eyebrows were trying valiantly to raise, but the flawless forehead only allowed her eyes to widen ever so slightly.

"Among other things, Mrs. Kilbourn."

Jacqueline looked like she was weighing whether or not she should be seen talking to the help.

"Well, enjoy your girl talk," she said, going nearly cross-eyed from looking down her nose at them. "I've got another party to attend soon, so I must say my good-byes." She swished away in satin and pearls.

"Let's hope the next one is slightly more tolerable," Cecily sighed.

"How did Ferris go from you to that?" Frankie asked. *Oh shit. When was she going to learn to keep her mouth shut?*

"It probably had something to do with her being pregnant with his child," Cecily mused. "Oops. Family secret. Pretend I said something really Zen and sweet instead."

"You're right. Jacqueline really is a *treasure*," Frankie said.

"Oh, Cecily!" A woman in a burgundy shawl waved from her up-close vantage point of a very naked statue.

"That's a friend of mine. Would you like me to introduce you?" she asked.

Frankie shook her head. "I hope you don't mind, but I'd rather stay incognito. I've only got one more catering gig to go, and it's just easier if no one knows my... connection to Aiden."

Cecily nodded. "I understand. Well, it was lovely to see you, and I'm looking forward to dinner tomorrow night."

"Me, too," Frankie said. And she realized she actually meant it.

Frankie headed in the direction of the kitchen to get rid of Jacqueline's dead shrimp. Nothing killed the appetite like someone else's chewed up food.

"Did you see who Cecily was talking to?"

Frankie heard Jacqueline's voice coming from a cluster of ladies who were lingering near the bar.

"Who?" someone asked, breathy with excitement over any tidbit of gossip.

"A waitress."

"Was she getting a recipe?"

"The waitress is her son's *girlfriend*."

"No!" someone gasped in horror.

Okay, that was a bit of an overreaction. It's not like she just announced Aiden was eating homeless dogs for breakfast.

"Yes!" Jacqueline announced gleefully. "Like father, like son, I suppose. They both have a thing for the help."

"Was Cecily a waitress too?" one of the other women demanded.

"Almost as bad," Jacqueline continued. "She was a secretary or something at the interior design firm he hired to do the house in the Hamptons. Can you imagine? Poor dear always thought we were friends. But that's what you do to help. You pat them on the head and tell them they're doing a good job and then count the silver when they leave."

They cackled like a flock of chickens.

"There goes the bloodline," someone sighed.

"I suppose I should have told my daughter to get a job at a fast food restaurant or as a janitor when she wanted to catch Aiden's eye all those years ago."

Frankie was amazed that the tray didn't snap in her hand from the pressure she was applying. She did a rapid calculation. Exactly how bad would the consequences be if she beaned the soon-to-be ex-Mrs. Kilbourn in the head with this tray?

Crap. Pretty bad. She seethed. *Okay, physical violence was out. But she wasn't about to let this go.*

Frankie grabbed a cocktail toothpick off of the bar and walked into the midst of the hyenas. "There you are, Jackie. You've got a little spinach stuck in your dentures," she said handing over the toothpick. "I'd hate for everyone to be laughing at you behind your back."

The laughter screeched to a halt. Jacqueline stared at her coldly.

"Oh, and I'm so proud of you for making an appearance tonight. I can't imagine showing my face in public after my husband dumped me for a woman fifteen years younger. Good for you, sweetie. Will you be at dinner tomorrow night to meet the new Mrs. Kilbourn with the rest of the family?"

Jacqueline's mouth was hanging somewhere down around her augmented tits when Frankie breezed away.

Okay, it wasn't as satisfying as popping her one in the face. But it felt good enough.

She stormed back into the kitchen, took a two-minute breather, and then plastered a professional smile on her face and returned to the thinning crowd. Jacqueline was gone, and it looked like she'd taken most of her cronies with her. Probably to prove she wasn't wearing dentures.

Everyone was looking at her, though, and laying on the profuse thank-yous when she passed with the tray. Ugh. She preferred it when they were too important to look at her. Word traveled fast in high society. *Aiden Kilbourn's girlfriend was slinging apps in an apron on a Friday night. What was the world coming to?*

"I'd love a piece of whatever it is you have." The voice was smooth with a practiced flirtatiousness that immediately put Frankie's back up.

"Stuffed mushroom caps?" she asked, shoving the tray between them.

He was leanly muscled and slight of frame, close to her own height. She guessed that she outweighed him by a good ten pounds.

There was something insolent about the way he perused her tray before popping the mushroom cap into his mouth and making a show out of licking his fingers.

"I'm Lionel, by the way."

"Hi, Lionel," she said, not interested in continuing the getting-to-know-you portion of their evening.

"I'm sure Aiden's mentioned me before. I usually beat him on the polo field," Lionel said, tossing his mop of blond hair off his forehead. "We like to compete against each other in everything." He lowered his voice as if he were imparting a secret.

"Good for you," she said side-stepping him. But he followed her, blocking her path.

"You're very beautiful, you know. I saw you from across the room and just couldn't take my eyes off you."

"Cut to the chase, Lionel," Frankie demanded with the minimum of politeness she could muster. She hated being restrained by the required professionalism of her current role.

He reached out and traced a knuckle over her cheek. "I

think you'd like being in my bed better than Kilbourn's. What do you say?"

Fuck off. Go fuck yourself. Go slather yourself with ground beef and walk into a grizzly bear den. "No thanks." There was enough chill in her words that Lionel should have gotten frostbite.

"Maybe you need a little convincing. I like it when a girl plays hard to get."

"Are you talking to me like this because I'm the help or because your wallet says you can?"

He threw his head back and laughed. "What a wildcat you are. Come on. Forget Kilbourn. Have a drink with me. I'll pay you for the rest of your shift."

Lionel made a fatal mistake by grabbing her wrist and giving her a tug.

49

*A*iden frowned at the text from Frankie.

Frankie: Can't make it tonight. Raincheck?

The last time they'd talked, they were both looking forward to a night together. Aiden drummed his fingers on the desk, a dread growing in the pit of his stomach. Had Elliot actually carried out his threat? Had he underestimated his sniveling, lazy coward of a brother? The fact that Elliot needed money was obvious. But as for the why? It was still a nagging mystery.

Aiden's investigation had barely begun, and he had yet to dig up any connection between Elliot and Donaldson.

He'd assumed it was an empty threat. Elliot was many undesirable things, but his quest to be an important asset to their father was equal to no other goal. And Aiden was counting on that consistency to buy himself some time. He needed to figure out just how to break the news to Franchesca that he'd caused their best friends years of misery.

He could either do that by meeting Elliot's financial needs or maneuvering his way out of his commitment to his father.

In short, he was fucked.

His phone rang, and Aiden snatched it up. It was his mother. He briefly debated letting it go to voicemail but changed his mind.

"Sorry for calling so late," Cecily said, her voice bright. "But I knew you were working anyway. I wanted to tell you I ran into Franchesca at an event tonight. She was working."

"Was Elliot there too, by chance?" Aiden pinched the bridge of his nose and hoped for good news.

"Not that I saw. But his mother was."

Aiden's lips curved at the slightest hint of derision in his mother's tone. She should have been awarded sainthood for her gracious acceptance of Jacqueline and Elliot after his father's philandering. Now that the marriage was over, Cecily had been sprung from the prison of politeness, of putting on a brave face.

"Anyway, Franchesca's so different from anyone I've seen you with before, Aiden. And I wanted you to know that I like her very much. And that assessment was already in existence before she put Jacqueline in her place tonight when she was running her mouth about father and son enjoying 'the help.'"

Aiden swore quietly. He felt twin pangs. One of relief and one of dread. Even at work, Frankie couldn't escape his family. And though it hadn't been Elliot telling secrets, Jacqueline could do enough damage on her own.

"What exactly did Jacqueline say?" he asked, his tone steely.

Cecily laughed. "No need to ride into battle. Your girlfriend handled herself well enough that Jacqueline left with her tail between her legs. She's a good match, Aiden."

"Dad doesn't seem to think so," Aiden admitted.

"Your father needs his horizons expanded. I hope you keep her."

"We've only been dating two months. Are you designing wedding invitations already?"

"Two months is the outside for most of your relationships, dear son. And I don't see any of the usual tells that you're growing bored with her."

No, if anything, he was more fascinated, more enamored by the day. And someone in his orbit had upset Frankie tonight. It was his job to protect her from that.

"Where was this Save the Whatever fundraiser?"

HE FOUND HER, finally, in a bar a block from the fundraiser. The crowds had thinned, and Frankie sat alone at the bar, still in her catering uniform, staring morosely into a glass of something. He barely registered the dark paneling, the soft lighting, and the subtle art under brass lamps. His focus narrowed to her, to the slump of her shoulders, the sweep of her hair, the pursing of her lips.

"You're blowing me off so you can drink alone?" he demanded, taking the stool next to her.

She didn't look up, her long hair hiding her face. Aiden could be a patient man when the situation called for it. He signaled the bartender and ordered a scotch.

That got a rise out of her. "So, you're drinking again?" she asked.

"I'm having one drink with you. A beautiful woman shouldn't have to drink alone."

She shook her head and lifted her face. He saw the red eyes, the tear-stained cheeks, and felt his body shift into fight mode. Someone had hurt her, and they would pay.

"What happened?" he asked, his voice low.

"First, you need to know that I'm mad crying. Huge difference from sad crying. I'm not weak."

"Franchesca," he said, turning her stool to face him and caging her between his legs. "There isn't a person on the face of the planet who would ever use your name and weak in the same sentence." His phone vibrated in his pocket with an incoming call.

She looked down at her bunched fists. "I got fired."

He reached for her hands and held them in his. "And you're mad."

She nodded.

"I heard about Jacqueline," he pressed. "Did she do this?" His phone signaled again in his pocket.

Frankie shook her head. "I'd actually forgotten about that. I know she's still technically your stepmother for a few more weeks, but I hope I'm not required to be nice to her. I probably should have checked with you first."

"Franchesca, I don't want you to ever feel like you have to be nice to someone who isn't treating you the way you deserve to be."

She looked at him, into him, and her eyes welled with tears.

"Shit, sweetheart. Tell me what happened."

"Oh, I can do better than tell you." She pulled a hand from his grasp and slid her phone in front of him.

Aiden glanced at the screen and then picked the phone up for a closer look.

The picture drew his attention first. Frankie was in mid-swing with a serving tray heading in the direction of a blond man's square jaw.

Aiden Kilbourn's girlfriend attacks business rival at fundraiser.

"Who is he, and what did he do?"

Frankie's eyes widened. "He made it sound as if you two were Lex Luthor and Superman."

"There are many people who feel that their relationship with me is more important than it is." If his phone didn't quit ringing, he was going to throw it in the bar sink.

"Ouch."

"You, on the other hand, keep downplaying the importance of our relationship," he pointed out.

"Nice save. Why aren't you freaking out? It's Lionel Goffman, by the way. Rivals on the polo field and business arena," she said, quoting the article.

Aiden had a vague recollection of the man. "What did he do, Franchesca?"

"He hinted that I should try out his bed instead of yours. I'm required to be polite, professional, at work. I needed that job. Needed the money. But he grabbed me—"

"He touched you?" Aiden's voice was dangerously calm, but it didn't fool her for a second.

"Don't you go all white knight and make this worse, Aide."

"What exactly did he do?"

"He grabbed my arm and started pulling. He said he was going to buy me a drink and pay me for the rest of my shift."

Aiden glanced back at the phone. "Did you break his nose?"

Frankie sighed and picked up her glass. "There's video," she murmured.

"I beg your pardon?" Aiden asked, leaning closer.

"There's video. Scroll down."

He did as he was told and watched as his Franchesca yelled a warning to the unsuspecting dead man. "You don't get to touch me! In fact, you don't get to touch any woman without her permission."

But Lionel wasn't in a listening kind of mood. He grabbed for her again. "Listen, let's go for that drink—"

Frankie was shaking her head and then the tray came up. With one hand, she bashed him in the head like the tray was a cymbal. Dazed, Lionel took a step back and tripped, falling on his ass.

"For your information, Aiden Kilbourn is a better man than you could ever dream of being. And if you ever insinuate otherwise, I will hunt you down!" The temper had exploded, and there was no putting it back in the box. She grabbed a tray of champagne from a cocktail table behind her and dumped the entire thing on him.

"There's your fucking drink, asshole!"

Shocked gasps and some laughter rose from the crowd of witnesses as Lionel tried to scramble to his sticky, humiliated feet.

"You'll be hearing from my lawyers!"

Aiden put the phone down and felt his own vibrate in his jacket yet again. If the Rumor Mill blog already had this, it was everywhere by now. Damage control would be... interesting.

He picked up his glass and shocked them both by starting to laugh.

Frankie looked at him like he'd lost his damn mind. "How can you laugh at this? I've humiliated your entire family? Your PR bill is going to be astronomical this month alone."

But he couldn't stop laughing. He had Franchesca Baranski in his corner. No smarmy competitor, no wicked stepmother, no idiot brother had scared her off. She stuck. And her fierce loyalty now extended to him.

Just as his heart belonged to her.

"Aiden, stop laughing and start thinking about how much damage I did. I assaulted someone on video. And if that isn't bad enough, now everyone knows that your girlfriend is a waitress."

"Was," he corrected her. "You got fired."

She gasped so hard he thought she might fall off her stool. "It's not funny!"

"There is no one like you in the world, Franchesca. I'm so glad you're mine."

"Aide! What do I do? Am I going to get sued? Do I have to apologize? Because fuck that. Do you know how long it's going to take me to pay off my credit card on just the development center's income?" She put her head down on the bar, her dark curls spilling over like a waterfall.

"Franchesca, you're not getting sued."

"Did you watch the end of the video when he starts howling about lawyers?"

Aiden sighed and pulled out his phone. Twelve missed calls. He skipped the ones from his mother, father, and Oscar and dialed his PR firm.

"Michael," he said by way of greeting. "Hold on while I conference in Hillary." He called his favorite of the family's attorneys. "Hillary? I'm on the line with Michael. Here's where we stand. I want a countersuit prepared and ready to file if this Goffman asshole is stupid enough to proceed. I also want a statement prepared that says Ms. Baranski and I are weighing the idea of pressing charges for assault. She felt physically threatened by his overtures and handled the situation as best she could to safely diffuse the threat."

Frankie gaped at him.

"I'd like to further add a statement about Kilbourn Holdings' recent stand on sexual harassment and bullying. Some standard wording about how this behavior won't be tolerated whether in a business or social setting, and we are proud of Franchesca and women like her who stand up to outdated patriarchal behaviors and call them out for what they are. Antiquated customs intended to value one sex over the other have no place in this day and age."

"Got it," Michael announced. "I'll coordinate with Hillary, and we'll get you a draft before it drops tomorrow morning."

"Good. Make sure you mention that Ms. Baranski is repped by Hutchins, Steinman, and Krebs."

"Looking forward to kicking some ass," Hillary announced.

"Thank you for the overtime," Aiden said and disconnected the call. His phone was already ringing again. It was his father. He ignored the call. Two texts popped up on the screen from Oscar. They were screenshots from other gossip blogs.

"Your dad is going to hate me even more," Franchesca moaned.

"The only Kilbourn you need to be worried about is me. And I'm proud of you for standing up for yourself. And I also owe you an apology. Our relationship is the reason you're dealing with this, and I can't tell you how sorry I am for that. But I will make it right."

"Oh, God. You're not going to kidnap him, are you?"

"Do I look like Elliot?"

She gave him a ghost of a smile. "So, you're really not mad?"

"I'm furious. But not at you. Never at you."

"You hide it well. I feel it, I blow up, and then I spend a day or two regretting it."

Her phone buzzed on the bar, and she picked it up, wincing. "Oh, God. Brenda, my boss. I can't lose that job, too."

"Let me pay off your credit card." Aiden knew it was a mistake as the words were coming out of his mouth, but he could do this for her, give this to her.

She was already shaking her head. "Uh-uh. Nope. Not happening."

"You know it's nothing to me," he argued.

"Just like you know it's something to me. I'm not some trust fund kid who goes to Mom and Dad to get bailed out."

"First of all, I look nothing like your parents."

"Har har. I'm not taking your money, Aide."

"Would you take Lionel's?"

"What?"

"Would you take Lionel's money if it came in the form of an apology for his behavior?"

"Oh, hell yes."

"Then I'll get you whatever it is he owes you. What's your balance?"

Frankie named a figure so paltry that Aiden had to close his eyes and take a breath. "You're really that close to not scraping by, and you won't let me do anything about it?"

"You're furious at someone else, not me. Remember?"

"You're going to give me a headache."

"Oh, sure. I bash one of your pals in the head with a tray and douse him in champagne, and you're totally fine with it. But I turn down your billions, and then you get a migraine," she pouted.

"What if there was something that I needed desperately that was in your power to give so easily?"

"Money is different. Money is power and control, and I want my own, not someone else's."

He hated to admit it, but he could see her incredibly misguided and stubborn point.

"Fine. I'll get you Goffman's money."

She shook her head and gave a soft laugh. "You're something, Kilbourn."

"Back at you, Baranski. Can we watch the video again?"

Girlfriend of Aiden Kilbourn has secret life of catering jobs and sexual harassment...

Aiden Kilbourn's girlfriend assaults Upper West Side fundraiser attendee...

Aiden Kilbourn's new girlfriend brings Brooklyn bar fight to art gallery fundraiser...

Aiden Kilbourn threatens lawsuit and charges against girlfriend's attacker...

50

"*I* have a name," Frankie muttered at her computer screen. Brenda and Raul had decided it would be better for everyone if she worked from home until the scandal and ensuing news interest died off.

"Damn right you have a name," Marco agreed in her ear.

"Aiden Kilbourn's girlfriend," Frankie snorted. "Every single one of these headlines call me Aiden Kilbourn's girlfriend."

"If they didn't know your name before, they will now."

"Are you eating?"

"Mmm yeah. Corned beef."

"I don't suppose you deliver?"

"Not with everyone in the neighborhood stopping by for gossip on our own Frankie B," Marco snorted.

"We usually only pull in these kinds of sales around the holidays. But you put us on the map. We got neighbors and reporters crawling out of the woodwork."

"Oh, God! No one's talking to the reporters, are they?" Frankie moaned.

"Only in glowing lies about your goodness. You've been dubbed Saint Franchesca."

"You are so full of shit."

"Relax. We take care of our own," Marco said, biting into what Frankie could only assume was a giant dill pickle. "Besides, Aiden and his PR guy stopped by earlier in the week and gave us all the standard line."

"Aiden came to the deli?" Frankie asked.

He'd been so busy in the week since "the incident" they hadn't seen much of each other. And he had definitely not mentioned the visit.

"Yeah, had a roast beef for lunch and took another one for the road. Didn't you see the pictures of him carrying the Baranski Deli bag around? Can't pay for that kind of advertising. Had a real estate developer call us up and ask if we'd consider opening a location downtown."

"Are you kidding me?" She'd been wallowing in her own stew of embarrassment and anger that she hadn't bothered to give two shits about anything else apparently.

"We're not gonna do it. Baranskis are Brooklyn, you know? But it was nice to have the opportunity to say 'No, thanks.'"

"What the hell else have I missed? The Pope pop by for a turkey club and a chat with Dad?"

Marco barked out a laugh. "Ha. I miss your twisted sense of humor. Stop by sometime, okay? Bring your guy."

Frankie sighed. "I will. Thanks for having my back."

"Family. Later, Frank."

"Later, Marco."

Frankie scrolled through the Google Alerts she received in the last week and pulled up a picture. There Aiden was in all his wealthy entrepreneur glory in a sexy navy suit, aviators, and a Baranski Deli bag. Looking at him in the picture, it was hard for her to reconcile the fact that she shared a bed with the man. He looked like he'd strolled off of someone's Perfect Guy Pinterest board.

She knew why he was working so much this week. He was cleaning up her mess, and he'd taken the time to make sure her family was prepared. Just like family would.

Tomorrow, he was taking her to a fundraiser supporting a children's cancer hospital hosted by his mother at her Long Island home. It would be their first "appearance" since the "incident," and Frankie was already feeling the pressure. He hadn't told her anything about his parents' reaction to her brief lack of judgment. All she knew is the family dinner last Saturday had been canceled, presumably because Aiden was working on cleaning up her mess. Or because his parents were horrified by her behavior.

Well, she'd find out soon enough.

She scrolled through some more pictures, finding a few of them together. Aiden escorting her out of her building for brunch after a night of mattress pounding sex. Aiden guiding her into his office building with a hand at her lower back. The two of them wrapped up in each other in line at a coffee shop.

How was this her life? The magnifying glass had lowered without her ever really preparing for it. Now she appeared in magazines. Her decision to smack Lionel with a tray had been debated on a morning talk show. The attention was oppressive. And all she could do was sit and wait for the next celebrity or gossip column favorite to do something outrageous before the rest of the city forgot all about her.

"Come meet me for lunch," Pru demanded.

"I'm not showing my face in that borough until someone famous gets arrested for prostitution."

"You can't let them push you into hiding. You're Franchesca Fucking Baranski. You don't hide from people!" Pru said, working her way into a halftime football coach pep talk.

"I'm not hiding," Frankie argued. "I'm laying low so I don't get sued by an asshole whose retainer for his lawyer costs more than my MBA."

Jesus. She wasn't safe anywhere. Her corporate social responsibility professor had pulled her aside and asked if Mr. Kilbourn would be interested in addressing the class on sexual harassment at the management level in the workplace.

She was one of those bugs on a white board with a pin in it. Collected and preserved by greedy fingers.

"Are you really going to let a little attention banish you from life? Or are you going to grow a pair, put on a gorgeous dress, and come eat lunch with me?"

"I'm not letting anyone banish me from anything."

"Good. Get your ass on the train."

"Pru—"

"Aiden's worried about you. He thinks he's ruined your life. I'm giving you the opportunity to prove to him that you've got a stronger spine than that."

"Do they teach manipulation as a Gen-Ed course in private school?" Frankie asked.

"I will eat a roll if you come to lunch."

"Ugh. Sold."

So, Frankie reluctantly threw on that beautiful red dress, slapped on some makeup, and strutted down Fifth Avenue with Pru. There were a handful of photographers shouting questions, but Frankie iced them out behind her oversized sunglasses.

And damn if it didn't feel good. Good enough that she ordered two pieces of apple pie to go.

"I eat one multigrain roll, and you're going to pound a

thousand calories worth of pie?" Pru asked, eyeing the tasty little to go boxes.

"They're not for me," Frankie laughed. "I'm dropping them off for Aiden and his admin at the office."

Pru shot her a smug look.

"What?" Frankie asked.

"You liiiiike him," she sang.

"You're so junior high," Frankie sighed. "I thought we'd already established the fact that I like him."

"Allow me my gloating time," Pru insisted. "I knew you two would be great for each other, didn't I?"

Frankie leaned back in her chair and crossed her arms. "You *may* have mentioned something along those lines."

"I can't wait to be your matron of honor," Pru said. "I've already got a proposal from a party planner for your bridal shower."

"We're dating and having sex, *not* getting married," Frankie insisted. The idea of a bridal shower like Pru's, with bitchy women whispering about how much they hated each other and useless, overpriced gifts like platinum ice cream spoons, gave her the heebie jeebies.

"We'll see about that," Pru mused, rising and sliding into her coat.

Frankie ignored her friend and buttoned her coat. They were halfway to the door when she stopped short. Pru ran into her back. "Hey," her friend muttered.

Frankie pointed at what had caught her attention. Tucked into a quiet corner in front of the window were Elliot Kilbourn and Margeaux the Dragon Lady.

Elliot had Margeaux's face cupped in his hand and was moving in for what promised to be an NC-17 kiss.

"Gross," Pru hissed. "Go before they see us!"

They hurried out of the restaurant, eyes straight ahead. And didn't stop until they were halfway down the block.

"Well there's a match made in heaven," Frankie said dryly.

"You said it, sister," Pru agreed. "An evil wench and her henchman. We should give them a couple name. Elgeaux? Margel?"

Frankie shuddered and clutched the apple pie to her chest. Nothing good could come from a union like that.

51

*A*iden rested his hand on Frankie's bare thigh in the darkened back of the limo. She'd chosen a short dark purple number with a tempting halter neck that made his fingers itch to untie it. All that stood between him and Frankie's naked, begging body was two hours at his mother's fundraiser and a short speech. There was also the ride home from Long Island to Manhattan, but with a privacy screen and condoms stocked in the small compartment under the bar, that wasn't necessarily a hindrance.

"Do you like your dress?" Aiden asked, skimming his fingertips over her inner thigh.

He watched her open her knees a little wider to accommodate his touch.

Since her lunch with Pru earlier in the week, Frankie had declared herself cured of any worry about what a bunch of strangers with cameras and gossip blog subscriptions had to say about her. Which meant she hadn't heard anything about what the paparazzi had dubbed Dress Gate.

"It's very beautiful," she said, playing with the tulle of the skirt. It nipped in at the waist before flowing into a full skirt reminiscent of 1950s elegance. She looked stunning, fuckable, regal.

"Do you like my hair?" she asked, pushing a pin back in place. It was pinned up in a curling mass leaving her neck bare.

"Very much," he admitted.

"I watched a YouTube tutorial," she said proudly.

"You did it yourself?" he asked, his eyebrows winging up.

"I didn't have time for the salon today."

"What will society say when they find out you do your own hair?" Aiden teased.

She rolled her eyes. "I don't care what they say. It's stupid to drop a couple hundred bucks once a week just to have someone else stab pins into your head. Besides, you'd think they'd have more important things to worry about."

"You'd think," he agreed.

She was one of the few people in the world who could be completely immune to the crush of disapproval orchestrated by the media. She'd survived the attention over the Goffman incident, though he doubted the news would let it drop, especially after today.

But she could survive it. Franchesca Baranski didn't care what a stranger behind a computer screen had to say about her style. And it was refreshing. He'd seen stray negative blog comments destroy entire weeks of the lives of women he'd dated before. "How could they say she wore it better?" "That's photoshopped," they'd howl at the screen while dialing their publicists.

It came with the territory of being considered important.

Frankie couldn't be bothered to care enough to read the drivel in the first place. People could have been singing her praises or tearing her down, and it wouldn't have interested her either way.

What remained to be seen was how she would feel about him going to bat for her. Aiden reached into his jacket pocket and produced the check.

"Here," he said offering it to her.

"What's this?" she asked peering at it in the dark. "Twenty-five hundred dollars? Aiden, I told you I'm not taking your money."

He tapped the top of the check. "It's not my money."

He watched her as a slow smile spread across her face. "Lionel Goffman. And how did you manage that?"

Aiden cleared his throat. There was a lot they had to talk about. But the car was easing up his mother's drive. "We'll talk about it later," he promised.

Frankie tucked the money into her clutch and leaned down to adjust the strap of her stiletto. Her breasts pressed against the fabric of the halter top, begging to be released.

He shifted uncomfortably as his dick hardened. Would he ever stop having that reaction to her?

Oblivious to his lecherous gaze, she sat up and reapplied her lipstick. Dark, sexy red. He wanted to see those lips wrapped around his dick, her big eyes staring up at him as she took him to the edge of reason with her magic mouth.

"Shit," he muttered.

"What's the matter?" she asked, snapping her compact shut and shoving it back in her bag. "You're not getting a headache now are you?"

"More like a cockache."

Not satisfied to take his word for it, she palmed his hard-on through his trousers.

"Damn it, Franchesca! You're not helping."

"Do you pop little blue pills for breakfast? You're hard twenty hours a day. I didn't even do anything to you... yet."

The car pulled up to the front of his mother's estate. He

watched her internally freak out over the opulence. Thick ivory columns graced the front of the house. The circular driveway was made from crushed shells and orbited a large fountain with white statues in various poses of what looked like grief or some kind of extra weird orgy. The cars already here made the driveway look like a luxury sedan showroom.

"Don't tell me what happens after 'yet,'" Aiden begged, closing his eyes and willing his body to relax.

"I won't tell you that I'm going to hold my boobs like this," she said, pressing her tits together, "and let you fuck them."

He hissed out a breath and reached for her. But she scooted out of his grip.

"Don't you dare! Someone is going to open that door in five seconds, and we both better have our clothes on." She wrapped her coat around her.

"Don't play with me, Franchesca."

"Or what?" she asked innocently. "You'll come in your pants?"

He growled and made another grab for her shapely ass. She was his tormentor, his angel, his enemy.

The car door opened, and Frankie winked at him as she slipped out in front of him.

She'd pay. He'd make sure of it. But for now, he'd be the one to suffer.

He caught up with her on the steps and tucked her arm through his. "Slow down, sweetheart, before you break an ankle."

"If you fall right now, you might break your dick," she mused.

"As soon as this is over, I'm going to fuck you so hard you won't be able to sit down tomorrow."

"Promises, promises," Frankie said airily.

"If I shoved my hand up your skirts right now, are you telling me I wouldn't find you wet?" he asked.

Her inhale was sharp, and Aiden knew he wasn't the only one looking forward to the end of the event. They'd be lucky if they made it back to the limo.

"Nice house," she said, her voice strained. Her coat gapped, and Aiden caught a glimpse of hardened nipple under the satin of her top.

"Tell me you're wearing a bra."

"I thought we weren't supposed to lie to each other?"

"Jesus. Franchesca. How am I supposed to get through two hours knowing the only thing between my mouth and your perfect tits is a scrap of satin?"

She shrugged as if she hadn't a care in the world. "I guess you'll just have to think about baseball."

He backed her up against the red brick of the entry way and flexed his hips into her so she could feel how hard she made him. She gave a little gasp and cuddled into him.

Aiden reached into her coat and shoved his hand into the top of her dress. Her nipple throbbed against his palm. He squeezed her breast and ran his thumb over the point.

"Fuck, Aiden," she hissed.

"That's right, baby. You're going to be begging me to fuck you," he promised. "I'm going to ride you until you're out of orgasms. Until you can't move. I'm going to ruin you."

She looked dazed. And Aiden felt like he'd gotten the upper hand again.

"Now let's go smile pretty for the camera," he said

She sagged against the wall when he stepped back. He adjusted himself to a slightly less painful position in his pants. His phone buzzed, and he glanced at the screen. He grimaced.

"What's wrong?" Frankie asked, righting her dress.

"My mother is reminding me that there are security cameras out here."

"Seriously?" she swore darkly. "She already probably hates me for causing a scene, and now I'm dry humping her son on the front porch!"

"There was nothing dry about that, Franchesca," Aiden grinned wickedly.

"Evil." She made a cross with her fingers. "Stay away from me with your magic penis and pheromones."

He laughed and opened the front door.

52

*H*is mother had limited the press to a few society reporters and bloggers. The media was confined to the entry hall, a two-story room in soft ivories and beiges with fussy accent chairs and tables.

It was a very civilized press gauntlet on home turf. Aiden kept Frankie glued to his side. His mother had made it very clear to the press that no one would be discussing Lionel Goffman. They suffered through the same questions over and over again. How did you meet? How long have you been seeing each other? And with each round, he could feel Frankie getting antsier.

"My subscribers wouldn't forgive me if I didn't bring up Dress Gate," the blogger had thick glasses and pink streaks in her hair and directed the question at Frankie.

"What's Dress Gate?" Frankie asked.

"The ongoing conversation about you repeating the red Armani dress you wore to dinner at The Oak Leaf and then again to lunch this week."

"Are you pulling my leg?" Frankie asked, bewildered.

The blogger flashed her a friendly smile and waited.

Frankie looked up at Aiden. She was practically vibrating next to him.

He opened his mouth to speak, but she shook her head. "Oh, I've got this one. Don't you all have more important things to do with your time? It's a beautiful dress. I like it. I'm going to wear it more than once, not throw it away. Deal with it. Why don't you ask me about the small business initiative the city is trying to pass or how survival rates with children fighting leukemia are five percent higher at this facility than any other in the country? Or, at the *very least*, ask Aiden here who he's wearing."

It occurred to Aiden that Frankie might be dangerously close to breaking another nose.

He slid his arm around her waist. "I have very fond memories of the first time she wore it. I hope I get to see it many more times in the future. And speaking of the future, I hope your questions for my girlfriend reflect both her intelligence, her sense of social responsibility, and her involvement in the business community."

He dragged Frankie away before she could add anything further.

"What the fuck? Dress Gate? Are they serious?" she hissed.

"Aiden! Franchesca!" Cecily Kilbourn, dressed in head to toe silver, glittered her way toward them.

"Mom," Aiden said, leaning down to kiss her cheek.

"I'm glad you two were able to make it inside," Cecily teased.

Frankie turned scarlet, and Aiden pulled her into his side and dropped a kiss on top of her head. "Sorry about the R-rating," he said, not feeling remotely sincere in his apology.

"I'm happy to see you happy," Cecily said, winking at them both. "Now, let me introduce you two to some people."

IT WAS the last time he had his hands on Frankie. She was dragged away for introductions and wine while Aiden made his own rounds. His mother had opened up the library, dining room, and grand hall for the event. He tried to stay in the same room as Frankie, but when Pruitt and Chip arrived, he felt like he was constantly chasing her from room to room.

He found her easily in the crowd when he got up to make his speech. He spoke of family and community and the responsibility they felt for providing for a better future. But he thought of Franchesca, naked and bucking under him.

She smiled up at him from her chair. Those red lips curving sinfully.

It was an obsession, her mouth. Listening to the words she would scream or pant or plead while he was inside her. Watching her wrap her lips around his cock as she took him to her throat. That dirty, smart, funny mouth.

He'd given up trying to anticipate exactly what she'd say. She was quicker with a jibe, wittier with a reply than anyone he knew. His Franchesca had the brains that made her even more appealing than her goddess-worthy curves did.

It wasn't just sex. It never had been with Franchesca. He loved watching her. He loved their late-night calls to catch up. He loved knowing he was going to see her and enjoying that painful edge of anticipation. He loved... *her*.

The thought echoed in his head, resonating like the chime of a bell. Resonating like the truth.

People were applauding, but only Frankie existed to him.

He stepped down from the riser his mother had positioned at the end of the grand hall and zeroed in on her. Ignoring the attempts to grab his attention, he reached her and tugged her from her chair.

"Come with me," he ordered, pulling her from the room into the empty hallway.

"Aide, slow down," she said breathlessly behind him. He slowed his steps so she could keep up.

"What's going on down there?" she asked, eyeing his crotch.

Aiden reached down and adjusted his erection that was threatening to tear its way out of his pants.

He turned on her. "This is what you do to me, Franchesca. You eviscerate a reporter, you cross those long, beautiful legs, you order a fucking pizza, and I'm hard."

"Too bad we're surrounded by a hundred people who didn't come to watch a porno," she said. And then she made a mistake. She reached between them and cupped him through the material of his pants.

He grabbed her by the arm, hard. "Don't tease me, Franchesca."

He saw that spark in her eye and recognized it. The woman loved a challenge almost as much as he did. Maybe even more.

"Or what? You'll punish me?" She dragged her knuckles over the ridge of his cock. "You'll fuck me? Where would the keynote speaker drag me off to—"

He didn't let her finish the sentence. He wouldn't have survived it. Aiden kept his grip on her arm and dragged her down the hall.

She was jogging to keep up with him, her short steps on those heels made her tits bounce against their confinement. If he didn't find an empty room in the next six seconds, his drycleaner was going to have a serious issue to deal with.

The kitchen and morning room were too open. There was too much traffic. The library was where the bar was and usually drew a small crowd over the course of an evening. But the music room with its glass doors and dark interior? That would work.

He pulled her inside and kicked the door shut behind him.

"Are you gonna lock it?" Franchesca asked, her voice husky.

"There's no lock," he said, drawing her across the darkened room to the white Chesterfield sofa. "So, if someone comes in here they're going to see me fucking you on this couch. They're going to see your tits bounce every time I drive my dick into you."

That excited her, that potential for exhibitionism. He saw it in the gleam of her eyes.

She always managed to surprise him.

He balanced her on the rolled arm of the sofa. Aiden reached up behind her neck and in one swift tug untied the halter neck of the dress. It was exactly why he'd bought it for her. That quick access. One hard pull, and her breasts were tumbling into his hands.

They were heavy and caramel tipped, the nipples already budding at just the thought of his mouth on them. He skimmed his thumbs over them and listened to her hiss of breath.

Yes, this was love and need and everything in between. He backed her against the couch and dipped his head to feed, first at one breast and then the other. She clawed at him, slipping her hands under his jacket, raking her nails over the fabric of his shirt.

"I don't have a condom, Franchesca," he said, unbuckling his belt.

"I don't fucking care, Aiden."

"Be sure," he warned her. "Because I'm not going to stop."

Her answer was to grip his cock through his pants with one hand while wrestling with his zipper with the other.

He was hard enough that his cock escaped the confines of his pants on its own and hung heavily toward her. He was going to *feel* her tonight. Every sensation would be magnified. Every squeeze of her pussy he'd experience with nothing between them.

He wouldn't give her foreplay or finesse. Not here. But he would finish her in the room in which he'd suffered through summer time music lessons. He'd pour himself into her and brand her from the inside.

Aiden pushed the skirts of her dress up until his fingers found wet satin. "So ready for me, baby. Aren't you?"

Frankie nodded wordlessly, her eyes glazed over as Aiden slid his fingers inside her delicate little thong. She was already spreading her legs for him. He tugged the satin down to her knees and let them fall the rest of the way. He took a moment to stroke his begging cock while Franchesca watched hungrily as his fist closed around his shaft. As he stroked, moisture pooled at the tip like tears of delayed gratification.

"You are so fucking perfect," he praised her as he guided the head of his cock between her legs. "I'm going to fuck you standing like this so I can watch you when you come on me."

She gave him a tiny nod, and he felt like he was back in control. He had won. And what a sweet victory it was with the tip of his dick pushing against her velvet wet.

"This is how I'm going to fuck you tonight in my mother's house with a hundred people on the other side of those glass doors. Anyone could see you. Anyone could watch you come for me."

"Aiden," his name was a strangled cry from her lips.

With one hand holding her hip and skirts, he pulled and thrusted at the same time.

The angle prevented him from going any deeper. But it was enough. Enough for the greedy little squeezes of her pussy to milk him like a fist. Enough for her to buck her hips against him and beg for more.

There was nothing between them and it was exquisite. Her slick flesh held his erection in a death grip. "You're so close already, baby."

"Who knew I'd like being bossed around?" Frankie murmured, a whisper of a laugh hanging on her words.

He needed more of her. Being fully clothed with just his dick hanging out of his pants wasn't enough. But it would get them through the party. He squeezed her hip tighter and hefted her breast with his other hand. Heavy and full, her breasts were a personal fantasy. He wanted to suck, to lick, to make her scream. But with the height difference he had to settle for tugging that perfect dark nipple with his fingers.

She answered by pushing into his hand and bucking her hips harder. She was riding his rigid cock standing up. Sliding back and forth on it taking a few inches each time.

"Aide. I'm coming," she moaned.

There was nothing more important to him than feeling Franchesca fall apart on his bare cock. He didn't care that there were footsteps approaching from the hallway. Didn't care that they could see Marjorie Holland, heiress to a coffee fortune, clear as day from the lit hallway as she wandered past the door.

"Jesus," Frankie hissed.

He needed her to come. Dropping her skirts, Aiden shoved his hand under them and used his thumb to press speedy little circles to her clit.

She went off like a rocket around him, bathing him in wet, gripping him like a fist. Squeezing him to within an inch of his life. And all the while he mimicked the waves with pulls of his fingers on her nipple.

"Ohmygod, ohmygod, ohmygod," she chanted in a soft, desperate whisper.

He wanted to tell her there in that moment, with her lips forming the perfect o. Her hooded eyes glassy as they stared in shock and joy into his own. I love you. He could say it right now. But a Kilbourn never showed all their cards at once.

She was still trembling through the last aftershocks when he spun her around and bent her over the rolled arm of the couch.

He pushed his way inside her, hungry to be welcomed again. This time, he slid all the way home. Frankie let out a sharp gasp that he could feel at the tip of his dick. He wouldn't last long. Not with her draped over a sofa for his pleasure. Not with those beautiful breasts hanging down, nipples brushing tasseled pillows.

Aiden gripped her hips and eased halfway out of her. She whimpered, and it went to whatever primitive part of his brain was responsible for fucking. It broke him. There was no control as he thrust back in. There was no finesse in the way he used her body to build himself to orgasm. He felt the tightening in his balls as they drew up against his body, felt the tingling at the base of his spine.

The sound of his flesh slapping against hers was music to his caveman ears. He was brutal with the power of his thrusts. But when he reached down, hinging over her to take handfuls of her breasts, Franchesca threw her head back and gave a silent scream of ecstasy. Her orgasm, a surprise to them both, destroyed him. There was no holding back or making it last. He poured himself into her, holding deep at the hilt and relishing the feel of his hot seed exploding inside her walls.

This is what had been missing. This is what he would never again do without.

He curled grunting softly through every wrenching spurt,

raining kisses on the bare skin of her back. "My beautiful Franchesca. You're mine now."

"Pretty sure I was before you filled me up with a gallon of your super sperm in your mother's cigar room." He slapped her lightly on the ass. And, liking the sound and her squirmy reaction, did it once more.

"Music room," he corrected.

"Whatever. From now on, I dub this room the secret party orgasm room."

Aiden slowly pulled out of her and watched his come drip out of her, wet and hot on her thighs. He found a box of tissues on a completely impractical secretary desk and returned to her. Franchesca seemed to feel no need to get up and put herself back together. And with her breasts bared, her ass in the air, Aiden was oh so tempted to put his half-hard cock back in her.

"Don't even think about it, Kilbourn. Clean up in aisle three."

He cleaned them both—and the floor—as best he could and pulled her underwear back into place. "I want you to spend the rest of the night with my come inside you."

Aiden Kilbourn gushes over girlfriend at hospital fundraiser...

Is Manhattan's most eligible bachelor officially off the market?

Love is in the air for Aiden Kilbourn...

53

*T*heir bliss lasted until Monday morning.

Franchesca steamed past reception, leaving the staff staring after her.

When Oscar rose from his desk, she shook her head.

"He better be in there, and no one better interrupt us," Frankie said, stabbing a finger at him.

Oscar bobbed his head. "Yes, ma'am!"

She heaved open the door and marched inside, ignoring the delighted expression on Aiden's face. He wasn't allowed to be delighted. He should be shaking in his boots.

She dropped her iPad on the desk in front of him with the offending article.

"You can't just buy a company because some guy was mean to me!"

Aiden's gaze flicked down to the headline and back up.

"Mean to you? Franchesca, he put his hands on you."

"So, you bought his company and *fired* him?"

"He's lucky I didn't do more than that."

"Don't put me in the middle of your pissing contest. Some guy thought he could beat you, so you *ruin him*?"

"Some guy thought he could touch you, drag you away from your work, and insult you, and I'm supposed to do what? Nothing?"

Frankie flopped down in the leather visitor's chair. Gio had called her on her way into work to tell her he always liked Aiden and approved of his methods. She'd only been at her desk long enough to corroborate the story before she took a personal day and rode the train downtown in a fit of rage.

She scrolled through more of the article.

"Oh, my God. He checked into *rehab*?"

Aiden looked so unconcerned with the fact that he'd ruined a man's life, Frankie was aghast.

"You're not going to convince me that I should have left him alone," he said coolly. "And I'm not the only one. Your brothers—"

"If you agree with my brothers, then we have a problem. They're idiots."

"They have your back, and so do I."

"You took it too far, Aiden!" Frankie rose and paced his office.

"Would it make you feel better if I told you he's a systemic harasser? That he's paid off previous accusers? That his company was weeks away from bankruptcy, and all those people would have lost their jobs?"

She flopped back down in the chair again, suddenly exhausted.

"You and I, Franchesca? We're in this together. We belong to each other. And if someone comes after you, they will live to regret it. I expect the same courtesy from you."

Her eyebrows shot up. "So I'm supposed to say thank you?"

The door to Aiden's office flew open. Ferris Kilbourn strode in with Oscar hot on his heels.

"I need a word with you," Ferris announced, zeroing in on Aiden behind the desk.

"Sorry," Oscar mouthed to Frankie.

"Why in the hell would you get tangled up in a mess like Goffman's company?" Ferris demanded, slapping down a newspaper where Frankie had only minutes earlier dumped her tablet. "You're not thinking with your brain, son."

Aiden rose and buttoned his jacket.

Oscar inched out of the room and quietly closed the door.

"If you think I'm going to let you throw away everything this family has built over a girl—"

Frankie cleared her throat and rose from her chair.

"If you have a problem with the way Aiden is running the company, maybe you shouldn't have dumped it on him," she snapped.

"Don't insert yourself in family business, Franchesca," Ferris said coolly.

"You'll watch how you speak to her," Aiden snapped, his voice was cold enough that Frankie shivered.

"You don't have the luxury of dabbling in pet projects, Aiden. You have a legacy to fulfill. People are counting on you. *I'm* counting on you."

"If you have a problem with my performance as CEO, take it to the board," Aiden suggested.

Frankie moved to stand next to him. "Or, you could trust your son to do right by you and the business," Frankie spoke up. "You may not understand or particularly like some of his decisions, but *you* put him in this position. Now it's time to trust him to do what's best for your family."

"I know what's best for the family. And you are not it."

Frankie crossed her arms. "Said the guy who dumped an empire on his son and said, 'good luck running it.' Oh and try to turn your sociopathic half-brother into a contributing adult. I'll be in the Caribbean."

"I've given this company everything," Ferris shouted.

"What have you given your son besides an impossible responsibility?" Frankie shouted back. "You owe him more than a job. And you know what? Even if he wasn't your son, what kind of sense does it make to hand over the reins and then expect him to do everything with one hand tied behind his back? You're sabotaging him because you're doubting yourself."

Ferris glowered at them both and snatched the newspaper off the desk. "You'd better think long and hard about the choices you're making." He was speaking to Aiden but pointed the folded paper at Frankie.

The message was clear. Choose family or choose hot mess girlfriend.

She felt Aiden's hand settle at the small of her back.

"Well, that was pleasant," she said dryly after Ferris stormed out. "Are you okay?"

Aiden put his hands on her shoulders and squeezed. "Come on," he said, nudging her toward the door.

"Where are we going?"

"I want air. And coffee."

"Air and coffee sound good." She watched him slide into his long wool coat, admiring the view of tailored suit, strong jaw, and unreadable eyes. "What if we run into your dad in the elevator?"

"Then you can hit him with a tray," Aiden promised.

Oscar was sitting behind his desk, pretending to be very busy.

"Oscar, we're going for coffee. Do you want us to bring anything back for you?" Frankie offered.

"Double espresso with soy," Oscar rattled off without looking up from his blank word document where he was typing gibberish. "Please."

Frankie wasn't sure if she or Ferris had scared Oscar more.

They took the elevator in silence, and Frankie let Aiden lead her through the lobby and out into the frigid first day of March.

He held her hand but remained silent on the half block walk to a café. Frankie's nerves all but crackled. Was he ushering her off site to politely explain that things wouldn't work between them anymore? That they'd had a good run, but family came first?

She swallowed hard. She couldn't blame him exactly. She'd been a disaster from the start. In the time since Barbados, she had assaulted his brother, insulted his stepmother, embarrassed his entire family with a public brawl, and now was to blame for Aiden using the company coffers to get even with someone who dared act like an asshole in her presence.

Maybe she should just do it first. *Thanks for all the amazing sex and being a really great, smart, funny, protective boyfriend, Aiden, but it's time to move on...*

Her heart was pounding so loud in her ears, she didn't hear him ask her what she wanted the first time.

"Franchesca?"

"Oh, sorry. Tea. Ginger?" She needed something to calm her stomach that was currently turning somersaults.

He ordered for them and led her to a small table in the corner. Solicitously, he helped her out of her coat. If he was letting her take her coat off, was he settling in for a long-winded break up? She'd rather he just rip off the bandage and let it weep pus in the open air.

Gross.

"Franchesca," he began.

She squeezed her eyes closed, bracing for the brush off.

But no brush off came. No words at all. She opened one eye to peek. He was watching her with amusement.

"What are you doing?"

"I'm bracing myself."

"For what?"

"For the 'it's been nice knowing you' speech."

"That's what you think?" he laughed. "I'm surprised you didn't try to beat me to the punch and dump me in the lobby."

She blushed.

"You thought about it?" he asked, somewhere between astonished and amused.

"I didn't know what this was. I thought you were mad. I— just shut up. Okay?"

The barista called Aiden's name, and still chuckling, he picked up their order.

He handed her the tea and sank back down in his chair.

"Thank you."

"For what? I've done nothing but create disasters since we met."

"For doing what no one else in my entire life has had the balls to do. You stood up to my father."

"What about your mother?" Frankie asked, blowing on the steam rising from her cup.

"Mom convinced, cajoled. She never yelled at him. Never called him on his bullshit."

"See, this is why people become assholes. They're insulated by trust funds or glass towers or titles, and everyone else is too scared to point out they've turned into a monster."

"But you'll call a monster a monster?"

"What's he going to do? Go open a deli next to my parents'

and run them out of business? Kidnap one of my brothers? I'm one of the little people. Not even worth the energy of flicking me off."

Aiden shook his head. "But you're important to me. That makes you important to him."

"You're not suggesting your father would go all Elliot on me, are you?"

"Kilbourns are ruthless," Aiden reminded her. "I've told you before."

"Ruthless or not, hurting me would only hurt you. And as shitty as his attitude is right now, I don't believe your father wants to hurt you."

"What did you mean he was sabotaging me because he's doubting himself?" Aiden asked, studying her over his coffee.

"A little psychology. No one walks away from their empire without worrying that they're making the right decision. He doesn't know who he'll be if he's not part of that empire anymore, and that reality is hitting him."

"So you pushed the button?"

"I Aidened him."

"When did you start playing so dirty?" Aiden asked, taking her hand in his and tracing his thumb over her palm.

"When I started hanging out with the ruthless, pillaging Kilbourns."

54

*A*iden checked his phone for messages from Frankie as he headed toward his waiting car. He'd just wrapped another round of meetings with management in Goffman's app development firm and could feel the excitement of momentum. With a few tweaks to the corporate structure, an overhaul of terrible existing policies, and a rebranding under the Kilbourn umbrella, he could see a very bright future for the company.

His father would have to eat his words on this deal eventually.

He was opening Frankie's text when he collided with someone.

"I'm sorry," he said, reaching out to steady the woman.

"Oh, Aiden!" Margeaux, the bitchy bridesmaid from Chip and Pru's wedding, stared up at him, her eyes welling with tears.

Of all the people to smack into on a busy sidewalk, it had to be the one who would probably sue him or try to blackmail him into bed.

"Are you hurt?" he asked curtly, looking her over. She wore

a camel-colored wool coat. Her blonde hair was curled in thick ringlets that hung down past her shoulders. Her missing eyebrow had mostly grown back.

She gripped him by the lapels of his coat and threw herself against his chest. "I just need a friendly face," she said in a tremulous voice.

Aiden looked over at his car and sighed. So close.

"I don't know what to do! My boyfriend and I just got into a fight, and he left me here," she said, her voice pitching into a wail.

Aiden gritted his teeth. She was a horrible human being but a horrible human being in need. "Can I offer you a ride?" he asked.

She nodded, looking up at him as if he were her own personal hero. He didn't like it. There was something slippery about this woman. Like an eel. He didn't think she'd appreciate the analogy.

He opened the door for her and, with a glance over his shoulder, slid in next to her. She crowded him on the seat, leaning against him. "Where can we drop you?" Aiden asked briskly.

"Oh, Fifth and East 59th. Please." She added the word like it was an afterthought. It sounded foreign from her lips.

She was fiddling with her phone, still leaning too close. He pulled out his own phone, using his elbow to dislodge her from his side, and scrolled through his messages. Frankie was leading another social media workshop, and thanks to her known association with Aiden, enrollment had skyrocketed with small business owners hoping the Kilbourn fortune would spread through osmosis.

Frankie: I think they're half expecting you to come strolling through the door doling out money bags.

Aiden: I should stop by with my money bags. I seem to have an excess of it since my girlfriend won't let me spend it on her.

Frankie: Funny guy. Gotta go teach people how to geographically target their Facebook ads.

Aiden: See you tonight, beautiful.

She responded with a heart emoji. And Aiden eyed it feeling like a king. She didn't know it, but she was falling for him. He just had to wait for the right time to bring it to her attention. And possibly come clean that he'd come to the conclusion weeks ago.

He was in love and, for the first time in his life, thinking about next steps in the relationship department.

He sent a glance in Margeaux's direction. She was reclining on the opposite side of the car, a sly smile on her face as her fingers flew over her phone's keyboard.

"So, you had a fight with your boyfriend?" Aiden asked, not really caring. But they had fifteen blocks to go, and her change in attitude unnerved him.

"Hmm?" she said, looking up from her screen. "Oh, yes. A fight. And it's the last one as far as I'm concerned. I deserve better, and I'll see that I get it."

"Mmm," Aiden murmured noncommittally. From his limited experience with Margeaux, she deserved to have lemon juice poured into paper cuts every day for the rest of her miserable life. But who was he to judge?

He had Frankie, and that was all that mattered. There would be no more trading one girlfriend for another, one heiress for another. He had what he wanted. Finally.

Aiden briefly entertained the idea of sending Goffman a thank you card for being an asshole.

He was feeling confident in the future. Franchesca was finishing up her MBA in the next two months, and they'd been discussing what she'd do professionally afterwards. He'd hoped she'd consider a position with his company. She'd laughed in his face when he suggested it. But he was persuasive. He could wear her down. And he could use her. Even if she didn't want to work with him directly, he had a number of new smaller acquisitions that could use her energy. She liked the small business arena. Maybe he could build something for her to manage?

He'd bring it up again in a week or so and test the waters.

"Here we are," Morris announced from behind the wheel. Whatever business Margeaux had was in a pricey art deco hotel. Morris hustled around and opened the rear door. Aiden stepped out and offered Margeaux his hand.

"Best of luck to you, Margeaux," he said.

"I don't need luck," she said with a smirk and then raised on her tip toes to press a kiss to the side of his mouth. "See you around."

She strolled into the hotel. Aiden shook his head.

Morris gave a shiver. "That one there's an evil one," he announced.

"You're not wrong," Aiden agreed.

Once a bachelor always a bachelor

Aiden Kilbourn caught sneaking into hotel with socialite

Aiden Kilbourn's girlfriend devastated by affair

55

Frankie locked the front door of the development center behind her and shouldered her bag. It was cold and dark. A typically depressing March evening. But she had Aiden and takeout to look forward to in a few hours. She'd let that thought keep her warm on the walk home.

Her phone vibrated in her pocket, but before she could dig it out, a shadowy figure pushed away from the wall one storefront down.

"Well, if it isn't my old friend Franchesca," Elliot Kilbourn said slyly, falling into step with her.

"How's the schnoz, Elliot?" she asked breezily. There was only one reason Elliot would be waiting for her. Trouble.

"I snore now, thanks to you."

"Consider it a souvenir that reminds you not to abduct people."

"Did you know that I'm not the only Kilbourn with dirty secrets?" he asked. His gleeful tone put her on edge.

Frankie stopped mid-stride. "Look. Let's get this over with, okay? I've had a long day. Just drop the subterfuge and spill it."

"I came to offer my condolences," he said, grinning devilishly as if he relished every word. "The news is breaking right now."

He handed her his phone and Frankie gave the screen a careless glance.

Once a bachelor, always a bachelor. Aiden Kilbourn throws over girlfriend for hotel fling with socialite.

The pictures. God. The pictures. Aiden with Margeaux Fucking Assface in his arms on a city sidewalk. Their heads were tilted toward each other, faces serious. It looked... intimate. Aiden in his limo with Margeaux cuddled up against his side. She was pouting for the selfie while he looked at his phone. Then Aiden and Margeaux getting out of the car in front of a hotel and Margeaux leaning into him, pressing a kiss to his mouth.

Frankie was going to murder someone. She just wasn't sure who to start with.

Wordlessly, she handed the phone back to Elliot.

"He's not the guy you thought he was," Elliot said. "He's selfish and cruel and only cares about himself."

Frankie started to walk away. Her gut was roiling with anger and pain and confusion.

"There's a SnapChat video too. But you probably don't need to see that," he said, picking up the pace to keep up with her. "And there's one more thing."

Frankie pinched her lips shut. She was going to throw up. Or scream. Or both.

"Aiden's the reason Chip dumped your friend all those years ago."

"What did you just say?" Frankie came to a screeching halt.

"He and Chip were talking at my parents' house. They

didn't know I was around. They never did."

Frankie saw the bitterness in Elliot's eyes.

"Chip mentioned he was thinking about proposing soon. But Aiden didn't like that. He told Chip that he didn't think Pruitt was a good match. That she wouldn't be the kind of partner he'd need. Chip didn't see what he was doing, but I did."

"What was he doing?" Her phone vibrated again, and she knew without looking it was Aiden.

"He was pulling strings like a puppet master. Kilbourns learn it from birth. How to make people do what you want them to do. He 'guided' Chip to the same conclusion, telling him Pruitt was too immature, too needy. She wouldn't be the right partner for him."

"Why would he do that?" Frankie asked, her voice barely a whisper. Why would Aiden ruin Chip's happiness? Why would he set into motion years of misery and pain for Pruitt?

"Who knows?" Elliot shrugged. "Maybe he wanted her for himself? Maybe he couldn't stand seeing his friend happy? The point is, he's not the man you thought he was."

"Go home, Elliot," Frankie said quietly. A ton of bricks had just leveled her. And worse, she hadn't seen them coming. She should have known better.

"Sorry to be the bearer of bad news," he offered, still smiling over whatever triumph he'd achieved by carving her out and leaving her bleeding.

"No. You're not."

She walked away, and this time, he didn't stop her. He left whistling a happy little tune.

Frankie's phone vibrated again. She pulled it out. Aiden.

He'd called four times so far. Pru called too. But she wasn't prepared to talk. She needed to go someplace. And home was no longer an option.

He'd find her there.

She turned around and let herself back into the darkened office. Locking the door securely behind her, Frankie took her laptop upstairs to the conference room and sat in the dark.

She brought up the first gossip blog she could think of and forced herself to read the article, to look at the pictures. "Oh, shit. There really is a video," she murmured to herself. Frankie didn't consider herself a coward under the worst circumstances, but it still took her nearly five minutes to push play.

It was Margeaux—that nasty asshole—laying across the leather of a limo bench seat. Her head was in a man's lap. He was wearing a gray suit, just like Aiden's in the pictures. She was toying with his tie, stroking his thigh. "Heading to the Manchester for some afternoon delight," she purred. Frankie wanted to break her laptop, snap it in half, set it on fire. Anything to get the image of Margeaux and Aiden out of her head. A hand in the video swooped down to stroke over Margeaux's jaw.

Frankie frowned and hit pause. She backed up the video and watched it again. The hand was wrong. So was the watch. Aiden wore a Patek Philippe watch that cost more than her parents' house when they bought it forty years ago. A sentimental and flashy gift from his father upon joining the company. The man in the video wore Cartier.

Son of a bitch.

She scrolled back to the pictures. The first one on the sidewalk. It was shot as if to highlight Margeaux's face as she looked up at Aiden. His face was angled away. It was definitely him, but there was something about the photo. It wasn't the blurry shot of a tourist or a rushed frame from a paparazzi. It looked crisp, clear, professional. Staged?

Frankie rubbed her temples. Her phone vibrated again on the table in front of her. It was Gio.

"What?" she answered.

"Dude, I don't know what's going on, but Aide's about five seconds from tearing Brooklyn apart brick by brick looking for you."

"You see the news?" she asked.

"Yeah, I saw it," Gio said, sounding more annoyed than furious.

"Front row at a Knicks game's enough to buy your loyalty?" Frankie asked.

"Jesus, Frankie. The dude in the video had a manicure. It ain't Aiden. The guy is losing his shit, sis. I know you're gonna hate me for this, but I think someone set him up."

She'd already come to the same conclusion, but that didn't explain the other pictures. The embrace, the kiss. And there was that whole other thing about destroying the happiness of her best friend in the world.

"I'm not ready to talk to him yet," Frankie said.

"Can I at least tell him you're okay?"

"Fine. Whatever. Look, I gotta go."

"Are you okay?" Gio asked.

For the first time, she felt tears prick at her eyes.

"Not really," she said, her voice breaking.

Gio swore. "Listen. You know I have your back, right? No matter what."

"Yeah. I know," she said, finding a sliver of comfort in that. *Family first.*

She hung up and dialed the only person who would tell her the truth.

56

*a*iden kicked open the door of his penthouse and strode inside. The desk had called to tell him that Ms. Baranski was waiting for him. He saw her, sitting on the leather sofa, a bag packed on the floor, two glasses of scotch in front of her. Relief, fast and fierce, coursed through him.

"Franchesca," he whispered her name.

She turned to him but didn't look him in the eye, and Aiden's stomach sank. He reached for her, but the chill she gave off stopped him.

"Tell me you don't believe it," he said quietly. He needed her to know him, to trust him. The idea that she could ever think that he'd—

"Some of the pictures are real," she said flatly.

He nodded. "Yes. I ran into her after my meeting this week. She bumped into me and acted as if she was crying. Said she had some kind of fight with her boyfriend."

"You gave her a ride," Frankie filled in.

"Yes. *Just* a ride." He reached for her again, but she leaned forward and picked up a glass and handed it to him.

He closed his fingers around the cold of the crystal and

wished it was her skin. If he could only touch her, everything would be all right. They couldn't lie to each other when they were touching.

"I believe you," she said simply, and the ball in Aiden's gut dissolved. He dropped to his knees in front of her dumping the scotch on the rug to run his hands up the outside of her thighs.

"I'm so sorry. I don't know why Margeaux would have done something like that. Attention or—"

"Revenge," Frankie filled in. "Did you know she was involved with Elliot?"

Aiden's spine stiffened. The alcohol soaked into the knees of his trousers. Elliot. It wasn't Margeaux and the fake scandal. It was Elliot and what he'd told her.

"I didn't know," he began, waiting for her to determine his fate.

"I'm not going to do this anymore, Aiden." Her voice was so calm, so flat.

"Franchesca, you can't leave." She couldn't. It was physically impossible for her to leave. She had possession of his heart. If she walked out, she'd leave with it.

She shook her head, and when she met his gaze, he saw the temper in her eyes. "Don't 'you can't' me. I'm sick of being in a fucking circus."

She rose, and he grabbed onto her hips, his forehead landing on her stomach. "Franchesca."

She pulled him to his feet. "Look at me, Aiden," she ordered.

He did as he was told and cupped her face in his hands. She closed her eyes for a moment. And when she opened them, he knew he'd lost her.

"I want you to understand I know you didn't have an affair

with Margeaux. I know that you wouldn't have done that to me."

"Then why..." he trailed off. He knew why. He wanted her to say the words that he deserved to hear.

"I want to hear you say it." Her words echoed his own thoughts. "I want you to tell me."

Aiden clenched his jaw. He felt powerless. Was this karma for all his years of manipulation, living for the pursuit of success at all costs? He could have had it all, and now he'd be left with everything he had before. Ironically, it added up to the equivalent of nothing without Franchesca.

"I was afraid she wasn't right for him. She seemed so young, so immature. He was my first real friend, and I was looking out for him. At the time, I didn't think she was the right partner for him."

Frankie flinched at his words, and he felt her pain like it was his own wound.

"Go on," she said flatly.

"He had just graduated and was talking about getting engaged. I thought... I thought it was a mistake. I didn't realize how strong her feelings were for him. I'd only met Pruitt a handful of times. I thought I was doing him a favor."

"Do you know how devastated she was?" Frankie asked, her voice low and strained.

"I had no idea until you mentioned it at the wedding. When they found their way back together again, they seemed so much better suited. She was steadier, more mature. She was good for him. I thought the time apart had been warranted."

"She didn't eat, Aiden. She couldn't get out of bed. She should have been hospitalized, but instead her parents pumped her full of anti-anxiety meds and put a full-time nurse on her. She thought she'd met *the one*. Thought her future was just starting, and then you took it away from her because she wasn't good enough."

Her voice rose sharply.

"Franchesca, sweetheart. I'm so sorry. I never meant to cause any harm. I was looking out for a friend and had I known how deeply Pruitt felt for him I never would have said anything."

"If she wasn't good enough, then what am I, Aiden? If Pruitt 'Blueblood' Stockton isn't good enough, why did you waste so much time slumming it with me?"

He gripped her arms. "You are everything to me, Franchesca. Everything I didn't know I was missing. Everything that I can't live without now. I love you."

He saw them, bright in her eyes. Shock and horror. "What did you just say?" There was nothing flat and dull about her tone now.

"I said I fucking love you."

"You do *not* get to manipulate me with that word! You don't get to pull it out and throw it down when you're in fucking trouble for hurting people that I love. You don't get to use love as a tool to get you what you want."

The panic was clawing its way up his throat. "It's the truth, Franchesca. Damn it. I'm no good at this. I've never told anyone who wasn't my mother that I—"

"Stop talking, Aiden! Christ. I'm a regular person. Regular people don't have photographers following them around or rich assholes trying to destroy their relationships. Regular people don't use love as a weapon."

"What do you want me to do? Tell me, and I'll do it," Aiden commanded.

"I want you to let me go," Franchesca shouted.

"No!" He would do anything for her. Just not that.

"You don't get to decide to keep us together. You hurt my

friends. You hurt me. And you didn't tell me yourself. I had to hear it from your creepy brother who was waiting to pounce outside my office. Everywhere I go, there's a Kilbourn telling me I'm not good enough."

"Elliot is my problem. I'll handle him."

"He cooked this up. He and Margeaux. I'd bet your big fat checking account on it. Pru and I saw them when we were out to lunch. I thought they were dating, but they were plotting."

"Elliot wants me to buy him out of the company. He said he'd tell you about Pru and Chip if I didn't close the deal."

"So why didn't you?" Frankie demanded.

"I thought he was bluffing."

"Wrong fucking answer, Kilbourn!"

"It's the truth!" Aiden roared.

"I *know* it's the truth! That's the problem! I can't deal with this, Aiden. I don't want to spend my life being outmaneuvered or lied to or constantly threatened or used because of your last name. I want a *partnership*. That's not what we have."

She made a move toward her duffle bag, and he stopped her, grabbing her arm.

"We can have it. I swear to you, Franchesca."

"You said you'd give me everything I wanted," she said, looking at him accusingly.

"Anything and everything."

"But you couldn't even be honest with me. Tell me, when Elliot came to you with what he knew, did it even occur to you to come clean? To tell me? To take your lumps and hope for the best?"

Had he considered it? Or had he just decided to handle it?

"Everything is a power play to you," she said quietly. "And I'm done being played."

She tried to free herself from his grip, but he held on tighter.

"You're hurting me."

"*You're* hurting *me*, Franchesca. Let's talk about this. Let me fix this!" If she walked out that door, he knew she'd never be back. It was like holding back the tide, but he'd be damned if he didn't at least try.

"I'm not lying when I say I love you. I really felt it and knew what it was at my mother's house. I looked at you in the audience, and you're all I saw. You're all I want to see every day for the rest of my life. Please don't let this break us, Franchesca."

"You've known you loved me for how many weeks now, and you didn't think to tell me? Like an ace up your sleeve? Your get out of jail free card? Do you see how fucked up that is? Do you think that's what I deserve?"

"No, of course not. I've never been in love before, Franchesca. So excuse me if I don't know how to process it. It took a battle just to get you to date me. I didn't know what it would be like to say those words to you and hear nothing but silence in return. I wasn't ready."

"Who said there would have been silence, you idiot?" Temper and tears glistened in her eyes. "Who said you were the only one who felt those feelings?"

He gripped her arms. "What are you saying?"

"I'm saying I loved you, too. You ass!"

Loved? How could it be past tense just like that?

"Why didn't you tell me?"

"Because you're Aiden Kilbourn, permanent bachelor and womanizer. You're married to your work. And I didn't know how to say it. I wasn't saving it up to tip the scales at the right moment. I didn't know how to tell you without breaking my own heart."

"Franchesca, we can make this work. We love each other."

"It's not enough."

"It has to be."

She shook her head and pulled free from his grip and held up her hands when he stepped forward. "Look at me. Understand me. I don't want to be here and I don't want you to come with me."

"Why can't we talk this out? Why can't you let me fix this?"

"Because a team fixes things together, Aiden. And we're not a team, and we're not together."

He took a step back as if she'd landed a physical blow. This couldn't be the end of it. But she was picking up her bag and moving to the door. She paused, her hand on the knob.

"Don't talk to me. Don't come see me. Don't call me."

God she meant it. He'd never seen her so serious, so hurt. And he'd done that.

"And one more thing. Elliot's trying to ruin you, Aiden. Be careful there."

She left, closing the door behind her with a quiet click. And all the light went out of his world.

57

*B*ack in her apartment, in the bed they had shared, she finally let the tears come. Hot and salty, they scorched paths down her cheeks and soaked the pillow beneath her. His pillow. She'd known, hadn't she, that this was how it would end? She'd taken precautions, but in the end, nothing could have guarded her heart from Aiden.

He'd looked so brokenly at her as she left. She felt his pain echo inside her. They were both to blame. She for falling for him and him for disappointing her. He would always be looking for a way to win. It was in his blood.

Frankie rolled over, clutching the pillow to her chest and cried until she slept.

The dull gray winter morning did little to coax her out of bed. She'd seen Pru in the depths of despair over Chip and had promised herself she'd never let a man wreck her like that. And here she was aching on the inside, eyes puffy from so many tears shed.

She couldn't today. She couldn't go out into the world, not with news of Aiden and Margeaux smugly splattered on every blog and news site in the city. Not with the truth of her loneliness.

She texted Brenda and sent her apologies saying she wasn't feeling well and couldn't come in today.

Great. Not even the threat of loss of income could tempt her out of bed. She was officially a broken woman. She didn't even want food. She just wanted to be left alone.

As if the universe heard that thought, there was a loud pounding on her door. Frankie's heart raced at the thought that it might be Aiden who magically found the right words to stop her hurt. She pulled a pillow over her head and pretended the world didn't exist.

Unfortunately, the world had a key to her apartment. Two big bodies hit her mattress, jostling her under the covers.

"Go away."

Her pillow, the one that smelled like Aiden's shampoo—oh God, his thousand-million-dollar shampoo was still in her shower—was ripped from her face.

Her brother Marco smiled down at her. "There she is," he said cheerfully.

"Get. Out."

"It's either us or Ma, and she's curled up in the fetal position crying about all those beautiful Kilbourn babies she'll never get to hold," Gio announced from the foot of her bed.

Frankie did the last thing her brothers expected her to do. She burst into tears. In all her adult years, she had never once cried in their presence. Not even that time when one of their buffoon cousins broke her arm playing flag football on Thanksgiving.

"Oh, shit," Marco whispered.

"What do we do?" Gio demanded.

"I can still hear you, idiots," Frankie sobbed, ripping the pillow out of Marco's hand and holding it over her head.

"She trying to suffocate herself?"

"I'm callin' Rach. She'll know what to do."

"You're not calling anyone! I'm fine!" Frankie wailed. If she was going to humiliate herself, she was going to commit to it. At least it would teach her brothers to never enter her apartment without an express invitation again.

Not that they'd be interrupting anything. New life plan: She was going to age badly and rescue a bunch of cats that would one day eat her in her sleep.

Frankie heard Marco on the phone in her living room through the paper-thin walls. "I never saw her like this before," he was saying.

"What can we do, Frankie?" Gio was asking. "You want us to go beat the shit out of him?"

She sat upright. "No, I don't want you to beat the shit out of him!"

He frowned. "You want us to beat the shit out of her?"

"Maybe." She shook her head. "No, I don't want anyone beating the shit out of anyone. It wasn't true. He was set up, but we're still broken up. Okay?"

"I'm confused."

She flopped back down on the bed and held the pillow over her face.

Marco came back in the room. "Rach gave me a really specific list. I'm gonna go get the stuff. You stay here. And don't let her look out the window."

"Why?" Frankie asked, sitting up again.

"Shit. I thought you couldn't hear me through the pillow."

"What's outside my window?" Frankie scrambled over the mattress, and Gio made a dive for her, but she dodged him. She pressed her face to the dingy glass. "You've gotta be kidding me."

"Fuckin' paparazzi," Gio sighed.

"Why are there cameramen outside my building?"

"I guess you didn't see the news today."

"What the hell could have possibly happened?"

"Aiden filed a lawsuit against that Mar-goat chick and every blog and news site that printed the story. Most of them already printed retractions."

"How is this my life?" she murmured to herself.

"I'm going out the alley. Be back in a few," Marco said, shrugging back into his coat.

Frankie drew her blinds, throwing the apartment into the gloomy kind of darkness she felt in her heart. She let Gio talk her into at least getting out of bed and brushing her hair, but when she spotted Aiden's comb and a stray pair of boxer briefs in the hamper, she lost all desire to behave like a human.

They slumped on the couch staring at a rerun until Marco returned.

"Okay, we got some glossy magazines that don't say anything about keeping your man on the cover," he said unloading the bag on her coffee table. "Some tissues in case that thing that happened in there happens again. Six different kinds of chocolate bars. Two pints of ice cream because any more than that and you'll hate yourself in the morning. And a quart of chicken noodle."

"What's in the other bag?" Frankie asked, with a sniffle.

"I bought a bunch of blow 'em up Blurays that we can watch. And the taco truck was two blocks over, so I got some of those, too."

"Thanks, Marco," she said. "Thanks, Gio."

Gio ruffled her freshly brushed hair and flipped her off. "Family."

AIDEN HADN'T CALLED. When she finally got the nerve to turn her phone back on, she had fifteen missed calls from him, but that was before the showdown at his penthouse. He hadn't called her since. But he had texted.

Aiden: I know you said no calling. But you didn't explicitly say no texting. And until you tell me otherwise, I'll keep texting. I miss you. I'm sorry.

Aiden: I have exactly everything I had before you, but now it feels like nothing.

Aiden: I wish we were on your couch. You cuddled up to me. Me playing with your hair. Leftovers going cold on the table. I miss you.

Aiden: I'm suing a bunch of people today. I thought you should know. No one gets away with hurting you, Franchesca. Not even me. I'm in misery without you.

The next morning the gifts started. No direct contact. Just little gifts with handwritten cards delivered by messenger. On Tuesday, he sent a stack of romance novels and a hefty gift card to Christian's salon to her apartment. On Wednesday, when she finally returned to work, he had gourmet hot chocolate delivered for her, Brenda, and Raul. Frankie didn't want to know how he knew she was at work. If he was still keeping tabs on her, he still had hope. Something she didn't.

On Thursday, Frankie found a bundle of fuzzy knee-high socks outside her apartment door. The kind she loved to wear under her boots.

Friday brought a silky soft set of pajamas. Not sexy lingerie but the kind you'd pull on after a long week and live in for the weekend. She'd put them on immediately and curled up on the couch with Aiden's Yale sweatshirt that she'd pulled from the laundry basket so it wouldn't lose his scent.

The week was a blur of "no comment" when she (rarely) ventured out in public and unenthusiastic "I'm fines" at work and around her mother's dining table. She felt cold inside as if she'd taken the winter within her and would never again warm up.

And every night, she fell asleep on the couch without ever turning on the TV, avoiding the big, beautiful bed and its memories.

*a*iden gazed out his office window, ignoring the pile of things that required his attention on the desk. He had nothing to give. Just showing up drained him. He was tuned out, shut down, and it was affecting his work. Oscar was walking on eggshells around him. Meetings were magically rescheduled for future dates. His mother spent their entire dinner together last night smiling sympathetically at him.

And Aiden couldn't rouse himself to care.

His desk phone beeped.

"Yes?"

"There are two burly gentlemen from Brooklyn here to see you," Oscar announced.

"We're comin' in, Aide." Aiden heard Gio's voice through the door.

Great. Just what he needed. The Baranski brothers ready to beat the hell out of him.

"Send them in," he sighed.

A second later, his door opened, and Gio and Marco sauntered in. They were probably playing it cool so Oscar didn't call security right away.

Marco slumped into one of the visitor's chairs while Gio prowled the office. Aiden couldn't tell if he was admiring the view or looking for security cameras.

He waited for one of them to speak first, hurling threats or accusations, demanding sacrificial kneecaps or whatever body part it was the Baranski brothers would break for their little sister.

"Bro, what the hell?" Marco asked, breaking the silence. "You gotta watch yourself around girls like that."

"Girls like what?" Aiden asked calmly.

"That Margeaux chick," Gio filled in, coming over to lean against the corner of his desk.

"She exudes evil, man. I'm surprised you fell for it and let her set you up like that," Marco sighed.

"Set me up? You believe me that nothing happened?"

Gio snorted. "Frankie's prime rib, and we're supposed to believe you'd go through the drive-thru for some Skeletor, pinched-face, ball buster?"

"So, you're *not* here to beat the shit out of me?" Aiden clarified.

The brothers threw back their heads and laughed but didn't give him a definitive yes or no.

Aiden's phone buzzed, and he glanced down at the screen.

Oscar: Do I need to call security?

Aiden: Not unless you hear me sobbing for my mommy.

He returned his attention to the brothers. "Then why are you here?"

"Frankie is wrecked," Gio announced.

"We figured you probably weren't doing so hot either," Marco chimed in.

"You could say that," Aiden said, looking down at the disorganized mess on his desk. "I need to get her back."

Marco sighed, and shoved a hand through his thick hair. "I don't know, man."

Aiden rubbed a hand over his brow. "No advice, no magic key to make her forgive me?"

"She ever tell you about our second cousin Mattie?" Gio asked.

Aiden shook his head.

"Yeah, that's because she won't speak his name. He got gum in her hair when she was nine, and Ma had to cut it out. She didn't speak to Mattie again until his wedding last year."

"She's not big on forgiveness," Marco said. "Like ever."

"It can't be over," Aiden said, pushing his phone around on the desk. She'd not once responded to one of his texts or gifts. Desperation made his chest ache.

"Ah, shit," Gio sighed, scratching the back of his head. "Look. You can't keep texting her and sending her stuff, okay? Anything you do is gonna look like psychological warfare."

"You want me to give up?" Aiden asked.

"Nah, man," Marco said. "Just make it *look* like you're giving up."

"Look, guys. I haven't been sleeping well. I'm not getting what you're trying to say," Aiden said.

"She's a smart girl, our Frankie. Stubborn but smart," Gio began.

Marco shifted in his chair. "You fucked up, pretty big. But so did she."

"She didn't do anything," Aiden argued.

"She's had one foot out the door your entire relationship because she figured it would end bad. She was scared, and if you ever repeat that to her, I'll fuck you up and lie about it," Gio said, pointing a finger at him.

"She was looking for an excuse," Aiden said half to himself.

"Yeah, but given her current level of misery, if you give her some space, she's gonna figure it out that she isn't the innocent party here either."

"How much space?" Aiden asked. He needed them to spell it out for him. The idea of abandoning his efforts—giving up control—was terrifying, but a tiny spark of hope lit in his chest.

"All the space," Marco said.

"No texting, no presents, no nothing," Gio added.

Aiden covered his eyes for a minute trying to wrap his head around the idea of giving up and hoping for the best. It went against everything in his DNA to leave things up to chance.

"I was thinking about paying off her student loans," he admitted. His small gestures hadn't gotten her attention. Maybe a bigger one would. She would have at least been compelled to come to his office and scream at him.

"Oh, Christ, no!" Marco said, looking horrified.

"She'd hate that, man," Gio agreed. "Do not, I repeat, do not go throwing piles of money at Frankie. She'll just set them on fire."

"So, I give up? Leave her alone?"

"You make it *look* like you're giving up," Marco said as if there was a difference.

"If I do this, do you think there's a chance she could forgive me?"

"Yeah," Gio said supportively. "I do."

"A real small one," Marco piped up. He shrugged when his brother shot him an incredulous look. "What? I don't want him to get his hopes up if she decides to Frosty the Snow Bitch him permanently."

"Listen, you gotta think of something else, Aide. Are you prepared to forgive her? She walked out on you instead of having your back—again, if you ever say this to her I will ruin your very nice face also probably your fancy suit—and if you're going to let that fester, you don't have a chance."

The philosophers of Brooklyn were sitting in his office giving him advice and the tiniest sliver of hope.

"I won't let it fester," he promised.

"Good." The brothers nodded.

"You got a nice place here," Marco said, glancing around.

"What? We're making small talk now?" Gio demanded.

"I'm being polite." Marco kicked Gio's knee where it rested on the desk.

"Ouch! Fucker!"

Oscar: Was that a body blow I just heard?

"Anyway," Gio said, looking at the clock on his phone.

Aiden felt himself tense. He didn't want them to leave. They felt like his only tangible connection to Frankie.

"You wanna go for a drink? Maybe some steak?" Marco asked Aiden.

Aiden nodded as relief coursed through him. They weren't abandoning him. "Yeah. Yeah, I do."

59

"I'm not sure how to tell you this, Frankie," Raul began for the third time, clearing his throat. Brenda sat next to him at the conference table stemming her tears with a third tissue.

Frankie saw her employee file on the table and had connected the dots within five seconds of walking into the room.

"We lost our grant," Raul announced. "Two of them, actually. They're not even being funded anymore, so it wasn't anything that you did in the grant writing. It wasn't anything that we did as an organization, it was just... bad luck."

Her life felt like it had been nothing but bad luck these past few weeks.

"So, what I'm trying to say," Raul took a deep breath, "is that we're shutting the office down. We can't continue to serve the business community without those funds, and we've been talking about retiring for a while now."

Brenda blew her nose noisily.

"And that means that your employment is also terminated." Raul choked out the words and reached for his coffee, managing to spill most of it.

"Okay, then," Frankie said, too numb to process anything. It was the trajectory of her life, plummeting straight down. By this time next week, she'd be warming her hands on the open flames in hell if her descent continued. "I'll just pack up my stuff and go."

Brenda's quiet sniffles turned into full blown wails. "We're so sorry, sweetie! And after everything that you've been through..."

Frankie rose and gave each of them a mechanical hug. They had been mentors, second parents, and friends to her. And now they, too, were out of her life.

"Can we take you to lunch or... something?" Raul asked.

She shook her head. "No, thanks."

"We'll send you your vacation pay with your last paycheck," he said, looking glumly at the table.

"Thank you," Frankie said, pausing inside the door and taking a last look at the room.

Downstairs, she shoved what she could from her desk into an empty paper ream box and stepped out into the mocking sunshine. The end of March was showing signs of the spring to come. But nothing could thaw the ice inside her.

She sat down on the curb in a scrap of sunshine that filtered between the branches of the trees. Was this rock bottom? No job, six weeks shy of finishing her master's, and she was going to have to decide between rent and tuition. Oh, and speaking of school, this job and her social media workshops had been part of her thesis project. So, graduation this spring was no longer an option.

And worse was the fact that Aiden had stopped contacting her a week ago. As if he'd vanished from the face of the planet.

But he was still here. Still working. Still existing. Still living his life.

She knew because she couldn't stop herself from opening those blasted Google alert emails every damn morning.

He went to work every day, had dinner in the city, made appearances. Meanwhile, she'd stopped talking to everyone. Her parents, her brothers, Pru. She was avoiding human contact because she no longer felt human.

The anger, the hurt, had shifted inside her making room for a new feeling. One she didn't understand. Guilt.

"Frankie!"

She winced at the cheery greeting. She couldn't do Pru right now. She was incapable of even pretending to be happy to see her best friend.

"Hi," Frankie said flatly.

"Why are you sitting on the sidewalk with a box of... Oh."

"I got fired. They're shutting down the center," Frankie said.

"Then you've got time for me to buy you lunch," silver-lining-finder Pru announced. "Let's go." She dragged Frankie to her feet and picked up the box. "I'm feeling like pizza."

Frankie stumbled over her own feet. "You're voluntarily eating pizza? Do I really look that bad?"

"You look like a zombie. Sort of alive on the outside but totally dead and gross on the inside."

"Gee, thanks."

Pru led the way to one of Frankie's favorite pizza shops, chattering about the weather and gossip. Frankie didn't bother responding. It took too much effort.

Pru slid into the booth across from her and interlaced her fingers, smiling expectantly. "I've got some things I need to tell you."

"Is everything okay?" Frankie asked, rousing herself into a minimal level of caring.

Her friend nodded.

"What can I get you ladies?" Vinnie the proprietor demanded, leaning on their table with a combination of charm and impatience.

"The biggest, greasiest pepperoni pizza you can make," Pru decided. "And how about some of those garlic twists?"

Frankie's eyebrows winged up. Her friend was serious about all the carbs today.

Vinnie took their drink orders and headed back behind the counter.

"So. I'm pregnant," Pru announced.

Frankie's mouth opened. Her brain wasn't prepared for new information of that magnitude.

"Wha...?"

"Pregnant. Like with my husband's baby?" Pru said, beaming at her. "Thanks, Vin," she said when Vinnie returned with their waters.

Frankie chugged half of hers, trying to get her brain back to functioning. "You're going to have a baby?"

Pru nodded again. "Honeymoon baby, which was a surprise. But we're so excited."

Frankie could see it. The sheer delight on her friend's face. And even though her own life was in the gutter, she still felt a stirring of happiness for Pru.

"Wow. Congratulations. Chip must be thrilled."

"He wavers between thrilled and hyperventilating. He ordered sixteen parenting, pregnancy, and baby books and wants to start interviewing nannies now."

"Wow," Frankie said again. A rush of memories washing over her. Pru dressed as Carmen Miranda strolling into their dorm room on Halloween. Pru dancing on the bar at Salvio's after one too many margaritas. Pru trying on her wedding dress for the first time. "I know I don't look it, but I am so happy for you."

Pru reached across the table and grabbed Frankie's hand. "I know your life sucks right now. But you're going to be an aunt, and that's worth something. And I want you to hang on to that aunt thing while I say this next thing."

"Uh-uh." Frankie braced herself.

"Why haven't you talked to Aiden?" Pru asked.

Frankie felt herself shutting down again. "Look, Pru. There are things you don't know. No, he didn't cheat on me with ol' one-eyebrow. But there was something else. Something much bigger."

"I know," Pru said, squeezing her hand. "He told me. He talked to me and Chip last week."

"He told you?" Frankie asked, astonished.

"He planted the seeds for Chip to break up with me."

"And you're okay with that? He robbed you both of years of happiness, Pru. Because he thought you weren't good enough for his friend."

"He thought I was immature and flighty, and to be honest, he may have been right. Not that I'd tell him that. I was fresh out of college and had diamond rings in my eyes. I had no idea what marriage was actually about. I just wanted a sparkly ring and a big party. If we hadn't broken up and both matured a bit, I don't know that we'd still be together. And I do know that this little low-carb baby wouldn't be growing in me. I'm stronger than I was then. Happier. Maybe the slightest bit more mature. And in the end, Aiden was just looking out for his friend. A friend who made the decision through no coercion, I might add."

"He *hurt* you," Frankie pointed out.

"And I forgave him. You should try it sometime."

Frankie snorted and stabbed her straw into her glass of ice. "Fool me once shame on you. Fool me twice..."

"Do you think relationships mean never screwing up at all?" Pru asked. "The insult was against me, the damage was done to me, and I've forgiven him. Why can't you?"

"Because you always had a soft heart. If I were you, I never would have forgiven Chip."

"And where would I be then? Not married to a man who makes me laugh every day. Not picking paint swatches for the nursery. Not sitting across from my best friend in the world desperately trying to show her what doors forgiveness opens. I could have played it safe. I could have married some boring guy who let me call every shot. But what kind of life is that when there's never any risk of getting hurt?"

Frankie stared down at the table, wishing Pru's words weren't landing direct hit after direct hit. "Being in a relationship with Aiden was so hard," she said lamely.

"It's not like you were doing yourself any favors there. You fought him every step of the way. You were just waiting for him to disappoint you, to give you the excuse you were looking for to leave."

"I was not," Frankie argued.

"Now you're lying to yourself."

"All in," Frankie whispered. Had she ever really been all in? She'd made the commitment, but had she really acted on it?

"You're the most loyal person I know, Frankie. Why can't you be loyal to him? Why can't you fight for him? Who does Aiden have in his corner that he can count on? Who has his back? You should have been out there attacking Margeaux. Instead, you holed up and hid yourself away."

Vinnie returned with a steaming pie. He dumped plates in front of them. "Enjoy, ladies."

Frankie stared at the swirl of sauce over bubbling cheese.

"I love him so much it scares me," she admitted, her voice low and shaky. She brought her gaze up. "I love him so much I can't breathe because I feel like a piece of me is missing."

"You are so damn stubborn," Pru said with a sliver of sympathy. "You'd ruin this just to be right."

The guilt in Frankie's gut stood up and saluted in recognition.

"My feelings for him terrify me. I'm living a nightmare. And it's all too late. He stopped texting, stopped sending me things. It's like I don't even exist to him anymore."

Pru slid a slice onto her plate and reached for the oregano. "Then maybe it's time you reminded him that you exist."

60

It took her an entire twenty-four hours to formulate a plan. And when she had it organized in her head, she started with Pru. Collecting names and numbers, making connections. She lunched with celebutantes, met with servers and maids and personal assistants in alleys by recycling bins, and pled her case.

They didn't all say yes, but enough did. And what they gave her would have to be enough to put it all into action.

When the chips were down, when there was a real chance at karmic retribution, women banded together.

She took everything they gave her and, pushing aside her now defunct thesis project notes, started a brand-new project.

Every word that she typed, every piece of information she gathered, she fit into the larger puzzle making her feel more hopeful, more in control. And when she was finally certain she had enough, she made one more phone call.

"Davenport, it's me Frankie. Do you still have that video from Barbados?"

FRANKIE COULDN'T SLEEP. She kept checking her phone to see if the gossip blogs had picked up the news yet. And when it finally landed on her newsfeed at seven, she danced a boogie in her kitchen.

There, on screens across the city, Margeaux screamed obscenities and drunkenly brawled in the pool with Taffany. There were hundreds of comments with more pouring in every minute.

Frankie danced over to the whiteboard she'd set up in her living room.

Step One: Discredit Marge.

She crossed it off with a flourish. And eyeballed step two. She was going to need some armor for this one.

She plucked the gift card off the board and dialed.

"Hi, I was wondering if Christian could squeeze me in today? I'm going to war."

An hour later, she was in a swiveling chair in front of a gilt framed mirror in a salon she couldn't afford. Christian was frowning at her tresses as he shoved his fingers through them. "You were supposed to come back last month," he chastised her.

"I didn't have to go into battle last month. Make me gorgeous and invincible."

Christian snapped his finger in the air. "Makeup!"

She kept an eye on her bag next to Christian's workstation as he and his minions set about endowing her with female weaponry. The smokey eye, contoured cheekbones, those gorgeous lowlights, and finally a blow out that made her look like she belonged in *the* red dress. If this didn't crush her enemy like a bug and prove irresistible to Aiden, she was going to swing by the shelter and get her first two cats... and then ask Gio if she could move in with him since she could no longer afford rent with no job and no degree.

Great. Really solid Plan B. But she was hoping that there'd be no need for it. She had a lot—everything—riding on Plan A.

"Christian? Christian's miracle workers?" she said, looking at the stranger in the mirror. "You guys are the shit."

She high-fived them down the line and handed over Aiden's gift card. Christian shoved an appointment card at her. "See you in six weeks."

"I'll be here," she said decisively. Positive mental attitude. She would win. Or she'd be curled in the fetal position being eaten by cats.

"Wish me luck!"

"Good luck!" they chorused after her as she strode out the door and into battle.

He was already there waiting for her at the bar. A double of something in front of him despite the fact that it was barely II in the morning.

"Good morning, Elliot," she said, sliding onto the stool next to him.

The younger Kilbourn straightened in his seat, leering at her cleavage. "I had a feeling I'd be hearing from you again. What can I do for you? Help you get revenge on brother dearest?" He straightened his tie.

"Oooh. I'm afraid you're about to be very disappointed," Frankie said, unpacking a file from her bag. She slid it across to him. "Here. This is for you."

With still too much confidence, Elliot flipped open the folder. It took a full four seconds for its contents to sink in. His eyes widened, pupils dilating. "What is this?" he demanded.

"This is every dirty deed I could dig up on you over the

past ten years. I don't know what Boris Donaldson has on you, but I'm willing to bet it's somewhere in this file."

"How do you know about Boris?" he asked, scrambling through the photos, the photocopies, and the interviews.

"You pushed for him for CFO despite the fact that he's currently under investigation for fraud and, as of about ten minutes ago, embezzlement."

"What?" He reached for his drink and drank it down.

"Well, what kind of investigation would I be doing if I didn't pry into my boyfriend's enemies? You people will never understand that your underlings see and hear things that your dirty money can't cover up. By the way, the SEC's anonymous tip website is *so* easy to navigate. Now, let's talk about you."

He was flipping through papers alternately going beet red and ashen.

"You've been a very naughty boy. Using your expense account to pay for prescription drugs and lap dances. Side note, they're not actually into you. Then there's these sticky consent cases that you paid off. Anything other than a yes is a no, Elliot. All of that I almost expected from you. But what even I was surprised by was you bringing a male prostitute back to your then-girlfriend's apartment and—"

He slapped the bar. "She signed a non-disclosure agreement! I paid her!"

"Oh, sweetie," Frankie said, laying on the phony sympathy. "She signed a non-disclosure, but her doorman and house-keeper and personal chef didn't."

He swore. "I'll sue. I'll sue you for defamation."

"Then Chip will press charges for abducting him. That's a felony, by the way. And I don't think your defense is going to be able to come up with any character witnesses for you. Not with all of this in your history," she said, tapping the file.

He picked up the file and ripped it in half.

Frankie sighed. "Is this a temper tantrum? Because you know I have copies of copies of copies."

He braced his elbows on the bar and put his face in his hands. She didn't feel the tiniest bit of guilt.

"What do you want?" he asked.

"I'm glad you asked. It's very simple. I want you to leave Aiden alone. Permanently. You don't have a blackmailer to pay off anymore. You're welcome, by the way. So, you can have a fresh start. Step down from the company, stop acting like a fuck-up, and don't so much as glance in Aiden's direction except for the occasional uncomfortable family dinner. Got it?"

"If I do what you want, what will you do with this?" he asked, pointing at the shredded paper.

"I'm going to hang on to it, very quietly. But if you step a fucking toe out of line if you take advantage of one more woman or buy one more bottle of pills, I'll know. And I'll go to every gossip blogger and society journalist in the country with this dirty little packet. Imagine what your mother would think. Or worse, your father. You're at my mercy. And with the SEC taking out your blackmail buddy, you basically won the lottery today. Don't fuck it up."

She slid off her stool and straightened her dress.

"Do we have a deal?" she asked.

He nodded glumly.

"Good. Now, there's just one more thing." She picked up his drink and tossed it in his face. "That's for every one of these women. Be better from now on."

61

"Your one o'clock is here," Oscar announced, poking his head in Aiden's office doorway.

"My what?" Aiden looked at his open calendar on his monitor. Who the hell was he supposed to—

She walked in wearing the red dress that haunted his dreams.

Aiden wasn't even aware that he'd risen from his desk so suddenly that his chair went spinning behind him.

"Franchesca?"

Had he finally lost his damn mind? Was he missing her so much he was now hallucinating her instead of catching the ghost of her scent, the echo of her laughter?

"May I come in?" she asked.

It felt as if a bolt of lightning struck the carpet that separated them. The room was charged with electricity. He knew by the parting of her lips, by the guarded expression on her face, that she felt it too.

It was pathetic how grateful he felt just to see her again. His heart pounded in his chest as if it knew that everything came down to the next few minutes of his life. And he wasn't in control.

Franchesca was.

Oscar quietly shut the door, and Aiden knew it must have cost him dearly.

"Of course," Aiden said gruffly. He wanted to cross to her, to take her in his arms and bury his face in her hair. Instead, he gestured toward one of the chairs in front of his desk. "Please. Sit."

She sat, crossing one leg neatly over the other, and he went rigidly hard. His cock had no shame. The woman who had destroyed him, who had turned the life he'd built into an empty shell, still made him want.

He'd crawl to her if he thought for a second it would work. But Frankie didn't want a man who crawled.

"I have a proposition for you," she began, slipping a folder from her bag.

She handed it to him across the desk, and when their fingers brushed, he knew without a doubt this woman would never leave his system. A storm was brewing between them, and he only hoped that when it broke, he wouldn't be alone.

"I'm listening," he said, his voice rougher than he meant it to be. He pulled his chair back and sank into it.

If she noticed, she didn't let on. Frankie cleared her throat. "Okay, there's a new gap in small business services in Brooklyn. I know the neighborhoods, I know the business owners. They need guidance, mentoring. They need education. They need loans and grants."

She was pitching him a fucking business proposal?

"I know you, Aiden. I know that all levels of entrepreneurship interest you. And it could start here," she flipped to a page in his packet and tapped a finger on a map of her parents' neighborhood. "Six storefronts are for sale on this block alone. The buildings themselves need some work, but they've got good bones. Most of the apartments are rented."

She talked real estate and revitalization, and Aiden felt his interest pique despite his profound disappointment.

She had photos of the street, detailed maps of neighborhood parking, the real estate listings, rental unit potential, and even an itemized list of types of stores that were missing from the neighborhood.

She talked about weekend farmers markets, about block parties and restaurants with outdoor seating. She painted a pretty picture.

"You could make a difference one city block at a time. You don't have that kind of real estate potential here in Manhattan. Not anymore. Think of the communities you could build, the small businesses you could support and watch grow. You'd need a development center. Something that could guide new businesses and help older owners take advantage of new technologies."

"And who would manage it?" he asked.

"Me."

Aiden's gaze flew to her face. "You're asking me for a job?" He didn't know whether to be impressed or furious.

"Oh, Aide, I want you to give me a lot more than that."

62

Her heart hadn't stopped hammering against her ribs since she walked in here. Seeing him was hard. So impossibly hard. He was just as beautiful as before. But there was a wall between them. One that she had built. One that was up to her to tear down.

Frankie took a deep breath and took the plunge.

"I let you down, Aiden. And I'm having trouble forgiving myself."

"And you think me giving you a job will make you feel better?" he asked in confusion. He didn't even sound angry. But she had to appeal to all of him, starting with the successful entrepreneur driven to win at all costs.

"You need me, Aiden. And damn it, I need you. Not your money. Not your family connections. You."

He was watching her intently now, and she watched him back, noticed him carefully hide the spark of hope behind those cool blue eyes.

"You're thoughtful. You listen, really listen. You're smart and charming and funny and surprisingly sweet. You're so fucking generous I worry that you're going to get hurt."

She couldn't catch her breath. The words were spilling faster and faster from her lips. She reached into her bag and her fingers closed around the next part of her plan.

"No one's ever touched me the way you do. No one's ever loved me the way you do. And I've never loved anyone the way I love you." Her voice broke, and she saw his knuckles whiten as he closed his hands into fists.

With a shaky breath, she pushed herself out of her chair and walked around his desk on jelly legs. She knelt down in front of him and held up the jeweler box.

His face gave nothing away, so she popped the lid of the box revealing the simple gold band. "It was my grandfather's," she whispered. "It's nothing fancy. But it's family, loyalty, love. And I can give you all that. So marry me, Aiden. Be with me. Give me forever."

She held her breath and blinked back the tears that were threatening to overflow her lashes.

"What about Chip and Pru?" he asked, staring at the band.

"The truth is, I had more trouble forgiving myself than I did you. I was looking for an excuse to end it, to be right, because I didn't want to get hurt. And I ended up hurting us both. Also, Pru called me the Upper West Side version of a chicken shit, and I hate when she's right."

She saw the ghost of a smile play at the corners of his mouth, and her heart sang with hope.

"What about my family?" he asked. "They'll always be a problem."

"I have a feeling there will be less drama. I've discovered that I fit in quite well with manipulative backstabbers."

"You're going to have to explain that cryptic statement," he said, reaching for her, his hands closing over her wrists. He stood, pulling her to her feet.

"First, answer me, please. Then I'll tell you anything you

want. Will you marry me, Aide? Will you take me as I am? Forgive me for being stubborn and proud and so very, very wrong? Because, damn it, Aiden, you fit in my life like you're the missing piece. I can fit into yours, too. I want you for an ally, a partner. I was wrong to hold back, wrong to be looking for a way out. And I'm so fucking sorry. But I promise you from this day forward, I will be your partner, and we can build something beautiful together. And I swear to you I will always, always, have your back."

She was shaking, with love, with fear, with hope.

Aiden nudged her chin higher and looked her in the eyes.

"We can't both be chicken shits, now can we?"

"Aide, if you don't give me a yes or a no right now, I swear to God I'm going to ruin your life like I just ruined your brother's."

He grinned down at her, the full wattage that made her weak in the knees.

"It's always been yes with you, Franchesca. There is no one I'd rather have in my corner."

"Yes?" she repeated.

He nodded. "Yes, and the sooner, the better."

"Well, we don't need to move *too* fast," she began, feeling hesitation rush up.

"You got down on both your knees—"

"I can't get down on one knee in this dress! You'd have been looking at my hooha during my very sweet and inspiring speech!"

He was laughing now and lifting her off the ground. She felt him hard against her hip and went quiet. Her brain shifted gears into sexy time.

"I love you, Franchesca," he whispered against her jaw.

"I love you, Aiden, you stubborn son of a—"

He covered her mouth with his, shutting her up with a

kiss. She struggled for half a second, determined to make her point, and then lost her damn mind when his tongue stroked into her mouth. She shoved her fingers into his hair, gripping the silky strands she had missed so much. Breathing him in, she told him again and again as his mouth slanted over hers just how much she loved him.

"How are we going to celebrate?" he asked, breaking free for a second.

"You're going to bend me over that desk and remind me of everything that I've been missing."

"I'm the luckiest man on the planet." He nipped at her neck, fisting a hand in her hair.

"Damn right you are."

EPILOGUE

(One month later)

"Cannonball!"

Franchesca rolled to her side to watch Aiden at the open terrace door. Sheer white curtains billowed in on the tropical breeze. He was naked, as he had been for most of the twelve hours since they'd been pronounced husband and wife. Her ring finger bore the weight and sparkle of their commitment to each other. A commitment they'd made on the white sand beaches where it had all begun and continued in the same bed where she'd first discovered Aiden Kilbourn's potency.

"Mmm," she sighed, stretching her arms over her head. "I could get used to this view for the rest of my life."

Aiden shot her a cocky grin over his shoulder. His muscled back, and gorgeous ass, showed evidence of the tracks her teeth and nails had taken throughout the night.

"I'm not sure if I'd want this view every day," he commented. "Your dad just did a cannonball over Marco and Gio and splashed Rachel."

Frankie snorted. "You did not have to bring them all along, you know."

"They're family."

Marco and Gio shouted something, and there was another loud splash.

"Antonio! Stop splashing. Don't you idiots encourage him, or they'll throw us all out of here," May Baranski screeched at Frankie's favorite underage cab driver and her brothers.

Frankie flopped back on the pillow. "You can't take the Brooklyn out of the Baranskis. When are they leaving again?" she asked.

"Tomorrow with Chip and Pru and my parents."

"I still can't believe your dad came to the wedding," Frankie said. She rolled out of bed and padded across the room to the small refrigerator where she found a bottle of water.

"He's getting used to the idea of letting me make my own decisions. In another five years, he might even like you."

Frankie laughed. "I'll hold my breath for that possibility. Did you tell him about Elliot?"

Aiden shook his head and met her where she stood, his hand stroking over her breast and down to the curve of her hip. He circled her body as if he were taking stock of it. "Some things are best left between brothers. But I did tell him I bought Elliot out of the company."

"A clean slate," Frankie sighed.

She felt his erection stir as it brushed her ass cheeks. "You're insatiable." She reached for him, gripping him at the base.

"The same could be said of you, my wife."

"Oh look! We can see in Frankie's room from here! Yoo hoo, Frankie!" May stood up on her chaise lounge and waved.

"Oh my God." Frankie shoved Aiden out of the line of sight and onto the floor. "I can't take these people anywhere!"

"I guess we can go be social until tomorrow," he sighed with disappointment.

But she was already sprawled on top of him. And he was already hard and pulsing between her thighs.

"Maybe we can spare a few minutes," she suggested, moving to straddle his hips.

He was laying on top of her discarded veil and the skirt of her crumpled wedding dress. Both of which he'd stripped from her last night.

He'd refused to tell her just how much the dress had cost, but she'd caught the estimate in the gossip blogs. Leave it to Aiden to spend that much on a piece of clothing worn for a few hours.

Aiden's blue eyes hooded with desire. He was a beautiful sight, and he was all hers. He hinged forward, bringing his mouth to her closest breast, his abs rippling with the motion.

As he sucked and teased, Frankie took him inside her in one languorous slide.

"God, you're so beautiful," he murmured against her flesh, teasing the nipple with his lips.

"You're everything I didn't know I wanted, Aide," she breathed.

His hips thrust up to meet hers, rocking into her in a slow, steady rhythm.

She moaned, and he clamped a hand over her mouth. "Quiet now, sweetheart. We have an audience outside."

Frankie tasted the metal of his wedding band, felt the drag of him inside her against her trembling walls.

"It's never going to be enough," he whispered. "I'm never going to have enough of this with you, Franchesca."

His words, sweet and strained, echoed in her head, her

heart. She dug her toes into the floor, rolling her hips against him.

He hissed out a breath, and she swore she felt him throb inside her.

"You'd better be with me," he growled, and with that, he rolled, trapping her between the skirt of her wedding dress and his unyielding body.

He drove into her powerfully, his hand still covering her mouth. But they didn't need words. Not when their gazes held, not when their souls locked into place and their bodies came apart at the seams. She felt the first hot burst of his release as she clamped down on his cock as her own climax bloomed like a flower.

"Yes, Franchesca. Yes." He chanted sweet and dirty vows as they came together.

All in. Forever.

EXTENDED EPILOGUE

ONE YEAR LATER

Aiden Kilbourn and Frankie Baranski revitalize entire city block

Aiden Kilbourn's wife wears Target dress to ribbon cutting

Aiden Kilbourn's wife chokes on sausage at inaugural event

"Those are ridiculous," Frankie insisted, pointing at the over-sized shears Aiden held in his hand.

"A big ribbon-cutting calls for big scissors," he said, slinging an arm around her shoulder. He'd left his trademark suits home today and wore jeans and a simple white button down. If it weren't for his panty-dropping face of perfection, he could almost pass for a normal human being.

"What?" he asked, noting her attention.

She grinned. "Just feeling a little extra lucky today."

"You should. It's not every wife who can talk her husband into buying her a city block."

"Us," she reminded him.

"Us," he agreed, squeezing her shoulder.

"I'm pretty impressed with us," she said eyeing the street. "A grocer, a coffee shop, a sandwich place, a tiny brewery, and a small business development center open all on one day? You're going down in neighborhood history."

"You mean like Saint Franchesca?" he teased.

"Well, obviously you won't be as revered as *me*. But close," she predicted.

In just over a year, the little strip of street in Brooklyn had gone from ignored and dilapidated to rejuvenated. There was a lively jazz band playing on the restaurant's patio, and the street was roped off with one big, red ribbon. Neighbors and business owners spilled out onto the sidewalks, ready for the festivities to begin. Aiden had hired local restaurants and food trucks to feed the crowds for the neighborhood's first ever block party. Proceeds would go toward the grant program managed by the brand-new business center, where Franchesca had an office and about six weeks of work ahead of her already.

"Shall we do the honors?" he asked, nudging her toward the end of the street.

"Let's do this."

They tag-teamed the speech with a natural rhythm. Frankie's parents and brothers waved from the front row. They talked about community and neighbors and pride, and then, together, to the raucous cheers of the crowd, they cut the ribbon.

The press was there in large numbers because it was a Kilbourn project. But Frankie didn't mind the attention. Not when they had, for the most part, learned to treat her like any other entrepreneur. No one dared to ask her who she was wearing anymore.

After the ribbon was cut, the speech made, and the doors

opened, Frankie and Aiden walked arm in arm down the revitalized street, mingling and munching, tasting and touring. They ate hot sausage from a food truck, drank Pilsner samples from the brewery, and toured each business with each owner. Frankie pinched herself and Aiden repeatedly just to make sure this wasn't one big, beautiful dream.

No, it wasn't, Frankie thought with satisfaction as she sunk her teeth into the Bratwurst Wagon's bestselling foot-long sausage. She had played a role in the redevelopment of an entire city block. Something that would benefit both the neighborhood and the business community. And Aiden had stood with her, guiding her, and trusting her throughout the process. She loved him desperately for it.

Her phone vibrated in the pocket of her smart sundress, and she pulled it out.

Aiden: You're giving me ideas with that sausage in your mouth.

She laughed, nearly choking, and then, spotting him in the crowd, made a private show of shoving as much of it into her mouth as possible.

"Mrs. Baranski," someone said, shoving a phone into her face. "Care to comment on the predicted revenue of your project here?"

The sausage and bun turned to sand in her mouth, and she started coughing.

Aiden was at her side in a moment, slapping her on the back.

"Sorry," Frankie gasped, tears stinging her eyes. "Too much sausage in my mouth."

The journalist, a woman in a trim blazer and glasses, gaped at her.

Aiden covered his laugh with a cough. "I'd be happy to answer any of your questions while my wife finds a drink of water," he said smoothly.

Frankie, still coughing, decided it was in her better interest to wash down the sausage wad with more beer to calm her butterflies. The public part of their big day was drawing to a close, but she had one hell of a surprise cooking for Aiden, and there was a good chance he would hate it. She took a steadying breath. He *had* to love it. If she had to love the expansive wardrobe he'd bought for her and the embarrassingly beautiful stash of jewelry and books and kitchen toys, he had to love her surprise.

She paused at the glass doors of the shiny new small business development center and traced her fingers over the lettering on the door. All her dreams had come true, thanks to the man who teased her about sausage. And she wasn't going to let him down. No, Aiden Kilbourn would have no choice but to be proud of his MBA-wielding, small business genius wife.

She ducked inside and found her parents, Hugo and May, huddled in the conference room over the cookie tray. Her brothers, Gio and Marco, were racing desk chairs around the four cubicles on the opposite side of the front desk. She'd hired a receptionist, a part-time employee, and an intern. Between the four of them, and the ever-growing list of resources Aiden was developing, they'd make a dent in the small business needs of Brooklyn Heights.

She glanced at the sign-up sheet on the front desk. Next week's workshop on business expenses and other accounting questions was already booked solid.

"There's our beautiful, amazing daughter," May announced as if it had been weeks rather than minutes since she'd last seen Frankie.

Gio cut Marco off with his chair and dumped his brother onto the floor.

"Winner!"

"You guys break it, you bought it," Frankie said, nudging Marco with her foot.

"Get your ass off the floor, you juvenile delinquents," Rachel snapped, bouncing little Maya on her hip. Frankie's niece was wearing a t-shirt that said My Aunt is Awesome.

Frankie liberated Maya from her mother's arms and held her aloft. She squealed in delight and clapped her little hands.

"Two of my favorite ladies," Aiden noted, poking his head in through the front door.

Frankie grinned at him. "How's it going out there, Mr. Mayor?"

"Everyone is eating, drinking, and shopping. I'd call it a success," he said, his eyes dipping to the V-neck of her dress.

May bustled out of the conference room and whacked her sons on the head. "Stop acting like wild animals," she snapped.

"Ouch!"

"Sorry, Ma."

"Why can't you act more like Aiden?" she demanded. "Look at him behaving."

When she turned to point at Aiden, Marco and Gio flipped him off.

May spun to shoot her sons a fierce frown, and Aiden used the opportunity to return the one-fingered salute.

Frankie and Rachel shook their heads and laughed.

"You two did good here," Hugo announced from the doorway of the conference room, a cookie in each hand.

"Thank you, Dad," Frankie said. "I think we're going to do a lot of good things here."

"Maybe you can show your mother how that Book Face Twatter works," he mused.

Gio snorted. "Frankie's real good at the Twatter."

Using the baby as cover, Frankie flipped Gio off.

Aiden plucked Maya from Frankie's arms and jiggled the little girl in the air before pressing a kiss to her chubby little cheek.

"Think you have a few minutes to sneak away?" Frankie asked. She was going for casual, but the words came out strangled.

She saw the spark in his eyes, knew he thought she had other intentions.

"I always have time to sneak away," he said, his voice husky.

"Hand over my baby before you say anything gross in front of her," Marco demanded.

Frankie grinned. A year into the marriage, and neither she nor Aiden had put the brakes on in the fucking-like-rabbits department.

Aiden gave the little girl another kiss and turned her over to her father. He slid his arm around Frankie's waist and pulled her into his side. "What did you have in mind?" he whispered.

"Let's go for a little walk," she suggested, pulling him toward the door.

She'd told no one what she'd done, and the secret was eating her soul. When they'd married, Aiden had opened an account in her name and dumped an obscene amount of money into it so Frankie never felt like she needed to ask for anything.

She'd refused to touch it on principal. Until now.

"Where are we going?" Aiden asked gruffly as he let Frankie pull him down the block, away from the festivities.

"You'll see," she said vaguely.

They followed the street west before skirting north and then west again into the historic district until Frankie came to a stop in front of a two-story brown brick building. It had a garage flanked by two doors.

"And what are we doing here?" Aiden asked indulgently.

Frankie pulled the key out of her pocket and took a deep breath. "Hopefully, being really happy and not yelling at me at all."

She felt the weight of his gaze as she slid the key into the lock.

"Franchesca," he said her name softly, questioningly.

She tossed him a shaky smile and gave the door a hard shove. It creaked open on rarely used hinges.

Aiden followed her inside.

Thick, worn floorboards drew the eye from the front to the back of the large space.

She waited while Aiden prowled, examining plaster walls and the rickety staircase up to the second floor. Everything was dirty and dusty. It was an abandoned construction zone. The beginning of a kitchen was tucked into a corner. But the back of the building with its series of arched windows that stretched from floor to ceiling were the wow factor.

Frankie waited, gnawing on her thumb while Aiden stood before one of the windows and stared out across the greenway to the murky summer waters of the river. Beyond it, the Manhattan skyline loomed.

"Well? What do you think?" she asked, breathlessly.

"Why don't you tell me exactly why we're here, and then I'll tell you what I think," he said, eyeing her with that probing look.

"I bought it. For us." She blurted the words out. "You've been saying you wanted to look for a place here, close to the development center and my family. It's a carriage house or was before someone started the renovations. They ran out of money and sat on it for a few years. Your dad thinks we got a great deal on it—"

"My father?" Aiden asked, swiping his hand over his chin.

It irked her that she couldn't read him. Frankie nodded. "Ferris helped me set up a corporation so I could buy it without you knowing. Surprise?"

He stared at the view once again and then returned to her face. Aiden started toward her.

"Tell me what you're thinking before I die. Do you like it? Do you hate it? I thought we could renovate it together. The Greenway is literally in our backyard, and we've got the square footage for a couple of bedrooms and bathrooms upstairs. The roof is sound. We could have one of those cool rooftop terraces..."

He reached her and gripped her hips, pulling her against him.

"Aiden, seriously if you don't say something right now, I'm going to freak out," Frankie said.

He didn't speak. He kissed her instead. A soft, sweet slide of tongues. A leisurely sampling that left her knees weak.

"You're not yelling," she said as she pulled back. Her hands fisted in his shirt.

"It's perfect, Franchesca," he said softly, nudging her chin up. She felt the knot in her stomach loosen. She met his gaze, saw the softness in his eyes.

"We can still keep your penthouse," she began.

"Our," he corrected her.

"Our," Frankie repeated. "But this will be nice too... eventually. I mean, it's kind of a pile of crap right now but—"

"I love that you did this," Aiden said, cutting off her rambling. He started to sway from side to side to music only he could hear. Frankie followed his lead, hypnotized by the love she saw in his eyes. "We'll make it our own. We'll watch the fights with your brothers here, host Thanksgivings here. You and I will curl up on the couch at the end of the day and eat Chinese food and complain about the fortune cookies. We'll argue about everything. You'll break dishes. I'll eat everything that you cook. We'll escape from it all here. You and me."

Frankie felt tears prick her eyes. He was painting her a picture of their future together, and she'd provided the canvas.

"All in," Frankie whispered to him.

He brushed a thumb across her cheek. "All in, my Franchesca."

AUTHOR'S NOTE TO THE READER

Dear Reader,

Where do I start? As always, I started the book with an idea of where it would go. I thought this was going to be just a light, funny, rom-com set in paradise. And then Frankie and Aiden got deeper, their conflict got more intense, their families got more complicated. Basically, I fell head over freaking heels for these two and their hot mess of a non-relationship.

I was so sure Frankie would get her heart broken and then she ended up doing the breaking. It's like I have no control over these people! I hope you loved them as much as I did!

I set the wedding in Barbados because it's one of my favorite places to go with Mr. Lucy. We went specifically so I could soak up the research for this book... also some sun. And all the rum. The white sandy beaches, the turquoise water, the insane minivan public transportation. It's ah-mazing.

Anyway, if you loved Frankie and Aiden, please feel free to hop over to Amazon and leave a gushing review. If you hated them and you're still reading this note, I admire your commitment.

Do you want to hang out and be BFFs? Follow me on Facebook and join me in my reader's group: Lucy Score's Binge Readers Anonymous. And if you want first dibs sales and awesome bonus content, definitely sign up for my newsletter! I hope to see you around!

Xoxo,
    Lucy

ABOUT THE AUTHOR

Lucy Score is a *Wall Street Journal* and #1 Amazon bestselling author. She grew up in a literary family who insisted that the dinner table was for reading and earned a degree in journalism. She writes full-time from the Pennsylvania home she and Mr. Lucy share with their obnoxious cat, Cleo. When not spending hours crafting heartbreaker heroes and kick-ass heroines, Lucy can be found on the couch, in the kitchen, or at the gym. She hopes to someday write from a sailboat, or oceanfront condo, or tropical island with reliable Wi-Fi.

Sign up for her newsletter and stay up on all the latest Lucy book news.
And follow her on:
Website: Lucyscore.com
Facebook at: lucyscorewrites
Instagram at: scorelucy
Readers Group at: Lucy Score's Binge Readers Anonymous

ACKNOWLEDGMENTS

- Jaycee at Sweet 'n Spicy Designs for this hella hot cover

- Dawn and Amanda for your editorial eyeballs of awesomeness

- Mr. Lucy for ignoring my Christmas request for knock-off Uggs and buying me my first real pair... and then not yelling at me when I immediately got a grease stain on them (can Uggs be dry-cleaned??)

- Jodi for once again turning my mangled chunk of a blurb into something exciting and one-click worthy

- Joyce and Tammy for being amazing in Binge Readers and in real life

- Sushi

- The Will & Grace reboot

- Tacos. Always tacos.